HOT BLOODED

DONNA GRANT

St. Martin's Paperbacks

NOTE: If you purchased this book without a cover you should be aware that this book is stolen property. It was reported as "unsold and destroyed" to the publisher, and neither the author nor the publisher has received any payment for this "stripped book."

This is a work of fiction. All of the characters, organizations, and events portrayed in this novel are either products of the author's imagination or are used fictitiously.

HOT BLOODED

Copyright © 2014 by Donna Grant.
Excerpt from *Night's Blaze* copyright © 2014 by Donna Grant.

All rights reserved.

For information address St. Martin's Press, 175 Fifth Avenue, New York, NY 10010.

ISBN: 978-1-250-06072-3

Printed in the United States of America

St. Martin's Paperbacks edition / January 2015

St. Martin's Paperbacks are published by St. Martin's Press, 175 Fifth Avenue, New York, NY 10010

10 9 8 7 6 5 4 3 2

Praise for the Dark Warrior novels by
DONNA GRANT

"Loaded with subtle emotions, sizzling chemistry, and some provocative thoughts on the real choices [Grant's] characters are forced to make as they choose their loves for eternity."　　　　　　—*RT Book Reviews* (4 stars)

"Vivid images, intense details, and enchanting characters grab the reader's attention and [don't] let go."
　　　　　　　　　　　　　—*Night Owl Reviews* (Top Pick)

MIDNIGHT'S KISS

5 Stars TOP PICK! "[Grant] blends ancient gods, love, desire, and evil-doers into a world you will want to revisit over and over again."　　　　—*Night Owl Reviews*

5 Blue Ribbons! "This story is one you will remember long after the last page is read. A definite keeper!"
　　　　　　　　　　　　　　　　—*Romance Junkies*

4 Stars! "The world of the Immortal Warriors is a thoroughly engaging one, blending powerful ancient gods, fiery desire, and touchingly human love, which readers will surely want to revisit."　　　　—*RT Book Reviews*

4 Feathers! "*Midnight's Kiss* is a game changer—one that will set the rest of the series in motion."
　　　　　　　　　　　　　　　　—*Under the Covers*

MIDNIGHT'S CAPTIVE

5 Blue Ribbons! "Packed with originality, imagination, humor, Scotland, Highlanders, magic, surprising plot twists, intrigue, sizzling sensuality, suspense, tender romance, and true love, this story has something for everyone." —*Romance Junkies*

4½ Stars! "Grant has crafted a chemistry between her wounded alpha and surprisingly capable heroine that will, no doubt, enthrall series fans and newcomers alike."
—*RT Book Reviews*

MIDNIGHT'S WARRIOR

4 Stars! "Super storyteller Grant returns with...A rich variety of previous protagonists [that] adds a wonderful familiarity to the books" —*RT Books Reviews*

5 Stars! "Ms. Grant brings together two people who are afraid to fall in love and then ignites sparks between them." —*Single Title Reviews*

MIDNIGHT'S SEDUCTION

"Sizzling love scenes and engaging characters fill the pages of this fast-paced and immersive novel."
—*Publishers Weekly*

4 Stars! "Grant again proves that she is a stellar writer and a force to be reckoned with." —*RT Book Reviews*

5 Blue Ribbons! "A deliciously sexy, adventure-some paranormal romance that will keep you glued to the pages…" —*Romance Junkies*

5 Stars! "Ms. Grant mixes adventure, magic and sweet love to create the perfect romance story."
—*Single Title Reviews*

MIDNIGHT'S LOVER

"Paranormal elements and scorching romance are cleverly intertwined in this tale of a damaged hero and resilient heroine."
—*Publishers Weekly*

5 Blue Ribbons! "An exciting, adventure-packed tale, *Midnight's Lover* is a story that captivates you from the very first page."
—*Romance Junkies*

5 Stars! "Ms. Grant weaves a sweet love story into a story filled with action, adventure and the exploration of personal pain."
—*Single Title Reviews*

4 Stars! "It's good vs. evil Druid in the next installment of Grant's Dark Warrior series. The stakes get higher as discerning one's true loyalties becomes harder. Grant's compelling characters and the continued presence of previous protagonists are key reasons why these books are so gripping. Another exciting and thrilling chapter!"
—*RT Book Reviews*

4.5 Stars Top Pick! "This is one series you'll want to make sure to read from the start...they just keep getting better...mmmm! A must-read for sure!"
—*Night Owl Reviews*

4.5 Feathers! "If you're looking for an author who brings heat and heart in one tightly written package, then Donna Grant will be a gift that makes your jaw drop. You don't want to miss *Midnight's Lover*."
—*Under the Covers Book Blog*

NOVELS BY DONNA GRANT

FROM ST. MARTIN'S PAPERBACKS

To Lara Adrian –
Extraordinary writer, special person,
and treasured friend!

ACKNOWLEDGMENTS

A special shout-out to everyone at SMP for getting this book ready, including the amazing art department for such a gorgeous cover. Much thanks and admiration goes to my fabulous editor, Monique Patterson, who I can't ever praise highly enough.

To my incredible agent, Natanya Wheeler—here's to dragons!

Hats off to Leah Suttle for all the design work she's done for me, and to my wonderful Dolls. Words can't say how much I adore y'all.

A special thanks to my family for the never-ending support.

And to my husband, Steve. For . . . well, everything! I love you, Sexy!

CHAPTER ONE

Laith leaned back in the chair with his hands behind his head as he looked around Constantine's office. There were only a handful of Dragon Kings in the large room. Some were on various missions regarding the Dark Fae, Ulrik, and others that only Con knew about.

Still other Kings were on the sixty thousand acres of Dreagan property tending to livestock, overseeing their famous Dreagan whisky, and patrolling their borders. Because even though their dragon magic kept most humans and other beings out, some still tried to gain entrance.

As a race of shape-shifting immortals who had been around since the dawn of time, the Dragon Kings weren't without their share of enemies. And the list kept growing as the months went by.

Each King was powerful in his own right or he would never have been chosen to rule his dragons, but there was one who was King of Kings—Constantine.

Con with his surfer boy golden blond hair and soulless

black eyes could be a cold son of a bitch. He did what was necessary, regardless of who was hurt, in order to keep the secret of Dreagan from leaking to the humans.

While turning the gold dragonhead cuff links at his wrist, Con sat patiently behind his desk staring at a file folder while everyone took their seats.

"What's up?" Ryder leaned over to whisper before promptly taking a bite of a jelly-filled donut.

Laith shrugged. It could be anything, and he learned long ago not to try and guess what was going on in Con's head or try to figure out Con's thinking when he did something. The fact that Con wouldn't look up from the folder meant that whatever was inside was troubling indeed.

Kellan was the last to enter Con's office. After a quick look around, Kellan closed the door behind him. The Keeper of the History remained as he was, leaning against the door instead of taking a chair.

Another sign that something bad had happened. Laith took a deep breath and slowly let it out. Besides Ryder, Con, and Kellan there were Rhys, Warrick, Hal, and Tristan. Everyone looked at ease. Except for Rhys.

There was something going on with his friend, but so far Rhys hadn't shared it with anyone. The lines of strain around Rhys's mouth said that whatever bothered him was taking a hard toll.

Rhys ran a hand through his long dark hair, his gaze meeting Laith's. A heartbeat later, Rhys's gaze skated away. Laith scratched his chin, the two-day's growth of beard itching, as he considered how hard to push to get Rhys to tell him—or someone—what was wrong.

"Come on, Con," Tristan said as he bent a leg to set his ankle atop knee. "Stop stalling. Why did you call us in here?"

Con's black eyes slowly lifted to meet Tristan's. He let

the silence lengthen before Con leaned forward and stabbed a finger on the file folder. "This."

"And what is that?" Hal's voice was calm, but as one of six Kings who had taken mates, he was anything but. His gaze was riveted on Con, his bearing anxious and worried.

Con sighed and got to his feet. He shoved his hands in the pockets of his navy slacks. "I'd hoped we would have a reprieve. I'd hoped that Kiril and Shara would have more time to themselves being newly mated."

"For the love of all that's holy, spit it out," Ryder stated, unable to wait any longer.

A muscle in Con's jaw jumped. "John Campbell was found dead this morning."

Everyone stilled, their faces expressing shock, surprise, and disbelief as Con's words penetrated. No one said a word as they comprehended what John's death meant to Dreagan.

Laith closed his eyes, feeling remorse for John's death. The Campbells had owned the fifty acres bordering Dreagan for countless generations. It began shortly after the war with the humans, once the Kings sent the dragons to another realm. There was a doorway onto Dreagan, it was hidden, but could be used by their enemies. Since no Dragon King's magic could touch the area around the doorway, it became apparent that they would have to trust a human to do it for them.

The Campbells, one of the few groups of humans who didn't wage war on Dreagan, stepped forward. And so the watch of the Campbells had begun.

Only the head of the family, the one responsible for ensuring that no one accidentally stumbled upon the doorway, knew the secret of Dreagan and what was being guarded. It continued in that vein for thousands of years through wars and invasions. The Campbells kept the Dragon Kings' secret, and the Kings, in turn, protected them.

How Laith was going to miss John's laughter and his jokes. John hadn't just protected Dreagan, he'd become a friend.

"Who's going to guard the land?" Laith asked.

Kellan glanced at Con. "John has a daughter, Iona."

"That's right. I forgot about her," Rhys said.

Hal frowned as he sat forward and rested his arms on his legs. "She's been gone for a while, aye?"

"A verra long while," Con said. "Twenty years in fact."

Laith shifted to get comfortable in the chair. "John often talked of Iona. He showed me her photographs when he'd come into the pub. For as long as I knew him, and as often as we chatted, he never told me what happened with his wife."

Con stood and walked behind his tall chair, leaning his arms upon the back. "One of John's responsibilities was to remain on the land."

"He remained when his wife left and took Iona," Hal said softly.

Laith shifted his gaze back to Con. "He could've left for that."

"He took his oath to us seriously," Kellan explained. "To help with the pain of his loss, he buried himself in his writing after that."

Warrick nodded slowly. "He was an excellent writer."

"That he was." Con looked at the file folder again.

Laith dropped his arms to his lap. "What's in the file, Con? If it was only a matter of ensuring his daughter take up her father's duties, we wouldna been called here."

"Iona stepping into her duties is another matter entirely. I'll get to that in a moment. What's in the folder is a report. John didna die by natural causes," Con said as he locked his gaze on Laith's. "He was murdered."

Tristan mumbled a string of curses beneath his breath and sat forward. Ryder remained as he was, his body going taut. Rhys kept his eyes on the floor, a hand clenched at his side.

Kellan pushed away from the door and walked to stand beside Con. "John's old Range Rover was found on its side coming down the mountain from his house. The SUV's fall killed him instantly."

"How do we know it's murder?" Ryder asked.

Con said, "The police inspector knew John and I were acquaintances and since Dreagan is such a large holding in the area, he came to me with the findings. John's death was first classified as an accident, but upon inspection of the vehicle they realized it was murder. The brake line had a near-invisible puncture in it enough to drain the brake fluid and cause the brakes to go out."

"That could happen to any vehicle," Warrick said. "Old vehicles like that need repairs. Perhaps he didna tend to the Rover."

"The hole in the line was a perfect circle. It wasn't frayed as it would be if the line was worn." Con straightened. "I've asked the inspector to keep things quiet. He was happy to oblige since he doesn't want word leaking just yet."

Laith inhaled deeply and slowly released it. "What do you want us to do?"

"Keep an eye out for anything," Kellan said.

Con nodded to Laith. "Especially at the pub. People will talk. I want to know who did this to John. He was well liked and didna have any enemies."

"Which means they're our enemies," Ryder said.

Rhys lifted his eyes to pin Con with a look. "You think it's Ulrik."

Con lifted a shoulder in a shrug. "It could be Ulrik, or it could be the Dark Fae. There's no doubt the Dark will be wanting payback for what Kiril did."

"And Rhi," Rhys added.

The silence that followed after he said Rhi's name was

filled with friction. Rhi, a Light Fae, who had been a lover to a Dragon King was a constant source of irritation to Con. Recently she had been kidnapped by a Dark named Balladyn, who happened to have been a close friend of hers before he turned evil. Rhi managed to get free, but no one knew where she was.

Since Rhi had risked her life against the Dark for Kellan and Denae as well as Tristan and Sammi, every King owed Rhi a huge debt—including Con.

"And Rhi," Con added tightly.

The hatred between Con and Rhi multiplied through the centuries instead of easing. It was to the point before the kidnapping that Rhi made it her mission to annoy Con at every turn. And she was very good at it.

"There's been no sign of the Dark," Tristan said. "Even Henry's tracking of them with his resources at MI5 have dwindled all of a sudden."

Hal twisted his lips. "We've tripled our watch at all times, and no one has even heard a whisper about the Dark. Something is up."

"And Ulrik hasn't left Perth," Ryder said.

Con let his gaze rest on each of them in turn before he said, "The authorities are going to want a culprit for John's death. We can no' hand them a Dark Fae, but I doona think it was a Dark. Their methods are more . . . heinous. This was the work of humans."

"If it's Ulrik, he's commanding it all from The Silver Dragon," Ryder stated.

Everyone knew Ulrik found a way in and out of his antiques shop undetected despite the array of cameras Con had surrounding the building.

"We'll learn if it's Ulrik soon enough. I'm no' going to wait around and hope Iona returns for her father's funeral. She hasna seen him in twenty years."

Tristan frowned. "Meaning?"

"Meaning, I'm no' taking any chances. Iona will be here soon. Ryder, please pull her picture and show it to everyone. As soon as she's spotted in town, I want to know. She's no' been here for John to pass on the Campbell legacy."

"Which means one of us will," Warrick said.

Laith hoped to hell it wasn't him. He didn't want—or need—to be bogged down with a human who would need to be convinced the Dragon Kings were good. He'd been down that road before.

And it had ended badly.

He just wasn't the patient type, nor was he the type to explain things calmly and rationally over and over again. For him, actions spoke louder than words. The one who needed to take Iona by the hand and show her the way was Warrick, or even Ryder. Hell, even Con would be better at it than him.

Laith was going to make damn sure he didn't get stuck with her. Why then did he have a suspicion fate was laughing at him?

Hal raised a black brow, his moonlight blue eyes filled with doubt. "Are you so sure you can force Iona here?"

Con's eyes narrowed. "She'll be here, but in the end it doesna matter. Iona Campbell can no' sell the land. It stays in the Campbell family through a direct line as it always has."

"Things change," Rhys said.

"No' this," Con stated icily. "No matter what Iona Campbell wants, she can no' sell that land. If we want to remain concealed from the humans, then we're going to have to continue using our few allies like Henry North and the Warriors. And the Campbells."

Laith didn't think he would ever be grateful to any humans other than the Campbells, but Henry North was an exception. The spy had come to their aid a few times and continued to help time and again.

Warrick cleared his throat and stood. He pinned Con with his blue gaze. "I doona give a flying fuck about decisions we made in the past. We need to look to the future. That doorway on Campbell land needs to be guarded."

"As only a Campbell can," Kellan said.

Con blew out a breath. "We made that pact with the Campbells with magic, Warrick. No matter what we might want, that can no' be changed."

Ryder gave a small nod. "None of us want our war to spill over into the human's world. We've kept ourselves secret for thousands of millennia. We can—and will—continue."

Laith had his doubts, especially with all the technology that abounded, but more importantly, their enemies weren't just trying to kill them, they wanted the Kings exposed to the world.

More troubling was that the Dark searched for something hidden by Con. No one but Con and Kellan knew what the weapon was, and neither was talking. Already the Dragon Kings had fought a war with the humans, a war that caused both sides immeasurable losses.

For one, there was Ulrik. A Dragon King who had been banished because he began killing humans after his woman betrayed him. That in itself was a terrible loss, but more than that was the fact that all the dragons were gone. The humans had been very good at killing, and in order to keep the peace, the Kings sent their dragons away.

Laith looked down at his hands. He knew in his heart he would never see his beloved Blacks again. They were gone for good. All he could hope for was that they prospered and lived.

"Be vigilant," Con said and returned to his seat.

Laith was one of the first to rise and walk to the door. He needed to return to the pub. The Fox and The Hound had been his idea over a thousand years before. Because he loved being there, everyone knew him, which meant he had to sleep for a generation or two before he could wake once more and take his spot behind the bar. No one knew it was owned by Dreagan. The people did know he was part of Dreagan, but the secret of who owned it had been held since the pub's inception.

Laith reached the stairs leading down to the first floor of Dreagan Manor when he heard his name. He looked over his shoulder and found Tristan hurrying to him.

"How is Sammi doing?" Tristan asked worriedly.

Laith shook his head as he laughed. "As I've told you for the past few weeks, she's doing splendidly. She owned her own pub, remember?"

"Is she happy?" Tristan pressed.

"Verra."

Tristan smiled goofily while they descended the stairs. "Thanks for giving her the job. She needed something to do, and she loves being behind the bar."

"It was as much for my benefit as for hers. No longer do I have to come up with lies when I need to leave. As your mate, Sammi knows our secret. That makes my life infinitely easier."

Tristan slapped him on the back, his smile even wider. "I know. She's amazing. I'm going to meet her for lunch."

Laith stopped at the bottom of the stairs and watched Tristan stride out of the manor. He was always amazed at how his fellow Kings managed to find mates at all, especially since they had gone so many thousands of years alone.

"I doona understand them," Ryder said as he stopped beside Laith. "Doona get me wrong. I love the feel of a woman's thighs around me, but to be bound to a single woman for eternity?" Ryder shuddered. "It's no' for me. Human or Fae."

Laith had to admit it was odd to see a King mated to a

Fae, and a Fae that was part of a powerful Dark family at that. But Shara proved herself and her love for Kiril to one and all. She was as much a part of Dreagan as the human females who had mated Kings.

"I agree," Laith said.

Ryder chuckled as he threw Laith a look. "I've seen you flirting with that redhead from the village when she comes into the pub."

Laith grinned. "I'm a pub owner. I flirt with everyone when I'm behind the bar."

"You keep doing that, and you'll find yourself mated quick enough."

"It's no' for me. I'm perfectly content just as I am."

Ryder made a face. "Are you insane? Why say something like that and tempt the cosmos?"

Laith watched him walk away, wondering if he had just drawn the interest of fate.

CHAPTER
TWO

After twenty years, Iona was back in Scotland. She drove the small rental through the winding roads of the Highlands ignoring the spectacular beauty around her that urged her to grab her camera and document it. But it was difficult.

It wasn't that she didn't love the scenery. Even when she tried to forget her childhood in Scotland, she felt something missing in her soul. It wasn't until she landed in Edinburgh that she realized that missing piece was the wild, mystical land.

Iona's hands were sweating as she gripped the steering wheel. The closer she got to her childhood home, the more her heart pounded. She wasn't sure if it was nerves or sadness that brought on such a reaction, and she didn't want to delve too deep into the emotions to find out.

Just last week while on assignment in Afghanistan, she'd nearly been killed. It was because of the U.S. Marines she was with that she managed to come away with only minor injuries, but it put things into perspective. It made her realize how very short life was, and regardless of how she felt about what her father did, she needed to talk to him, to see him.

No sooner had she packed her belongings and booked a flight out of Afghanistan to Scotland than people began asking her about her family and where she was from. It was . . . odd.

Almost as if fate stepped in and gave her another nudge to return home.

As if she needed it. The near-death experience was enough.

But she was too late. During a layover, she was notified by the company she worked for about her father's death.

Iona hadn't shed any tears. Instead, anger welled up within her. She was furious that her father had died before she got to see him. Yes, it was silly and irrational, but it didn't change her feelings.

No sooner had she found out about her father's death than she got a phone call from her father's attorney wanting to know when she would be in town for the reading of the will.

Iona focused on the winding road as she passed through a cluster of rain clouds. The windshield wipers were loud and squeaky as they diligently worked to keep the windshield clear of rain.

Everything grated on her nerves. She felt raw, exposed. And she hated it.

She was used to being completely independent, moving from place to place with just her backpack. Iona had learned very quickly in her early years that the only one she really could depend on was herself. There was no use putting her faith or trust in anyone else, because they always disappointed her.

It began with her mother and father, and it continued on through school and university. She liked being alone, and despite what some people thought, being alone didn't mean she was lonely.

Which is why she loved her job. Photography was her

life. For as far back as she could remember, it's all she had ever wanted to do. She was lucky enough to work for the Commune—a group of wealthy business owners from around the globe who hired experts in various fields for any number of things.

For Iona, her assignments could be nothing more than photographing a horticultural exhibit in Paris or, like her last mission, deep in the middle of battle to get a firsthand view of the war being waged.

She bounced along the roads, encountering a car or two in the otherwise quiet mountains. She might have been only eight when her mother took her away from Scotland, but she recalled how quiet and still life had been.

A glance at the directions next to her had her turning left onto a dirt road that was more mud than anything. She drove around puddles not knowing how deep the holes might be and not wanting to get stuck.

Even after so many years since she lived in the Highlands, she still recognized the gate ahead of her. Iona stopped the car and put it in park, staring at it. Her father had set her atop the gate when he had opened and closed it. It was one of the few memories she allowed herself to remember, because opening that floodgate would do her no good.

Iona unbuckled her seat belt and threw open the door. Her hands shook as she walked to the gate and unbolted it before she pushed it wide. It creaked loudly, silencing the birds chirping around her.

She looked around at the dense forest. Her photographer's eye noticed the deep green of the pine needles, the paler green of the ferns that blanketed the ground and how they added contrast against the dark-colored bark and the sun filtering through the tree limbs.

It would make a beautiful picture, but documenting her trip was the last thing she wanted to do.

Iona returned to her car and drove through the gate before getting back out and shutting it behind her. She then drove slowly down the narrow road through the woods. Twice she had to stop to miss a pine marten that darted across the road.

When the trees thinned and she came upon the clearing with the small cottage, she had to stop the car, she was so overcome with memories.

Iona drew in a breath, her throat tight with emotions. Her eyes welled with tears, but she refused to shed a single one on a man who hadn't tried to contact her in twenty years. He was her father, and she would bury him since she was his only relative, but she wouldn't cry for him.

Or for the memories of the past.

The last time she saw the cottage was in the middle of the night during a vicious thunderstorm. She was drenched by the time her mother dragged her screaming to the car. All the while her mom kept telling her what a good life they would have in Kent, and that while England seemed a long way, it really wasn't.

Iona hadn't paid much attention to her mother. All she could do was stare at the silhouette of her father in the doorway as he stood watching them leave. She screamed for him to stop her mother. She held out her arms to the man who had never let her down.

But that night she discovered the man her father really was.

He watched them leave without uttering a single word. He didn't try to stop her mother or even attempt to keep Iona with him.

For weeks afterward she knew her father would come for her. He would take her back to the cottage and their woods, but the days turned into weeks and weeks into months. He didn't call, he didn't write, and he never came to see her.

Iona blinked away the sudden rush of tears and drove

the last few hundred yards to the house. She was slow to exit the car. Once she had, she didn't move. She wasn't sure she could go into the house.

Leaning against the rental car, she slowly perused the area. The cottage itself was in neat order. There were bird feeders everywhere, something that had been added after she was gone.

How many times had she begged her parents for a bird feeder? She hadn't had a camera at that age, but seeing the birds had been just as good.

Iona straightened and walked around to the back of the house. A wooden deck had been extended from the back door. A wrought-iron table and two chairs were perched on the deck as well as a book, opened and lying facedown.

The wind riffled the pages, damp from the frequent rain showers. The book had been set aside as if her father planned to return. Which meant his death had come about suddenly.

That was one thing she hadn't asked—how he died. Iona hadn't thought she wanted to know.

The sound of a motor broke the peace of the forest. Iona was instantly on guard when she walked back to the front of the house. Her steps slowed, and then halted when she saw the tow truck come to a stop with her father's 1972 Range Rover hooked to the back.

The door to the truck opened and a balding, heavyset man with graying hair and a bushy beard got out. He flashed her a smile. "I was told to return the vehicle now that the authorities are done inspecting it."

"Inspecting it?" she repeated.

He looked up from his clipboard. "Aye. That's usually the case when an overturned vehicle is found."

"Overturned vehicle?" Iona couldn't stop repeating his words. She knew she sounded like an idiot, but that was before she discovered how her father died.

The driver raised his gaze to her and slowly lowered the clipboard. "Forgive me, lass. I thought you knew."

"I just arrived." She swallowed, hoping he didn't hear the catch in her voice. "Please tell me."

He hesitated as if he were trying to think of a way to get out of explaining. Finally, he pursed his lips for a moment and then said, "John's Rover was found on its side about two miles from town the day before yesterday."

Two miles? That meant he was coming off the mountain. There were no guardrails, just boulders and more mountain, if someone went off the side.

"I'm sorry to say, lass, that John was found deceased."

Iona blinked and nodded. "Did you know my fa . . . John?"

"I did. I considered him a friend. He would hate to know that you'd finally come home now that he's gone."

She couldn't stand the censor in his dark gaze, nor did she care that her father had a friend. "Was John drunk?"

"Nay," the old man said, affronted. "He came into town three times a week for dinner and then went to the pub for a dram with me and a few other lads."

It seemed odd to find out such little things about her father's life now that he was gone. She grew uncomfortable standing there talking about her father.

The driver must have sensed her unease because he went back to writing on the clipboard. A few seconds later, he tore off a portion of the paper and handed it to her along with the keys. "It'll take me just a moment to unhitch the vehicle."

Iona didn't move from her spot while the Range Rover was freed from the constraints, nor did she move until the truck was out of sight. Only then did she let her shoulders sag. Now that she knew her father died so unexpectedly and harshly, she felt bad for thinking so callously of him just moments before.

With the trees blocking most of the light, the shadows began to lengthen, urging Iona to get her things and go inside the house.

The key was on the fob with the others of her father's. She let herself in, and then closed and locked the door behind her. Paying little attention to the house, Iona walked to the first door on the right and came to a sudden stop.

Her old room was just as it had been the night she left. Nothing had been moved, though everything had been recently dusted. Even the red plaid comforter was still draped across the bed.

Iona dropped her bags next to the bed. It was like walking back in time, except she couldn't pick up her life at eight. She was twenty-eight.

She spent the rest of the evening going from room to room looking through everything. Her father's office, next door to his room, was a complete mess. Just as she recalled from her childhood. There were papers stacked everywhere. His computer was on, the cursor blinking in the middle of the page where he had stopped writing.

When she next looked up at the clock, it was well past midnight. Iona shuffled to her bed and fell upon it, still fully dressed.

She only meant to rest for a moment, but exhaustion won out. The night was passed filled with dreams of her mother and father, and when her life was turned upside down. Iona would wake up and roll over, only to be woken with another dream.

She tossed and turned all night, and finally gave up trying to sleep. It took two cups of coffee before she could even glance at the clock to see it was just after six in the morning. The sun was shining as she set aside her cup and made her way into the bathroom.

After her shower and a change of clothes, she felt more human. She would give the cottage one more night, since it could have been all her snooping that caused the dreams. But if she had another sleepless night, she would book herself into the nearest motel or B&B until all of her father's belongings were taken care of.

Iona dropped her head forward to bang against the mirror in the bathroom. She still had the funeral, and since she was his only living relative, it would be up to her to arrange everything. Not to mention the reading of the will.

The sooner she got everything over with, the sooner she could move on. She lifted her head and smoothed aside her wet hair before she reached for the blow dryer. As she dried her hair she made a mental note of all she needed to take care of like the funeral, his will, his bank accounts, selling his Range Rover and the property.

Iona didn't think there would be much in his bank accounts since her father had never been good at controlling his funds, but with the sale of the land and the SUV, she figured it would be enough to reimburse her for what she would have to shell out for the funeral.

She looked at herself in the mirror. Attractive, that's what men called her, but not a great beauty. She didn't turn heads or cause men to forget themselves. Occasionally she would catch a man's eye, but with her schedule of travel, she didn't go looking for a relationship. Of any sort.

Her parents might have played a huge role in that decision-making process, however, when it came to men and relationships.

Iona ran her fingers through her pale blond hair. It took her forever to straighten, and with the humidity of the Highlands she didn't even bother to try. She opted to go with her natural state, which were waves. Not pretty curls, but waves that did whatever they wanted.

To help fortify herself, Iona pulled out what little makeup she carried with her. The small village wasn't London or Sydney, but she wanted to make a good impression.

Less than an hour later, she walked out of the house to her car. Another thirty minutes and she was in town. It took her two passes through the narrow street where most everything was located before she found the police station.

Iona parked and took a deep breath before she stepped out of the car. She closed the door and realized that several people had stopped and were staring as if she were some oddity.

She put a smile on her face, pulled her purse on her shoulder, and went to collect her father's body.

CHAPTER
THREE

It was the longest day of Iona's life. Everyone wanted to talk to her about her father. John Campbell had been admired, respected, and even loved among the people of the village. Odd since it went against everything she remembered her mother saying of him.

Iona was dead on her feet by the time she returned to the cottage in the late afternoon. All she wanted was a sandwich and a beer. She tossed her keys and purse on the kitchen counter and kicked off her shoes. Then she opened the fridge looking for a beer.

"Of course," she mumbled when she didn't see one.

It never dawned on her that she might need to pick up some groceries. She made her sandwich before going outside to sit at the table. As she ate, she watched the birds flying from feeder to feeder, their singing soothing. One by one, they settled for the night. Dusk was upon her, and yet she didn't want to go inside and be reminded of her childhood.

Not that sitting outside was any different. She recalled playing among the trees as a young girl and hunting the wild cats in hopes of getting a glimpse of the elusive animals. She hadn't had the entire forest to play in, however. The forest was huge, covering several hundred acres, but she had been confined to a small portion near the house.

Campbell land, her father called it. The land beyond belonged to Dreagan Industries. She still didn't understand why one company would need so much land.

Iona finished her sandwich and sat back in the chair. She remained until it grew so dark that she couldn't see anything. As she rose to return to the house, she paused, sure she heard something in the forest.

She listened intently, but didn't hear anything else. With a shake of her head, she walked inside the house and closed the sliding glass door.

She was walking to her room when she saw her keys on the floor. Iona bent and picked them up, sure they had landed by her purse. Or maybe she was just too tired to realize they had fallen.

It was after midnight when the mobile phone rang. He rose from his bed and the warm body of the woman to pad naked to the coffee table where all six of his mobile phones were lined up.

He sat on the cream leather of the Chesterfield sofa and reached for the fourth phone. He answered with a curt, "Yes?"

"She's arrived just as you said she would, sir," came the Australian accent across the line.

"Good. What other news do you have?" he asked.

The mercenary said, "She visited the morgue and talked to many of the villagers before returning home. I looked through her purse while she was outside, but I've not found anything yet."

"Keep looking. John will have left her something."

"Yes, sir."

"What about the other group of men I sent? Have they spotted you?"

The merc chuckled. "No, sir. It's working just as you told me it would."

"Excellent. Have they been seen?"

"Not yet, but they've remained hidden in the trees behind the house with only two as guards watching who comes up the drive."

He leaned back against the couch and smiled. "Keep me posted."

The call ended. He replaced the phone back with the others. Everything was falling into line perfectly. Next, Con would send one of the Kings to get close to Iona in the hopes of determining how much she knew.

Then the King would notice the group of men following Iona, just as he had set up. The Kings would be so focused on the group that they would never realize what was really going on around them.

He could almost taste the victory.

Con flew amid the clouds, loving the feel of the wind against his scales. As much as he wanted to enjoy his time, he was on patrol. Though it gave him time to think over his next step with Iona Campbell.

Just as he'd asked, he was notified as soon as she arrived in town. It was going to take one of the Dragon Kings to make a connection with her to discover if John left her instructions on what to do. Because if John didn't, then it was going to be up to the Kings to fill her in.

How Con hoped that wasn't the case. He didn't know Iona, but he expected her to be like most humans and scoff at the idea there were other beings on the planet with them. The fact that the land was crucial to Dreagan didn't help matters.

He dipped a wing and circled back around, his gaze

scanning the ground. The only thing he spotted was a herd of red deer nestled in a glen. Things had been quiet, too quiet. John's death and the Dark Fae movements suddenly becoming difficult to track only spelled bad news for everyone at Dreagan.

Whether Iona wanted it or not, she was part of something she couldn't escape.

All Con could hope for was that Iona and a King made some sort of connection. Even if it meant the King found his mate.

He grimaced. Constantine hated to even think along those lines, but if that's what it took to get Iona to believe them, then Con would parade every unmated King in front of her if he had to.

Iona was numb. Not from lack of sleep for a second night, though that was part of it. But because it was the only word she could come up with to describe what she felt as she watched her father's body being lowered into the ground.

Even as she dressed for the service, it hadn't hit her until she arrived at the church that she was burying her father. That she would never hear his voice again or see his smile.

Halfway through the service she stopped paying attention to anyone. She stopped hearing everyone's condolences. She saw their mouths moving, felt their sympathetic touches, but everything was drowned out by the ringing in her ears.

Once the service was concluded and the body was in the ground, she wanted to run to her car and get away, but she couldn't. People kept stopping her wanting to talk, to tell her how much they liked John Campbell. She nodded and smiled cordially, unable to utter a single word.

"Miss Campbell," said a deep voice beside her.

She turned her head to stare into a face so gorgeous he

almost didn't seem real. His blond hair was short and wavy, reminding her of the guys she watched surfing in Australia. His penetrating black eyes scrutinized her carefully.

"I'm Constantine from Dreagan Industries. I'm verra sorry for your loss," he said.

She nodded, glancing down to see his perfectly tailored black suit and the starched white shirt beneath with the black and silver tie.

"I'm sure you have many pressing things to do, Miss Campbell, but please know if you need anything, you need only to come to Dreagan and ask. I considered John a friend. His loss will be felt for years to come."

She simply looked at him, unable to fathom that her father was friends with someone like Constantine from Dreagan.

Constantine gave a quick bow of his head to the gravesite. "John Campbell was a good, honorable man."

Before she could say anything, he walked away, his long strides eating up the ground. He stopped beside a bright blue Maserati GranTurismo MC Stradale and got inside before driving away.

Iona knew she should be happy her father apparently had so many friends, but she couldn't manage to feel much of anything. She took a deep breath and spotted her father's lawyer, Thomas MacBane. He was the one who called to tell her about the will. He gave a nod, waiting for her. Iona made her way to Mr. MacBane.

As soon as she reached him, he began to speak of her father fondly, but Iona tuned him out as they walked down the flower-laden path by the church to the sidewalk that took them to his office two blocks over.

Mr. MacBane opened the door and waited for her to walk through before he entered his building. He smiled and motioned her forward into his office as his receptionist greeted them.

Iona settled into the comfortable chair before his large desk. She sat back and crossed her legs. She'd had to buy a black dress when she landed in Edinburgh. It seemed odd to see herself in heels when she normally wore hiking boots every day.

She looked into Thomas MacBane's face, noting the laugh lines around his eyes. He was around her age, with a thin frame and pasty white skin. But he had a kind look about him. It was no wonder her father trusted him. "I want to apologize beforehand, Mr. MacBane, but if I seem rude, it's just that it's been a tiring few days."

"Of course," he said, his dark eyes locking with hers, his interest plain. "And please call me Thomas."

She forced a smile. Thomas wasn't bad looking with his light brown hair and infectious laugh, but she couldn't even muster up an attempt at flirting. "Thank you, Thomas."

He cleared his throat and gathered the papers in his hand. "Your father's will is pretty straightforward, Iona. He leaves all his possessions to you, including the entire sum of money in his three accounts."

"Three?" she questioned in shock.

"Yes, three. He also had several investments in stocks. All of that will now go to you."

"I didn't think he had much money."

At this, Thomas glanced away from her face. "John had the three accounts since before you were born. Your mother had access to only one of them, which he rectified when she left."

Iona tightened her grip on the arms of the chair. She distinctly remembered the arguments late in the night between her parents over money. Specifically her mother complaining that there was never enough. "And the stocks? Have they always been there?"

"A few. Others he invested in over the past few years."

"How much money are we talking about?"

Thomas hesitated a moment before he replied, "They total just over five hundred thousand pounds."

"I didn't think he made that much with his writing."

"He's made verra good money with his novels. Most of his income went to support the village and charities. He's always lived verra frugally."

Iona was beginning to feel ill. The image she had of her father and what her mother had told her over the years was conflicting with things she was learning now.

"I hate to be the one to tell you this, but your father received a large chunk of his money from inheritance," Thomas said. "He put most of it aside for you."

Now she really was going to be sick. Her stomach churned as she broke out into a cold sweat. Why hadn't he contacted her? Why hadn't he tried to see her? She would've learned the truth about him then.

Money didn't matter to her because she made a very good living, but it would've been nice to know his side of the story.

Iona needed time alone. "Is that all?"

"No," Thomas said with a shake of his head, his eyes sad. "There is one stipulation in the will. The fifty acres of land can never be sold or leased. It must remain in Campbell hands. It can no' be transferred to another Campbell except upon your death."

She rubbed her temple trying to take it all in. "Does it say why I can't sell?"

"Your father left you a letter. Perhaps this will explain everything."

Iona doubted it. There were dozens of questions bouncing around in her head. She took the letter as she stood and walked from the office in a daze. If she'd felt numb earlier, she was overwhelmed with emotions now.

By the time she reached her car parked at the church,

she managed to calm down a degree. Then she noticed the letter in her hand.

Her father had been rich, rich enough to keep her mother happy and content. Rich enough to have kept them all together. But he hadn't. He let them leave that night, destroying her perfect world and the only home she'd known. He hadn't fought for her.

Perhaps that's what hurt the most. It wasn't like she could ask her mother any of this. The lies her mother told were stacking up hour by hour, and Iona was tired of being lied to. She wanted the truth.

Or did she? She squeezed her eyes closed and battled against the emotions choking her. She and her father had been close. He was her hero. Until he let them leave.

Iona opened her eyes and threw the letter, along with her purse, in the passenger seat of the car as she got in. She started the car and drove out of the village, but she didn't go to the cottage.

Instead, she steered the car in no particular direction and followed the road, needing to think. Twenty minutes later she pulled over when she saw a scenic spot atop a mountain and rolled down her window.

She gazed at the rolling mountains with the sun shining through the clouds. The clouds made amazing shapes along the slopes. Iona turned around in her seat and grabbed the two bags that were always with her—her camera bag, and a travel bag.

It took her a bit, but she managed to change out of her black dress and heels into a pair of jeans and plain white tee. It wasn't the first time she changed in a car, and she doubted it would be her last.

She stuffed her feet into a pair of hiking boots and laced them up before grabbing her camera and exiting the car. Just being away from town helped to ease her somewhat.

There was really only one way for her to relax, and that was to take pictures.

Iona walked about twenty paces from her car and got down on one knee. She unzipped her bag, and carefully brought out her camera before lifting it to her eye. She adjusted the lens to focus on the spread of yellow flowers. Several snaps later, she shifted the camera and took more pictures of the mountains, zooming out to get as much of them as she could.

She was smiling by the time she lowered the camera. Some people exercised or drank to calm down, but all she had to do was have her camera in hand. The world looked different through the lens of her camera.

Unable to stay away, Iona traveled farther down the slope to a stream in the valley. At the water she took pictures of the rocks along either side, as well as the larger ones in the middle of the stream that caused the water to flow around them.

Iona snapped away as a butterfly landed on a stone on the opposite bank. She was enthralled by the blue and purple colors on the butterfly's wings. For the next hour, she explored the area and filled up her camera with pictures.

The hike back to her car was as enjoyable as the trip down. So much so that Iona was already planning to do more hiking while she was in the Highlands. It would be a pity not to take advantage of the beauty surrounding her.

She got into her car and started to set her camera bag on the passenger seat. Her gaze caught on the envelope from her father, but that's not what caused her heart to miss a beat. It was because the envelope was setting atop her purse whereas it had been beneath it when she left. It was still unopened, the globe of the red wax seal in place, but it looked as though someone had messed with the edge.

Iona glanced at her open window. If the wind had come through, it wouldn't have put the letter there. Had the wind been fierce enough to pull it from beneath her heavy purse, it might have flipped it to the floorboard or even out the window.

That meant someone had been in her car. Iona hastily looked around as she locked her doors and rolled up her window. There were few trees where she was, leaving no place for someone to hide behind.

Iona didn't wait around. She started the car and turned the wheel to effortlessly pull a U-turn to head back to the cottage. The farther she got from the place, the easier she was able to breathe.

"So much for the peace I found," she mumbled to herself.

On her way through town she saw a sign for The Fox & The Hound pub. Since she didn't want to stop at the store just for alcohol, Iona decided a drink in the pub might be nice. She could sit and review the photos she'd taken while sampling a good ale.

Iona saw the wooden sign swinging from the metal pole on the side of the road and slowed. Parking was difficult since nearly all the spots were taken, even in early afternoon. It still didn't dissuade her as she parked.

She put the letter in her purse and looped the strap over her shoulder as she got out of the car. She made sure to lock it before heading into the pub. Iona opened the door and stepped inside, instantly taking in the place. The floors and tables were clean, and the walls were covered with news articles and photos from the people of the village.

Iona's gaze locked on a tall man behind the bar in a dark blue T-shirt leaning with his hands on the bar as he spoke to someone. He laughed, the sound hitting her straight in the gut, before he grabbed a glass and tilted a spigot of ale to fill it.

She tried to swallow as she took in his dark blond hair that hung just past his chin. He ran his hands through his hair, causing the thick muscles in his arms to bunch and move.

Even from the distance, Iona knew he was the kind of man that would cause her infinite trouble. The kind that left a trail of broken hearts wherever he went.

She told herself to walk away, to forget about the drink. But she wanted a closer look at him, to see the color of his eyes.

So she walked up to the bar and took a seat, her breath locking in her chest when his gunmetal gaze turned to her.

CHAPTER
FOUR

Laith set Keith's ale in front of him and caught a glimpse of someone out of the corner of his eye. He turned with a smile, ready to pour them a drink, and then stopped cold. Iona Campbell had walked into his pub.

He knew her by her picture, but the photo was nothing compared to the woman in the flesh. Her lips, wide and tempting, were quirked in a half-smile, giving her an air of mystery. Her shoulder-length, wavy blond hair was wind-blown, as if she had been walking among the heather.

She had an air of independence about her that was . . . enticing. She was tall and slender, her white shirt just tight enough to cling to her breasts. There was a smudge of dirt on her elbow as if she had been lying upon the ground recently.

His gaze returned to her face as she claimed a stool at the bar. She tucked her hair behind an ear, her coffee-colored eyes directed at him. Her skin held a golden glow, denoting that she was often in the sun.

Laith took a step closer, noting the sprinkle of freckles over her nose. "Welcome to The Fox and The Hound. What can I get you?"

"Your best ale," she said, her lips curving into a deeper smile.

Laith was powerless not to respond. He returned her smile and turned to get her ale. Surely it was a trick of the light or something to cause him to react as if she were the first female he'd seen in a millennia. Once he looked at her again, he would see she was like every other female who walked into his pub.

He finished filling the glass and hesitated for a moment. Laith twisted to the newcomer, and was hit once again by her earthy appeal. If someone asked him, he would call her a child of the forests.

Her smile fell a bit as he stared. Laith shook himself and set the ale in front of her. Their eyes met again, held. He felt an uncontrollable, undeniable pull to this woman and he fought against it. Hard. It was more than just lust. This . . . feeling . . . was on another plane altogether.

Nay.

He didn't want to feel anything for Iona. If he did, he might be tempted to be the one to show her the magic of Dreagan and what she guarded.

Bloody hell.

"Thank you," she said and reached for the ale.

Their fingers touched briefly, but that was all it took for a current of pure, utter desire to heat his blood. She jerked her hand away, proving she felt it as well. Her eyes darted to the left before skating back to him.

Laith wasn't sure if he wanted to scream in fury for fate calling his bluff, or jump over the bar and claim Iona's mouth in a kiss hot enough to set the pub aflame.

Whether or not he played a role in Iona's future, he had a part to play right then. "I have no' seen you in here before. Are you a tourist taking a stop in our beautiful village?"

She took a sip of the ale when he released the glass. "I was born here, though I've been away a few years."

"You must be Iona Campbell. My condolences about your father. I liked John a lot."

"It seems everyone did," she murmured with a hint of confusion.

Laith wanted to walk away and cut whatever ties might begin, and yet he found himself asking, "Do you intend to remain in town long?"

"Actually, no. Once everything is taken care of, I'll be back to work."

"And where is that?" Laith couldn't begin to understand why he kept asking questions. He told himself it was information for everyone at Dreagan, but in reality, he was more than curious about her.

Damn, damn, damn.

She laughed softly, the sound shooting straight to his cock. He glanced around and noted that he wasn't the only one who couldn't take their eyes from her. The rest of the patrons were staring with interest.

"I'm a photojournalist. I travel the world taking photos of people and events."

"I'm impressed." And he truly was. It couldn't be an easy life, but she obviously loved what she did. "The arts run in your family."

It was the wrong thing to say because a small frown formed on her brow and the smile disappeared. She ran her fingers along the condensation of the glass. "I guess it does."

Laith gave a nod and reluctantly returned to his other customers. Several times he caught her staring at him through the mirrors behind the bar. No matter how much he tried not to look her way, he found himself doing it again and again.

A little later he saw her with a camera as she scrolled through photos. Somehow he managed to keep his distance until her ale was almost finished.

"Would you like another?" he asked.

She glanced up and grinned. "Please."

He poured her another ale and placed it before her. Just as he turned to leave, she caught his eye. "Aye?"

"How well did you know my father?"

Laith shrugged and leaned his hands on the bar. "Pretty well. He came in three times a week every week. There was a small group of men he was with, though occasionally he would be by himself."

"I'm having a bit of trouble reconciling who I thought my father was with who he really was."

Laith couldn't imagine being in her shoes. By the pain she couldn't quite hide in her dark eyes, he found himself wanting to give her comfort. The kind of comfort he'd seen Kellan give Denae.

No' good news at all. I'm getting in over my head.

Why then didn't he leave?

If only he could answer his own question.

"Your father spoke of you often."

A slight blush stained her cheeks. "You mean you knew I was a photographer?"

"Aye. Everyone does. John showed us your work often. You're verra good."

She took another long swallow of the dark ale. "You seem to know a lot about me, and yet I don't even know your name."

"It's Laith."

"Laith," she repeated, letting it fall slowly from her lips, almost like a caress.

He was instantly, painfully hard.

It's your last chance. Run. Run now.

"An unusual name," she said.

"It's a family name."

Her brows rose. "Do you have family around here?"

"No' for a long time."

"I'm sorry." She turned her glass around. "Can I ask you something?"

He gave a nod. "Of course."

"This pub borders Dreagan. What do you know of them?"

Laith was completely taken aback by her question. He thought she might ask something about her father, but not about Dreagan this soon. Could she already know? Could John have told her?

"They distill the best whisky around, and they're good to the people."

"And my father knew them?"

"He did. John knew everyone."

She worried her bottom lip with her teeth. "It's odd, isn't it? To think you know someone, only to learn everything you believed was wrong. Scotland isn't my home. Hasn't been for twenty years, but I don't want to stay here."

"You doona find it beautiful?"

Iona smiled. "I took plenty of pictures today to prove that I do, but I don't have time to take care of land."

"You inherited your father's land," he said, putting enough inflection in his tone so that she might believe he just guessed it.

"I did. I want to sell it, but it appears that I can't."

The door to the pub opened and Sammi walked in, her powder blue eyes crinkled from her smile and her sandy-colored hair pulled back in a ponytail. "Hey, Laith."

"Hey, Sammi," he called.

She came around the bar and put her purse beneath it, and then flashed a smile to Iona. "Hello there. You must be who everyone is talking about."

"That's me," Iona said ruefully with a lift of the ale.

Sammi stuck out her hand. "I'm Sammi. I work with Laith."

"Nice to meet you," Iona said as they shook hands.

"Same to you. We should have a dr—" Sammi began, but was cut off when the door opened again. "Hang on," Sammi said and rushed around the bar to Tristan, who grabbed her against him for a quick kiss.

Iona watched the scene before she turned her head to Laith. "Who is that?"

"That's Sammi's husband, Tristan, who just happens to be a part of Dreagan." It was the perfect opportunity for him to push Iona onto someone else, but as soon as the words were out of his mouth, he wanted to take them back.

Iona watched the pair carefully. "They seem to really care for each other."

"They genuinely do," he said, unable to keep from frowning at her choice of words.

She turned back to him. "I'm usually on my own. I sometimes forget that I say things out loud that I should keep to myself."

"Doona worry about that here." He spotted Sammi bringing over Ryder and Tristan so he nodded in their direction. "You're about to meet more people."

Iona sat up straight and swiveled on the stool to face the three.

"Iona," Sammi said. "This is my husband, Tristan, and our friend Ryder."

Iona wore a friendly smile as she greeted them. "Hello."

Tristan bowed his head, but Ryder took her hand and gave her a charming smile. Laith didn't like the way she blushed in return. He took a step back. He should be grateful, relieved even that another King had taken an interest in her. That meant Laith was off the hook. He didn't want to look after Iona.

Did he?

"I was just telling Iona that she and I needed to get a

drink sometime." Sammi turned back to Iona. "I used to be on my own, and then I met Tristan. Now, I can't seem to have enough friends."

"You got me, love. Is that no' enough?" Tristan asked Sammi with a wink.

Sammi pulled on his long brown hair. "You know it is."

Tristan yanked her against him. "When do you get off work?"

"No' until closing," Laith said with a chuckle. "You'll have to wait to have some alone time with your wife."

Ryder sat on the stool next to Iona. "Have you been to Dreagan yet?"

"No," she said and glanced at Laith. "I did meet Constantine however."

Laith tossed aside his towel. "At the funeral."

"We wanted to speak to you," Ryder said. "But Con asked us no' to overwhelm you."

Iona frowned. "I'm sorry. There were so many people there that I don't remember many of them."

"No one blames you," Sammie said. She put a comforting hand on Iona's arm. "It's probably better that only Con approached you instead of a slew of men from Dreagan."

Laith watched Iona fidget under her embarrassment before she asked, "What do you do at Dreagan?"

"Many things," Tristan answered.

Ryder raised a blond brow. "We doona just make whisky, lass. We run thousands of sheep and cattle."

"I had no idea," Iona said, a hint of awe in her voice.

"Most of the land Dreagan uses for conservation," Tristan added. "The forests, the mountains, and such are all protected natural habitats."

Her eyes widened a fraction. "Really? That's nice to hear. I've run into plenty of people who could care less about conserving nature."

"No' everyone is a bad person," Laith said. Though there were more of them out there than she could guess.

Her coffee-colored eyes softened as they shifted to him. "No, they aren't."

CHAPTER
FIVE

Rhi didn't know why she returned to Earth. The realm held nothing for her anymore, but then again, she hadn't found any peace since Balladyn tortured her.

As she stood on the Ponte Milvio in Rome, she looked down at the blue water of the Tiber River. The bridge was famous in Rome for couples to attach padlocks to as a show of love. Once the lock was clipped on, the couple then threw the key into the river.

Rhi wondered how many wished they could retrieve those keys. Being chained to someone—or some*thing*— was the worst sort of torment.

Even now that she was free of the Chains of Mordare, she was still living a nightmare. Where once she found joy in shopping like humans and driving around in her Lamborghini, now she couldn't stand any of it.

She looked down at her fingers. Before her kidnapping, she hadn't let a day go by without having her nails painted. She collected nail polish in every shade.

In a fit of rage she destroyed them all before leaving her sanctuary in the mountains—a sanctuary that no one was supposed to know about. Yet, it had been Ulrik who had not only rescued her from Balladyn, but brought her to her secret cabin. She still didn't know how he discovered her place, but she was going to.

Her nails drew her gaze once more. The color, some pale pink shade, was all but gone now.

Rhi loved Rome. Or she used to. She would wander the streets watching the locals and tourists alike. She had been to the Coliseum countless times from its inception right up until last year.

There were many things on the realm that she had seen from their origins. It was one of the advantages of being Fae. Rhi closed her eyes and lowered her head. She was Light Fae, or she was supposed to be.

Balladyn had done a good job of pushing evil upon her. She wasn't an unforgiving person, and yet, it took the slightest thing to set her off now. Many times she had to hold herself back from retaliating against someone.

The light inside her was . . . diminished. Luckily it was still there, but it was getting harder and harder to sense. That was Balladyn's doing. Once so close she considered him a brother, he was now Dark Fae, blaming her for his turning Dark.

Rhi halted her thoughts and opened her eyes. She spent enough time thinking of Balladyn. It was time to move on.

She turned away from the side of the bridge and started walking. Right on cue, she heard her queen call to her. It was a call Rhi had been ignoring for several weeks, but Usaeil's request was growing more and more demanding.

Rhi could only put her off for so long, but she wasn't yet ready to face the queen or those of the court. Everyone knew what happened to her. They would be looking for a defect, a thread of darkness.

A weakness.

Because no Light had ever come back after being taken by the Dark.

Rhi hadn't expected her own people to come for her. There was too much at stake for them to try a rescue. She hadn't thought the Dragon Kings would help her either. They were already knee deep in their own Dark Fae war.

Not to mention the hatred between her and Con. Constantine would sooner let her rot than look at her. Yet, a small part of her had held out hope that the few Kings she considered friends might help. Out of everyone, she knew Phelan would try.

Thinking of the Warrior brought a smile to her face. He had a primeval god inside him that made him immortal, but even before that he was a powerful Highlander since he was part Fae. Rhi had been the one to find him and introduce him into the Fae world.

Phelan reminded her of the brother she had lost to one of the countless wars the Fae were always involved in. Yes, Phelan would have tried to help, and the Kings would have stopped him, just as she would have wanted.

If the Dark ever learned of Phelan, it could be a game changer. It was worth enduring all of Balladyn's torture to keep Phelan's identity a secret.

Rhi wanted to talk to Phelan, to let him know she was all right. If she did, it would alert the Light as well as the Kings that she was back. Was she ready to return to everything? Could she act as if she was the same Fae as before? More importantly, could she ever enter a Dark stronghold again?

Rhi quickly turned to the left and went down a narrow alley. She rested her head against the stones of the building as she struggled to breathe. Every time she thought of seeing the Dark, a panic attack would hit.

She hadn't even known a Fae could get a panic attack, but there was no denying that's exactly what was happening to her.

There was no telling how long it would last this time,

and she didn't want anyone to see her. Rhi vanished from the alley and reappeared at her cabin overlooking the Italian lake. She dropped down on the grassy hillside and sank her fingers into the dirt. It seemed to take an eternity before she was able to stop shaking and take a calming breath.

Blinking at the bright sunlight, Rhi shaded her eyes and remembered why she had fallen in love with the place. Light twinkled off the lake as birds chirped nearby. A soft breeze danced around the poplar trees and pulled her hair into her face.

Rhi pushed the locks aside and got to her feet. She threw a quick look at her cottage to make sure no one was there. Once she was certain Ulrik wasn't sitting on the porch, she faced the cottage for a closer inspection.

She was going to have to find a new location. This one was ruined now. It was supposed to be a place she didn't have to worry about being found, not one that she needed to inspect to see if someone awaited her.

After a check, Rhi stepped onto the porch and then inside the house only to come to a surprised halt.

The last time she had been there she had destroyed everything. Every piece of furniture, every item of clothing, every bottle of nail polish—all three hundred bottles. She anticipated returning to clean up, but it was immaculate. Someone had been there repairing furniture or replacing it.

Apprehension coiled tightly within her. She closed the door and quietly walked from one room to another until she reached her bedroom.

A new comforter of soft cream covered her bed. Dozens of pillows of all different sizes and shapes in various shades of peach, pink, and gold were stacked against the headboard. She didn't dislike the colors. In fact, she found them soothing. Not too bright or flashy.

Then she turned to the right and peered inside her closet.

There were two outfits hanging. One was a white lace shirt paired with light denim and brown heels.

The other was a sheer black shirt with black jeans and black booties.

Whoever cleaned her house was giving her a test with the clothes. If she chose the white set, she was still the person from before. If she chose the black, she was more Dark.

Rhi twisted away and her mouth fell open when she caught sight of the nail polish. Every bottle she had collected—and some new ones—were lined on the shelves clustered by color. She walked to the colors and ran her finger along the bottles. If it was a test, then she would give them an answer.

Rhi grabbed a bottle and teleported to her favorite nail salon in Austin.

Laith leaned his hip against the table with his arms crossed and listened to Tristan and Ryder tell Con of their conversation with Iona.

"Interesting," Con mumbled. He shifted his gaze to Laith. "How long did you talk to her before they arrived?"

"A wee bit. She's no' sure how she feels about the things she's learning regarding John. She's thought of her father one way all these years, but she's seeing him in a new light."

Con leaned back in his chair behind his desk as he steepled his fingers. "So she doesna yet know what she guards?"

"No' that I can tell." Laith dropped his arms to his sides and crossed his ankles. "She doesna want to stay in Scotland."

"That can pose a problem," Ryder added.

Con frowned and asked Laith, "Do you think she's that determined to leave?"

Laith clenched his jaw and nodded.

"She took a shine to Laith," Tristan pointed out. "Maybe he can turn her around."

Laith glanced at Tristan before turning back to Con. Here was his chance to point out that Ryder might have a chance with her. But those weren't the words that came out of his mouth.

"She doesna know I'm from Dreagan. That could be to our benefit. I can learn what she does or doesna know. If John has told her what she guards, then I'll tell her who I am and hopefully convince her to remain."

"Do whatever it takes," Con said matter-of-factly.

Laith knew Con would do whatever it took to convince Iona, but he wanted to do things his way. The only kink in that plan was that they didn't have a lot of time. "Aye," Laith finally agreed. "I'll see what I can do."

Tristan shifted in the chair and grinned. "You may no' have to do too much. She's pretty taken with you."

Laith could still recall in exact detail the scorching desire that raced along his skin and through his veins. It hadn't lessened after Iona left. He didn't like how he felt disoriented near her, or how he tried to think of ways he could touch her without her realizing it.

"If she doesna want to stay, we'll have to set up extra patrols," Con stated.

Laith braced his hands on the table on either side of his hips. "And if she stays, but John hasna told her what she's guarding?"

It was Ryder who blew out a breath and got to his feet. "She'll need to know how important that piece of land is. She'll need to know the truth. Frankly, I'm glad I'm no' the one to tell her."

Would Iona be so frightened that she didn't let him near her again once she saw him in dragon form? Or would she welcome the dragon that he was?

Every Campbell that guarded the secret doorway knew of the Dragon Kings. It was only right that Iona did as well. The Kings only had to tell the first Campbell. The burden then fell to each Campbell before the land was passed down.

"There's something about her that's familiar," Tristan said, breaking into Laith's thoughts.

Con lowered his hands to his stomach. "John. She has the look of her father."

Tristan shook his head, frowning. "Nay. Someone else. I can no' place it right now, but it's as if I should know."

Laith uncrossed his ankles and straightened. "I think she'll return to the pub. I'll try to talk to Iona more and see what I can learn."

"Oh, she'll return," Ryder said with a chuckle.

"Bugger off," Laith said, but there was a smile on his face. "I'm going to take to the skies."

Laith and Ryder were walking out of Con's office when Tristan blurted out, "Hayden."

Laith stopped in his tracks and exchanged a look with Ryder before they turned to look at Constantine. Con had his forearms on the desk, and a frown of concentration on his face.

Tristan smiled widely. "That's it. She reminds me of Hayden. Look at her eyes. They're no' black as Hayden's, but they're dark. It's the shape of them as well, and her hair color."

"I'll be damned," Con whispered.

The Warriors had all been mortal once, and if they tried, many of them could trace their families through the centuries. Tristan himself had been a Warrior before he was beheaded and reborn as a Dragon King.

"We have to tell Hayden," Tristan insisted. "He'd want to know."

Ryder slowly nodded. "It might be a good idea. He isna a part of Dreagan, and he's her family. She doesna have anyone else."

"She has her mother," Con broke in.

Laith found all of their gazes on him. "Since when did I get voted the one to look out for her?"

"The moment she ignored me for you," Ryder said with a sly smile.

Laith was eager to see her again, excited to hear her sexy voice, and impatient to touch her. And wholly confused as to why he was enormously happy that she chose him. "She just buried John and is learning he's no' the man she thought he was. She's going to need someone. Let's bring in Hayden."

CHAPTER
SIX

Iona sat at the kitchen table staring out the window to the woods beyond. She was supposed to take an assignment next week, but oddly enough Iona found she wasn't ready to leave Scotland.

The decision had come in the long hours of the night as she stayed awake looking at the ceiling. After all that she learned about her father, she couldn't leave yet. It wasn't because she couldn't sell the land. It was because she needed the time at the cottage to reconcile who her father really was.

Iona sent off a quick text to Abby, her contact with the Commune, declining the next assignment. Iona had never refused a project, but it seemed the right thing to do. She wasn't even sure if anyone declined the Commune. It wasn't like she or any of the other employees spoke to each other. She knew of some, but for all she knew, her refusal could mean she was fired.

That made her grimace, but it wasn't like it would be the first time. She always managed to land on her feet no matter what life threw at her. Oh, she might stumble a bit, but she refused to fall. She would survive whatever came next.

Iona looked down at her teacup, noting that it was no longer warm in her hand. She sat back with a sigh. She probably should call her mum and tell her about John. Every time Iona thought of talking to her mother she got heartburn. Her mother was as high maintenance as they came.

On her fifth husband, Sarah was in Morocco. The marriage wasn't even two years old, and already her mother was talking divorce. The one thing her mother never did was work—at anything. Whether it was a job or relationships, the moment things began to get difficult or demanding, she was gone.

Perhaps that's why Iona worked twice as hard at everything. Iona had known the truth about Sarah for a long time. However, Iona always assumed her parents' marriage crumbled because of her father not handling their money correctly and leaving them poor, as her mother had always claimed.

Iona looked around the cottage. There wasn't extravagance, but everything was nice and clean. And neat. Obsessively neat—just as she was.

Her mother? Just the opposite. Iona learned to do laundry at the age of nine because she'd had no clean clothes and Sarah didn't know how to work the washer. The cleaning then fell to Iona soon after, as did the cooking, shopping, and bill paying.

Iona felt that her mother had needed taking care of because she was so distraught over the divorce and loss of her beloved husband who had wronged her.

Was it all a lie? Had Sarah fabricated everything?

She refused to think about that as she rose from the table and changed out of her PJs into jeans, a tee, and hiking boots. After running a brush through her hair, she quickly wound a ponytail holder around her hair into a bun.

A brush of her teeth, and she was walking out the door with her camera bag over her shoulder. Iona didn't get far before she took out her camera. The sight of a squirrel sitting on a limb as he ate a nut caused her to smile. He looked at her, cocking his head to the side. Iona snapped a couple of quick photos before he scampered up the tree and disappeared.

The sky was filled with thick, puffy clouds that rolled lazily across the summer sky. Being out in the forest eased the knot of stress between her shoulder blades.

It was several hours later after wandering all over that she heard the waterfall. Iona quickened her footsteps, anxious to see the water. She burst through the trees as the roaring grew louder.

She came to a sudden stop, struck by the beauty. She had forgotten the waterfall, had forgotten that it was a place she and her father would go to alone. The beauty of the water cascading down the rocks before filling a small pool and then drifting down into the stream was breathtaking.

Had she hated her father so much that she blocked out the memories of their times at the waterfall? The picnics, the laughter?

The small pool was where he taught her to swim. The stream had been a place of endless hours of fishing. The waterfall had been a source of fantastic tales involving dragons and magic.

Iona sat down and simply stared at the waterfall. She had no idea how long she remained that way before she shook herself out of her memories. She brought the camera to her eye, and then lowered it.

It took two more tries before she was able to take any pictures.

The buzz of his mobile vibrating on the desk pulled his attention from an e-mail he was reading. He glanced down at the row of mobiles until he saw the one lighting up as it announced a call.

He accepted the call and said, "Yes?"

"She's in the woods, sire," came the reply in a whisper.

Just as he had known Iona would be. "Do you have eyes on her?"

"Aye, sir," came the Australian reply.

He drummed his fingers on the desk. "Keep watching her. I want to know everyone she speaks with. I'm certain Con will make a move soon. Where all has she been?"

"To the church, lawyer's office, and the pub."

He smiled. "The pub. She's making this too easy."

"The word about town is that Campbell's death is still an accident."

He sat forward in his chair and gripped the phone tighter. "You might be ex-military, but you're dealing with people you can no' even begin to understand." Anger surged through him as he let his brogue slip through. It always happened when he grew irate. "Dreagan will be on guard. They'll be looking for anyone and anything out of the ordinary. I've prevented them from seeing you, but if they get wind that you're out there, nothing will stop them from finding you."

There was a beat of silence before the mercenary cleared his throat. "They won't have reason to find me."

"And you're remaining close to Iona?"

"Of course."

"Keep it that way," he stated. "I'll be waiting on your next call."

He ended the conversation and set the mobile back in place. It hadn't taken Iona long to go to the pub. She was a pretty enough human that she would most likely gain a Dragon King's interest.

Now that she would be remaining in Scotland a bit longer,

it would give whichever Dragon King time enough to seduce her.

That's when he would make his move.

"So predictable, Con," he said smugly.

The granola bar Iona ate was long gone by the time she returned to the cottage at noon. Her stomach rumbled with hunger as she entered the house. After setting her camera bag down, she opened a bag of chips and popped one in her mouth while throwing together another sandwich.

It was only her second one, and she was already getting tired of eating them. Except there was little else in the cupboards. If she wanted to cook, she was going to have to go into town.

Then she thought of the pub, of Laith. Now him she didn't mind seeing. He was easy on the eyes, had a devilishly sexy smile, and a body that she yearned to photograph. Naked. She knew just by looking at the way his clothes fit that he had a body that would make her mouth water.

Iona paused, the sandwich lifted halfway to her mouth. She could go into town and grab a few things, then eat a late dinner at the pub. Perhaps Laith would be there.

A thread of excitement ran through her. It had been a long, long time since a man caught her interest as Laith did. Not that she wanted anything more than a few days in his arms.

Her mother ruined her for any sort of relationship. Iona only saw the failures each time her mother tried to find love, proving to Iona that there wasn't such a thing as love. It was also why she didn't get involved with anyone for more than a night or two. Anything longer allowed the men to think there could be more.

"Never going to happen," she mumbled before taking a bite of her sandwich.

Iona didn't just keep her distance from men, but people in general. She knew a lot of people, but no one she considered a friend. It was better that way, because then no one could let her down. More importantly, it made her rely only on herself. That way she was never disappointed in thinking someone would do what they said they would—because most people didn't.

People made promises as easily as wishes, and thought nothing of forgetting or breaking a promise.

Life was a hard lesson, but she learned much while still a teenager watching one man after another rotate out of her mother's life like a revolving door.

Iona finished eating and cleaned up the kitchen. Then she went into her bedroom and took a look at her clothes. She wanted to dress a little nicer than what she had worn so far, but she had nothing.

She flopped down on the bed and looked at her clothes—hiking pants, solid color tees, rain jacket, and two pairs of jeans—with a frown. Was that really all she had? Had she been so involved with work that she hadn't bought anything nicer?

There wasn't any place in town for her to get more clothes, nor would she have room to pack them. She had so few items because they fit in the backpack easily. Not to mention she would have no other cause to wear them once she returned to work.

Iona pulled out her second pair of jeans and her best shirt, a black tee. It was going to have to do. Besides, it might be better since she might like the way Laith looked and spoke, but her interest was too deep already. That should put the brakes on anything she might think about.

Kicking off her boots, she removed her clothes and tossed them next to the washer before she headed into the bathroom for a shower. Twenty minutes later she shut off the blow dryer and dressed. She double-checked the back door to ensure it was locked before walking out the front and locking it.

It was a nicely laid out plan that went to shite as soon as she pulled up in front of the co-op and got out of her car. The priest from the church walked up and asked if she was all right. It took ten minutes to assure him that she was fine. Then she walked into the store and was stopped five different times by the owner and shoppers.

All Iona wanted to do was get a few items. What should have been a quick errand was turning into an event. It was everything she could do not to just walk away from them all. She carried her basket, filled to the brim, to the counter and checked out without another incident. A glance at her watch showed it had taken almost an hour.

Iona was carrying her purchases to her car when someone called her name. She looked to find Thomas MacBane, her father's attorney.

"Hello," he said with a smile as he walked up. "I was going to call you tomorrow and let you know the bank is ready for you to come in so they can sign over John's accounts."

She nodded woodenly. "Right. I can get there sometime tomorrow."

"Would you like me to come with you?"

Iona stilled and tried not to read anything into his question, but there was no doubt he was asking for much more than to accompany her by the look in his eyes. "I appreciate that, Thomas, but I think I can handle it."

"There will be taxes that need to be paid as well on the inheritance."

She adjusted her bags in her hand and forced a smile. "And you have the paperwork needed?" she guessed.

He beamed. "I do. We can go over it tomorrow and get that out of the way."

"Sure," she said. The sooner she finished her dealings

with Thomas the quicker she could distance herself from him.

"Perhaps we could have lunch?" he offered.

"Hey, Iona," Sammi said with a bright smile as she walked to them. "I was hoping I'd run into you."

Iona could have kissed Sammi she was so happy to see her. "Hey there."

Thomas looked from Sammi to Iona. "So what do you say, Iona?"

Iona hesitated, and Sammi quickly said, "Oh, Thomas, I'm sorry. Iona and I have lunch plans tomorrow."

"That's too bad," he said, his face downcast. "Another time then."

Iona waited until he was out of earshot before she looked at Sammi and said, "I owe you big time."

"Come to the pub and grab a bite with me and we can talk about that," she said with a wink.

Iona wondered if the excitement coursing through her was because she wasn't going to eat alone, or if it was all at the prospect of seeing Laith again.

CHAPTER
SEVEN

Sammi grabbed a booth in the back corner and slid into the seat with a smile. Iona was slower to join her, though Sammi noted how Iona made a point of looking at the bar. The disappointment that showed wasn't hidden fast enough for Sammi. She took note of the obvious interest Iona had in Laith. Even more intriguing was the way Laith was fascinated by Iona.

Sammi wasn't into matchmaking. As a mate to a Dragon King, she knew the importance of their secrecy, but there was something about Iona she liked immensely.

It might be Iona's aloofness or her reserved nature that reminded Sammi of herself before she came to Dreagan. At least Iona's life wasn't in danger—a first in a while for a woman who came to Dreagan.

"What?" Iona asked as she raised a brow at Sammi.

Sammi shrugged. "What do you mean?"

"It's the way you're looking at me. You're deep in thought, and I've a suspicion it's about me."

Sammi smiled wide and motioned to Glen at the bar for drinks. "You're good. I'll give you that."

"Are you going to tell me what you were thinking?"

Sammi waited until Glen set the ales in front of them and walked away. "I was just thinking how you remind me of myself before I came here."

"How's that?" Iona asked before taking a drink of ale.

"I owned a pub near Oban."

Iona's brows rose. "Really? Why did you leave?"

"My business partner laundered the Mob's money through my pub. I didn't know about it until he began skimming money from them."

"That's something you hear in the movies, not real life."

Sammi's lips twisted. "I can attest to how very real it was. I was shot while trying to escape."

"And you came here? Why here?"

"My half-sister." Sammi smiled and played with the edge of the coaster. "Jane is married to Banan, who is part of Dreagan, and they took me in and sheltered me."

"And you found Tristan."

Sammi couldn't think about her mate without her blood heating. "Yes."

"I find it curious that you say Tristan and Banan are part of Dreagan instead of saying they work for Dreagan."

Sammi looked into Iona's dark eyes and realized Iona was much more observant than ordinary people. "That's because they own part of Dreagan. They do work the land with the others, but Dreagan is them, and they are Dreagan."

"I see," Iona said softly and sat back.

"Would you like a tour of Dreagan?"

"You want to show me how beautiful it is, I suppose."

Sammi shrugged and held her gaze. "Of course. Dreagan is beautiful. It's also my home. However, I thought you might like a personal tour of the distillery."

"Why?"

"I was being nice, Iona."

"People aren't nice unless they want something."

Sammi snorted and shook her head. "You're reading things into this that aren't there. I'm extending a hand of friendship."

"I don't have friends."

Iona said it so unemotionally that Sammi knew she was speaking the truth. "I see. That's too bad."

"That came out terribly rude. I apologize," she said and grabbed one of the menus stacked against the back of the table. "Is the fish and chips any good here?"

"The best," Sammi answered without missing a beat. If Iona wanted to change the subject, she would comply. The more she was with Iona, the more she learned about her.

Without a doubt, Con wanted Laith to get close to Iona, and it wouldn't be difficult. But Sammi knew there were things a woman would only tell another woman, which was why she had taken it upon herself to befriend Iona. Though she hadn't lied. She would have befriended her regardless.

Iona set aside the menu. "I think I'll get that then."

Sammi slid out of the booth and went to place the order herself in the kitchen. She was walking out when she heard Laith's voice coming from the back office. He would leave as soon as he was finished placing the orders with his vendors, but she knew once he saw Iona he would stay.

Sammi walked back out to the pub and returned to the table. Iona's ale was half gone and she was busy looking at all the photos along the walls.

"It's been a long time since I've been in Scotland," Iona volunteered.

Sammi set down her glass after a long drink and asked, "How long exactly?"

"Twenty years."

"That explains why you don't have the Scottish brogue."

Iona licked her lips. "I lost it pretty quick after two years in Kent, four in London, three in Paris, and then two in Spain."

"You got to see a lot of the world while still young," Sammi said, impressed.

"I got to see my mother go from one relationship after another."

That one statement summed up Iona more than she realized.

"I didn't know my father. He's an American who had an affair with my mother, but chose another woman to marry. He lives in the States, and has for years. Jane is the one that found me. Before her, it was just me and my mum."

"You were close?"

"Inseparable," Sammi said, sadness weighing on her heart as it always did when she thought of her mother. "She died a few years back."

"I'm sorry."

Sammi lifted the glass, but stopped short of bringing it to her lips. "Are you close with your mum?" she asked and then drank.

Iona rolled her eyes. "Lord, no. She texts me about once a week, to let me know where she's at. She likes men, and she likes money."

"Relationships with our parents are never as cut-and-dry as we'd like to hope."

Iona chuckled loudly. "No truer words have been spoken."

Sammi was happy to see Iona smiling again. It was time to turn the conversation away from her mother, which was obviously a sore subject. "So how did you get involved with your photography?"

"I've been fascinated with cameras for as long as I can remember. I received my first one when I was seven. It was a Christmas present. I was never without it. When Mum and I left Scotland, I hid behind the camera much as other children did their favorite stuffed animal."

"And you found a passion," Sammi guessed.

Iona's smile was slow but wide. "Yes. I worked relentlessly to hone my craft, and entered countless photography contests. I knew I wouldn't win, but I always got incredible feedback from the judges. I then took what they said and poured it back into my art."

"You have a gift. There's no denying that."

Iona looked down, but the pleased smile remained. "Thank you. I'm lucky to get paid to do something I love."

"I know what you mean," Sammi said and looked around the bar. "My pub was bought with the help of my mother. It was precious to me, and when I lost it, I didn't know what I was going to do. Then there was Tristan, and luckily Laith offered me a job. It feels good to be back behind a bar."

"Mixing drinks isn't exactly an easy thing to do. That takes talent as well."

Sammi laughed and looked at her. "Perhaps. I learned a lot about others behind my bar. You discern to read between the lines of what people say to what they really mean."

"Ah, so you're a psychologist, only with drinks instead of a couch?" Iona asked with another chuckle, this one louder.

Sammi threw her head back and laughed. "I've never thought of it that way."

"But you help them, don't you?"

"I suppose I do. I listen. Most times that's all people need."

"Is that what you're doing to me?" Iona asked, her dark eyes still crinkled in the corners.

Sammi shook her head, and then smoothed her hair out of her face. "Of course not. I'm not behind the bar," she added with a sly smile.

That had Iona laughing out loud, and just as Sammi suspected, it brought Laith out of his office. From the corner of her eye, she could see him standing in the doorway staring at Iona.

"What about any men in your life?" Sammi asked, knowing Laith could hear them.

Iona snorted as she set down her glass and swallowed the last of the ale. "There aren't any men."

"Thomas MacBane would like to be one."

"Ugh." Iona dropped her head in her hand and groaned. "He's persistent, I'll give him that."

Sammi glanced at Laith to see a small frown on his face. "Thomas will ask you out again. I'm afraid you might have to be very firm with him."

"Most likely."

"Do you have this kind of problem often?"

Iona ran a hand through her long hair and studied her empty glass. "No. I tend to keep my distance from men as a general rule."

"Because you don't trust them?"

"Because of how I watched my mother go through man after man as if they were pieces of candy. She showed me there is no such thing as love or soul mates or any of that nonsense."

The smile was gone from Sammi's face now. She was looking at Iona with new eyes. "I hate to disagree with you, but there is such a thing as true love and mates."

"It's what everyone wants to believe. A few even manage to keep their vows, but take a look around, Sammi. How many people stay married? How many of them actually work at a relationship? How many take the vows seriously? Not many. People live with each other as if it's no big deal. Moving in with someone isn't just important, but significant. We went from living with one man after another constantly. It's why we moved around so much."

"Did you ever think it might just be that your mother can't love?"

Iona hesitated for a moment and then sighed. "Yes. Unlike my mother, I'm not going to go through a string of men. I have my work. That's enough."

"Is it?"

"I'm sorry?"

Sammi leaned forward. "I'm not saying what your mother put you through is right. It wasn't, but that was only one kind of relationship. Love exists, Iona."

"I'll take your word for it."

"Have you had a relationship with a man before at all?" Sammi asked, unable to help herself.

Iona smiled, but it didn't reach her eyes. "Not really."

"Do you mind if I ask how long you stayed with one man?" Iona stared at her long enough that Sammi added, "I'm sorry. I'm just trying to understand your view on things, that's all."

"A month."

A month. Sammi slowly let out a breath. That wasn't a relationship. That was a fling. How could Iona know if she was like her mother or not if she didn't try?

"I've shocked you," Iona said.

Sammi started to deny it, and realized that Iona would know she was lying. "A wee bit, yes. It takes longer than a month to know if a relationship can work out, and even then it took me a good half dozen before I met Tristan. It was only by me learning from mistakes and what I knew I didn't want from those earlier affairs that I saw what could be with Tristan. I knew I would walk through Hell itself for him, and in some ways I did just that."

"Love isn't meant for everyone," Iona said softly. "It isn't meant for me."

CHAPTER
EIGHT

Laith braced a hand on the doorway and listened to the conversation between Sammi and Iona. It had been Iona's laugh that pulled him from his office. He knew it was her without even looking.

Her wavy blond hair looked like spun gold next to the black shirt she wore. She sat straight against the back of the booth, her posture denoting that she had closed a wall between her and Sammi.

Though he was guilty of having a string of human lovers, Laith also kept relationships from developing. That hadn't always been the case, however. At one time he thought he had found his mate. It was eons ago, right before Ulrik's lover tried to betray him.

After what the female did—and consequently the Kings' retaliation against her—Laith hadn't been able to look at his woman the same. Then the war with the humans broke out, and the strain on their relationship was like the straw that broke the camel's back.

He might have had difficultly trusting humans with more than helping him run the pub, but he never despised them as Ulrik and even Kellan had. Matter of fact, Laith didn't think much about them at all. The Dragon Kings were meant to protect the humans, and they did to a degree. The Kings didn't protect the humans from themselves. Not once had the Kings stopped a human war.

The Kings had, however, stopped the Fae from taking over the realm. It was one of many wars the Kings fought for the humans without them ever knowing it. Unlike others, Laith had done his duty without much fuss simply because he had given his oath. And an oath, once given, was binding.

He couldn't take his eyes from Iona. She lured him, enticed him without even trying. Laith didn't want to think what she could do to him if she tried. His body vibrated with uncontrollable need and uncontainable desire.

Every fiber of his being told him to leave, but he couldn't. Iona was appealing in ways he couldn't begin to describe, exciting in ways he didn't try to define.

There was no denying her beauty, but it was more than just her flawless sun-kissed skin. She had an air of confidence that hid the uncertainty and trepidation within. That combination of self-assurance and vulnerability was a heady mix indeed.

In all his millions of years of living, Laith had met all kinds of humans, but there had never been anyone like Iona. She was a beacon, a light that led him straight to her. As much as Laith might want her, he knew better than to get entangled deeply with her. It wasn't in his nature.

He dropped his arm and took a step toward Iona when Sammi's eyes suddenly went wide. She was looking at the door of the pub, not Iona. Laith followed her gaze. As soon as he caught sight of Rhi, he wasn't sure whether to shout with joy or call Phelan and let the Warrior know Rhi was all right.

Rhi's gaze slowly moved around the pub until she spotted him. She didn't smile, or even acknowledge him.

Instead, her eyes kept roving until she noticed Sammi. The heels of Rhi's black heels were loud in a pub that had suddenly gone silent at her arrival.

For men who had never seen her before, they were struck dumb by her ethereal beauty, not realizing they were gazing upon a Fae.

For the women, there was a blend of envy and desire.

Rhi came to a stop beside Sammi and Iona's table and offered a small smile to Sammi. Sammi jumped up and threw her arms around Rhi. Laith watched as Rhi stood as still as a stone for two heartbeats before she hesitantly returned the embrace.

That's all Laith needed to see to know that Rhi was still somewhat herself. It was a relief, even if he knew the Rhi that had always been might not be the Rhi standing in his pub now.

Laith walked to them just as Sammi was stepping back and wiping the tears from her face.

"Damn you, Rhi," Sammi said with a sniff. "You know I don't cry."

Rhi's smile was wider as she glanced at Laith and focused on Sammi. "It's good to see you as well."

"We were worried. I'm glad you dropped by," Laith said.

Rhi looked to the ground before she swiveled her silver eyes to him. "Not everyone was worried, I'm sure."

"The ones who count," Sammi hastened to say.

Rhi smirked and tossed her long black hair over her shoulder. Laith noticed the tips of Rhi's nails were painted black.

The black shirt wasn't what caused Laith's concern because it wasn't the first time Rhi wore black. It was her nails. Rhi loved her polish. Everyone knew that, and for the most part, you could discern her mood by the colors she chose.

The black was significant. Mainly because she often

used it as an accent, but she had never painted her nails that color.

When he looked up from her denim-clad legs, her brows were raised as she watched him. Laith lifted one shoulder in a shrug. She took a deep breath, and when she released it, her shoulders sagged a little, as if she had decided something.

"I'm not the same," she said softly.

Laith couldn't even imagine what she had gone through while in the Dark's dungeon with Balladyn, her once closest friend, torturing her. Phelan had described what Rhi looked like when he saw her chained, as had Kiril and Shara, but none of them could really know what she endured.

Without a word, Laith wrapped an arm about her shoulders and gave her as much of a hug as he knew he could get away with. Rhi was leery of the Dragon Kings, after she and her King lover had ended their affair.

Rhi patted his hand on her shoulder.

He leaned close and whispered, "If you need anything, let me know."

"Who is this?" Rhi asked as she looked at Iona.

Laith shifted his gaze to Iona to find her staring. He cleared his throat and tried to drop his arm, but Rhi kept ahold of his hand. "This is Iona Campbell. Iona, let me introduce you to a good friend, Rhi."

"Rhi," Iona said, glancing at Rhi's hand atop Laith's.

Rhi grinned slyly. "Iona."

Sammi looked between the two women. Then she asked Rhi, "Have you seen Tristan yet?"

"No," Rhi said and pulled her gaze from Iona to Sammi. "I stopped here first."

"Here?" Laith said and managed to pull his hand from Rhi's. "Why?"

She shrugged and waved at Glen who immediately brought her a glass of whisky. She smiled brightly, causing

Glen to blush to the roots of his red hair. He tripped over a nearby chair on his way back to the bar.

"Rhi," Laith mumbled.

"It's not my fault," she said with a smile.

And for the first time Laith grasped that her smile didn't reach her eyes. She was trying, but failing miserably. The concern he'd had earlier returned tenfold.

As if sensing his scrutiny, Rhi's smile faded altogether as she tossed back the whisky and slammed the glass facedown on the table.

Laith had to take the attention off Rhi. He jerked his chin to Iona and told Rhi, "Iona is here for a wee bit settling her father's estate."

"Campbell you say?" Rhi asked and looked closely at Iona.

Iona lifted a brow and asked saucily, "Is there something on my face?"

"Do you have any family?" Rhi asked.

Iona frowned as she looked to Sammi and then back at Rhi. "Just my mum, why?"

"No other Campbells?"

"No," Iona stated tightly.

Laith knew Rhi had seen what others had—that Iona looked a lot like Hayden Campbell. He opened his mouth to stop whatever Rhi was going to say, but it was too late.

"I know a Campbell," Rhi said.

Iona chuckled softly. "There are many Campbells in Scotland."

"True enough," Rhi said before she turned on her heel and walked away.

Laith looked to Sammi to find her brow furrowed deeply as she stared after Rhi. After a glance at Iona, Laith hurried after Rhi. He managed to catch her outside the pub before she could vanish, as the Fae were wont to do.

"Rhi," he called.

She stopped, sighing loudly as she slapped her hands on her thighs and looked dramatically at the stars. "Go back inside and flirt with Iona, Laith. There's nothing for you out here."

He halted beside her and waited for Rhi to look at him. "You have no idea how worried everyone has been. Phelan and Aisley have been beside themselves."

"Phelan is a Warrior and half-Fae, and Aisley is a Phoenix. They're married and can find many ways to occupy themselves other than to worry about me."

"You really don't have any idea how much you mean to them, do you?" Laith asked.

Rhi hurriedly looked away and crossed her arms over her chest. "I needed time."

"Anyone would. We doona hold that against you, but we thought you were dead. After Con told us Ulrik took you, we thought the worst."

She stood silently for so long that Laith didn't think she was going to say more. Then she spoke in such a low whisper that the wind couldn't even find her words. "I'm not the same."

"You freed yourself, Rhi. You broke the Chains of Mordare. Do you know how strong you have to be mentally to do that?"

She snorted and jerked her head around to him. "Strong? You think I'm strong?" she all but yelled, her eyes bright. "I'm broken!"

As soon as the last word left her lips, she was gone.

Laith put his hands on his hips and dropped his chin to his chest. He hadn't handled that well. All he could do was hope that Rhi went to see Phelan soon. The Warrior and Aisley considered Rhi family. What was more, Rhi knew that. Perhaps that's why she hadn't gone to see them.

Not because she didn't care, but because she cared too much.

Was that why she hadn't been to Dreagan yet? At first glance, he assumed she had managed to get past whatever happened to her, but it was apparent she was far from that. Going to Dreagan would put her too close to her past and the love she'd lost.

And might very well send her over the knife's edge she walked upon.

Laith lifted his head when he heard the pub door open and saw Sammi and Iona rush out.

Sammi was the first to him. She looked around expectantly. "Where is she?"

Laith dropped his arms and sighed. "Gone."

"Gone?"

"She needs more time."

Iona finally reached them. "Rhi needs time for what?"

"Um . . ." Sammi hesitated, glancing at him. "She was recently kidnapped. She's still dealing with all of it."

Iona looked down as she kicked the toe of her hiking boot against the rocks. "I didn't know. I feel bad for giving her attitude."

"Trust me, Rhi didn't mind that," Laith said.

Sammi blew out a breath. "I guess we better return for our food."

"Yeah," Iona said.

Yet she delayed even as Sammi went back inside. Laith faced Iona, wondering what would keep her outside with him. It was the first time they had been alone, and in the cool night air under the stars, he was having a hard time thinking of anything other than tasting her lips.

"Did you and Rhi date?" Iona asked.

"Date?" he repeated in shock. "Nay."

Iona smiled. "Good," she said and pivoted to go back into the pub.

CHAPTER NINE

Laith waited until Iona was back inside the pub before he peered into the shadows and saw a shape. It shifted and walked out from the tree line. He sighed when he recognized Rhys.

"How long have you been there?" Laith asked.

Rhys shrugged. "Long enough."

In other words, he had seen Rhi. "What's your take on Rhi?"

Rhys was quiet for a long moment before he said, "She's trying to be what she was before, but something has changed her."

Laith glanced at the ground, because he knew Rhys was also talking about himself. Ever since the wound he received while fighting the Dark Ones in Ireland, he hadn't been the same. No one had.

Because his wound had been delivered by a Dragon King.

They had yet to determine who it was, but no one was more aware of it than Rhys. Though he pretended everything was fine, it wasn't even close.

Laith let him lie. He wanted to push Rhys to talk, but if Rhys was going to talk to anyone, it was Kiril.

"Aye. You've the right of it," Laith said. "I'm happy she's back."

"The question is: how long was she with Ulrik?"

"It couldna have been for long. Con has him under surveillance."

Rhys snorted derisively. "As if that makes a difference. He's the one who took Rhi out of that hell."

"Are you saying you believe Rhi might have turned against us?"

"Rhi has never let us down. We really can no' trust anyone else."

Laith frowned and took a step toward Rhys. "You can trust us. We're your brothers."

"Really? It was a King who sent that blast of magic toward me."

"This is what our enemies want, Rhys. They want us fractured from within."

Rhys looked at the pub. "Are you returning to woo the lovely Iona, or are you taking to the skies?"

"Iona is here. I'll meet up with you later."

Rhys turned on his heel and faded back into the shadows. Laith remained where he was for a time thinking over Rhys's words. It was true that Rhys's wound had been dealt by a Dragon King. Dragon magic was recognizable by a King, but Laith couldn't believe it was anyone at Dreagan.

Which left Ulrik. He was the likely culprit, and yet his magic—as well as his ability to shift into dragon form—had been taken when he was banished from Dreagan. Ulrik let everyone know he would come for Con one day to exact his revenge, and yet Laith couldn't imagine Ulrik attacking anyone else but Con.

Ulrik might have escalated the war with the humans, but he was honorable. Or was he? For thousands of millennia, Ulrik had been confined to his human form to wander the earth and never return to Dreagan.

If the same had been done to him, Laith knew eventually the anger and resentment would change him. It was possible the same could have happened to Ulrik. The fact of the matter was that Rhys was healed, and until Laith knew for certain that Ulrik was the one trying to expose them, he wasn't going to go after him.

"Doona let me be wrong," he whispered to the night.

Laith returned to the pub. Once inside, his gaze fastened on Iona who had taken her seat across from Sammi. Iona had her back to him as she laughed at something Sammi said and took a drink of ale.

He walked to them, his eyes never wavering from Iona. As he approached, she turned her head and flashed him a welcoming smile. His lips tilted up in answer. He didn't want to like her, didn't want to notice how her shirt hugged her curves or how good her long legs looked encased in the denim.

"My shift has begun," Sammi said and slid out of the booth. "Take my spot, Laith," she said and waved at Iona before walking away.

Iona laughed and shook her head as she watched Sammi. "She's something else."

"Aye, she is. Everyone likes her."

"I can see why. She has a way about her. I wish I didn't like her."

"Why do you say that?" he asked before he thought better of it.

Iona shrugged and turned her head back to him. "I move around a lot, and I'm never in one place too long. It seems pointless to become friends with anyone only to leave them behind."

"You could see them again."

"It's doubtful. It just saves time."

Laith leaned back, one arm resting on the back of the booth and the other on the table. "That's a lonely way to live your life. Everyone needs someone."

"No, not everyone. There are those who prefer to be alone."

"And you're one of them?" he asked with one brow lifted.

She chuckled lightly. "I am."

"I doona believe that. I saw you with Sammi. You were laughing and talking, just as everyone else is."

"I can't deny that. It's not something I normally do, but Sammi was . . . persistent."

Laith glanced at Sammi as she moved from one customer to another, a smile always in place. "She is that."

"Is that how she got Tristan to fall for her?"

It was an odd question, but Laith would play along. He shook his head. "Tristan pursued her, and then she pursued him before they finally came together."

"If two people were meant to be together, why must it be so difficult for them to reach that point?"

"The best things in life are rarely easy. The harder you work for something, the more it will mean."

"Are you Buddha now?"

Laith grinned. "No' even close."

"You've lived a very different life than me," she said, her tone suddenly serious as she took a swallow of ale.

Laith watched her carefully. "In a way, perhaps. I think we all make our own way, and along that path, we make decisions depending on where we are at the time."

"Yes. Though my decisions were made based on things my mother told me."

"About your father?" Laith guessed.

Iona rolled her eyes as she nodded. "I truly believed everything she told me about him."

"Until you returned and learned that some things were no' true?"

"I didn't want to believe it, but the more people that came up to me and spoke of my father led me to realize the man I remember from when I was eight is not the man he was."

"A child sees their parents in one light, while the rest of the world sees those same parents in another. It's the way of things."

Her coffee-colored eyes locked with his. "Is it the way for a child to think the worst of her father?"

"Is that why you remain here?"

"Perhaps. There are other things I need to take care of regarding my father's things anyway."

"The time off will be good for you, I think."

Her face suddenly brightened. "I did take some amazing photos today. I can't wait to load them on my computer and see how they turned out."

"There's plenty around for you to photograph. That will keep you busy."

"I'm going to go deeper into the woods behind the house tomorrow," she said before taking a drink. She swallowed and set the glass down. "I can't remember ever going past the waterfall as a child."

Because she hadn't. Laith didn't tell her that, however. The waterfall was one of the boundaries of magic between Campbell land and Dreagan. The magic should be enough to keep Iona out, but Laith had his doubts. She was tenacious enough to push through any reservations that assaulted her.

"How are things progressing with John's estate?" Laith asked to get the talk off the forest.

Her face fell. "As well as can be expected. I'm to go to the bank tomorrow and get the accounts signed over, then I'll need to pay the taxes."

"It sounds all under control."

"I suppose."

"And the estate? What will you do?"

She smiled softly. "Everyone is curious, aren't they?"

"Of course. The Campbells have been a part of this village for generations."

"I was so sure I was going to sell when I came. Then I learned I couldn't."

"What's wrong with that?" he asked.

She sighed loudly. "Nothing, I suppose."

Laith waited, but she didn't continue. So he prodded further. "You might find it's a good home for you."

"What do I need with the land and cottage? I don't have time to take care of it or worry about it."

"It could be a place for you to holiday at, a place where you could return home."

She lifted one shoulder in a shrug. "I have a flat in London."

"Are you there often?"

"No," she replied. "I can't remember the last time I was."

He shifted so that both arms were on the table as he sat forward. "It sounds as if you need a place to get away."

"Probably," she said with a half-smile.

Her words hung between them as Laith found himself drowning in her gaze. She had seen more of the world than others would ever guess existed. She had been in the midst of battle and deep in the African plains, and yet she was withdrawn from everyone and everything. She might not talk, but her pictures did, whether she knew it or not. Iona was remarkable, brave, and astonishing.

She suddenly looked down at her ale. "We've been talking about me. Why not tell me more about you?"

"There isna much to tell."

"I'm bad at this," she said with a laugh as she glanced

up at him. "But I do know that people normally like to talk about themselves."

Laith was enamored. Totally, completely. Utterly. "What do you want to know?"

"Everything." Her gaze slowly lifted to meet his once again.

He couldn't tell her everything yet, but he would talk, if for no other reason than to keep her there. "The pub has been in my family for what seems like an eternity."

"Did you always know you wanted to take over ownership?"

"No' really. It kinda fell upon me, and I wanted to see where things went."

She nodded as he spoke. "So there is someone else in your family that can take over if you no longer want it?"

"Something like that," he said evasively. "I've found the work pleases me. I enjoy interacting with people and learning about those who work for me."

"You think you'll remain here then?"

"Without a doubt." He smiled at her and caught her gaze when she tried to look away. "Have you seen the beauty that surrounds us? Why would I want to leave this?"

She laughed as she said, "I don't know."

"You've walked the woods today. Tell me there isna something about this land that doesna take hold of you and sink into your verra soul."

Her smile slowly faded. "It did. How did you know?"

"You were born here, Iona. You were part of this land, just as it's a part of you. You've been gone a long time, but it still remembers you. You just needed to remember it."

CHAPTER
TEN

Iona couldn't remember the last time she woke so . . . happy. Her thoughts immediately went to Laith. It couldn't be just him. Could it?

She smiled with laughter following as she rose from the bed. Try as she might, she couldn't recall the last time she'd had a night of conversation as she had with Laith.

It amazed her that he could be so open and willing to talk when she had such a difficult time doing the same. Yet, he managed to set her at ease as he had from the first moment she saw him. Whether he did it naturally or he actively set out to lessen her discomfort, it worked.

Iona walked into the kitchen and inhaled the aroma of freshly brewed coffee. She poured some into a large mug, added a bit of cream and some sugar, and looked out the window to the forest.

She had told Laith things she hadn't told another soul, and though that took her aback, she didn't regret it. In the crowded pub, they had been left alone, cocooned in the booth. Laith told her stories of her father and of the town.

Iona laughed more in one night than she had in . . . years.

She blinked. Could it really have been that long? Surely that wasn't right. Surely she laughed. Didn't she?

"What has my life turned into if I can't remember laughing?" she asked herself.

With all the traveling she did, she didn't watch TV. She did catch a movie every so often on a flight or in a hotel room. Being so disconnected from the world kept her privacy as she wanted it, but she was then left completely out of the loop on, well, everything.

Did Laith notice? Had he realized how much she shunned the world? Suddenly she forgot about the good time she'd had and began to worry that she hadn't been witty enough.

He had laughed. She recalled that, because the sound was infectious and had her joining him more often than not. And his smile. Lord, did he have the best smile. It was in turns sweet, seductive, and downright sexy. How could a man look so good without even seeming to try? Laith was charming, enticing, handsome, and fascinating.

If she had to classify him, it would be sex-on-a-stick.

In the space of one night while talking to him, she had pictured herself having sex with him so many times she lost count. She wondered how his lips would feel as they kissed, how his hands would feel on her skin.

More importantly, she wondered how his skin would feel beneath her hands.

Iona closed her eyes and imagined lying down as he rose above her, his cock sliding inside her, stretching her. She bit her lip and moaned. Need tightened low in her belly.

She snapped open her eyes and pulled her mind out of that fantasy. It could do her no good. Iona went back to drinking her coffee and staring at the woods. After some toast and jelly, she changed and threw her hair up into a ponytail. She stuffed some water and granola bars into the camera bag, then slung it over her shoulder as she walked out of the house.

Iona took her time walking in the woods. This time she headed to the right, away from the house. With her camera out and ready, she snapped photos as she walked.

A glance at the sky told her it wasn't going to be the beauty yesterday had been. Overnight, clouds had come in and it was all the sun could do to peek through them every so often.

As overcast as the sky was, it didn't deter her from the hike. She knew how easy it was to get turned around in places, which is why she had a compass on her watch, one on her phone, and another in her camera bag. It was an unfortunate event that had taught her one compass was never enough.

She shuddered just thinking of that time in Iraq when she had gotten turned around in the desert and her watch, which had the compass, smashed on the rocks when she fell. Had the unit of U.S. Marines not stumbled upon her after she was separated from the British troops, she didn't know where she would've ended up.

It had been one of her most embarrassing days, but a day full of lessons as well. She was always prepared, and sometimes over-prepared for things, but she never wanted to be in a situation like that again.

The morning waned to noon as she continued her trek. She managed to catch a herd of elk grazing in a field before they caught her scent and ran off.

She stopped beside a stream and saw salmon swimming in the shallow water. It was when she was checking the photos on her camera that a pine marten came bounding to the stream on the opposite bank. Iona stilled and watched as he drank, his gaze riveted on her. After a few seconds, he turned and sprinted away.

The more time she spent in the forest, the harder it was

for her to think of leaving. Laith was right, there was something about the land that seeped into a person's soul.

Iona laughed at her thoughts while she climbed to her feet. She found a narrow part in the stream that was piled high with river rocks. They were smooth and all different colors as they glistened just beneath the surface of the water.

She crossed on top of the rocks, with her boots barely getting wet. In her camera bag, she had even stuffed a windbreaker. It might have been a long time since she lived in Scotland, but she remembered how wild the weather could get in the Highlands.

Suddenly, Iona stopped, unable to go any further. Something kept telling her to return to the cottage. Instead of listening to her subconscious, she remained, staring into the forest.

A memory, long buried, sprang up of her father warning her never to cross the stream and go into the forest.

"The Dragonwood," she mumbled.

How could she have forgotten the Dragonwood? Her father had explained that it wasn't their land, and that dangerous animals lurked in the shadows.

His words had scared her enough as a child never to venture past the stream. As an adult, she wasn't as fearful of the shadows as she had once been. Still, there was a part of her that wasn't so keen on going into the Dragonwood.

"I've been in the middle of battle, faced lions, and scaled mountains. I can walk into the Dragonwood."

It took her two more times of stating those words before she was able to lift her foot and walk into the forest.

Laith bit back a string of curses and dropped his head against the bark of a pine tree. Just as he expected, Iona hadn't stayed out of the Dragonwood.

He had been following her from the opposite side of the

stream for miles. She meandered through the trees with no purpose, going wherever something caught her interest.

But she wasn't blasé about anything. She checked the sky and the compass on her watch often. Many times she would stop and turn around to look back at the way she had come as if memorizing things, and then she would pivot back around and continue on her way.

Laith didn't worry about her becoming lost. He worried she might venture onto Dreagan. It wasn't so much that she would see something during the day, but if she were brave enough to do it in the daylight, she would eventually try it at night. That's when she really might see something.

It wouldn't matter once she knew everything, but until then he had to keep an eye on her. The last thing anyone at Dreagan wanted was a picture of one of them in dragon form plastered everywhere.

He focused on Iona and moved from tree to tree so she wouldn't see him. Her movements slowed, and she looked around more often, as if someone were watching her. Which he was.

Laith didn't get too close. He kept his distance, but it was difficult. He spent the entire night thinking of Iona instead of sleeping. He'd lain awake picturing her blond waves and dark eyes, her smile, and her body.

He gave a shake of his head and focused on Iona. It would be the worst kind of mistake for them both if he continued along that path of thinking and didn't concentrate. The farther into the woods Iona got, the more anxious Laith became. He had to somehow get her back onto Campbell land.

A sound behind Iona drew Laith up short. He opened his hearing and detected at least four sets of footfalls approaching.

Whoever was following Iona was good. They kept hidden, which alerted Laith that it wasn't the Dark Fae. They rarely hid. They were more of the smash-and-grab types. That meant the fellows following Iona were human.

In some ways, they were as bad as the Dark. After the war with the humans, the Kings had come to Dreagan and let talk of dragons turn to legend and myth. They hid, protecting their secret from anyone not a Dragon King. It had worked for millions of years.

Until recently.

No species was without enemies, but the Kings seemed to have more than most. Laith clenched his teeth when he saw an arm poke out from behind a tree. The mercenaries could be sent by their enemy to try and find a dragon. Or they could be after Iona.

Either way, Laith wasn't going to let that happen. He counted five in camouflage fatigues, their faces painted green and black. The men moved as one toward Iona. He was ready to kill every one of them, until they suddenly veered away from him.

He frowned. There was no way they could know he was waiting. Laith jerked his head to Iona and spotted her twenty yards ahead of him as it began to rain. That's when he realized the men were following her right onto Dreagan. If they were the ones who had killed John, then Laith was going to make them pay.

Laith hurried after Iona while still remaining hidden from her and the men. Every time he would get close to Iona, she would suddenly turn the other way. Even with the rain, she stopped and took pictures.

It began to rain harder, the sky turning dark. The wind howled, as the trees swayed in response. Laith stood against the force of nature looking from the mercenaries to Iona. When Iona packed away her camera and turned to retrace her steps, her path took her right to him. Laith let out a sigh of relief. Then he saw the mercs set up position in order to surround her.

"Bloody hell," he whispered.

Laith watched Iona tilt her head back to look up at the sky. At that moment, thunder boomed and a split second later lightning zigzagged across the darkening sky. Iona started running, weaving her way through the trees while the mercenaries moved from place to place to try and catch her.

The shadows were lengthening, and the rain and wind made it difficult for a human to see properly. As soon as Iona was even with him, Laith reached out and clamped a hand over her mouth as he yanked her back against his chest. She struggled against him like a cornered dog.

"Iona," he whispered. "It's me. Calm down."

She stilled, though her chest continued to heave. Her hands were on his arm, and she tried to pull it away from her mouth.

"Listen. There are men following you. We need to get you back to the cottage," he said in a low tone. Then he removed his hand from her mouth.

She leaned her head back to meet his gaze. Her eyes were wide with fear and shock. "Are you sure?"

"There," he said and pointed to a merc who was peering around a tree at her.

"Oh, shit," she whispered.

"I can get you back home. Do you trust me?"

She nodded.

Laith slid his fingers into hers. "Ready?"

"No."

He smiled and pulled her after him as they raced through the forest.

CHAPTER
ELEVEN

Iona's mind was swirling in confusion. What was Laith doing in the Dragonwood? Why were men following her? Where was Laith taking her? And how was he moving so quickly?

Several times she lost her footing only to have Laith tug her in one direction or the other and help her right herself. She was running as fast as she could on the slick—and sloping—ground and she wanted to slow down. Yet she could tell Laith wasn't moving nearly as fast as he wanted.

With her panting breaths, she couldn't discern if the others followed or not, and she didn't dare chance a look over her shoulder for fear of falling. Then she spotted the stream through the trees. A smile formed, because she knew where they were.

However, that smile died a quick death when Laith suddenly stopped and jerked her against him as he hid behind an oak tree.

Iona swallowed, her fear mingling with the desire that suddenly heated her body as she found herself forced against Laith's front. He looked down at her, his gunmetal eyes giving nothing away. His hands were steady as he held her while her palms rested on his chest—a very firm, very defined chest.

With her breasts pressed against him they were so close, she couldn't help but notice his fine body. She watched as Laith's lids slowly lowered over his eyes while his head cocked to the side as if he were listening. She did the same and realized that there was no sound other than the rain. It was as if the world had gone silent.

Iona tried to peer around Laith's shoulder, but he hastily pulled her back. She looked up to find him frowning down at her. The rain was coming faster, causing Iona to have to blink repeatedly to keep the water from her eyes.

Laith stood still as a statue. His gaze was on her, but she knew his attention was on the men. She looked back at the stream and noticed how open the area was. The stream wasn't wide. But they would need to go from the tree line to the stream and then across it before they could run across another ten feet of rock until they reached the opposite bank of the forest. It was a prime opportunity for someone to take aim and simply wait for them to cross.

Laith's big hand moved to her neck and slowly tilted her head up to him. His gaze searched hers while water dripped from his long eyelashes. His voice was barely above a whisper as he said, "When I say, run to the cottage and doona look back."

Iona shook her head and opened her mouth to speak, but he placed a finger over her lips to silence her.

"I'll be right behind you," he promised.

She'd been in enough war zones to know she would be better served doing as he asked. But once at the cottage, if the assholes dared to come closer, she wouldn't hesitate to use any weapon she could get her hands on.

Iona gave a nod of acceptance, and Laith's answering smile was enough to boost her courage. Laith turned her so that her back was to him. He rested his hands on her shoulders and leaned down so that his lips were by her ear. His warm breath skated over her skin, sending goose bumps rising and causing her to shiver.

"Doona look back," he whispered.

Iona was surprised when he gave a squeeze of her shoulders. She licked her lips and adjusted her camera case, her gaze on the stream as she searched for the easiest way down the slope to the water.

Then he shoved her.

Iona ran as hard and as fast as she could, her arms pumping and her gaze straight ahead. She didn't look back, though she wanted to desperately. She waited for the pain from a bullet, but none came. As soon as she cleared the forest, she leapt over larger rocks in her haste to get to the water. It didn't take her but a second to find where she originally crossed the stream and run to the other side.

Laith didn't watch Iona to see if she made it to the stream. He stepped away from the oak and took three long strides to the next tree where he grabbed the mercenary by the back of his collar and slammed him face-first into the bark.

The merc crumpled to the ground as three others stepped out from their hiding spots. Laith didn't waste time in toying with them. There was one missing, and he knew the arse had gone after Iona.

The mercenaries didn't use guns, as they didn't have any. They had knives and Tasers, both of which they had at the ready.

Laith smiled coldly at the three remaining men as they closed in on him. He contemplated using his power of paralyzing gas, but the need to punch something was too strong. It took all his patience to wait until they were close enough, and then with a quick shift of his weight, he knocked one out with a punch to his jaw, and kicked the other back into a tree, slamming his head against it.

With only one left, Laith leaned to the side to avoid the Taser. Before the merc even knew what was happening, Laith was behind him, choking off his air.

As much as Laith wanted to kill the guy, he didn't. He waited until the merc was unconscious, and dropped him next to the others.

Before the man hit the ground, Laith was running after Iona. While he raced toward her, he opened the mental link between all Dragon Kings and told the others what happened in quick order, as well as where the four unconscious mercenaries lay.

Then Laith severed the link. He needed to focus on Iona, not be bogged down with questions he knew Con would have. Laith was faster than Iona. Even with losing the few precious moments fighting, he easily caught up with her.

He didn't rush to her. Instead, he held back, watching the mercenary trail her. Laith didn't understand what the man wanted. There was ample opportunity for him to attack.

It almost looked as if he were trying to catch Iona instead of kill her. Laith changed his position so that he would come up behind the merc. The rain kept the man from hearing Laith's approach. Laith waited until Iona turned down the path that led to the cottage, and then sprang at the mercenary.

The momentum took both him and the mercenary to the ground. They rolled while the man tried to stab Laith. They came to a sudden stop, putting the mercenary on top, but Laith got the upper hand and landed two quick punches to the man's kidneys and another in his throat. With the merc wheezing, Laith took the opportunity and slammed his elbow into the side of the mercenary's head. With a quick inhale, Laith released the paralyzing gas, watching it billow around the mercenary as he jerked before falling over.

Laith shoved the man off him and got to his feet. He

stared down at the man. "You came onto the wrong land.
And you messed with the wrong woman. Doona worry. I'm
no' going to kill you. You'll be detained by my friends, and
we'll keep you until you give us all the information we
need."

Next, Laith leaned over the man, and punched him to
knock him out. Not because the gas would wear off anytime soon, but because Laith needed to vent some of his
anger.

It took no time for Laith to catch up with Iona before
she reached the cottage. She turned around swinging before he had a chance to say anything. Laith deflected her
blows, impressed that she knew enough to defend herself.
She gasped when she recognized him and lowered her
arms. Her chin dropped to her chest as she stood shivering in the rain.

She didn't fling her arms around him or faint. She was
frightened, but she held her own. A strong woman in a
world filled with evil, danger, and death.

"It's over," he said above the thunder. "They willna be
bothering you again."

She raised her coffee-colored eyes to him. "Are you sure
it was me they were after?"

"Positive." He motioned to the cottage. "Let's get you
inside."

Iona was never more conscious of a man as she was of Laith
in her house. A wall separated them, and she found she
hated that wall. She also hated that she couldn't stop thinking about Laith. How she looked for any opportunity to
get close to him that he might touch her. How sad was that?

She closed her eyes and groaned. She was sad. Sad and
depressed. Was she that hard up for some attention that
she was willing to practically throw herself at a man who
might not be as interested as she hoped he was? She sighed

and opened her eyes. Laith was a man who went after what he wanted. If he wanted her, he would have made a move already.

With the towel in hand, she wrung out her hair and stripped out of her clothes before wiping herself down. She put on a new pair of panties and a bra. As she looked in her bag, she realized she didn't have anything to wear. All of it was in need of washing.

Iona wrapped the towel around her and hurried from her room to her father's. She opened three drawers before she found a pair of sweatpants and a shirt. She let the towel drop to the floor and stepped into the sweats that were several sizes too big. She rolled them up repeatedly at the waist. Iona reached for the shirt she had tossed on the bed when she looked to the doorway and found Laith.

He said nothing, simply stared, his eyes slowly drifting down her body before moving back up again. Her mouth went dry. Iona slowly straightened as their gazes locked, held.

Laith stepped into the room and closed the distance between them. He halted in front of her, his hands resting on her hips. Iona shivered again, this time for an entirely different reason.

Heat infused her wherever Laith touched. Breathing became difficult as he caressed up her sides until he cupped her face. His head lowered, and she rose up to meet him. Their lips met, sending sparks of desire and need zipping through her. He moaned, low and needful, causing her knees to weaken. She wrapped her arms around his waist and simply held on.

There was nothing else to do. Laith captured her interest, her mind, and her body with simply a look. Iona was out of her element, adrift in a sea of passion she couldn't navigate.

And for once, she didn't want to.

He kissed her again, pulling her lower lip into his mouth before releasing her. Iona sunk her nails into his back, silently begging him to continue. His lips found her again, except this time he wasn't content with just tasting her lips. His tongue slid into her mouth while his arms moved to wrap around her and tug her tighter.

The kiss deepened as Iona opened for him. The longer they kissed, the hotter the fire inside her burned. His hands were all over her back, in her hair, and on her hips pressing her against his arousal.

Iona was trembling with fierce need the like she hadn't known existed. She was reaching for his shirt when a pounding came from her front door.

Laith ended the kiss and stared down at her, not bothering to disguise the desire darkening his gunmetal eyes. She didn't want to stop, didn't want anything to interrupt whatever had taken them.

But Laith was already releasing her.

"Get dressed," he said softly and ran his thumb over her bottom lip.

He turned to walk out when she tried to stop him. "Wait. You don't know who's out there. It could be more of those guys."

"It's no'," he said without stopping.

Iona threw on her shirt and rushed out of the bedroom as Laith opened the door. She slid to a stop when she spotted Tristan, Ryder, and another man she didn't recognize. Two of the three were from Dreagan, and she was willing to bet everything she had that the third was as well.

She looked from the men to Laith and watched how they greeted him. It was there before her all along, she just hadn't realized it. Laith turned to her then and waited. The room grew quiet as the group stared at her.

Iona wrapped her arms around herself and lifted her chin. "You're part of Dreagan too," she stated.

Laith gave a single nod. "I am."

"Why not tell me from the beginning?"

He glanced at the floor, a small frown furrowing his brow. "There is much more going on than you know, Iona. Those men in the forest for one. These are verra dangerous times."

"In more ways than one," she mumbled to herself.

CHAPTER
TWELVE

Rhi was thankful that she could remain veiled longer than most Fae. It allowed her a few minutes to wander her queen's estate on the west side of Ireland to make sure there were few Fae about.

Usaeil liked her privacy, and though she had a palace on the Fae realm, she spent a lot of time on Earth. Mostly because for the last five years she was posing as one of the most famous actresses in the world.

Rhi waited until the antechamber outside of the queen's throne room was empty before she dropped the veil and appeared. She took a deep breath and looked around at the high ceilings, ornate crown molding, and priceless art.

The room was small and narrow compared to others throughout the estate. It was where all Fae came if they wished an audience with Usaeil, or if the queen requested your presence.

It seemed like a lifetime ago that Rhi was there, when in fact it had only been over a month. She had been alive thousands of years, and yet one simple month drastically changed her life.

Rhi remained on her feet despite the cushioned benches

set along the walls in various places. There was no need to inform anyone of her arrival. Usaeil already knew.

Almost on cue, the twenty-foot-tall double doors opened behind her. Rhi turned and stared through them to the throne room. There were two rooms in Usaeil's estate that no Fae could teleport into—the throne room and Usaeil's private quarters.

Releasing a deep breath, Rhi clasped her hands behind her back and walked to the doors. Her steps slowed a fraction right before she passed through them, because once inside the throne room, the queen would decide just how long Rhi remained.

Rhi spotted the white high-backed chair with a cream velvet cushion, but no Usaeil. She immediately halted, waiting for whatever punishment the queen deemed necessary because Rhi hadn't come when summoned.

"Rhi."

She closed her eyes at the happiness she heard in Usaeil's voice. The greatest day of her life had been when she had become part of the Queen's Guard. Usaeil wasn't just her queen—she was a friend.

When Rhi opened her eyes, Usaeil stood before her wearing jeans and a flowing yellow shirt that set off her long black hair. Usaeil's silver eyes were filled with tears while her smile was bright. She threw her arms around Rhi and held her tight. "We didn't think we'd ever see you again. You don't know how happy I am you've returned."

Rhi had never been very good with showing emotion, and she was always uncomfortable with displays of affection—except with *him*. She stopped that train of thought in its tracks. Thinking about her Dragon King lover wouldn't help matters.

She returned her queen's hug and waited for Usaeil to pull back. Rhi let out a thankful breath when she finally did. Usaeil wiped at her eyes and studied her.

Somehow Rhi remained still under the scrutiny. Only her family and Balladyn knew her better than Usaeil. Her family was dead, and Balladyn — she was going to kill him for what he did to her.

Usaeil's smile slowly faded. "I came for you."

Rhi frowned, unsure of what to say. No Light Fae, especially the queen, ever ventured into the Dark. For anyone.

"I did," Usaeil repeated. "I was with Con, Rhys, and Phelan. I wasn't going to let the Dark take you. I . . . I had no idea Balladyn was alive, Rhi. I'm sorry."

"You didn't free me," she said.

Usaeil swallowed and turned away to walk to a couch set against the far wall in a light brown distressed leather. "I was told Balladyn put the Chains of Mordare on you."

A tremor of fear raced through Rhi at the mention of the hated chains. They were thought to have been lost, until Balladyn locked them on her. The Chains of Mordare were only to be unlocked by the Fae who shackled them. Any time a Fae would try to use magic to remove them, unimaginable pain would shoot through their body.

The worst part was that the chains helped to drain a Light Fae of the spark within them, the light that made them who they were.

"No one has survived the Chains of Mordare," Usaeil said in a low tone. "No one but you, Rhi. I knew the first time you walked into my palace that you were special."

"Because I was foolish enough to fall in love with a Dragon King?" Rhi asked sarcastically.

Usaeil didn't bother to acknowledge her comment. "You have battle skills better than many who have trained their entire lives to serve me. You have a quick mind, your loyalty is without question, but it's the light within you that truly sets you apart. It's why Balladyn fell in love with you."

"What are you talking about? Balladyn hates me."

"There is a thin line between love and hate." Usaeil

smiled dejectedly. "He was in love with you before he and your brother went off to war. He was waiting until the right time to approach you. Then he had to return home and tell you and your family about your brother's death. It put everything on hold."

Rhi's chest began to ache as she recalled all the times she spent with Balladyn talking about her brother. While she grieved, Balladyn had been patiently waiting.

"He was beside himself when you fell for the Dragon King. He kept it from you, though it killed him to do it."

Rhi shook her head. "Stop. Balladyn was my closest friend. I'd have known if he had feelings. He thought of me as a sister."

"He wanted you for his wife," Usaeil insisted. "We spoke about it. I was the one to caution him to stand beside you instead of trying to talk you out of your affair with the Dragon King."

"Balladyn was the one to comfort me after . . ." Rhi couldn't even say it thousands of years later.

Usaeil waved Rhi to her, then tugged Rhi down beside her on the couch. "When Balladyn was injured in the war, we all saw him fall. You weren't the only one to try and reach him. The battle lasted days, Rhi, with scores of Fae— Light and Dark—dying. We fought for survival, intending to return for our dead."

"Except Balladyn was gone," Rhi said.

"His wound was fatal. None of us could've known that Taraeth wanted Balladyn as one of his men."

"Balladyn blames me," Rhi said and focused on the thirty-foot painting hanging on the far wall of the Fae realm. "It's why he kidnapped me. It's payback for leaving him on the battlefield."

Usaeil snorted. "That's shite, and you know it."

"Is it?" she asked, turning her head to look at Usaeil. "He was all the family I had."

"You're Light, Rhi. You're never without family."

Rhi lowered her gaze to the white marble floor with veins of dark gray running through the marble. "My light was almost taken."

"But it wasn't. You're here with us now."

She paused a second before returning her gaze to Usaeil. "I'm not the same. I'm . . . different."

Usaeil took one of Rhi's hands in her own and ran a finger over Rhi's black-tipped nails. "How do you think the Dark Fae began?"

"Their need for power."

The queen's smile was forlorn as she shook her head. "It began because there were some who couldn't control the darkness that's in all of us. They weren't strong enough to hold onto the light. No realm is merely black or white, good or evil. It's a mixture. Always has been. Always will be."

That didn't help Rhi. It wasn't as easy as making a decision. She had been inexplicably altered.

"It was the light within you that broke the Chains of Mordare. Do you understand what that means, Rhi?"

She looked at the queen. "It means I'm a liability."

"No, my dear. It means you hold more light inside than the entire Light Fae combined. It means you are powerful, but more importantly, it means you fought—and won—against the Dark."

Could it be that simple? Was she worried for nothing? There was melancholy and rage inside her as well, and Rhi didn't know how long she could hold those emotions back.

"What is it?" Usaeil asked.

Rhi looked at the black on her nails before she turned her head to gaze out the window. "I can't find happiness as I used to. There is such anger inside me."

"Look for the light inside when such feelings come. It will help to center you."

Rhi nodded, since it was expected.

"I was told Ulrik carried you from Balladyn's fortress."

"Apparently he did." Rhi withdrew her hand from the queen's. She didn't want to talk about Ulrik, but she knew Usaeil would eventually get to him.

"Is that where you've been? With him?"

Rhi chuckled as she looked at Usaeil. "No."

"Be careful there," her queen warned. "There is a war coming between the Kings and Ulrik."

"He is a King," Rhi corrected her.

Usaeil raised her brows, her silver eyes seeing everything. "Not according to Constantine. Ulrik was banned from Dreagan, stripped of his magic, and unable to shift into dragon form. He has revenge in mind. Don't get in the middle of what is coming between them."

"It seems I wasn't the only anomaly recently. For the first time a Dark has become Light," Rhi said, changing the subject.

Usaeil shrugged and leaned back against the arm of the couch. "A Fae chooses to become Dark. Up until now, we've never found one who wanted to return to Light. Shara's love for Kiril helped her find her way to overcome the darkness. She's the first, but hopefully not the last."

Shock waves reverberated through Rhi. "Tell me you aren't going to do what I think you're going to do."

"What is that?" Usaeil asked innocently.

"You want to try and change Balladyn back to Light."

Usaeil drew in a deep breath and slowly released it. "He was turned against his will."

"Trust me when I say he is fully Dark. He's second in line behind Taraeth. Balladyn wants to rule the Dark, and one day he will. You can't bring him back from that path."

"He was a great warrior for the Light," Usaeil said, her voice rising.

Rhi jerked to her feet, rage flooding her. "He's not the

same! He is evil to the core. There's no light within him, only darkness and cruelty."

"If a Light can be changed to Dark with torture, a Dark can be changed to Light."

"If you believe that, you're going to put every Light Fae in danger. You don't know the Balladyn I was tortured by."

Usaeil's eyes narrowed before she stood and faced her. "You're blinded by your hate. And lest you forget, Balladyn used the black smoke to torture you."

"How would you know that?" Rhi took a step back. "How do you know anything that happened to me? Unless . . ."

How could she have been so stupid? The Light Fae and Dragon Kings had a shaky truce, and she assumed Con and Usaeil didn't interact. Apparently, she was wrong.

Usaeil didn't respond. She merely held Rhi's gaze. Rhi laughed, though there was no humor in the sound. She was so wrapped up in her thoughts she hadn't realized what Usaeil had let slip earlier, but she did now. "So I didn't misunderstand when you said you were with Con and Rhys looking for me?"

"No."

"And Con then told you what happened."

Usaeil clasped her hands in front of her and nodded.

"There are three people who know what happened at the end, excluding me. Balladyn, Ulrik, and Con. Balladyn is Dark. Ulrik is banished. Of course you would believe whatever Con said."

"Why would he lie?" Usaeil asked.

Rhi turned on her heel and started out the doors. "Why does Con do anything?"

Usaeil waited until Rhi vanished and the doors closed before she turned toward the hidden doorway behind her throne and waited for Con to step out. "Well?" she asked him.

His lips flattened. "I think she's right. She's not the Fae she used to be. Before she was reckless, wild, and uncontrollable, but she was always . . . happy, for lack of a better word. Now, she's controlled, easily enraged, and oppressed."

"I lost Balladyn, Con. I can't lose her as well."

"You won't. I promise."

CHAPTER
THIRTEEN

Laith laid upon the ground and stared up at the ceiling of the cavern. There were dozens of candles lit and reflecting on the water from the hot springs. The ripples of light playing from the movement of the water bounced on the walls and ceiling.

It normally calmed Laith, but he wasn't finding any peace today. Ever since Iona threw him out of her house, he had been in knots. Not even securing the prisoners and ensuring no one else would bother her helped.

He understood Iona's feelings. An omission was a lie. Laith purposefully didn't tell her he was a part of Dreagan. It wasn't to hurt her but to determine how much she knew about her ancestors. But it backfired on Laith. He should've known Iona wouldn't appreciate such tactics. She found it difficult—nay, impossible—to trust, and he just gave her reason not to trust him.

"I knew I'd find you here," Warrick said.

Laith didn't bother to look at his friend. "What do you want?"

"Ryder said the men you knocked unconscious are

finally waking. Thought you might want to be there to question them."

"It's been almost twelve hours."

"Apparently you hit hard," Warrick said, a drop of humor lacing his words.

Laith sat up and looked at the doorway. "I do want to question them."

"Then get your arse moving. Rhys is already on his way."

Laith jumped to his feet and followed Warrick. They trekked through long corridors and past caverns of various sizes before they reached the tunnel they had carved millions of years before to connect one mountain to another.

"Is it just Ryder watching them?" Laith asked.

Warrick grunted. "As if the buggers would be able to find their way out of the mountain."

"True, but we've encountered men like this before."

Warrior glanced over his shoulder at Laith. "They're mortal, and we have them where no Dark Fae can get."

Laith had been so upset after Iona wouldn't let him talk that he had taken to the skies—and remained there until dawn—once the prisoners had been secured. "I know exactly where they are, Warrick. It was my suggestion we put them there."

"Then you know they are no' going anywhere," he stated.

Laith didn't bother to say more as they reached the turn in the corridor that would dead end at the small cavern. He quickened his pace, ready to get some answers as to why they were following Iona.

Warrick was the first to enter, and then came to a dead stop. Laith had to shove him out of the way so he could step through the doorway, and then he too halted and simply stared.

"It happened so fast," Ryder said as he stood over one of the five men who was prone on the ground, white foam falling from his mouth.

Laith looked from one man to the next and found the same foam. He was in shock at what he saw. "Cyanide? They had cyanide pills hidden in their mouths?"

"We were finally going to be able to get some answers," Warrick mumbled irritably.

Rhys ran a hand down his face and scowled. "We're no' getting anything now."

"I didna think to check them for poison," Ryder said.

It was a setback, but Laith wasn't too worried. "There will be more. Whatever reason they were after Iona, as soon as these come up missing, more will arrive."

"I hope you're wrong," Rhys said. "I've had my fill of our enemies getting so close."

Warrick kicked the feet of one dead mercenary. "Why do they want to harm Iona Campbell? She's no' associating with any of us." He then looked at Laith. "Much. I doona think she even knows about her heritage."

"John was murdered," Laith reminded them. "Possibly by the same men. Who's to say they willna try the same on Iona?"

Ryder hefted a merc over his shoulder. "Good point. You need to find some way back into her life, Laith."

He blinked at Ryder. "She's made it clear she doesna trust me now."

"And you're going to let that stand in your way?" Rhys asked, then made a sound at the back of his throat. "Since when do you give up so easily?"

Warrick grinned from ear to ear. "I think the point, lads, is that he fancies her."

"I doona fancy her." The lie sat heavy on Laith's tongue, and all of them knew it. "She intrigues me."

Rhys met his gaze, his face somber. "Then doona waste

time. Find a way to earn her trust once again if you want to keep her alive."

"Go," Ryder said. "We'll clean this up."

Laith started to turn away when he stopped. "I thought Con would be here."

"We all did," Warrick said.

Rhys bent and flung a mercenary over his shoulder, then straightened. "No one has seen Con in a few days. He's off on another of his mysterious trips."

"After Ulrik, perhaps?" Ryder asked.

Laith said, "I doubt it. He'll wait until we can all see the battle."

"If you think that, you doona know Con," Rhys said before he walked out.

Warrick gave Laith a shove before he hefted another of the mercs and followed Rhys. Laith stared at the two remaining dead bodies and pivoted. He couldn't remember a time he had ever tried to gain the trust of a female. He wasn't even sure if he knew how.

Iona walked around her father's Range Rover for the second time that morning, stopping on the driver's side as she looked at the huge dents and scrapes caused by the boulders when the SUV fell off the mountain.

The driver's door was stuck, but the others worked fine. There was no sense in her keeping the rental car when she had a perfectly good vehicle to drive the few times she went into town.

Her decision made, Iona walked to the passenger side and climbed in before settling in the driver's seat. Once behind the wheel she put the key in the ignition and tried to start it. The battery wouldn't even turn over.

Iona dropped her head to the steering wheel for several moments before she climbed back out and opened the hood.

Part of being independent meant that she knew how to do a little of everything. It was by necessity that she learned to work on vehicles, but she discovered she liked it.

She found where the battery had been disconnected quickly enough. Just as Iona was about to reconnect it, she took a look at the rest of the engine, a frown forming. Someone wanted to make damn sure no one could drive the Rover.

Iona looked in the small shed out back and found the tools she needed. Then she got to work on the Rover. She meticulously checked everything as she went. Despite the vehicle's age, her father had taken good care of it, replacing parts as required.

She stopped long enough to grab something to eat at noon before she was back under the SUV. A check of the water hose proved that all was good, as was the radiator. It wasn't until she got to the brake line that she noticed all the brake fluid gone.

There were a few other things she needed to pick up from town, so once her initial check was done, Iona took a shower and changed. She made a list of all that she required, then drove into town in her rental.

Iona pulled into M&M Auto Repair and parked. She had the list in hand when she got out of the car. No sooner had she closed the door than Michael MacDonald, the owner, walked out of the garage, wiping his hands.

"Hello, again," he called with a cheery smile.

Iona noticed the smudge of grease on his cheek as she returned his smile. She handed him the piece of paper. "I've made a list of things I need to repair the Rover."

His smile disappeared and a frown creased his brow as he looked from her to the paper. "You're repairing John's Rover?"

"I am. I do know what I'm doing."

His gaze jerked back to hers. "Oh, I didna mean to imply that you didna, lass. Are you sure you want to handle this yourself?"

Sammi wasn't the only one who learned to read people. Iona hadn't had the pleasure of learning behind a bar like Sammi. No, Iona learned out in the real world hunkered down with different military squadrons during war, or asking tribal leaders to allow her inside their borders where one wrong mistake could get her killed.

That's how she knew Michael was hiding something from her. "I do. Do you have everything I need?"

"Uh . . . I believe so." He waved her to follow him into the adjacent shop , and then proceeded to look through the shelves.

Iona leaned her forearms on the counter as she watched him. "Once I have her running, I'll drop by so you can beat out the door panel. I'm hoping that's all it'll take to get the driver's door working again."

"It'll take a wee bit more than that," he said as he walked around the aisle, a rag hanging from the back of his pants pocket.

"Maybe. We'll see."

"Um, hm."

She continued with the mundane questions and statements, putting him at ease. Then she asked, "Why do you think the battery was disconnected?"

Michael stilled for the barest of moments, then he walked to her with his arms loaded with items. "You say the battery was disconnected?"

"I did. The brake line was dry as a bone as well. What are your thoughts on that?"

His gaze lowered to the left. "I doona know."

It was a classic sign of someone lying. She straightened and kept her gaze locked on him "It was my father who died."

"I know, lass," he said and met her eyes. "Everyone liked him."

Honesty reflected in Michael's brown eyes. "You're speaking true now, but you didn't a moment ago. What aren't you telling me?"

"Lass," he began.

Iona immediately cut him off by lifting her hand. "If you're going to try and feed me more lies, don't. I'm not in the mood."

His shoulders sagged, and the lines on his face deepened. "I was hoping you'd never find out."

"Find out what, exactly?"

"Please doona make me tell you."

A knot of unease formed. "Who else knows?"

He wouldn't meet her gaze, which meant several others. "Iona, lass, perhaps it's better if you let this go."

As if that would happen now. "Was it an accident that killed my father?" she pressed.

Michael sighed and looked at her for several moments before he gave a single shake of his head.

If it wasn't an accident, that meant it was on purpose. Iona held herself in check, refusing to give into the scream of denial that formed in her throat, as she asked, "Was he killed?"

"Aye."

One word. One simple word had the ability to set her on her ear. She began to sweat the same time ice ran in her veins. Her ears rang, and her hands shook. She clenched her hands into fists to keep Michael from seeing how upset she was.

"How?" she croaked.

He put his weight on one foot and moved the items he had pulled for her around on the counter. "It took me a bit, but I found the pinhole in the brake line. It drained slow enough that John wouldna have known until it was too late."

Oh God. She was going to be sick. Someone had murdered her father, but why? Was that why those men had come for her yesterday?

"John didna have any enemies," Michael said. "We doona know why he was killed."

Iona found something to focus on, something that she could cling to instead of drowning in the guilt. "Who is we?"

"Those at Dreagan. Constantine himself wanted me to look closely because he suspected something."

"Is that so?" Iona had a destination. No longer would she be kept in the dark. She gave a nod to the items on the counter. "I'll be back for those."

CHAPTER
FOURTEEN

Lily Ross thanked the tourist exiting the shop with their purchase of Dreagan whisky, two whisky glasses, and a sticker of the Dreagan logo. She came around the counter ready to see if the other customers needed help when the door opened and a tall blonde walked in. She removed her sunglasses and pinned Lily with her dark brown eyes.

"Welcome to Dreagan," Lily said with a smile. "Have you just come from the tour?"

The blonde shoved the sunglasses on top of her head. "I haven't."

"It's all right. You don't need to do the tour to buy from us. Is there something I can help you look for?" she asked, noting the way the woman's eyes scanned the shop.

"You can actually. I'd like to speak to Constantine."

Lily blinked, her lips parting. She herself had never met Con. The closest she came was seeing him from afar, but he had yet to come into the shop when she was there. From the little time Lily had worked at Dreagan, she knew the people there liked their privacy, which worked great for her. There were things she wanted kept private as well.

"Do you have an appointment, Miss . . . ?" Lily asked.

The woman's lips quirked at the corners. "Campbell. Iona Campbell, and no, I don't."

"Oh." It hit Lily who the woman was. "I didn't know your father, but I'm very sorry for your loss."

Iona briefly closed her eyes and adjusted her purse on her shoulder. "Thank you. About Con?"

"I'm sorry. If you don't have an appointment, I can't help you."

"Is he here?"

Lily smiled to the customers browsing and touched Iona on the arm so she would follow her to the counter where their conversation could be a little more private. "I don't know where he is, I'm not privy to that information."

"I would appreciate if you could get me someone who can help."

Lily had encountered demanding customers before, but this was a first. No one had ever barged into the store and demanded to speak to someone from Dreagan.

She grabbed a pen and paper and gave them to Iona. "If you'll leave your contact information, I'll make sure it gets to Con."

"There's no need. Just tell him I know what really happened to my father."

Lily watched her walk out of the shop. She set the paper down, perplexed. Without a doubt, Iona Campbell was furious.

"Well, that was interesting," came a deep voice she recognized instantly.

Lily shivered in pleasure and looked over her shoulder to find Rhys standing just inside the doorway behind the counter. His dark hair was loose about his shoulders, and his aqua eyes ringed with dark blue were made brighter by the blue Affliction shirt. His head was cocked to the side as he stared at her, as if waiting for her to speak.

Lily was forever being stupid around him. She hastily nodded. "Yes it was. Did you hear the entire conversation?"

"Aye."

"Why didn't you come out?" she asked.

He shrugged nonchalantly. "I didna want to talk to her."

Lily knew better than to read too much into that statement. Rhys liked women, and he normally had a different woman on his arm every night. Matter of fact, he loved blondes, and Iona seemed just his type. "Can you deliver that message to Con?"

"Have you met him, Lily?"

God, how she loved the sound of her name on his lips. "Not yet."

"You're no' missing anything. Trust me on that," Rhys said crossly.

Lily wanted to scream in frustration when their conversation was interrupted by not one, but two customers checking out. By the time the last one left, Lily was certain Rhys would be gone.

She was more than surprised to find him standing exactly as he had been. Her stomach fluttered, and still she cautioned herself to remember she was nothing more than an employee at Dreagan.

"Are you happy here?" Rhys asked.

Lily's grin was uncontrollable. "It's the first time in a long time I've been happy."

"And people are treating you good?"

"Very. Cassie and Jane are amazing, and though I don't see Elena or Denae much since they work in other parts of the distillery most times, they are great."

One side of Rhys's mouth lifted in a grin. "I'm glad to hear it. You know we're here if you need anything."

For a moment, Lily thought Rhys might have discovered her past. Her heart pounded against her ribs, but as the seconds passed and he said no more, she realized she was wrong. "Of course," she hurried to say.

His aqua eyes studied her. "You have nothing to fear here."

"There is always something to fear."

The words were out of her mouth before she could stop them. It was a symptom of her past, a past she feared she would never be able to outrun.

"That's true," Rhys said softly. "Unless you have friends."

And with that, he turned on his heel and walked away. Lily sighed, because she knew that was as close as she would ever get to the handsome Rhys.

Laith sat in his office at the pub staring off into space as he wracked his brain over how to fix things with Iona. For the past several hours, he'd come up with absolutely nothing. The fact he wanted to be near her set warning bells off in his head. He'd told himself he wouldn't get close.

But one kiss, one scorching kiss changed everything.

He finally blinked and noticed that someone was standing in the door. Laith straightened in his chair when he saw Rhys. "How long have you been there?"

"Long enough," Rhys said as he entered and sat in one of the empty chairs. "There was a visitor at Dreagan today."

Laith gave him a droll look. "There are always visitors at Dreagan. They're called tourists."

"I'm talking an actual visitor, you wanker," he snapped.

Laith rested an elbow on the arm of his chair. "Who?"

"Iona."

It was a good thing he was sitting down, because he might have fallen over. "What? Why?"

"She asked to speak to Con, and she was furious."

Laith pinched the bridge of his nose with his thumb and forefinger. "What else did she say?"

"That she knows how John died."

"Shite."

"Do you think it was a guess after yesterday?"

Laith shook his head as he looked at Rhys. "She's been in dangerous situations before, and she's intelligent. It wasna a guess. She discovered the brake line."

"Damn," Rhys muttered. "This could scare her off."

"It'll take more than this to send her packing. Besides, she told her bosses that she was taking some time off."

"Bosses?" Rhys asked.

"She said bosses. From what she told Sammi, it's a group of high-powered people who send her on assignments all over the world."

Rhys idly rubbed his chin. "Why?"

"Why?" Laith repeated. "What do you mean?"

"I'm asking why does it require a group of people to hire a photojournalist? I thought some photographers were independent and sold their photos to the highest bidder, or at the very least contracted with companies."

"I think that's what Iona is, contracted."

"And the company name?"

Laith began to see where Rhys was going with his questions. "I doona know."

"With as many enemies as we have, Laith, we need to be suspicious of everyone."

Laith knew Rhys was right, but that didn't mean he liked what he heard. "The pub is covered. Let's return to Dreagan. If anyone can find out this information quickly, it's Ryder."

"We best stop and find him some donuts," Rhys said as they walked out the back entrance of the pub.

Thirty minutes later they were striding up the stairs to the third floor of Dreagan Manor with a box of jelly-filled donuts in hand. Laith was the first one through the door. He handed Ryder the box over the rows of monitors and waited.

Ryder gave him a suspicious look, but at the sight of the donuts he waved them around. "I doona need to be bribed for whatever you need, but I appreciate the treat."

"We need you to look into Iona Campbell," Rhys said as he sank into a chair.

Laith noticed how Rhys still favored his right side, but he didn't point it out. "I thought we were interested in her bosses."

"It's better to start with one person," Ryder said. He stuffed a donut in his mouth, leaving it hanging there while punching something into the keyboard.

A second later and one of the screens filled with a picture of Iona, her credit rating, banking and medical information, university scores and classes, and employment history.

Rhys let out a whistle. "She makes good money for spending her time taking photos."

Ryder leaned back in his chair, donut in hand as he chewed and swallowed the bite. "Aye, she does verra well for herself."

Laith pointed to the last listing of employment. "These are the people we want to look into."

"The Commune," Ryder said and typed it in.

On another screen information on the Commune slowly pulled up. At first glance everything looked to be legit with nothing standing out that would raise eyebrows. The list of employees wasn't long, only about fifty people. It took only a few clicks for them to determine that each name was the top in their field, which ranged from rocket scientists to mechanics.

But that's what made Ryder so good at what he did. He

recognized simple things, or things that were missing, and kept digging.

Laith took a chair and waited as Ryder stuffed the last of the donut into his mouth and kept typing with more pages of documents continuing to pop up on the screen. Laith exchanged a look with Rhys, because the longer it took Ryder to dig, the worse it was going to be.

Twenty minutes later, Ryder pushed back from the keyboard and swiveled the chair around to face Rhys and Laith. "It isna good."

"Just spit it out," Laith demanded.

Ryder laced his hands behind his head. "Whoever these bosses are, they are going to extremes to hide their identities. I can find names, but just like Con, there isna a picture anywhere."

"Damn," Rhys muttered.

Laith stared at the computers as he gathered his thoughts. "Why was John murdered now? All these years, why now?"

"Because whoever did it must know about the pact," Ryder pointed out.

Rhys ran a hand through his long hair. "Which means they wanted John out of the way so they could use Iona."

"But why? They need her for something," Laith said.

Ryder lowered his hands and leaned back in his chair. "So you doona think she's spying for one of our enemies?"

"You mean like Shara did? Or Denae?" Laith asked.

"Aye. The only place our dragon magic willna keep people out is right there on Campbell land. A clear way for our enemies to get onto Dreagan."

Rhys stretched out his legs and crossed them at the ankle. "I agree with Laith. I doona think she's spying. Whether she's a willing accomplice is another story."

"Accomplice to what?" Laith asked, his frustrations

growing. "We can no' keep thinking everyone is our enemy."

Ryder's lips twisted. "We have to, because if we doona, we set ourselves up to have everything we've strived to keep hidden released to the world."

"Think about what she inherited, Laith," Rhys said. "She now owns property that borders us, along with a doorway anyone can get through if they find it."

Laith got to his feet. "I knew that spot was going to come back to haunt us. We should've done it somewhere else."

"There wasna time, and then there was the matter of Ulrik," Ryder pointed out.

Laith slumped back into the chair. "We need to talk to Iona, to learn how much she knows."

"Nay, *you* need to talk to her," Rhys said.

CHAPTER
FIFTEEN

Iona listened to her voice mail as she sat on the couch and cringed. She completely forgot her meeting with the bank to sign the needed documents to have her father's accounts turned over to her.

After the day she'd had, she wanted to be alone and think about the fact her father had been murdered. Murdered. That word settled heavily in her stomach, roiling and churning.

Based on everything she learned about John Campbell from those around town, he had been friendly, caring, and honest as the day was long. Not a single person said an unkind word against him.

So why would he be killed?

Iona set aside her mobile and rose to walk into her father's office. It was in direct conflict with the rest of the house. In the office there was nothing neat and tidy. It was like he forgot himself inside the room.

She sat behind the desk staring at the stack of papers on either side of the laptop. Taking a deep breath, she reached for the first stack and shifted through it seeing red pencil marks throughout and comments in the margins from her father's editor.

She found a rubber band and bound the papers together before setting them on the wide windowsill behind her. The next stack was a series of documents printed from the Internet on various things he was researching for his next book. Some pages had portions highlighted, while others had paragraphs circled.

Iona paper clipped those, and set them in a new stack on the opposite side of the windowsill. Pile by pile she went through, learning more about her father as she did. His neat handwriting was easy to discern amid all the papers.

By the time she finished cleaning off the top of his desk an hour later, she had four distinct stacks. There were the research stack, the copyedits, the rough drafts, and the galley proofs.

Her father didn't throw anything out. He kept it all. A glance at the bookcases on her left exposed additional clutter that she suspected was more of what she had just gone through.

Iona put a bright green sticky note on the book waiting on copyedits and a second one on galley proofs for another book. She would finish up both for her father and turn them in to his publisher. After years of rejecting him, it was the least she could do. It wasn't nearly enough, though.

She made a note to call his publisher the next day and posted it on the screen of his laptop. Then she pulled open the first drawer of the desk. It was shallow and held nothing more than pens, pencils, highlighters, paper clips, and rubber bands.

The second drawer was much deeper and held file folders. Iona ran her fingers along the tabs, her brow furrowing deeper as she recognized dates and locations of places she had been. She pulled out one file and stared in shock at pictures of herself standing with a U.K. military team on patrol in the Middle East.

She shoved that file back and pulled out a second. Once more there was a photo of her. This time she was on her stomach, adjusting her lens right before she took a picture of a group of children jumping into a river in India.

File after file was the same, and included notes of how long she stayed, what she took pictures of, and who she was with. All written on letterhead from a private detective firm in Edinburgh.

Tears filled her eyes, because while she had refused to acknowledge him, her father had made sure he knew every aspect of her life that he could.

She wiped her face and reached for the folder nearest her. Her throat clogged when she saw pictures of herself from the time her mother took her away until she graduated school, and then went on to university. There was even a listing of her scores in all her classes.

Iona returned the file. That's when she spotted the box in the back of the drawer. She took it out and removed the lid. The tears came faster when she saw card after card marked *Return to Sender* in her mother's handwriting.

All those years Iona thought her father hadn't wanted her, and it had been her mother who ensured there was no contact. Her father quit sending the cards, but he didn't stop buying them. They were labeled for Christmas, New Year's, Easter, and her birthdays, all with messages written inside.

Iona covered her face with her hands and sobbed for the father she hadn't known, the father who hadn't given up on her.

She didn't know how long she cried. When the tears finally dried, she felt drained, empty. Depleted. But there was also anger.

Iona picked up the handset at her father's desk and dialed her mother's mobile. She wondered if her mother would pick up, when on the fifth ring, she answered with a curt, "What do you want, John?"

"Hello, Mum," Iona said.

There was a beat of shocked silence before Sarah asked, "Iona? Honey, what are you doing in Scotland?"

"Dad's dead." It hurt to say the words, but somehow she got them out.

"John's dead? How?"

Iona made a decision right then not to reveal everything to her mother about his death. "There was a car accident."

"When?"

"A few days ago."

Sarah sighed heavily. "You should've called me. I'd have gone to that nasty place and taken care of everything for you so you wouldn't have to be reminded of that awful time in our lives."

"Was it so awful? Really? Was it?"

"I've told you repeatedly how it was."

Iona tucked her legs against her chest in the chair and closed her eyes. "Why did you return all of Dad's cards unopened? Why didn't you let me see them?"

"I didn't want to hurt you more. You know that. You would've asked for him, and there was no returning to him."

"What I know is that you love money and men. You move from one man to the next more often than I change locations in my work."

Sarah tsked. "Now, Iona, you know men can't be trusted. They're to be used. I thought I taught you that."

"You did, and for the longest time I believed you. However, I don't believe you about my father. You didn't leave him because he couldn't manage money."

"I certainly did," her mother said, affronted. "He spent everything."

Iona felt more tears coming as she opened her eyes. "I think you've told yourself that so many times that you believe the lie now. I think it was because he wouldn't give you access to all of his money."

"All of his . . . " Sarah trailed off and laughed. "Iona, your father never had any money."

"He did, actually. Lots of it he inherited, and more he made for himself with his novels. He lived simply, but the money was always there."

Just as Iona expected, her mother was speechless. It wouldn't last long. Sarah had a knack for knowing how to obtain money easily. This time, she wouldn't be using her body. She would try something different.

"Why don't I come and help you sort all this out?" Sarah asked. "You shouldn't be going through all of that on your own."

Iona knew her mother too well. "I'm an adult, and I've been handling this by myself just fine."

"You've always been independent, Iona, but there's no need for you to not take help when it's being offered. We could sell the land and make a pretty penny off of that. I'll leave Illias, and we can travel together like you've always wanted."

It was a prime opportunity for Iona to put her mother in her place once and for all. After all Sarah had done to keep Iona from her father, it seemed a perfect retaliation, but Iona couldn't do it. Regardless, Sarah was still her mother, and now her only surviving parent as well as her last living relative.

"I think you should remain in Morocco or wherever you're at."

"You're not going to share the money, are you?" Sarah asked tightly.

Iona crossed her legs and leaned her head back. "Yes, I'll give you money. If you want to be on your own for a while, I'll make sure that you don't have to sleep with a man to have the things you want."

"You're such a good daughter, Iona. I knew I raised you right. When can I expect the money in my account?"

"A week, two at the most."

She squealed. "How exciting. I've got to go. There's so much to do now."

There was a click and the line went dead. Iona hung up the receiver and sat in silence. The sounds of nature penetrated the house, lending a kind of peace and calm Iona recalled from her childhood.

It was no wonder her father had remained on the land. It wasn't just the legacy of his family, but part of his soul. The sad part was that she hadn't gotten a chance to experience it with him.

The more she sat there, the more her mind wandered and caused her to start crying again. Iona couldn't stand another minute of it. She rose and headed to the bookcase to sort through the stacks there before she tackled the second file drawer in her father's desk.

Rhi stood outside the cottage watching Iona. Over the centuries she made a point of checking in on whoever the current resident Campbell was. It began with her infatuation with the Dragon Kings, and developed from there to helping protect them after she got involved with her lover.

Since then, it has been something she was so used to doing that it became a habit. Perhaps if she hadn't been dealing with her own issues she might have seen what was going to happen to John Campbell and prevented it.

There was a new Campbell in charge now, but Rhi suspected the mortal had no idea what it was she had. If she did, she would be much more cautious about who she spoke with and about what.

The Dragon Kings had made one of the worst decisions ever by creating a doorway in which anyone—mortal or immortal—could cross and enter Dreagan undetected.

All because Con had been too angry to realize the consequences. It wasn't his first mistake, and it hadn't been his last. But it was his worst.

There were few who knew of the spot's existence because the Campbells so tightly guarded it. However, there was one who knew it, one who would use it to his advantage.

With a thought, Rhi vanished from her place and reappeared inside The Silver Dragon antique store. She was veiled, but revealed herself as soon as she saw Ulrik was alone. He looked up from his desk the moment she appeared. His golden eyes held a flash of surprise before he set down his pen and leaned back in his chair, watching her.

Rhi took her time looking around the store at the various items from suits of armor to teapots to the bookcases filled with books on the second floor. Neither said a word until she faced him once more. His mouth was lifted in a hint of a grin, one that said he had known she would eventually show up.

"You're looking well," Ulrik said.

She shrugged and ran a finger along the edge of his desk to the corner where she then sat, crossing one leg over the other. When he looked at her clothes, she asked, "Were you the one who cleaned up my cottage and set out the clothes?"

"Nay." He frowned and sat forward, his arms resting on his desk. "It appears I'm no' the only one who knows of your cottage."

"Perhaps not." She didn't entirely believe him, then again, why would he have the need to lie? She hated when she couldn't sort out a problem, and this was definitely a conundrum. "Maybe now you'll tell me why you had John Campbell killed."

Ulrik's smile was cold, calculating. "Who is John Campbell?"

"You know full well who he is."

"Why the interest? I thought you were done protecting the Dragon Kings?"

She lifted her chin. "Who says I'm protecting them?"

CHAPTER
SIXTEEN

Laith got out of his car and closed the door to the black Audi R8. He half expected Iona to stand at the door with a shotgun, ordering him off her property. When the front door didn't fly open, Laith glanced down at his clothes to make sure he looked all right and started to the door. He reached the front steps and gave three quick raps of his knuckles against the wood.

Then he waited.

And waited.

Laith looked at John's Rover and Iona's rental car. Either she didn't want to talk, or she was out in the woods again. He didn't take her for the type to avoid someone. No, Iona would have come to the door and told him herself to bugger off.

He backed off the steps and walked around the house, looking for any sign of her. When he didn't find her at the back of the house, he peeked in a window, but wasn't able to see her.

Laith then looked to the forest. Somewhere among the trees, ferns, and moss was Iona. It wasn't difficult to find her tracks leading from the deck. She didn't venture the same way she had the day before.

It was easy for him to deduce that she was headed toward the waterfall. Laith followed the well-worn trail John and his ancestors had made over the years. The sound of the waterfall could be heard well before he spotted Iona standing by the shore staring into the pool of water.

He stopped several feet away and simply watched her. She stood silently in her jeans and hunter green shirt. He almost hated to disturb her. She looked dejected and lost. Despite what he saw, he had to talk to her. Too much rode on learning answers, least of which were the lives of every Dragon King.

"Iona," he called.

Her head turned so that her gaze clashed with his. There was no welcoming smile, but she didn't tell him to leave either. After a moment, she looked back at the water.

Laith took that to mean he could approach. He waited until he stood beside her before he said, "I'm sorry about yesterday. I should've handled that better. I thought you were in trouble, and I reacted."

"Why didn't you tell me my father was murdered?"

He drew in a breath and shook his head. "Dreagan has enemies, powerful enemies, and we didna know if we could trust you."

"You mean you thought I might have killed my father?" she asked, anger deepening her voice as she faced him.

Laith turned to her, trying to find the right words. "We know you didna kill John, but we had to be careful. We would've told you the truth."

"Yeah, I bet you would've."

"I would have," he insisted.

Her shoulders drooped and she looked down as she kicked the dirt. "I believe you."

"Good."

"Did you find out anything from those men yesterday?" she asked and looked at him expectedly.

"I wish I could say we did. Turns out they had cyanide hidden in their teeth. They used it before we could question them."

Her eyes grew large. "Are you kidding? That doesn't happen in real life."

"It does actually. We have a close friend in MI5, and an ex-agent who is married to another of my friends."

She put her hands in the back pockets of her jeans. "What is going on around here? My father is murdered, men hiding out in the forest tracking me, and committing suicide by poison."

Instead of trying to explain, he asked, "Do you know the history of your family and Dreagan?"

"I remember my dad telling me stories about Dreagan, but I can't remember them."

Laith looked from the waterfall to the forest beyond. "Dreagan was here long before anyone settled the area. The Campbells were one of the first, and your family and Dreagan made a pact of sorts. They protected each other."

"From what?"

"Anything. Everything," he said, looking back at her. A strand of hair caught in the wind and tangled in her eyelashes. He pulled the hair free and tucked it behind her ear. "For hundreds of years that pact has remained."

Her gaze skated away when he touched her, and then slid back to him. "Which, I suppose, is why my father's will stipulates I can't sell?"

"Aye. It's in the will of every owner of this land."

"Why?" she asked, frowning. "I don't understand."

Laith wasn't sure what was told from one Campbell to another when they inherited, and he was loath to muck it up. "Your father should have left you something explaining things."

"Oh," she said in surprise. "He did. I completely forgot about it." She ran her hand through her hair and sighed. "I was distracted about his death and learning he wasn't who I thought he was. Then I discover he was killed."

"I'm sure the letter will explain everything."

"And those men? My father's murder? Can those be explained as easily?"

Laith gave a shake of his head. "I'm afraid no'. I wish I could, but as I said, we have enemies."

Her head cocked to the side. "What do your enemies want? And don't you dare say it's the recipe to your whisky."

"Corporate espionage is real," Laith pointed out.

"True."

"And people have been killed for less."

She gave a nod of agreement. "Again, true."

"We're the top seller in Scotch whisky, and we outsell most of the Irish whisky."

"If it was just the recipe your enemies wanted, why would they kill my father and track me? What are they really after?"

Laith smoothed a hand over his hair to the queue at the base of his neck. "You wouldna believe me if I told you. Trust me when I say that these people will kill anyone who stands in their way."

"I've been around dictators, generals, and tyrants too many times to count, and I know how those kinds of people think. This 'pact' you speak of between Dreagan and the Campbells is a weakness for Dreagan, isn't it?"

Damn, but she was smart. Laith wished she hadn't figured it out so soon. He really wanted her to read the letter before they spoke, because he had never told a human what he was. He didn't know what words to use so he didn't scare her.

"I see," she said. "Which means, I'm a liability, just as my father was."

"We protect our friends."

"Like you protected my father?"

Laith looked away. She had a point, and it pained everyone at Dreagan that John Campbell died because of them.

"I don't blame you," Iona said. "I blame the people who did it. You can't protect everyone, no matter how hard you try."

Laith then made a decision to tell Iona some of what they had pieced together, if for nothing more than to keep her aware of the danger. "We believe your father was killed to bring you here."

"I was already on my way here," she said with a snort. "There was an . . . incident at my last assignment where I almost died. I couldn't stop thinking of my father, so I decided to come see him."

"I wish you'd had the chance to talk to him, but then you might have been in the Rover with him."

Iona shrugged. "Why do you think someone wanted me here?"

"We're no' yet sure why it was important that you come, but whoever is pulling the strings has a purpose we've no' yet discerned. It's the only reason to kill your father so they could get to you."

"They are going to be mistaken if they think they can use me." She met his gaze. "Thank you for telling me, though that doesn't make things easier."

Laith bent and grabbed a rock. He tossed it in the air a couple of times, and then threw it over the water so it skidded thrice before sinking. "I need to ask you something."

"Go ahead," she urged.

"What do you know about your employers?"

She chuckled and moved to sit on a large rock. "What does anyone really know of their employers? I know they're a group of people who have unlimited wealth, and they hire the best people in their fields."

"Why?" His gaze returned to her as it always did. She drew his attention like no one else ever had—or ever would.

"Why?" she repeated, her face scrunched in confusion. "Why does anyone do anything? Because they can."

Laith grinned. "Why do they want the best people in their fields? Why are they no' content to let you work with a magazine or other company?"

"I was approached by a representative for the Commune through e-mail," she stated. "Abby explained the job offer. When I asked if I needed to submit something, she said I had already been chosen. I just needed to accept or decline the position."

"And you didna think that weird?"

"Not at the time when I was submitting my work everywhere to find a job. The money offered was more than I ever thought to make."

Laith considered her words. "What was the job description exactly?"

"That I would be given assignments—places, people, and things—that they wanted photographed. It seemed innocent enough. My travel and hotels were paid for, plus I got a massive fee. Next thing I knew, my work was showing up in national magazines, the news, and on the Internet."

"Have you met any of your bosses?"

Iona's eyes crinkled as she smiled. "Oh, no. Everything is sent through their assistant, Abby."

"Everything?" he asked.

"Everything. My assignments, travel itinerary, pay, and any correspondence."

Laith took a step toward her as worry set in. "You've never even spoken to these people?"

"No," she said slowly.

"You've no' seen or spoken with them? How do you know they're real?"

"My pay is real enough," she said as she got to her feet. "Why do you think the Commune is bad? They like to keep their identities hidden. There's nothing wrong with that. Con does the same thing."

Laith should've seen that one coming. "You checked out Con?"

"And you. Or I tried," she muttered. "Hard to do when I can't get a surname. However, Constantine is another matter entirely. There's no picture of him anywhere. His name is rarely mentioned, and only his first name, never his surname."

Laith couldn't exactly tell her they didn't have surnames. Some Dragon Kings picked up ones through the years, but changed them as needed. Laith was one who hadn't bothered with a surname. And of course Iona would notice that.

"Is Con hiding something? Are you?" she demanded.

"All I came here for was information on your company. We've no' been able to find much, and that worried us."

"As if you refusing to tell me your surname doesn't worry me?" she asked with a raise of her brows.

There were too many correlations between Dreagan and the Commune for Iona to notice the difference between them, and Laith couldn't explain without telling her everything.

"That's what I thought." She stared at him, as if daring him to contradict her.

His gaze lowered to her mouth, and he recalled all too clearly the taste of her lips beneath his, the way her body melted against him.

The way she opened for him.

Laith lifted his gaze to her eyes and noticed her features had relaxed. Her lips softened, parting slightly. He knew he should return to Dreagan and report what he discovered, but he remained where he was.

"Am I safe with you?" she asked.

"You have my vow that you are."

As one they closed the distance. Her arms wrapped around his neck as he splayed his hands on her back holding her close as he bent her over his arm and kissed her.

He was ravenous for her, the hunger growing with every touch of her tongue against his.

CHAPTER SEVENTEEN

Desire blazed, passion raged. Both reigned, controlling Iona as nothing and no one else had. This time she wanted . . . everything.

She shifted her feet to get closer, and a rock slipped beneath her foot, causing her to lose her balance. Since she was already leaning over Laith's arm, she began to fall backward. In an instant, Laith lunged forward, his leg stopping their tumble. The kiss ended as they looked into each other's eyes and began to laugh.

Iona had never gone from such scorching passion to laughter before, while still in a man's arms. It was such a different experience that she wondered what else she had missed out on.

She wound the locks of his dark blond hair around her finger, trying to decide if she liked it better in the queue or not. Even with Laith holding most of her weight in their difficult position, his hold was steady, his gunmetal eyes watching her. In a blink, their laughter died as desire ensnared them once more.

Iona licked her lips, the taste of Laith still upon them. It scared her how much she needed to feel him, to touch him. If there were ever a man to make her consider the idea of love—it would be Laith.

She loosened her grip on his hair and lightly scraped her fingernails over his cheek to his incredible lips. "I could kiss you all day."

Laith's gaze intensified. "All right."

His head lowered to hers. Iona lifted her face, anxious for more of his kisses when Laith suddenly looked to the waterfall, a sad, dejected expression falling over him. Laith set her on her feet and then took a step back.

"What's wrong?" Iona had been in awkward situations before, but this was the first time she hadn't wanted to just walk away and forget everything. "Is it something I did?"

"Nay," he quickly answered. "It's no' you, Iona. It's me. It's memories, actually."

He was staring at the top of the waterfall, his remorse visible for anyone to see. Iona saw nothing but beauty and wonder at the waterfall, but it obviously held something bad for Laith. Had she gone anywhere else but there, they would probably be kissing once more.

"Do you want to talk about it?" She glanced at him as she spoke.

He finally looked away from the waterfall to her. "I do, but I doona think you're ready."

"Me?" she asked, now thoroughly confused. "I thought this was about your past."

"It is." He paused, his lips flattening for a moment. "I'm mucking this up badly. You need to read your father's letter."

"I will."

Iona didn't want to think of the letter, her father, or anything other than Laith and the passion they shared. Just as she knew he didn't want to remain at the waterfall. With reluctance, she started back to the cottage, and he fell in step beside her.

For several minutes, they walked in companionable silence with Iona aware of his every move. Twice their hands brushed, sending currents of longing snaking through her like lightning, building her longing, heating her blood.

"Are you still angry that I didna tell you I was part of Dreagan?" he asked.

She thought about that a moment, then gave a half-hearted shrug. "No one likes being lied to, even if that lie was by omission. I get the feeling there is more to Dreagan than you're telling me. It doesn't help with all the secrets and secrecy either."

"I know. Read the letter John left you. I think that will help answer most of what you want to know."

"And the rest?" She turned her head to him to see his reaction.

His gaze met hers. "I'll fill in the rest."

It was more than she had gotten before. Iona hadn't cared about such things previously, but then again she hadn't met a man like Laith or had someone close to her murdered.

"The enemies you spoke of, do you know who they are?" she asked.

Laith's brow furrowed as he helped her navigate over an outcropping of large rocks. "We have our suspicions."

"So no one knows who killed my father."

He came to a stop and grasped her arm to turn her toward home. "No' yet, but I give you my vow we'll learn the truth."

"Why do I get the feeling you won't turn the information over to the authorities?"

"Because they wouldna be able to do anything."

She frowned, worry filling her stomach. "Who are these people?"

"They're dangerous. Just remember that. I want you safe. Unfortunately, just being here puts you in danger."

"Because I'm the last Campbell?" Why hadn't she put that together sooner?

Laith nodded solemnly.

"And since this land can never be sold since it has to remain in a Campbell's hand, I'm screwed."

"There could be another alternative."

"How, if there isn't another Campbell in this direct line?" she asked in confusion. His hesitation spoke volumes. "More secrets? Let me guess. My father had more children with another woman? Not that I would blame him."

Laith moved his hand to her lower back and urged her onward. "No' exactly. It's difficult to explain."

"Everything seems to be difficult to explain. It wouldn't be if you just told me."

"You're frustrated."

"Bingo, Sherlock. Why all the secrets? Why not just tell me?"

"There are reasons, Iona. We doona tell anyone."

"Someone must know or you wouldn't have enemies."

All too soon the cottage came into sight. Iona wasn't ready to face the letter from her father, not after all she had been through since learning how he died.

"Do you want me to stay?" Laith asked.

Iona blinked and looked up at him. When had she stopped walking, and when had he moved to stand in front of her? She did want him to stay. It was so unlike her that it took her aback. Independence was a virtue she'd cultivated early on in her childhood. She had faced all sorts of situations by herself and came through fine. Why would she want Laith to stay now?

His kisses. That was definitely one possibility, but she suspected it had more to do with how protected and secure she felt when he was near.

"No," she finally answered. "I need to read the letter by myself."

If she let him stay, it would be a step she hadn't ever taken before. He could get close, leaving her vulnerable. She refused to allow that to happen.

He gave a nod and walked her to the back door. Even as Iona was unlocking the door, her mind screamed for her to invite him in. Iona fought against the urge, and somehow succeeded.

"You know how to find me if you need anything," Laith said and gave a gentle tug of her hair.

Iona watched him walk around the house. She hurried inside and ran to the front to look out the window for a glimpse of him. With her arms wrapped around herself, she stared after him, loving the predatory way he moved.

When he reached his black Audi, he opened the door, but paused before he got inside. His head lifted so that he looked right at her through the window. Laith gave her a reassuring smile.

Oddly enough, Iona found it easy to return the smile. Then he got in the car and drove away. Once more leaving Iona by herself. She used to love the solitude, but she was beginning to hate it.

She turned from the window to look at her purse that sat on the end table next to the couch. Iona walked to her purse and found the envelope inside. She tucked a leg beneath her and sat on the couch, staring at the white envelope with her name written in her father's neat script.

During her years with him, she recalled him saying that handwriting was a lost art, one that he loved as much as writing his books. Iona smoothed her hands over the envelope, and then turned it over. On the back was a globe of red wax with the Campbell coat of arms imprinted in the wax. Iona broke the seal and opened the envelope.

She unfolded the pages to see more of her father's handwriting. Then she began to read.

My dearest Iona,

I hope that we've reconciled, and I've already explained some things to you, but just in case that doesn't happen, I've written down what I could.

This piece of land is always to remain with the Campbells. It can never be sold or given to anyone but a direct descendant of our line. I'm sure you're wondering why. There's no easy explanation. It goes back thousands of years. We Campbells were lucky to have found such friends as those at Dreagan. They are good people. Trust them, because they have been trusting us for generations.

I really hope I get to tell you this in person instead of just in this letter, because there's no easy way to explain who those at Dreagan are. They are different than us, lass. They are protectors, guardians if you will. The longer you remain on the land, the more you'll come to understand. You might even get a glimpse of something if you look to the night skies hard enough.

As with everything, those at Dreagan have enemies. During my time it's been relatively quiet, but I sense a change coming. There will be people who want on your land. You can't allow them access, because if you do, the consequences could be catastrophic.

That's all I can say in the letter in case it falls into the wrong hands. I'm praying that I get to ex-

*plain everything in detail in person, because there
is so much I'm having to leave out.*

*Be safe, be vigilant, and above all else, trust only
those at Dreagan.*

Your loving father.

Iona read the letter twice more before she set it aside.
If only she had come to see him sooner, if only she had
set aside her resentment and visited earlier she might have
learned who he was. She might have seen the man beloved
by everyone, and she would have learned what Laith was
hesitant to tell her.

Her father was adamant that she only trust those at Dreagan. That wasn't difficult after knowing Laith, but she
needed more. Her father spoke of dangers and enemies,
which meant he had seen things that worried him. Had he
seen his murderers?

Now Iona really wished Laith was there. Perhaps then
he could tell her what he'd refused to earlier. How was she
supposed to keep a secret confidential when she didn't even
know what the secret was?

Look to the night skies, her father had written. What
could possibly be in the sky besides stars and the occasional
airplane or helicopter?

She would have all day to think about that. Iona folded
up the letter and put it back in the envelope. She set it down
beside her, and then changed her mind and returned it to
her purse.

If she didn't get her thoughts off of the contents of the
letter, she would go insane. She wanted to jump in her car
and find Laith, and that made her remain where she was.
She was getting too close to Laith, her desire too profound
to be controlled. Even with the worry over whatever secret her father kept, she knew she had to have some time

alone to think and digest everything—including her yearning for Laith.

Iona got her camera and laptop and plugged in the camera to start uploading all the pictures she had taken.

A chime sounded from his computer, alerting him that Iona Campbell was uploading more pictures. He clicked on the folder labeled with her name and scrolled through each picture as it came through.

The silly chit had no idea she was doing exactly as he wanted. Of course she also had no idea that her photos were sent directly to him. She had been one of his best acquisitions since he put together the Commune, but her usefulness was coming to an end. She was now in possession of the plot of land that had been in her family for untold generations.

Iona wasn't as vigilant as her father. It was going to be easy to get on the land and find the doorway onto Dreagan. And he knew exactly where to start looking—the waterfall.

CHAPTER EIGHTEEN

Laith ran through the motions of pouring one drink after another, but his mind wasn't in it. No, he was squarely, firmly thinking about Iona.

Leaving her the day before had been difficult after their kisses. Staying away had been nearly impossible. Laith filled yesterday and today with anything he could think of that might take his mind off of her—to no avail.

She was resolutely a part of him now whether he wanted it or not, and frankly he didn't want it. That wasn't entirely true. He wanted her, craved her as he ached to see his Blacks again, pined to see the dragons they had sent away.

Laith took the money from a customer and put it in the register, but he wasn't seeing the currency, he was thinking of Iona's yielding lips, her honeyed taste. He could spend eternity kissing her, and he wanted to do much more than that.

Had they been anywhere else, Laith knew he would have made love to her. But they hadn't been anywhere else, they had been at the waterfall. It was a spectacularly beautiful place that was scarred by what they had done there.

"Laith?"

He blinked and came back to the present to see Rhys standing across the bar. "Aye?"

"I was beginning to wonder if you could hear me. I've been calling your name for a while."

Laith grabbed a towel and wiped down the bar around him. It had been a long day, and he suspected another long night awaited him. "I was thinking."

"I doona have to use magic to know your thoughts center on one mortal."

Laith glanced around quickly to make sure none of the humans had heard Rhys. He speared Rhys with a glower. "Lower your voice," he said through clenched teeth.

Rhys raised a dark brow. "You sound just like Con."

"I doona," he mumbled grumpily.

"Con disappears and everyone takes over his . . . attitude."

"You doona."

Rhys rolled his eyes. "Thank goodness."

Laith frowned as he leaned his arms on the bar. "Con still hasna returned?"

"You'd know that had you come to the manor this morning or even at lunch."

"I had things to do."

Rhys smirked. "Right."

Laith whistled and tossed the towel to Sammi when she turned to him. She caught it easily, her usual bright smile in place.

"You leaving?" she asked as she joined them.

Rhys gave a grunt as he pushed away from the bar. "I'm attempting to get his arse moving."

"I'm leaving, I'm leaving," Laith said as he threw up his hands.

Rhys paused and turned back to Sammi. "By the way, Tristan said to remind you that he'd meet you when your shift was over. He'll be in his usual place."

Laith watched Sammi's smile broaden, if that was even possible. Tristan's usual spot was out back in the woods where he waited for her in dragon form. Sammi would then climb onto Tristan and he would fly them back to Dreagan.

The only way they were able to do that was because the pub was so far from town, otherwise people might see them. Since Sammi usually closed up, all the customers were long gone by the time she met Tristan.

Sammi gave them a wave before she filled another glass of ale. Laith walked to the back of the pub and past his office and the kitchen to the back door. He drew in a deep breath when he stepped into the night, Rhys on his heels.

"She's fine," Rhys said. "We've been keeping an eye out."

Laith knew that, but it wasn't the same as seeing her himself. "I want to see her."

"Then go to her."

"I'm giving her time. She's got a lot to deal with."

Rhys grunted as he walked past him farther into the woods. "That's a load of shite, and you know it. If you want her, go to her."

Laith narrowed his gaze on his friend. "Where is your usual horde of women, Rhys? You've only been out twice in the last month."

"Keeping tabs on me now, aye?" Rhys asked and glanced over his shoulder.

The smile was forced, and it concerned Laith more. Rhys had always had women, flocks of women. He flew from one bird to another, and yet they kept rushing to him. Rhys was one of the few who loved to flaunt his wealth and his charm, which worked well with his love of women.

Things had changed ever since he was injured in Ireland. Rhys had been telling everyone he felt fine, but actions spoke louder than words—especially when it came to Rhys.

"What's changed with you?" Laith asked.

Rhys stopped and faced him. "Everything. You didna see what I have in the times I've gone after our brethren in the pits of the Dark Fae burrows."

"Nor was I recently struck with a blast of dragon magic," Laith added.

Rhys looked to the sky and sighed. Laith stood beside him and followed his gaze. The Kings had gone thousands of eons with no one coming close to hurting them. They were the most powerful beings on Earth, but they did have weaknesses.

A blast of Dark Fae magic while they were in dragon form could revert them back to human, unable to shift again for a short time. But the only thing that could kill a Dragon King was another Dragon King. Not only was their dragon magic some of the most powerful in the universe, but they couldn't be killed.

"I almost forgot how painful it was," Rhys said into the quiet. "The last time I was wounded by another King was in the war with the humans when we were split for a time."

Laith crossed his arms over his chest. "I had a glancing blow, but nothing serious. Hurt like the devil though."

"We got too complacent. We're no' prepared for a battle of that magnitude, Laith. That small skirmish in Ireland proved that."

"The Dark were defeated," Laith said, confused.

Rhys made a sound at the back of his throat. "If they were truly defeated, they would no longer be a threat. We know they're most definitely a threat. They want something Con has hidden, and they willna stop until they have it."

"I've no idea what it is they search for, do you?"

"Nay, but no' for lack of trying." Rhys shrugged and pulled off his shirt. "I can no' shake the feeling that our time here is coming to an end."

Laith took off his boots and set them next to a tree.

"We've been here since the dawn of time. We're no' going anywhere, Rhys. We're supposed to be protecting the humans, remember?"

"The humans doona want our protection. We sent our dragons away for them, and for what purpose? To hide who we are, to forget the fierce magic that runs through our veins?"

Laith didn't have an answer for him, nor did he attempt to follow Rhys. They had to patrol tonight on the east border of Dreagan. It would take him near Iona, enough to get a glimpse of her cottage from the clouds.

He stripped out of the rest of his clothes and took off running. As soon as he reached the top of the hill, he leapt from the cliff and shifted midair. He spread his wings, letting them catch the current before he flew straight up and into the clouds.

Rhys's words were replaying in his head as he dipped his right wing and circled around to head east and keep an eye out for Dark Fae or human mercenaries. They had no shortage of enemies, but that's not what put a thread of fear in him.

It was Rhys's proclamation that the Kings wouldn't remain long. Earth was their home. Where else were they to go? Even if they could find their dragons, that didn't mean everything would return to how it had been before.

Laith wasn't going to give up their realm without a fight. The dragons had willingly shared it with the humans, but it had been the humans who hadn't wanted to share. Now the Fae were added into the mix as well, and though Laith wanted to deny that Ulrik was part of the problem, he wasn't sure he could anymore.

Ulrik wanted revenge against Con, and if Laith were fair, Ulrik deserved it after what they had done to him. Laith cringed as he thought of that day that altered the course of every dragon.

A day seared upon each Dragon King's mind and soul.

It made Laith sad to know that one of his brethren was bent on destroying everything they had built. It also made him angry.

Ulrik was a brother, but one that had attacked the humans, igniting the war. Ulrik was now focused on ending everything. Con wanted to kill Ulrik before things progressed further. Laith had been one to caution Con against such a drastic action, but now Laith realized it might be the only thing that could save them.

If Ulrik was the one uniting the Dark Fae and the humans to attack the Kings, with Ulrik dead, that unification would disintegrate. The Kings had battled the Dark before and won. They could do it again.

Laith didn't want Ulrik dead, but he didn't want Iona hurt either. Iona was innocent, just as John was. The Kings were meant to protect the humans—even if that meant protecting them from other Dragon Kings.

Rhys stood naked in the woods. He wanted to take to the sky, but the last time he tried to shift, the pain had been too much to endure. If he didn't get on patrol soon others would notice his absence and come looking.

No one could know the agony he endured every day. Rhys couldn't stand to see their pity or hear their sympathetic words. He was a Dragon King, more powerful than any of the other Yellows. He was the largest of his kind, the strongest, and the one with the most magic. It's what made him King, and what would get him past the hell he was in.

Rhys only had to think about shifting for his body to begin to change. It happened in an instant, his skin changing to scales, his hands and feet into massive taloned digits.

There was normally no pain, but nothing was normal

anymore. The discomfort began softly and increased as more of his human body disappeared and the dragon took shape. A bellow formed, but he held it back, suffering silently. He shook, sweat covering him. The agony persisted, growing exponentially.

This was as far as Rhys got the previous night before he gave up. He wasn't going to give up this night. He would push through the pain and return to his true form.

With the last scale in place, Rhys slammed his huge dragon head from side to side to shake away the pain that was blinding him, unknowing that he was knocking down trees in the process.

Con jerked as he heard Rhys's bellow of agony through his mind. He said not a word to Usaeil as he ran to her balcony and shifted. He flew high and fast, his wings beating quickly to take him home to Dreagan.

Even without any clouds, he was high enough that no one could see him. He should've known Rhys was still in pain, no matter what he had said. Con took a direct path to Dreagan, one that could make him visible to any who bothered to look.

Fortunately when he finally reached Scotland, there was cloud cover. His wings ate up the air, getting him to Dreagan quickly. He knew by the way the others circled an area that Rhys was there. Con flew straight for them.

"*Con!*" Laith shouted as he came up alongside. "*Rhys isna moving.*"

"*I know. I heard his shout.*"

A flash of deep red scales flew below Con. A moment later Guy asked, "*What the bloody hell is going on, Con?*"

Con didn't answer as he glided down and landed beside Rhys who lay on his side, his eyes closed. "*Rhys? Can you hear me?*"

"*We've been trying that,*" Ryder said as he stood beside

Rhys. He nudged Rhys with his large head of smoke-colored scales. "*He's no' responded.*"

Constantine rested a taloned hand on Rhys and felt his magic surge from him and flow into Rhys. Con's dragon magic could heal anything. The one thing he couldn't do was bring someone back from death. There was only one King that had ever been able to manage that—Ulrik.

No matter how much magic he poured into Rhys, nothing was happening. "*Rhys, damn you. Wake up!*"

CHAPTER
NINETEEN

Lily.

Rhys remained as still as he could as the agony pulsed through him in immeasurable waves, threatening to swallow him whole. He searched his mind for anything that he could focus on. First it was a memory of flying with a group of Yellows, but that didn't help for long. The second was fighting against the Dark, which didn't help at all.

An image of Lily popped into his mind that he quickly moved past, and then instantly went back to her. She was smiling, her eyes so dark they were almost black.

Rhys focused on Lily, on her jet black hair that fell like a curtain down her back. She was shy and wary, but had more courage and spirit than he could remember seeing in a mortal.

Anytime he was with her, the world slowed and he remembered the Dragon King he had wanted to be. He loved listening to her voice and how when she got excited her words came faster and her eyes twinkled with merriment.

Women looked at him with eagerness—for his money or his body—but never for anything else. Part of it was his fault because of the women he hung around. He would admit it only to himself, but he went to the gift shop as often as he did simply to get a glimpse of Lily. She was a good soul who could change his day with her smile. Her quiet nature was what first drew his attention to the remarkable beauty that she was.

Even with the oversized, ugly clothes she wore, there was no missing the gorgeousness. She was the antithesis of the women he flocked to, and yet he desired her more than he had any other.

It was too bad he would never do anything about it.

Rhys sighed. Lily was untarnished, a boon in an otherwise gray world. He wouldn't sully her by dragging her into their fucked-up world. He cared too deeply to have her mixed up with evil. As it was, she was already in danger by being affiliated with Dreagan.

He should have Con fire her.

Then who would be there to calm the raging inside you?

That was true. Rhys couldn't let her go. Not yet at least. The power of Lily Ross was evident as he belatedly realized the pain had ceased. Rhys cringed as he was bombarded with yelling from his brethren's voices in his head. He opened his eyes to see Con standing next to him in dragon form with a scowl.

"*About time,*" Con stated coolly.

But Rhys wasn't fooled. The King of Kings had been worried if the frown dimpling his gold scales said anything. Rhys got to his feet and felt better than he had in weeks. "*I'm all right now.*"

Laith gave a loud snort as he circled above them as he blended in with the night sky. "*That's why you bellowed? Why you fainted?*"

"*I didna faint,*" Rhys said, affronted. He glanced around at all the other Kings either flying overhead or surrounding him. "*I was merely concentrating.*"

Con open his gold wings halfway, then snapped them

shut. *"Everyone get back to your posts. I'd like a word with Rhys. Alone."*

So not what Rhys wanted. He closed his mind to all but Con so no one else could hear their conversation. *"I'm really all right. I'm no' lying this time. I feel . . . great."*

"Like Laith, I heard you all the way in . . ."

He trailed off, but Rhys wasn't going to let him off that easy. *"Where, Con? Where did you disappear to this time?"*

"It's no' relevant. The fact is, you're no' well."

"I was no', you're right, but I am now. I was in severe pain when I shifted. That's what you heard, but it passed. All of the pain—and I mean all of it—is gone."

Con's frown didn't disappear. *"That doesna ease my worry, Rhys. Something is off."*

"Something was, but it's all corrected itself now. Go worry about something else like Iona learning her father was murdered."

The only indication that his words irritated Con was the flick of Con's long gold tail before he leapt into the sky and flew to the manor that was partially built into the mountain.

Rhys followed Con into the air and twirled around, feeling his old self once more. It was a relief, because Rhys had begun to think the dragon magic used on him had damaged him somehow. Now he knew he worried for naught.

Everything was right as rain.

Iona checked her mobile for the time, and flinched when the phone lit up the area around her. She hastily turned it off and stifled a yawn. For four hours she had been looking at the sky hoping to see something.

It began on the porch at the back of the cottage, but the trees prevented her from seeing much of the sky. Iona then trekked two miles to a clearing, but still that didn't help. Then she went to the waterfall where she spread a blanket and lay back to stare at the stars winking down at her.

Her eyes were growing heavy, and all she managed to see was a shooting star. She decided to call it a night since she had to be at the bank first thing in the morning to sign the papers.

Iona climbed to her feet and folded the blanket. She let her hand skim over the Taser in her pocket, hidden by her jacket. Having a weapon helped to ease her somewhat, but since someone had gone to extreme measures to kill her father, she knew they could do the same to her.

She shut off the flashlight before she reached the cottage and stopped to look around and see if anything was amiss. When she didn't notice anything, she slowly walked toward the house.

All the lights were out, and she wished she had left some on. Her thought was to let anyone watching her believe she was asleep, but she hated to walk into a dark house. More so now than ever.

As soon as Iona was inside, she flicked on the lights in the kitchen. She then pulled the Taser out and had it at the ready as she walked from room to room checking the windows and locks.

With a sigh, she undressed and pulled on her nightshirt before climbing into bed. The sun would be up in less than two hours, but she still left every light in the house on.

When the alarm went off a few hours later, Iona reached blindly over, attempting to hit snooze, and only managed to knock it off the table. She blew out her cheeks in frustration and flung off the covers to get out of bed and shut off the annoying alarm.

"Well, I'm up now," she grumbled to herself.

Iona shuffled into the kitchen bleary-eyed and was grateful the coffee was already ready and waiting. She poured a cup and turned to the counter where her purse sat with a corner of the envelope sticking out.

Her heart missed a beat, because she knew the letter had

been fully inside her purse. Several seconds went by as she tried to calm herself. It took a while, but finally she was able to breathe calmly. With as many times as she read the letter the day before, taking it in and out of the envelope, she could have moved it and simply forgotten.

The doors were locked when she returned last night, as were all the windows. No one had been in the house. Of that she was sure. She was just overly jumpy.

Iona took her coffee into the bathroom as she turned on the shower to heat the water. She had a long day ahead of her, and she planned to stop by the pub in the hopes of seeing Laith. She took one last sip of coffee and took off her nightshirt before stepping into the shower.

He tossed the blonde her clothes and pointed to the door as the phone rang a second time. Ignoring her pout and stomping as she left the room, he walked to the table where his mobile phones were lined up and grabbed the one lighting up.

"Tell me you have good news," he stated.

"Aye, sir," the mercenary stated in his Australian accent. "I followed her last night, and then broke into her house early this morning."

"And?" he urged impatiently.

"She stared at the sky most of the night," came the reply.

Now wasn't that interesting? "Did she see anything?"

"There was nothing to see."

If only the stupid mortals knew what dangers lurked so close to them, they wouldn't be so confident of their abilities. "So you think she was just stargazing?"

"It appears as if she were looking for something."

"Did you find the letter?"

"I did. I took a photo of it. You should already have it in your e-mail."

"And everything went back just the way it was so she didn't have any idea you were in the house?"

"Of course. I'm very good at what I do," the mercenary declared.

"With as much as I'm paying you, you better be. As I told you, the other team is already dead after having been discovered by Dreagan. You're on your own. Doona . . ." He paused and cleared his throat. "Don't screw this up."

"You have my word."

"I want you to check in every six hours from now on. Follow Iona Campbell everywhere."

The mercenary was silent for a moment. "She's getting ready to head into town."

"Follow her *everywhere*. The toilets, to eat, shopping, or whatever else she does. I want to know who she speaks with and what the conversations are. Do I make myself clear?"

"Crystal," came the clipped reply.

He ended the call and set the mobile back in place. If there was one thing he could count on with the ex-military types it was that they followed orders perfectly. The type of men he hired didn't ask questions or blink at what he told them to do. It helped that he paid them very well.

Anxious to see the letter, he pulled on his silver silk robe and walked around the desk. With one click his e-mail pulled up. He scrolled through the many messages and found the one he was looking for. He opened the message and quickly read the letter.

"Bloody hell," he bellowed and threw an empty glass that was nearby across the room.

The letter told him nothing that could be used as proof against the Dragon Kings. And it was irrefutable proof he needed. So far his attempts to get pictures had failed by using his mercenaries, but that's what Iona was for.

He had expected John to tell Iona what it was she protected, but he should've known John wouldn't reveal such a secret in a letter that anyone could steal. With Iona's lack of knowledge, she wouldn't be watching her land as she should, thereby giving him ample opportunity to get more men on her land.

It wouldn't be long before Laith told her what it was she guarded. She would then want to see it, and that's when he would learn the exact location of the doorway. Then he could get a crew across and onto Dreagan without being detected.

It was a flawless plan.

He rose and walked into the bathroom to stare at his reflection in the mirror. For countless millennia he had watched the world change around him, unable to be who he was meant to be.

Soon the scales would tip in his direction. He smiled, his gold eyes shining with the excitement of what was about to come.

The biggest change was about to hit the Dragon Kings like a nuclear bomb. Right now they thought everything was well in their ranks, but they would learn very soon just how wrong they were.

CHAPTER
TWENTY

Iona signed the last of the papers and pushed them across the desk to the bank manager. The woman smiled courteously and then rose from her chair to take the documents to someone else.

The manager's sharp black pantsuit was another reminder to Iona of how lacking her own clothes were. They were perfect when she was traveling on assignment, but it made her realize how deficient her wardrobe was.

She sat back in her chair and bit her lower lip with her teeth. If she was going to keep the cottage, there was no reason she couldn't use it as her home instead of the flat in London. Which meant she could buy some clothes and keep them at the cottage.

That also meant she would need to go shopping—something that couldn't be done in the small village. It wasn't that Iona didn't like to shop, she just didn't know fashion anymore. Luckily for her she had met someone who did.

Iona pulled out her mobile and scrolled through her contacts until she came to Sammi's name. She hadn't wanted to exchange numbers, but now she was glad she had.

A quick text to Sammi asking if she was free to shop soon was sent before the manager returned. Iona forgot about the text as each account of her father's—now hers—was explained.

It was an hour later before she finished. She had her phone in hand as she exited the bank, so she didn't see the person she ran into.

"Umph," she grunted as she staggered backward.

"I've got you."

She looked up into Thomas MacBane's face and forced herself to smile. "I'm sorry. I didn't see you."

He shrugged, and then looked down at his hands that held her. Thomas laughed and released her, but he didn't step back. "I was hoping I'd catch you here."

"Were you?" Iona knew she was going to have to come up with another excuse to refuse him, because to accept his offer of lunch would only give him hope there could be more—when that wouldn't happen.

Iona knew men like Thomas. He wouldn't stop until she told him in no uncertain terms that she wasn't interested. The problem was, she didn't want to be mean. Thomas had been kind to her and helped after her father's death. But she didn't want to have to avoid him when she came into town, or continue to lie to him.

His smile grew. "Aye. I looked for you yesterday and assumed when you didna come that you would reschedule."

"Yes, that's right. I had to reschedule." She took a step back to put some distance between them.

"How about some lunch? My treat?"

Iona saw the hope flare in his eyes. She would have to stop this now, for the both of them. "Thomas, you've been very kind. I appreciate all of your assistance during this difficult time."

As she spoke, his smile began to fade. "You'd rather no' share a meal with me."

"You've been a good friend," she began.

Sadness fell over his face. "A friend."

Iona's heart broke because she didn't want to hurt him. He wasn't bad looking, but he wasn't Laith. "A person can never have too many friends."

"Quite right," he said and then cleared his throat.

"I need friends." The lie didn't seem like such a lie after she said it. Iona had always considered herself a loner, but she wondered if she had been wrong all those years.

Thomas's smile returned, albeit dimmer. "If you ever need anything, Iona, doona hesitate to call."

"Thank you."

He gave a nod and walked around her. Iona leaned back against the building and sighed.

"Very well done," Sammi said as she came around the corner.

Iona jumped, her hand on her heart. "You scared me to death."

"Apologies," Sammi said with a smile.

Iona rolled her eyes. "No, you're not. How much of that did you hear?"

"All of it, I'm afraid." Sammi came to stand beside her. "I got your text as I was making a deposit for the pub, so I decided to wait for you. I have to say, you handled Thomas wonderfully. You told him no without actually telling him no."

Iona still felt badly about the entire incident. "I hope you're right."

"I am. Now, about this shopping," Sammi said with a bright smile.

Iona fidgeted under Sammi's watchful gaze until they began to walk. "I'm in need of a few things if I'll be remaining."

"So you are staying." She nodded in delight. "I'm happy to hear it."

"It's just that I always pack so few items. It's time to update what I have."

Sammi laughed and shook her head. "You don't have to convince me. I've never been a big shopper or had many friends. My mom and I did everything together. She was my best friend, so after she died and I came here, it took some adjusting to having a sister around all the time. Then there is Cassie and Elena who love to shop like it's nobody's business. However, Denae and Shara are good at it as well. Shara could be a personal stylist."

"I'm not a shopper." Iona's head began to spin at the thought of looking at all the different clothes. "At all. I mean, I can't remember the last time I went into a department store."

"I didn't mean to frighten you off," Sammi said mildly. "It took me a bit to become accustomed to having all the women around, but now that I know what it means to have girl friends. I wouldn't trade it."

Iona was about to tell her she didn't need friends when she recalled her words to Thomas. She did need them. How else would she discover who killed her father? She suspected her excuse for friends went deeper than what she was willing to admit, but it was a place to start.

Sammi waved to someone across the street before turning her attention back to Iona. "Going to a store might overwhelm you since it's been so long. Why not tell me what you're looking for and I can grab a few things and bring them over."

"Are you sure you're not just trying to keep me from leaving?" Iona teased.

"That's part of it."

The fact Sammi didn't smile or tease had Iona's own grin disappearing. Then she put it together. "Because my father was killed."

Sammi nodded and glanced around.

Iona suddenly stopped walking. "I don't know what I want for new clothes. I want something more than the plain tees and pants that I have. Perhaps a casual dress. I don't even know what size I am anymore."

"Leave it to me," Sammi said with a wink.

Iona wanted something new for that night when she planned to go to the pub and talk to Laith, but that was asking a lot of Sammi. "What do you need from me?"

"Just tell me any colors you don't like."

"There aren't any."

Sammi gave a nod and pulled her mobile from her purse. "I'll be by tonight," she said and turned away as she began calling someone.

Iona wasn't upset at her departure. In truth, she had errands of her own to run. Her first stop was at Michael's garage where she purchased all the items she needed to fix the Rover. Then she headed to Thomas's office to put something in order that should have been done years ago.

Rhys stood in his mountain looking through the arched opening to the water that fell from high above down the jagged rocks to a pool of crystal clear water. It had been months since the last time he was in his mountain, but he had a suspicion that now that he was back, he wouldn't be leaving again.

He drew in a deep breath and felt the fire stir within. Rhys directed the fire at torches set along either side of the water. Smoke curled from his nostrils as flames sparked in the torches and flared to life.

There was no need for him to have the torches. A dragon could see in any light. In his human form, his vision was three times that of a mortal, but even then it wasn't the same as his dragon eyes. It was one reason he set up the torches. The other was because he loved the look of the fire reflecting off the water.

As a yellow dragon, he was drawn to waterfalls. It was where any Yellow could be found. When they inhabited Earth. Now, it was a reminder of the past, of a time when dragons ruled.

Behind him was an outcropping of rock that rose up thirty feet in the air as if reaching for the hole that he flew into. Sunlight filtered through the large opening so that moss grew on the rocks, mixing with the gray and brown of the mountain.

Rhys walked to the water and entered. The pool was deep enough to submerge him ten times over, but there would be no playing for him today. He swam unhurriedly to the waterfall, then climbed up more rocks and walked beneath the waterfall to his cave.

He turned and lay down so that he could see out the waterfall. His return to the mountain could be permanent. He had been crazy to think that shifting to his true form and getting past the pain would solve everything.

It hadn't.

Rhys made sure he was alone when he tried to shift back to human form. He wasn't certain what made him think there might be pain. Regardless, he was glad he took the action, because the agony had been horrendous.

He immediately stopped trying to shift, and when he had, the pain ceased. That's when Rhys knew if he was going to try it again, he needed to be somewhere private, somewhere the others would know to leave him alone.

It wasn't that he was afraid of pain. He was a Dragon King, after all. It was the fact that it felt as if he were splitting in two.

The pain was ten times what it was the first time they shifted from dragon to human. Every muscle shredded, every bone broke, every tendon severed only to knit back together in a new shape. That pain had lasted but a moment. This . . . this lasted for what seemed like eons.

Rhys didn't want to lose control as he did the first time and shout. He refused to have anyone surrounding him worrying that he might be dying.

He was in misery. Not just because he was lying to everyone—including himself—about the extent of the injury, but the ache of it grew each day. Now he couldn't shift between forms without searing anguish. It would have been better had his brethren let his wound kill him, because this wasn't a way for a King to live.

There was an option. He could go to Ulrik. Rhys didn't want to see his old friend, but if Ulrik was the one had who injured him, Ulrik could be the one to fix him. If he even would.

At one time Ulrik would have given any of the Kings whatever they needed. But this was an entirely different Ulrik, one that had been banished, one who had been stuck in human form for ages.

One who hadn't been able to take to the skies as the other Kings could.

Rhys sunk his claws into the granite beneath him and closed his eyes. He immediately brought up the image of Lily. For several minutes he concentrated on her, and even daydreamed about pulling her close and sinking his hands into her thick hair. He dreamed of lowering his head to her lips and imagining how sweet she would taste.

Then he tried to shift.

CHAPTER
TWENTY-ONE

Laith paced the hallway, stopping every so often to look in Rhys's room, but Rhys had yet to return.

"Have you been here all night?" Kiril asked as he walked up.

Laith halted and turned his head to Kiril. "Aye. He's still no' back."

"You know Rhys," Kiril said. "He likes his privacy."

Laith raised his brows. "There's something wrong, Kiril. Something Con knows and willna tell us."

Kiril's shamrock green eyes narrowed. "If there was something wrong with Rhys, he'd have told me."

"I doona think so. You saw Rhys last night. You saw him lying still as death after he yelled out in pain."

Kiril ran a hand through his wheat-colored hair. "He told me he felt great. He was laughing and joking last night as we patrolled."

"I know. Right up until we all returned to Dreagan. I've no' seen him since, nor will he answer me when I try to contact him."

"Rhys doesna ignore people. That's Warrick."

"If we're going to get to the bottom of things, we need to talk to Con."

"Talk to me about what?" Con asked as he approached.

Kiril turned to face Con. "Where is Rhys?"

"In his room getting ready for the day, I suppose."

Laith shook his head. "Nay. He's no', nor has he been since patrol last night."

Con walked past them and threw open the door to Rhys's room. He stood there for a moment before Con looked at them and said, "He's no' answering my call."

"Apparently he's no' answering any of us," Kiril said. "I doona like this. I want to know what's going on with him."

Laith took a step toward Con. "We both do."

"I promised him I wouldna," Con said.

"That was before last night. And before he disappeared," Kiril said tightly.

Con looked away and put his hands in the pockets of his black dress slacks. His pale gray shirt was starched and his French-cuffed sleeves were held with his favorite cuff links—gold dragon heads. "Rhys has been in pain since the battle in Ireland."

"He's no' been verra good at hiding that fact," Laith said.

Kiril scrubbed a hand down his face. "He's no' been the same since Ireland. He came to help me and Shara, and in return he's been besieged by something we doona understand."

"He's been plagued by dragon magic," Con stated emphatically, his black gaze swinging to them.

Laith held up a hand. "We're no' going to get into who did this to Rhys now. We need to find Rhys and make sure he's all right."

"I know where to start looking," Kiril said sadly. He blew out a breath. "His cave."

The three wasted no time in hurrying from the manor

into the tunnel that led to their mountain. From there they rushed through the back entrance of the mountain. As one, the three shifted into dragons and flew to the mountain Rhys chose for his own.

It was miles away. One of the farthest from Dreagan. They flew quickly with no words between them. The bad feeling that descended upon Dreagan weeks ago when Rhys was first hurt had only worsened after John Campbell's death.

When they finally arrived at Rhys's mountain, the three circled the entrance before Kiril dove through the opening, shifting into human form and landing next to the water. Con went next, flying through the opening and waiting until he hovered next to Kiril before he shifted.

Laith took one more flight around the entrance that looked as if a giant had slammed a fist into the side of the mountain and created an opening. When he saw nothing of concern, Laith flew into the gap and swooped down over Kiril and Con to glide over the water.

One of his black wings sliced through the waterfall as he did. Normally, that would be enough to bring Rhys out if he was there, but nothing happened. Laith landed next to the waterfall and shifted.

Kiril and Con had already dove into the water and were swimming toward him. Laith navigated the rocks to stand beneath the cascade of water. A moment later Con and Kiril joined him.

"He could be sleeping," Laith said.

Kiril made a guttural sound. "No' Rhys, and no' now."

"Why do you say that?" Con asked.

Kiril shook his head and stepped through the waterfall. Laith looked at Con and shrugged, then followed Kiril. He came to a halt immediately.

"He didna tell me," Con whispered, shock and anger thickening his words.

Laith could only watch as Rhys kept trying to shift to human form. He would flicker and begin to shift, before he would revert back to a dragon.

"The yellow of his scales has dimmed," Kiril said sadly.

Con pointed to Rhys's right flank. "His wound has returned, as if it never healed."

Laith grimaced when he saw the wound open every time Rhys attempted to shift. Each time the injury opened, he saw a glimpse of something inflamed within Rhys.

"Why can he no' shift?" Kiril demanded.

Con walked closer to Rhys and peered at the wound. "Dragon magic or no', it shouldna be prohibiting him from shifting."

"Heal him," Laith demanded of Con.

Con put his hand on Rhys to use his magic, and the instant Con's flesh came in contact with Rhys's scales, Con was flung backward, crashing into the rocks.

Kiril squatted next to Rhys's head and closed his eyes. Laith knew Kiril was trying to reach Rhys however he could, but nothing was working.

Con climbed to his feet and wiped the blood from a healing cut on his forehead. "There's something more than dragon magic doing this."

"How do we combat it?" Laith asked.

"I can help."

Laith and Con turned to find Rhi standing behind them. Her long black hair was pulled back in a low ponytail. She wore a black and white horizontally striped shirt and black jeans. Water pooled around her black boots from the waterfall, and yet she didn't take her eyes off Rhys.

"Rhi."

Laith glanced at Con, because he hadn't called the Fae's name with his usual scorn. There was no mistaking the surprise in Con's black gaze, but Laith couldn't pinpoint the exact emotion in Con's voice. If Laith didn't know better, he'd almost think it was delight.

Rhi cut her silver eyes to Con before she looked at Laith, unfazed by their nudity. Her lips softened into a half smile. "Who is looking after the pretty Iona while you're here?"

"Is she in danger?" Laith asked, more harshly than he intended.

Rhi held out her hand and caught a drop of water on the tip of her nail. She turned her wrist so that the droplet ran between her fingers into the center of her palm. Her gaze watched the water until she closed her fist around it. Then her eyes lifted to him. "Not that I'm aware."

Laith didn't know whether she was teasing or not. Just as he was about to demand she check, Con gave a shake of his head. Laith held his tongue as Rhi walked past him to stand beside Kiril.

She put her hand on Kiril's shoulder. His head immediately jerked to her. He rose and enveloped her in a hug. Laith noticed she didn't return the embrace. Her hands hung by her sides waiting for Kiril to release her.

"Can you help him?" Kiril asked as he released her and stepped back.

Rhi took a deep breath and slowly released it. "I can try."

"We would be grateful," Con said.

Rhi's head turned slightly in Con's direction, but she didn't look at him. Instead, she focused on Rhys and walked to stand next to his head. She put her hand on his forehead while her gaze drifted from Kiril to Laith, and then finally Con. Then her lids closed and she began to glow.

"Con," Kiril said worriedly.

They all knew that for Rhi to use that kind of magic that she could destroy the entire mountain as she had the dungeon in the Dark Fae prison. Or she could use that magic to give life to a planet.

Con walked quickly and quietly to stand on the other side of Rhys's head and watched Rhi intensely. Laith glanced at Kiril, and the two shared a shrug, unsure of what was going on since no one was acting like themselves.

Several minutes ticked by before Rhi stopped glowing, and she lowered her hand. She opened her eyes to focus on Con. "There is Dark Fae magic mixed with dragon magic."

"We know. Our magic is stronger," Con said. "Rhys should be able to overcome it."

Rhi swallowed and ran a hand across Rhys's yellow scales in a caress. "He has a choice to make. I've told him as much."

Laith then noticed that Rhys was no longer trying to shift. As long as he remained in dragon form, the wound stayed closed.

"What choice?" Kiril asked.

Rhi let her hand drop to her side and lifted sad eyes to Kiril. "The mix of dragon and Dark magic has done something to Rhys. It's what is causing him such pain when he shifts. I've dulled the Dark magic enough to help manage the pain for him to shift once more."

"Once more?" Laith repeated, not wanting to comprehend what Rhi was trying to tell them.

Rhys blew out a breath and opened his orange dragon eyes. Then he lifted his massive head. He gently nudged Rhi with his arm, causing her to grin up at him.

It was Con who said, "You mean he can shift into human form, but he will never be able to take his true form again?"

Rhi nodded and rested her head against Rhys. "Or he can remain in his true form, never able to take human shape again."

Con hung his head, his fists clenched at his sides. Laith had seen that kind of fury only one other time—when Ulrik's woman betrayed Ulrik.

"It's your decision, Rhys," Kiril said. "We'll stand beside you whatever you choose."

When Con finally lifted his head, there was death in his gaze. "Ulrik will reverse this, Rhys. I swear it."

They watched Con walk to the waterfall and shift into a gold dragon before flying away. Kiril strode past Laith and slapped him on the shoulder. He jumped through the water, shifting into a burnt orange dragon as he did.

Laith turned back to Rhys and Rhi to find both looking at him. "Was it Ulrik that did this to Rhys?"

"Who else could it be?" Rhi asked.

"Doona do that," Laith said rigidly. "Doona answer my question with a question. If you doona know, then just tell me."

"The answers are more complicated than that," Rhi said as she pushed away from Rhys and walked toward Laith. "Only a dragon can use dragon magic."

Laith gave her a flat look. "We know. Every Dragon King except for Ulrik has been accounted for."

"Not every dragon."

Laith gave a loud snort of derision. "Rhi, Ulrik's Silvers are caged and asleep. They have been for more millennia than I can remember. They didna do this to Rhys."

She simply smiled and looked at Rhys over her shoulder. "I know. Regardless of what Rhys tells you, it's more than his wound that troubles him. The last time the Dragon Kings were in such discord was when the war with the humans erupted."

She vanished before he could respond. Laith looked to Rhys and frowned. Discord? There was no discord in the ranks of the Dragon Kings.

Or was there?

CHAPTER
TWENTY-TWO

Working on her father's Range Rover helped Iona pass the hours, but it did nothing to stop thoughts of Laith's kisses or the fact that someone killed her father. Murder wasn't new to her. She witnessed it while in Africa, Iraq, and Palestine.

Not at all times had she been protected by the military. There were cases when she had been alone with only a guide, and though she had been scared, she always got out alive with her assignment complete.

She wasn't on assignment now, but the terror was doubled. All because of some secret her family kept. A secret that she didn't know.

Iona tightened the last bolt after installing the new brake line. She looked up at the motor with all the new parts in place and wondered if she would ever get into a car again without worrying that her brakes might fail or if it would be the steering or something else.

"A person could go mad thinking about such things," she told herself.

She was alone on fifty acres. Anything could happen at any time, and no one would be around to know. No one was there to watch her back. It had Iona reassessing her lifestyle.

Those thoughts brought her back to Laith. He occupied most of her mind of late, especially after their kisses. Even now she could still feel his tender lips as they skillfully seduced her, because that was exactly what he did.

It should be a sin for someone to kiss so expertly that she forgot everything except him. She closed her eyes and thought back to their last kiss by the waterfall. Her stomach fluttered and desire coiled within her.

She didn't attempt to deny the need clawing through her. There was something compelling and altogether captivating about Laith. It could be his gunmetal eyes, the way the steel gray color was ringed with black. His stare was penetrating, as if he could see into her mind and sort through all her wishes and desires.

It could be his long dark blond hair. The color wasn't just blond. There were traces of gold, copper, and light brown through the strands. She didn't know if she liked his hair better down, or when he pulled it back in a queue, but she itched to sink her fingers into the length regardless.

It could be his lips. No man should have such full lips that, with just a smile, could make it feel as if a thousand butterflies had taken flight in her stomach. His lips were a heady combination of tender and forceful as they kissed. And they did incredible, wonderful things to her.

It could be his body. She hadn't seen him without his clothes, but even in them, there was no denying the hard sinew and bulging muscle. She was tall for a woman, but he towered over her. He moved with an ease that reminded her of a lion stalking his prey.

It could be his accent. As much as Iona wanted to pretend that she detested anything Scottish, she had always loved the sound of a brogue. After traveling the world over a dozen times, it felt good . . . right even . . . to be back in

Scotland listening to a man with a deep brogue that caused goose bumps to rise along her skin.

Iona was jerked out of her thoughts by the sound of a car approaching. She slid out from beneath the Rover and peered around the tire to see a newer-model black Range Rover come to a stop behind her car. The door opened as the engine shut off. That's when Iona heard the laughter.

She smiled when she recognized Sammi's laugh. Iona dusted herself off as she stood and started toward Sammi. That smile faltered when she noticed two other women with Sammi. The one with chin-length auburn hair tripped over . . . nothing, and Sammi quickly held out a hand to steady her. As they both laughed, Iona saw the similarities between the two women, which meant she must be Sammi's sister.

Iona's gaze shifted to the second woman and was completely taken aback by her beauty. The woman had long black hair with a strip of silver falling next to her face. That silver didn't take away from her exquisiteness, but added a hint of mystery. That silver also brought out her unusual silver eyes.

"Iona!" Sammi called when she saw her and held up bags in both hands. "I brought reinforcements."

Iona glanced down at her dirty, grease-stained pants and wished she had known Sammi planned to visit because she would have showered and changed. As it was, her attire made it more obvious how out of place she was.

"You know how to work on vehicles?" the black-haired woman asked in surprise.

Iona wiped her hand on her jeans and nodded. "I made myself learn after I was stranded in the Arabian Desert for a day."

"I wish I knew what to do with them. I'm hopeless. My talents lie elsewhere," Sammi said with a grin. She nodded to the woman beside her. "This is my half-sister, Jane.

And the stunning one beside her is Shara. Jane, Shara, this is Iona Campbell."

Jane held out her hand, a warm smile in place. "I've heard so much about you, Iona. It's good to finally meet you."

Iona shook her hand. She released it only to have Shara hold out her hand. "Hello," Iona replied.

Shara's silver eyes watched her closely, even as her lips lifted in a smile. "I've also heard a lot. It seems you've caught Laith's interest."

"I'm sure many women do." Iona wanted to kick herself. "I didn't mean that he was a womanizer, just that he was a handsome man who women would notice."

Sammi laughed. "We know what you meant."

Shara didn't release her hand. She took a step closer and said in a low voice, "Laith isn't like other men. It says a lot that you caught his eye."

"Does it?"

"Certainly." Shara dropped her hand to her side and lifted her other that held several bags. "I love to shop. Let's see if I picked anything you might like."

"I doubt it'll fit," Iona said as she turned and started toward the house.

Shara was beside her as she said, "We'll see."

Iona was the first inside. She kicked off her shoes and said, "Make yourselves at home. I'm going to take a quick shower."

"Take your time," Jane called before she ran into the side table.

Iona was unsure what she felt as she stepped into the shower. She wasn't used to being around women. Her assignments usually had men guarding her or guiding her wherever she needed to go. The fact she didn't have friends made her anxious that she might do or say something wrong.

By the time she finished showering, she regretted ever saying anything to Sammi about shopping. Iona should have done it herself so she would be the only recipient of her embarrassing lack of fashion sense.

Iona ran her fingers through her wet hair and shrugged on her robe. When she came out of the bathroom, all three women were in her bedroom.

"There you are," Sammi said. She pulled Iona farther into the room so she could see all the outfits either laid out on the bed or hanging in various places in her room. "We weren't sure what you were looking for, so we got a bit of everything."

"Shara got a bit of everything," Jane corrected.

Sammi elbowed her sister playfully, then turned back to Iona. "Shara is amazing, and has a true knack for choosing the perfect outfits for people."

"I'm not most women," Iona said.

Shara straightened from putting a necklace with a dress. She gave a halfhearted shrug. "I suppose that means you're perfect for Laith since he isn't like most men."

"Good point," Jane said. She rubbed her hands together. "I'm dying to see you start trying things on, Iona."

Sammi shooed Jane out and waved at Shara to follow. "We'll be waiting. Remember, what you don't like or doesn't fit can easily be returned."

When the door closed behind Sammi, Iona slowly faced her room and stared wide-eyed at the clothes. There really was something for every occasion. There were a couple of sets of jeans and shirts, three casual dresses, two dressier dresses, a chic after-five black dress, and even a few sets of pants and jackets.

They hadn't just stopped at the clothes. There were shoes and jewelry to go along with each outfit. Iona had no idea how the three of them had done it, or even why, but she was overwhelmed with all they had done for her.

She removed her robe and dug for a pair of panties and a bra before she reached for the first set of clothes. It was a navy sweater with navy sequins scattered across it. The sweater was light and draped over her becomingly. Iona then pulled on the pair of skinny navy slacks, surprised to find they fit as well.

Iona turned one way then the other in the mirror, liking what she saw. She checked the shoes, and merely laughed when she discovered they were her size. Once the heels were on, she donned the long gold necklace and gold earrings before stepping out of her room.

"I knew it," Shara said with a bright smile when she saw Iona.

Jane's eyes widened. "Wow."

"You look amazing," Sammi said from her spot next to Shara on the sofa. "What do you think?"

Iona looked down at herself. "I like the clothes. I like the way they make me feel. I like how they feel on." She looked back up at the three women staring at her. "I want this."

Jane tucked her auburn hair behind her ear, her amber eyes alight with glee. "There's more. I'm dying to see what you choose next."

Iona had a hitch in her step as she returned to her room. All the anxiety she had was gone. She looked at the clothes—and her blossoming friendships—with new eyes.

Laith had a difficult time paying attention to his customers. He didn't want to be at the pub. He wanted to be at Dreagan waiting to see what Rhys would decide, but he was also hoping Iona would visit. He tried to distract himself, but every time the door of the pub opened, he expected Iona or someone from Dreagan with news.

The dinner crowd packed The Fox & The Hound, and he found his temper running short. Laith walked to his office for a break and sank into his chair with a sigh. He dropped his head into his hands and wondered if the Kings had missed something when fighting the Dark Fae recently.

Con was sure Ulrik had managed to align the Dark and the humans to go against them. It made sense, especially since MI5 had sent Denae into Kellan's cave hoping that he would attack her and they would have footage of it. Kellan didn't attack Denae, but it hadn't stopped MI5 from doing their utmost to get onto Dreagan.

Then there was the Dark Fae. They had taken more risks in the past few months than they had in thousands of years. What was their hurry all of a sudden? Why had they lowered themselves to work with the humans, who they considered nothing more than entertainment and food?

If Ulrik was doing all of this, why hadn't the Kings seen anything from the dozens of cameras installed around The Silver Dragon in Perth, where Ulrik lived and worked?

Many of the times the Kings had been attacked, Ulrik had been inside his antique shop. At least the cameras hadn't caught him leaving. No Dark Fae were seen in the store, nor could the Kings match faces from visitors to any of the mercenaries they had run across.

Yet, if Ulrik got enough of his magic back to wound Rhys, he could easily hide himself long enough to evade the cameras watching him.

If Ulrik now had magic, it was only going to be a matter of time before he got it all back. Then all hell would break loose, because Ulrik would release his Silvers that were kept caged inside the mountain. With the Silvers loose, they would rain death and destruction upon the humans.

"Am I interrupting?" came a sultry voice.

Laith jerked his head up and spotted Shara leaning against the doorway. "No' at all."

"There's someone on their way to see you. I thought you might want to be out there waiting for her."

He tried to hold himself in check, but it was useless. He couldn't contain the excitement or anticipation. The delight. "Iona is coming?"

"She is."

Laith was up and out of his chair in a flash. He pushed past Shara but made himself slow before he entered the front of the pub. His gaze scanned the occupants, but didn't see Iona's head of golden hair.

Then the door opened and his gaze caught on a vision of beauty that would be stamped in his mind for eternity.

CHAPTER
TWENTY-THREE

Laith zeroed in on Iona as she paused just inside the pub while she looked around. As soon as she saw him, her amazing lips turned up in a smile that was as sexy as it was warm.

He was surprised to see her wearing something besides her solid-color tees and hiking pants. But he certainly enjoyed what he saw. The fluttery cream-colored shirt flowed around her gracefully and dipped low in the front so he saw the swell of her breasts, and the sleeves that trailed to her elbows were entirely of lace.

His gaze traveled lower to the khaki pants that hugged her legs and made them appear even longer down to the cream wedges. Laith leisurely let his eyes travel back up to her face where he spotted large gold hoops hanging from her ears.

He liked that she could appear feminine in hiking boots and jeans as well as decked out in heels and jewelry. No doubt she would be just as stunning without a stitch of clothes. How he wished he knew.

Laith started toward her, ignoring his name being called

from the bar. After the day he'd had, he wanted something that could make him forget his troubles. That was Iona.

"Hi," she said nervously when he reached her.

He couldn't help but smile. "Hi."

"I read the letter. If you aren't busy, I was hoping we could talk."

Laith only dimly remembered that they were in the pub and not alone. "No' here though. Give me a second."

He left her standing there as he told his staff to handle things until Sammi arrived in a few hours. Then Laith grabbed his keys and hurried back to Iona.

"You look amazing," he said as he put his hand on her lower back and guided her out the door.

By the way she beamed, his praise had been just what she needed. "Thank you. I can't take all the credit though. I needed to replenish my wardrobe, but I haven't been shopping in years. I happened to ask Sammi, and things went from there."

Now he understood how Shara knew Iona was on her way. Laith was curious to hear what Shara thought of Iona, and if he knew Sammi, Jane had also been there. That was someone else he would have to talk to as well.

"They might have helped, but they're no' the ones wearing the clothes."

Her dark eyes slid to him. "I can't remember the last time I felt so good in clothes."

And he wanted to get her out of them. Laith walked her past her father's green Range Rover to his Audi R8. "Any particular place you want to go?"

"You choose."

Laith opened her door and waited for her to climb inside before he closed it and walked around to the driver's side. Once he was behind the wheel, he smiled at her and started the engine.

The Audi purred as he started it. Laith backed up the car and pulled out of the parking lot onto the road as Iona leaned her head back in the seat and stared out the window to the darkness beyond.

"The letter was short," she said into the silence.

"Did it help?"

She snorted softly. "In some ways, but not everything."

"I thought perhaps you got all you needed since I didna see you."

Her head turned to him. "It's a lot to take in. Every time I think I have a handle on things, I remember my father was murdered. Then I start thinking I'm seeing things."

"Seeing things?" Alarms went off in his head at her words.

"Oh, it's nothing," she said with a wave of her hand. "I think I put something one place when I find it in another. I'm trying to see every detail of things, and I know there's a possibility I could be in danger, so my mind plays tricks on me."

Laith wasn't so sure of that, but he wouldn't say anything until he was sure. He didn't want her any more scared than she already was. He would do some investigating first. She had been through enough as it was.

Besides, Dreagan had failed John. He wouldn't allow that to happen to Iona.

He slowed the car and turned down a road that led to a secluded spot to lend them privacy. Laith suspected Iona had questions, and he wasn't so sure he could put her off anymore. They drove for another few minutes before he came to the gate and shut off the car.

"Where are we?"

"East of your place. It's abandoned, but I always found it a quiet place to go."

She gave him a droll look. "You have sixty thousand acres. Why would you need this?"

"Everyone needs a place. Want to see it?"

Her smile was wide as she opened the door and got out. Laith followed suit and closed the door. They were parked toward the top of the hill, and it afforded them spectacular views of Dreagan.

"Come," he said and held out his hand.

Iona took it, and he led her to the gate where they had to climb through it. He then walked her to the top of the hill where they could see lights from the few houses scattered before them.

"I wish I had my camera," she whispered.

Laith was pleased. "I knew you would like this, but that's no' the only reason I brought you."

"We could've returned to my place," she said and glanced at him out of the corner of her eye.

He looked up at the moon and swallowed a moan. It took a few moments, but he was finally able to say, "You said you wanted to talk, and I'm providing a place that you can do that."

Her forehead puckered in a frown. "So I couldn't talk at Dreagan? Or my home?"

"There are others at Dreagan, and I knew you wanted privacy." So did he, for that matter.

"And my home?"

Laith inhaled deeply. "I'm sure it's fine."

She held his gaze for long minutes, and then looked away as she shook her head. "My father's letter was vague about what I'm supposed to do. He told me that I have a secret to protect."

"But he didna tell you that secret?"

"No," she said, frustration lacing the word. She turned to face him fully. "He said he couldn't, that he hoped he would see me to tell me in person. He said it wasn't safe to put it on paper. He also said I could trust those from Dreagan. So I'm going out of my comfort zone and trusting you." She licked her lips. "Laith, what was my father trying to tell me?"

Damn. He hoped John might find a way to tell Iona, but it appeared it fell on his shoulders. Just as he had prayed it wouldn't. Laith ran a hand down his face. "What else did the letter say?"

"He told me to watch the night sky, and I might get lucky enough to catch sight of something. I spent all of last night looking at the sky, but I didn't see anything except stars. Please. Tell me what my father couldn't."

Laith was trying to find the right way to tell her. He couldn't just blab that he was a dragon. Iona would think he was daft.

"Can't you just tell me?"

"It's no' that simple."

She briefly looked away. "Is it illegal?"

"Nay, but you'll have a hard time believing it."

"I've seen a lot of things. I can handle whatever it is."

He wasn't so sure of that. Where to start though? "I told you we have enemies. Some of them are no' mortal."

"Not mortal?" she repeated with a deep frown. "You mean not . . . human?"

"Exactly."

"That's not possible."

Laith rubbed the back of his neck. "You've met two that are no' human already."

"I think I'd know if someone wasn't human," Iona said with a little laugh. "Who?"

"Rhi and Shara."

She rolled her eyes. "Is that some kind of joke? Because it isn't funny. Those women were human or mortal or whatever you want to call them."

"They're Fae. Light Fae to be exact, and trust me, they're no' mortal."

Iona's face went slack. "Did . . . did you just say Fae?"

"Aye."

"You're not joking," she said as she began to breathe heavily.

"There are two kinds of Fae. Light and Dark. If the Dark are no' using glamour, they have silver and black hair along with red eyes."

Iona bent over, her hand on her chest. "Shara has silver in her hair."

"Her family is one of the most powerful of the Darks, but she left all of that behind to be with Kiril," he explained.

Iona's head swiveled to him. "Why would a Fae want to be with a mortal?"

Laith held her gaze, waiting for her to answer her own question. He knew the moment it came to her because Iona paled and hung her head so that her hair covered her face.

"I'm going to be sick," she whispered.

Laith moved so that he stood beside her and gently rubbed her back. He waited for her to shove him away, and was relieved when she didn't. "Breathe, Iona. It'll be all right."

"My father knew?"

"He knew about us, but no' about the Fae."

She took several deep breaths before she slowly straightened. Her face was pale under the light of the moon when she looked at him and asked, "What are you?"

"Your father told you to look to the skies, because that's when you'll see us in our true form."

"You can't stop there."

"It's a secret we've kept for thousands of millennia, and it's no' easy to say." Laith looked into her dark eyes and found he was afraid to tell her.

If she reacted so harshly to learn that there were Fae, what would she do when she saw him in dragon form? Laith discovered he didn't want to find out.

"Laith, please. If I'm to carry on with what other

Campbells have done, I need to know. You say my father knew, and obviously it's something important if he couldn't put it down on paper. I'm sorry for"—she made a motion with her hand—"a moment ago. I never considered there were other beings here with us."

"This realm was originally ours," Laith said. "We ruled it for thousands of years before the first human arrived. We were then commanded to protect humans."

"Commanded?" Iona asked, interrupting him. "Ordered by who?"

Laith lifted a shoulder. "Our creator, of course. He created you as well."

"What were you?"

He took a deep breath, hoping, praying that she didn't run away screaming. It wasn't just that she was a Campbell and needed to protect the doorway. It was because it would kill him if her beautiful eyes suddenly looked at him with disgust. "Your father should've told you this. The Campbells always hand down the information. I doona know what they say or how it's done."

"I find it's best to keep things simple," Iona said softly, a note of apprehension in her voice.

"We're dragons. Where do you think the myths came from?"

She put her hand to her forehead and dragged in an unsteady breath. "Dragons? You're a dragon? Oh, my God."

"A Dragon King, actually."

"Shit. Dragons," she mumbled again.

Laith had to get her past that, and the only way he knew how was to explain more. "There were dozens of dragon factions."

Her gaze focused on him as she dropped her hand. "Factions?"

"It's what we always called them. Each set was divided by color and size. The strongest dragon of each faction, the one with the most magic was chosen as King. We were the ones able to shift from dragon to human and back again to keep the peace between our kind and humans. We took an oath to protect humans."

She swallowed hard. "Since I've never seen a dragon, I'm betting something went wrong?"

"There were some Kings who chose to take human females as lovers. Ulrik, King of the Silvers, was one of those. We discovered that his woman planned to betray him by leading him into a trap to start a war."

"Why would she do that?" Iona asked in confusion and shock.

Laith looked out over the land. "There were some humans who were jealous of the power we had, so they wanted to be rid of us. The humans didna realize the Kings couldna be killed so easily."

"What did Ulrik do?"

"He and Con were as close as brothers. It was Con who sent him away on a mission, and while Ulrik was gone, every Dragon King descended upon the female. Each of us sank our swords into her. We were protecting Ulrik and ourselves, but that day we broke a vow that had dire consequences for each of us."

CHAPTER
TWENTY-FOUR

Iona searched her mind for the right words. What did one tell a Dragon King? A dragon. Her mind still reeled from the knowledge that Laith wasn't human. Not to mention there were apparently Fae as well.

Until she saw a dragon for herself, she wasn't sure she could believe Laith. Her mind—no, her world—was rooted in facts, proof. She had to have proof of a dragon and Fae before she could so blithely accept them. Besides, there was no way such beings could exist in the world and others not know.

But others did know. Her father had been one of the few. No wonder he hadn't put it down on paper. She would have thought he had lost his mind. Of course, she was in doubt about her own mind at the moment.

She rubbed her hands along her arms and looked at Laith. "You broke your vow to help one of your own."

"Ulrik didna need help. None of us did. We have magic, Iona, the humans didna."

"So you're saying the only magic on Earth was yours?"

He started to speak, then paused. "Nay. There is other magic."

"Like the Fae?" she asked.

Laith gave a small shake of his head. "The Fae hadna found this realm at that time. The other magic came from the Druids."

Would the surprises ever stop coming? Iona waited for him to laugh and tell her it was a joke, but he didn't. "You're telling me there are Druids as well? Real Druids?"

"Real Druids. Doona always believe everything you read, especially history written by the conquerors of a nation," he cautioned.

Druids, Fae, and Dragon Kings. "Are there any other type of . . . beings around?"

His gaze held hers a long time, but with the darkness Iona couldn't make out his emotions. "There are Warriors."

"There are warriors everywhere."

"Nay. Warriors."

She rubbed her temple as her brain clogged at all the information. "Forget the Warriors or warriors or whatever for the moment. Let's get back to the story. So, if there was other magic, was it enough to hurt one of you?"

"Nay, but we didna want a war, and she was determined to start one. That's why we put a stop to the female."

"What was her plan?" she asked.

Laith rubbed his eyes with his thumb and forefinger. "We didna know at the time, but the humans had begun hunting and killing dragons. They were going to try and kill Ulrik. It was Con who called us to action."

"Con? Who is he to you exactly, except the CEO of Dreagan Industries?"

"He's the King of Kings. Most of us didna want that position. We were content to rule our own dragons, but Con wasna like us. He wanted to be King of Kings."

Somehow Iona wasn't surprised to hear that about Con. She might not know him personally, but it took a certain type of man to run a company such as Dreagan. "What does it take to be King of Kings?"

"You have to fight anyone who challenges you to the death. You also have to be extremely powerful. There were only four others who ruled as King of Kings before Con, and each came from either the Golds, which were Con's dragons, or the Silvers."

"Which are Ulrik's," Iona said as comprehension dawned. "Did Ulrik challenge Con?"

"Nay. Ulrik was happy ruling his Silvers. He was the only one who matched Con in strength and magic. I suspect it had something to do with them being so close, but Ulrik was much different back then."

Iona heard the pensive tone in Laith's voice and tried to picture what the world would have been like with dragons. It seemed as alien to her as Druids. "So Con became King of Kings, and it was his decision to bring Ulrik's lover to justice."

"We could've—nay, we *should've*—handled things differently, but no other human had ever sought to betray one of us."

"It wasn't just any human. This was Ulrik's lover, the woman he claimed as his own."

One side of Laith's lips lifted in a wry grin. "Are you defending us, lass?"

"It appears so," Iona said with a soft laugh. "Betrayal is betrayal no matter if you're human or dragon. Ulrik took the woman as his, sheltered her, clothed her, and fed her."

Laith gave a grim nod. "That was Con's argument as well. I doona regret thinking action needed to be taken, but I regret how we went about it. First, Ulrik wasna there."

"Why didn't Con want him there?"

"Con claims it was because he was looking out for his friend."

"That wasn't right."

Laith blew out a deep breath. "Aye. It was an action by every Dragon King save one. It was a show of force to the humans that we will live in harmony, but try to harm us, and we'll take action."

"What happened when Ulrik discovered what all of you had done?"

"He was furious with us, but it quickly shifted to the humans who bore the brunt of his wrath. The humans wanted to rule everything, and they truly believed they could be rid of us. Ulrik and his Silvers decimated the humans in quick order to an extent that shocked all of us, but still the humans sought to kill every dragon they could. And they killed so many."

Iona swallowed hard at the sorrow in Laith's voice. "How did you stop Ulrik?"

"With difficulty. First, Con tried to talk to him, but Ulrik didna listen. Then we tried a surprise attack, only to subdue Ulrik. The result was a huge divide in all dragons and the Kings. Half sided with Ulrik, and the other half with Con."

"Which side were you on?" Iona asked in a low voice, enraptured by the story.

"Ulrik's, for a while. We battled humans and our own, but it felt wrong. Con came to each of us individually and convinced us to return to him one at a time. While Ulrik was reminding the humans how we had been on this realm for over a millennia alone, Con was protecting them. Protecting humans who slaughtered dragons."

Iona wrapped her arms around herself and looked at the ground. She couldn't imagine protecting someone who was murdering her family. It was wrong in every sense. No wonder Laith sided with Ulrik at first.

"Even when Ulrik was the last one fighting the humans, he and his Silvers couldna be reasoned with. We were charged with keeping the peace, and yet we couldna manage it. In order to try to find some harmony, the killing had to stop. The humans, however, had become more aggressive in their killing. Drastic action had to be taken."

She lifted her gaze to find Laith looking at her. Half of his face was visible by moonlight, and the remorse and regret that lined his features made her heart clutch. "What did you do?"

"The humans were finding our dragons no matter where they hid. No matter how small or how large the dragon, the humans were out to divest themselves of every last one. We began to use magic to hide them, but the dragons hated being confined. We were protecting them, but they felt it was a prison. We couldna keep them locked away, and we couldna allow them to fly free, so we had no choice but to send them to another realm."

"And Ulrik?"

Laith smiled, but there was no humor in the action. "We surrounded him and the Silvers. Many of the Silvers we were able to send with our dragons, but three of the largest refused to leave Ulrik's side. We declined to kill them or let the humans have them. By that time we had already been using Dreagan as our home. We brought the Silvers back with us and used our magic to make them sleep, caged deep within a mountain."

"There are dragons here?" she asked in shock with a little fear mixed in.

Laith leaned back against a tree and lifted his eyes to the sky. "They've been there for millions of years. You doona have to fear them. We willna let them wake, because if they do, they'll return to killing humans."

"You still haven't told me what happened with Ulrik."

"Because I hate to even think about it, but it seems it's all I've done of late." Laith exhaled loudly. "Without his Silvers, Ulrik was like a madman. He felt we betrayed him by killing his woman without him present, turning against him in the war, and then taking his dragons. He wasna wrong. We did betray him."

"How is it a betrayal if you were trying to save the world, and he wouldn't listen?"

Laith glanced at her before returning his gaze to the sky. "We could've done things differently. Perhaps if we had, our dragons would still be here. Regardless, we had to stop Ulrik. Since he wouldna halt his killing of humans, we Kings once more gathered and banished him from Dreagan."

"Why do I get the feeling he wasn't just forbidden from returning to Dreagan?"

"Because it was much, much more than that. We took his magic, Iona. He can no' shift into dragon form, his true form. He's had to remain as a human for untold eons. He can no' communicate with any of us, and we doona talk to him."

"That's . . . extreme. Is he one of your enemies?"

Laith pushed away from the tree and looked down at her. "We believe so, but we've yet to find proof. Ulrik shouldna have any magic, and yet there's no denying there has been dragon magic used."

"Maybe one of the other Kings used it."

"Nay. We live as one with many of the Kings sleeping away the centuries. We've all been accounted for."

She gave a small shake of her head as she shrugged. "Perhaps there's another Dragon King roaming around out there."

"I wish. It would make things simple, but that's no' possible. Every King is inexplicably drawn to Dreagan. There are only so many Kings, and we know all of them."

"One could've been killed and someone else took over."

"It isna that easy," he said and slowly walked around her. "Only a dragon can be a Dragon King. Since all the dragons are gone, that makes it impossible. Then there is the fact that we can no' be killed by anyone or anything other than another Dragon King. When something like that happens, every King knows of it."

Iona blinked, her mind still whirling from everything. "This still comes back to my father and his murder, doesn't it?"

"Aye. Our enemies want onto Dreagan. Our magic prevents that from happening, except in one spot."

"My land," she guessed.

Laith gave a single nod.

"What's so special about Campbell land?" she asked, unsure if she really wanted to know.

"Because that's where we killed Ulrik's woman."

She blinked and shifted her weight to her other foot. "And?"

"You guard a doorway onto Dreagan land, Iona. Anyone can pass through and we'd never know they were there."

CHAPTER
TWENTY-FIVE

Laith's words haunted Iona even in sleep. Dreams of a dragon chasing her woke her several times during the night. At one point in her dream, the day faded to a night so black not even the moon could penetrate the darkness. A silver dragon parted its mouth and issued a roar as it dove from the sky toward her.

Just before she was clamped in its jaws, a dragon with scales the color of onyx swooped in and knocked the silver one away.

That was Iona's last dream. After that, she hadn't bothered to attempt sleep again. She rose and changed so she could walk the property.

If the woman who had betrayed Ulrik was killed on her land, then there had to be some kind of marker to indicate the space. At least she assumed there was. How else would Dreagan's enemies know where to go?

Before she walked out of the house, she sent a text to Laith asking him to meet her later. Her mind was still full of all the information Laith had imparted. She wanted to deny there were dragons, but why then would her father urge her to look to the skies? If only she had been brave enough to ask Laith to see him in his true form the night before. Iona hadn't let the words past her lips, because she was afraid he would've done just that.

Once she saw him, there would be no denying the truth. The fact she knew that meant that in the back of her mind she had already accepted his words as fact. If it hadn't been for her father's letter, Iona wasn't so sure she would have taken Laith seriously. The letter, combined with her father's murder, and the men chasing her put everything into perspective.

Iona packed some food and her mobile into her camera case and left the cottage, making sure to lock it behind her. She faced the woods and let her eyes roam the trees. More men might be out there, but if someone wanted her dead, no amount of hiding would change that fact.

It would be so easy to stay in the cottage and pretend she was safe, but that wasn't her way. Iona liked to face any obstacles in her path. Hiding wasn't an option. This was her land, and she wouldn't be afraid to walk it. Nor would she rest until her father's murderer was found—and punished.

Iona put her hand on the camera case. Tucked neatly inside the lining were two throwing knives she had purchased while in Hong Kong three years before. She was regularly searched wherever she went, but no one paid any attention to her camera bag once they looked inside. It was the safest place for the knives, even if she would rather have them on her person.

She stepped off the porch with her head held high. Hopefully Laith would arrive soon. The night before hadn't gone nearly as she had hoped. Mainly because she had wanted more kisses with Laith.

She got a history lesson instead, and though she was glad she knew the secret now, it weighed heavily, awkwardly on her shoulders. No wonder her father never left the land. It was a great honor—and a burden—the Campbells took on for the Dragon Kings.

The tale had taken a toll on Laith. Once he finished it, he was somber and withdrawn as he drove her back to the pub with the promise that Dreagan would keep an eye on her. When she left him and walked to her car, she spotted Warrick standing outside the pub. Laith hadn't been kidding. Dreagan was watching over her. Perhaps that's why she wasn't afraid when she returned to the cottage.

Iona took in a deep breath while she walked her land. She couldn't help but try to put herself in the shoes of the humans who had lived before, the ones who existed alongside the dragons.

She could understand her kind being afraid of a species who shape-shifted and had magic, but that didn't hold up since some of the humans were Druids who worked magic themselves.

Of course, she was getting a one-sided story. It was too bad there wasn't a record from a human's perspective so she could compare the stories.

Laith claimed the Dragon Kings were protectors, peacekeepers between both species, but how partial could they be since they were dragons first and foremost? She tried to find a reason to distrust Laith and the others from Dreagan, but she kept coming back to how they sent their dragons away.

What Laith hadn't mentioned was how the Kings had then hidden away. She pieced it together late in the night as she thought over his story. How else would they remain secret and the legend of dragons be born?

He said many Kings slept away the centuries. With their magic, they could easily have hidden within the mountains waiting for a time when the humans forgot the Dragon Kings. Then it would be just a matter of keeping their secret from ever getting out.

Iona looked up from the path and realized she had returned to the waterfall. She frowned as she recalled how odd Laith acted when he had been here. She found the spot they had kissed and shifted positions so she stood were Laith had been. He kept looking at the waterfall, but all she saw was water and rocks.

Then her gaze traveled upward.

"Of course," she said as she looked at the top of the waterfall.

Iona opted not to climb the rocks to the top and instead found a way around and up that part of the mountain. The trek was steep and littered with rocks of all sizes, but she trudged onward until she finally reached the top.

She straightened and took in the beauty as she gasped for air. The scene before her was simply awe-inspiring. All she wanted to do was pull out her camera and capture the spectacular sight before her. But Iona hesitated. There would be time for pictures. She had come up here for another reason.

Iona pulled out a water bottle and drank deeply as she looked around for some sign of something. When she found nothing at first, she didn't give up. She walked the top of the waterfall time and again.

After an hour of searching, she wiped the sweat from her face with the back of her hand and looked longingly at the water below. Iona scanned the area below seeking anything that might cause her concern.

When she didn't see anything, she hurried back down to the water and set her camera bag aside as she stripped and dove into the pool.

Laith shuffled through the receipts from the night before as he sat in his office trying not to think about the fact that Rhys decided to remain in dragon form. Not that he blamed

Rhys. The thought of never being able to shift to his true form again made him nauseous.

However, it wasn't just his friend in his thoughts, Iona occupied the majority of his mind. Laith knew he'd handled telling her badly. He should have thought more about it and started at the beginning instead of just spitting things out.

Laith made notes on what supplies needed to be reordered. Out front Shara was with Elena restocking the bar. Elena had asked to help out at the pub when she first came to Dreagan, and Laith had understood. She was from the corporate world and needed something to do.

He wasn't surprised that Shara joined Elena. Shara came from a Dark Fae family that had kept her prisoner in her own room for hundreds of years as punishment. She was finding her way again, with the help of Kiril.

Mates. Laith shook his head. He didn't want a mate. He didn't want the worry about a female. He certainly didn't want the apprehension that came at discovering a mate and wondering if she would accept him.

Laith ran a hand through his hair and sat back in his chair. Why is it he kept thinking about mates and Iona in the same sentence? Iona wasn't his mate. She was beautiful and alluring, but she wasn't his mate.

But was he telling himself that because he truly believed it, or wanted it to be true?

The phone in the pub rang, but Laith didn't bother to answer it. He wasn't in the mood to talk to anyone, and he knew either Elena or Shara would answer it. The phone cut off in the middle of the second ring. A second later, Elena's alarmed shout had Laith up and running into the main room.

He came to a halt as Elena hung up the phone. His heart pounded as he prayed it had nothing to do with Iona. "What is it?"

Elena's face was pale, her eyes wide as she looked from Shara to Laith. "That was Cassie. Lily didn't show up for work this morning, and they couldn't get ahold of her. So they went to her flat. Someone broke in, and they can't find Lily."

Laith didn't know Lily well, but he knew all of the women liked her. "What do they want us to do?"

Elena shrugged. "Cassie and Hal can't find her. They are on the way to the police and called to let us know."

At that moment, there was a slight buzz in his head, and then Con's voice said, "*It could be nothing, but I want everyone to keep their eyes out for Lily Ross. She didna come to work this morning, and her flat has been burglarized. We have many enemies, and we all know they doona care who they hurt to get to us.*"

Laith thought of Iona and how vulnerable she was. The fact John had been murdered without them even knowing someone was that close was a wake-up call for all of them.

"I doubt Lily will come here," Laith told the girls as he headed toward the door, "but both of you remain just in case. The rest of the crew will be in shortly. Open the pub as normal."

"I can help search for Lily," Shara offered.

Laith gave a nod of appreciation. "We may need you. Until then, stay with Elena."

"Good luck!" Elena shouted as he hurried out of the pub.

He got in his Audi and drove through the winding roads to Dreagan. The tires slid on the rocks when he slammed on the brakes and shut the engine off.

Laith stepped out of the car as Guy and Kiril were walking quickly toward him. "Anything?"

"Nothing," Guy said with a frown.

Kiril's lips flattened as he glanced at the gift shop.

"Sammi and Banan are with Jane now who is beside herself with worry."

"It seems all the women have taken to Lily," Laith said.

Guy gave a nod. "They have. She's sweet and shy."

"And brings out the protective nature in some," Kiril said.

Laith looked between his two friends. There was something in Kiril's voice that said he knew something. "You're talking about someone in particular. Who?"

At that moment, Laith caught sight of Rhys in human form angrily throwing open the door to the shop as he entered. Laith was so shocked that for a moment he could only stare, wondering if his eyes were deceiving him.

"I knew it," Kiril said between clenched teeth and started toward the shop.

Laith wasn't about to miss the confrontation. He fell into step beside Guy and followed Kiril. They entered the shop in time to see Banan's thunderous expression directed at Rhys while Rhys glared at Jane.

"What was the last thing Lily said to you?" Rhys demanded of Jane who stood behind Banan with Sammi beside her.

"Shouting willna do any good," Tristan said as he came out from the back. He looked at Sammi and waited for her to nod before he walked slowly to stand beside Banan. "We'll find Lily."

Rhys didn't pay Tristan any attention. "Jane, did she say someone was following her? That she was afraid?"

"No," Jane said with a shake of her auburn head. "She was in good spirits when she left last night."

Rhys jerked away and ran a hand down his face. Laith looked at Kiril who lifted a brow as if to ask, "Do I need to spell it out for you?"

Rhys and Lily. Laith hadn't noticed anything between

the two, but there was obviously something or Rhys wouldn't have given up flying.

It was Kiril who approached Rhys and put his hands on his shoulders. "We'll find her. I'm sure it's nothing."

"Nothing?" Rhys asked, his aqua eyes darkened by anger. "Would you think it was nothing if Shara's home was broken into and she was missing?"

Laith's thoughts immediately went to Iona. He knew he'd be losing his mind with worry, and he had simply kissed her a few times. The others who were mated—Hal, Guy, Banan, Kellan, Tristan, and Kiril—would kill anyone who dared to hurt their women.

Kiril dropped his arms and took a step back. "Nay. I'd be readying to kill. Let's go find Lily."

"There's no need," Con said as he walked from the back. He had a light brown suit on with a cream shirt and a tan and gold tie. He leaned against the door with his hands in his pants pockets, his gaze fastened on Rhys. "Hal and Cassie found Lily with the police."

Rhys's shoulders sagged. "As long as she's safe."

Laith expected Rhys to want to go to Lily, but Rhys walked past all of them to exit the shop and walk sedately to the manor.

"He'll never be able to shift again," Con said.

Banan turned on his heel and walked to Jane. He gave her a quick kiss and said, "A sacrifice I would make for Jane."

The nods from Guy, Tristan, and Kiril confirmed that the others who were mated felt the same.

"Do you think Rhys realizes what he's done?" Guy asked.

Kiril rubbed his chin thoughtfully. "I doona believe he does. He reacted at the thought of Lily in danger."

"And when he discovers he'll be in human form for all time?" Tristan asked.

Banan held Jane tighter. "He's going to need us more than ever."

Laith walked out of the shop to his car in a sour mood. He opened the door and saw his phone sitting in the cup holder. In his hurry that morning, he must have left it in the car instead of bringing it into the pub with him.

He slid behind the wheel and checked the mobile for calls and messages when he saw Iona's text. That had been hours ago. Laith shut the door and started the car as he sent Elena a quick text that he wouldn't be in until later. Then he drove straight to Iona's.

Laith knew she wasn't going to be at the cottage, but he did a swift check of it anyway. Afterward he walked to the waterfall. Laith didn't know how he knew that's where she would be, but he did.

The closer he got to her, the faster he walked until he was jogging and then running. Laith needed to see her, to hold her. He hadn't tried to touch her last night after all he had told her, but now he wished he had.

All night he yearned to hold her, kiss her. Each night that went by without having her in his arms was a new torture that no amount of cold showers could lessen. Until a King took a human as his mate, she was vulnerable and exposed to their many enemies. How could Laith continue to leave her on her own after what happened to John?

I thought you didn't want a mate.

Laith ignored his conscience. He didn't want a mate, but it wasn't like a King had a choice once he found her. Was Iona his mate? He wasn't sure, but he knew he had to know she was safe, had to feel her in his arms.

It didn't matter that Iona didn't believe in love. Right now he wasn't sure of anything but the need pounding through him. He needed—nay, he *hungered,* he *craved*—more of her sexy mouth, her tantalizing taste. Her irresistible body.

Laith slowed to a walk as the waterfall came into view. He spotted Iona lying atop a boulder with the fingers of one hand trailing in the water. Her skin glistened with a golden, sun-kissed hue while her damp hair clung to the rock and her shoulders in tousled waves.

All the blood rushed to his cock when he saw the pink tips of her nipples. He fantasized about seeing her naked, of stripping her clothes from her piece by piece, but this was even better.

She was a nymph, an enchantress sent to drive him mad with desire. And she was doing an excellent job. Laith couldn't take his eyes off her golden skin from her breasts to her waist past her hips to the blond curls hiding her sex to her long legs that seemed to go on forever.

Suddenly, she stilled and slowly sat up, her head turning so she looked at him over her shoulder. She didn't hide her nudity, which made him yearn for her all the more.

She smiled and stood before diving into the water. Laith jerked off his clothes as he walked to the pool. The rumble of the waterfall was drowned out by the roar of his desire. Every instinct within him demanded he claim her, that he mark her as his.

Mate, a voice whispered in his head.

Iona's head broke the surface as he reached the water's edge. Their gazes locked, held. She treaded water, waiting. Laith stepped into the water and made a shallow dive, gliding beneath the water until he reached her.

Laith broke the surface, wrapping an arm around her as he did. "You've no idea how much I want you."

"You've no idea how I dreamed of you just like this," she whispered.

Laith pulled her close, her breasts pressed against him. She was breathing heavily and her lips were parted. He splayed his hand on her back and took her mouth in a savage, wild kiss.

CHAPTER
TWENTY-SIX

Iona's blood ran hot, scorching her veins as Laith kissed her senseless. She clung to him, helpless to do anything other than hold onto him. She had been dozing when she knew with a certainty she couldn't explain that Laith was near. When she sat up and saw him, her legs went weak. She was still shaking when she stood and dove into the water.

Her trembling hadn't stopped there. In fact, it had worsened. The cool water lapped against her heated flesh, and she only belatedly realized that she had stopped treading water. Somehow Laith was holding them both up with one hand around her.

Iona sucked in a breath when he ended the kiss. It took her a moment to focus, and then she was looking into his beautiful eyes. The desire reflected in the gunmetal depths sent her passion soaring.

"I wondered if you would come," she said.

His arm tightened around her. "As if I could stay away." He kissed her again briefly. "I wasna sure after last night what you thought."

Last night? That's when she recalled his story and the

fact he was a dragon. It was difficult for her to think of him as anything other than a man since that's all she had seen him as, and what a magnificent body it was.

Iona licked her lips while she ran her hands over his thick shoulders, up his neck, and into the wet strands of his long hair. She had only gotten a glimpse of him, and she wanted to look him over at her leisure so she could touch and kiss every inch of him. That's when she recalled the glimpse of a tattoo on his back she had gotten when he dove in.

"Let me see your tat," she urged.

He smiled and drew her closer to shore so that she could stand, then he released her and turned his back to her. Iona gasped. The tattoo took up his entire back from his neck to his waist. The ink was a spectacular and unique mixture of black and red.

She touched the head of the dragon that rested on Laith's left shoulder. The dragon was standing on his hind legs, the wings semi-spread toward his right shoulder blade. Her eyes roamed down the body of the dragon to its tail that stopped at the top of his left butt cheek.

"I've never seen such beautiful and meticulous work before," she said in awe.

Laith's head turned to the side. "It's no' work. Each Dragon King has a tat of his dragon upon his body somewhere."

"Each of you have one of these?"

"Aye," he said with a smile.

She traced the tattoo until Laith turned around and took her in his arms again. He brought her against him so that their foreheads touched, their mouths breaths apart. Her heart pounded, her chest heaved. Nothing existed but the two of them and the craving for each other.

"All I can think about is you. All I want is you." Those

were private musings, but when it came to Laith, there were no boundaries anymore.

He moaned and kissed her.

"I can't explain it."

"Stop talking," he murmured and cupped the back of her head with his other hand.

Iona's toe hit the bottom of the pool. Sometime in all the kissing and talking Laith swam them toward the side of the pool. With both of his arms available now, Iona was crushed against his chest.

But she loved every minute of it. The closer she was to him, the hotter she burned. The only one who could soothe her, the only one who could ease the ache inside her was Laith.

Iona opened her eyes long enough to see they were in an alcove with boulders rising high around them, shielding them from any eyes. The water lapped lazily against shore, as if the seclusion slowed time.

She wound her arms around his head as he kissed down her throat and across her chest. His tongue was searing, his lips tender. Then he cupped her breast and skimmed his thumb over her already aching nipple.

A deep moan flew past her lips as desire shot straight to her core. She lifted one of her legs and wrapped it around him, sucking in a breath at the feel of his hot, hard arousal pressing against her stomach.

Iona reached between them and wrapped her hand around his cock. Laith stilled, his body going taut as a deep, hungry groan rumbled in his chest. She opened her eyes to find him watching her greedily. Her hand moved up and down his length, her movements causing the water to swirl around them.

"Tease," he growled, a small smile playing about his lips.

"As if you expect me not to touch as well."

He chuckled and squeezed her nipple. "Careful, lass. The teasing goes both ways."

Iona's smile grew when she reached the top of his rod and slid her thumb over his head. His eyes darkened as his cock jumped in her hand. Her victory was short-lived however. Laith removed her hand and bent her backward so that his lips latched onto one of her nipples to suckle at the same time his finger slid inside her.

Her mouth opened, but no sound came out. She was helpless to do anything other than lay there as his hands and mouth worked her into a frenzy. The harder he sucked, the more she moved her hips. His fingers were busy stroking her while his thumb circled her aching clit. The leg she had wrapped around him tightened as he continued to pull her closer and closer to her climax.

She was on fire, burning from within, the desire was so intense. Her nails dug into his arms as his muscles bunched beneath her palms. She heard someone moan loudly, and realized the sound was coming from her.

His lips moved to her other nipple and he flicked his tongue back and forth over the hard nub. All the while, he added a second finger inside her.

The next instant, he sat her up so quickly water splashed on him. Iona leaned forward and licked a droplet that ran down his cheek to his jaw.

"I'm trying to take my time, but you're no' helping," Laith said tightly.

She smiled and framed his face with her hands. "Good. I want you to feel as I do. I want you to crave me as much as I crave you."

"I do," he said softly.

Iona normally took charge any time she was with a man, but with Laith he not only didn't give her a chance, he took charge. And she loved it. It made her desire him even more because of that.

He removed his hand from inside her. Iona felt bereft, needy without his touch. He grasped her hips and lifted her. Without being told, Iona wrapped her other leg around his waist.

They were staring into each other's eyes when he gradually, deliberately lowered her. Iona sucked in a breath when the blunt head of his cock met her sex. And when he pushed inside her, stretching her, she moaned.

"I want you screaming," he whispered in her ear.

"I don't."

He leaned back and smiled. "You will."

His promise sent a thrill of anticipation rushing through her. If anyone could make her scream, it would be Laith, but it just wasn't her. She rarely made any noises during sex. As if to seal his promise, he thrust his hips forward, seating her firmly upon him. Iona's lips parted, but only a small groan sounded.

Laith pulled out of her until only the tip of him remained, then he plunged inside her. Again and again he repeated the move, sometimes thrusting hard, sometimes slowly filling her. Her eyes were glazed and half-open, her lips parted, and her chest heaved, but she wasn't screaming yet.

He shifted them so she was backed against a boulder worn smooth by the water. The driving, powerful hunger inside him grew with each moment Iona was in his arms.

The more he kissed her, touched her, filled her, the more he had to have. She had become an addiction without him even realizing it.

She eased him when he hadn't known he needed such tenderness. She inflamed him when he hadn't known he was capable of such desire.

She made him long for something he was sure he would never have considered—a mate.

Laith's chest constricted at the thought, but he couldn't release her. Iona was a part of him now for better or worse.

He increased his rhythm, sliding in her faster, harder, deeper. Her eyes were fully closed now, her nails drawing blood as they sunk into his back and shoulders.

She hadn't turned away from him after learning what he was, but even if she had, Laith would have pursued Iona. He had claimed her, whether it was just for the day or forever, that was up to her.

Laith held her hips steady as he pounded within her. Small cries began to fall from her lips as her head moved side to side. He smiled and moved just enough to slip a hand between to find her swollen clit. The first touch of his finger and she cried out.

Laith pulled out of her long enough to turn her so that her back was to him. She gripped the boulder, her face turned to the side so that her cheek was pressed against the rock. With one thrust, he entered her. For a moment, he held still as her body trembled and she tried to move her hips. She was close to peaking, but not nearly close enough to screaming.

Laith remained deep within her and reached around to fondle her breasts, pulling at the tight buds of her nipples.

"Laith," she whispered, her voice low and full of need.

Still he continued teasing her breasts, massaging them and rolling her nipples between his fingers. Only when she was panting, her hips bucking against him did he turn his focus to her sex.

He parted her with his fingers and briefly closed his eyes at the feel of her arousal. Then he focused his attention on her clitoris, alternating flicking his thumb over it and circling the swollen nub.

She continued to try to move her hips, but he held her steady. Her lips were parted, small moans and cries coming from her.

He knew the instant she was about to orgasm by the way her body tightened. Laith kissed the back of her neck and removed his hand. She let out a cry and tried to move, but he trapped her between him and the boulder.

"Are you ready to scream for me?" he whispered in her ear as he slowly withdrew from her.

"Yes. Oh, yes," she said with her eyes still closed.

He let his hand skim over her lips and then down her throat. "Open your eyes, sweetheart."

Her lips lifted and her eyes focused on the waterfall. She swallowed and waited for him to speak.

"Look at the water and doona take your eyes off it. Doona close your eyes, but more important, doona move."

She started to look at them, then changed her mind. "I have to move."

"You'll remain still," he murmured as his hand caressed down the side of her breasts. He wanted to fondle them again, to feel the weight of them in his palm, but that would mean moving her from the boulder, and that's not what he wanted right now.

"Laith?" She whispered his name with a mix of longing and fear.

Good. She was in complete control of every aspect of her life, including the men she took to her bed. He was going to be different. He was going to force her to go places she hadn't dared before.

Because there were aspects of Iona she kept locked away, even from herself. Laith was going to blow open those doors. She was going to have to be strong both mentally and physically to deal with what was coming.

"Trust me."

He smiled as she gave a small nod. That's all the acceptance he needed. Laith pushed into her about an inch before he halted and pulled back out.

Her gaze never wavered from the waterfall, though she was biting her lip and shaking from trying not to move. Laith wanted to draw this out much longer, but being inside her was too much. He wanted to bury himself deep and give in to the desire riding him. So far he had managed to hold on to his control, but it was fast slipping through his fingers.

Laith's grip on her hips tightened right before he filled her fully. He moaned at the feel of her sheath tightening around him. She held her word and didn't move her body. The walls of her sheath squeezed him, and it was Laith's turn to shake. He was too close to the edge, too far gone to prolong the pleasure that awaited both of them.

He began to move his hips, his thrusts slow and short at first, but it wasn't long before he was burying himself deep within her with fast, hard strokes. Laith felt his climax growing near even as he heard Iona's first shout. He was relentless as he pounded into her body, her screams of pleasure pushing him to bring them higher.

"Laith!" she screamed as her body convulsed with the beginning of her orgasm.

He continued to thrust, even as his own orgasm overtook him and he poured his seed into her.

CHAPTER
TWENTY-SEVEN

Rhi wasn't sure what brought her back to her secret cottage. Perhaps it was catching Laith and Iona locked in each other's arms kissing after such rousing sex. She knew it was a lie even as she thought it. Rhi walked into the house and closed the door behind her so she could lean back against it.

No, she returned to this place because it had helped to comfort her in the past. She once spent many nights curled up on the bed crying for her lover, for what could have been. It was worse now that Shara was mated to a King. A Fae, and not just any Fae, but a once Dark Fae. When it had been said that there could never be a union between the Fae and the Dragon Kings, what had eventually happened?

Rhi had been foolish enough to think she would have been the one to shatter that supposed rule put in place by her queen. Yet it was Usaeil who had been responsible for helping Shara and Kiril.

Why hadn't Usaeil done the same for her? Why hadn't any of them helped her and her lover as everyone had done for Shara and Kiril? Could it be because they didn't approve of the relationship she'd had with her King? Was it because they didn't like her? What was the reason her life had been destroyed?

She had to know.

She *needed* to know.

After so many thousands of years, the pain should have diminished, and even stopped. But it didn't. She didn't help matters by returning to Dreagan again and again. Each time she set foot on that land it was a reminder of what she'd once had, of what was the happiest time of her life. A time that had ended all too quickly.

Rhi pushed away from the door and walked past the living and kitchen area to her bedroom. She came to a halt in the bedroom doorway when she saw the bottle of nail polish sitting in the middle of her bed.

She drew in a breath and released it before she dared to step farther into the room. It hit her like a blast. *He* had been there, in her room. His scent of sandalwood and wind was one she could never forget. It brought back memories of his kisses, of how he knew just where to touch her to bring her the most pleasure, the fiercest orgasms.

Rhi walked to the bed and bent to lift the polish. It was her favorite brand, OPI. Unable to resist, she turned the bottle over to read the name.

"Gaining Mole-mentum," she said with a little laugh.

The shredded gold and chunky pink glitter looked fabulous in the bottle, and she couldn't wait to see it on her nails. She wondered why he chose that particular color. Rhi turned and sat on the corner of her bed. The light on in her closet caught her gaze. There was another set of clothes hanging there.

The ones from earlier that she hadn't chosen were pushed to the side so that she would see only the new set. Rhi had to admit she liked the goldish khaki skinny cargos. Paired with the soft pink, silky, sleeveless shirt and cream jacket with three-quarter-length sleeves, it would make a beautiful outfit. Just as before, there was a pair of shoes. These were a pair of Vince Camuto open-toed booties in a camel-colored leather.

But it didn't stop there. Around the hanger, draped down the shirt was a long necklace of various shades of pink from pale to magenta, with gold beads throughout. Rhi didn't have to look to know there was a pair of earrings and a bracelet to go with it.

The old Rhi would have jumped to wear such an outfit, but she wasn't the old Rhi. She was still trying to figure out who she was.

She stood and set the new polish with the other pinks on the shelf.

It wasn't time for pink yet.

Not even when *he* wanted her to wear it.

Lily watched as a new door and locks were installed. She knew it wasn't an accident that her flat had been targeted. Oh, she told Cassie and Hal exactly that, and thankfully they bought her lie. But Lily knew the truth.

The past she had tried to elude had found her again.

Her first instinct had been to run. It took her years to get up the courage to leave the first time, but once gone, she hadn't looked back. She reached around with her right hand and traced the scar on her left shoulder. It was a reminder of what her life had been—the fear, the terror, the anxiety.

It took her six months to be able to sleep after she ran away. Nearly a year later the nightmares finally stopped. She had no doubt that when she attempted sleep that night that the nightmare would return.

Running had gained her freedom. The safest thing would be to leave again, but she didn't want to. She had found a new life, a job, and friends all at Dreagan. No one there knew how much that job meant to her, or how much knowing she felt safe while there helped her carry on each day.

It was all an illusion. She knew that, but whatever helped, right?

Run or stay and fight? Lily hadn't been so cowed when she was younger. She had been strong and determined. It was time to find that Lily again. She liked the person she'd once been, and hated what she'd turned into before she left . . . the past.

"Ma'am?"

Lily jumped and jerked her gaze to the two men who were installing her new door. "Yes?"

"We're all done here." One of the men, the younger of the two with short dark hair held out her keys. His kind brown eyes held a hint of concern. "You have three locks now. Are you sure you'll be all right?"

"Yes, thank you." She took the keys. "I appreciate you working so quickly."

The men gave a nod, gathered their things, and left. Lily steeled herself by straightening her back before she entered the flat. She quickly locked all three bolts.

She set her purse by the door and turned to look around. Everything had been overturned, broken, and scattered. Nothing had been hers since she rented the flat fully furnished, but there was still something so . . . discomfiting about someone going through her things. She felt violated.

A knock on the door startled her. Lily whirled around, afraid to even approach. How could she expect to stay and stand her ground if she couldn't even go see who was at the door?

Her knees were knocking as she tentatively walked to the door and rose up on her tiptoes to peer through the peephole. She dropped her head to the door when she saw Cassie. Lily unlocked the three bolts and opened the door.

Cassie wore a bright smile as she enveloped Lily in a

hug. "You didn't think we would let you do this yourself, did you?" Cassie asked as she stepped back.

Lily looked from Cassie to the flat. Since Cassie and Hal had returned to Dreagan hours ago, Lily expected just that. She opened her mouth, trying to form words, when Hal, Jane, and then Banan walked in. They began to clean before Lily could tell them otherwise.

She hadn't had anyone help her since she walked away from her family. Her eyes filled with tears that she quickly blinked away.

"Is kindness such a foreign thing that it brings you to tears?"

She stilled at the sound of the silky, deep voice she heard even in her dreams. Her skin warmed, her blood heated, chasing away the cold numbness that had been with her since she found her door standing ajar.

Lily turned her head and saw Rhys leaning casually against the doorway, his arms crossed over his chest. As usual, he looked gorgeous with his long, dark locks loose about him and his aqua eyes ringed in navy focused on her. Every time she looked at him her stomach fluttered.

"The world isn't exactly a nice place," she finally answered.

He glanced down and gave a small shake of his head. "Nay, I'm sorry to say it isna. Was anything taken?"

"No." She was thankful to have something to think about rather than how she would do anything to have his arms around her.

"If they didna take anything, then why did they destroy your flat?" he asked with a deep frown.

Lily shrugged, turning away so he wouldn't see her face. "Good question."

"You doona know who did this?" His footsteps indicated he had pushed away from the wall and walked toward her.

She had suspicions, but she couldn't be sure. Nor would

she tell him anything, because it would lead to questions about her past that she didn't want to answer. "No."

When he didn't say anything else, Lily looked at him to see his gaze pensive as he stared at her counter. There was something different about Rhys. Gone was the sardonic smile, the easy swagger. "Are you all right? You've no' been yourself lately."

"Myself?" he questioned as he raised his aqua gaze to hers.

Lily shrugged. "You used to go out every night with such beautiful women. Has someone finally stolen your heart?" she asked with a smile she didn't feel.

He stared at her for several seconds before he said, "I've just had a lot to do lately."

Lily didn't know whether to be excited that no one woman had taken his interest, or upset that he would continue bringing the women around.

He turned away then and righted the couch. Lily sighed and grabbed the broom to sweep the dishes that had been broken.

Iona basked in the sun as she lay curled next to Laith. He had promised her she would scream, and she had. Multiple times.

"You're still smiling."

She looked up to find Laith's eyes slit open as he gazed down at her. Iona laughed. "I am, aren't I? I can't seem to stop."

"Good," he said and pulled her tighter against him.

It was a first for her that she was thinking about how long she could spend with him instead of coming up with a way to leave as she usually did. "I've never met another man like you."

"That's because I'm no' just a man," he teased.

But it made her remember what she had been doing at the waterfall. "The spot is close, isn't it?"

His smile faded. "Aye."

"Where?" When he didn't immediately respond, she said, "Laith, if my father knew, then I need to know as well to keep an eye out."

Laith sat up and pulled her up with him. The fact she could sit there with him completely nude and not want to cover up, said a lot about how comfortable she was around him. Another first.

"There," he said and pointed to the top of the waterfall.

Iona shook her head. "I was up there. I didn't see anything."

"Because you can only see it at night."

Her head swung around to him. "Why only at night?"

"I doona know, or ever cared to know really. It's how it's always been."

"Will you take me to see it?"

Laith moved a lock of damp hair away from her face. "If you really want to see it."

"You believe someone is trying to find it, right?" At his nod she said, "Then I need to know."

He got to his feet and held out his hand. "Come. Let's get some food."

She let out a shriek when he swung her up in his arms and then jumped into the water. Iona broke the surface laughing. That's when she spotted Laith swimming ahead of her.

Her competitive side took over and she swam as fast as she could. When she reached the shore he already had his jeans on. Iona threw him a glare. "That was a dirty trick."

"All's fair," he said with a wink.

Iona put on her bra and panties over her wet skin and then shrugged on a new red shirt and white shorts. It wasn't until she had on her shoes that she looked around for her camera case.

"What is it?" Laith asked.

"My camera case. I put it right here with my clothes."

She began to spin around looking for it, her heart hammering in her chest. That camera meant everything to her. Sure, she could buy another, but it had been a gift from her bosses after her first year with them.

"Here it is," Laith called.

Iona whirled around to see him standing near a tree holding the case. She hurried to him and clutched the camera to her. "I don't remember leaving it here."

She saw the way Laith's stance instantly changed as he surveyed the area.

"It's okay," she said and put a hand on his arm. "I'm sure I did it. I've been doing a lot of stupid things like that lately. Besides, if someone were here, wouldn't you have known?"

Laith's response was a grunt that only made her nervous.

CHAPTER
TWENTY-EIGHT

Laith was still disconcerted by Iona's camera case not being where she said she'd left it. He then brought her to Dreagan, the place he knew she was the safest. He couldn't take his eyes off her as she sat in the kitchen at Dreagan Manor eating. She glanced up and saw him, a smile forming as she popped a raw baby carrot in her mouth.

All Laith could think about was making her his mate. Iona was a Campbell, a guardian to the hidden doorway of Dreagan. She was part of their world now, but that's not why he wanted her. He wanted her because she made him burn, made him long for things he never wanted before.

He wanted to see the dragon eye tattoo on her arm, branding her as his. He wanted to always have her near. No, that wasn't right. He didn't want . . . he *needed*.

"That satisfied look will last how long?" she asked slyly.

"You mean the look of a sated man, or the look of a man who got you to scream?" He asked the last part in a whisper.

Iona rolled her eyes. "Both. But I think it's more of the second part."

"So you've really never screamed before?"

She laughed and leaned back in her chair. "Never."

"I'll have to make sure you do it every time from now on," he vowed as he put his arms on the table and leaned forward.

Her head cocked to the side while she stretched out her long leg and rubbed her foot on his thigh. "I like the sound of that."

Laith reined in his desire. Barely.

"Uh-oh," Iona said as she dropped her foot to the ground. "That's a very serious look you're now wearing."

"Because there's a serious issue still at hand. I can no' be with you all the time."

She frowned as she sat up. "Why not?"

She had tossed out the question nonchalantly, but Laith knew there was nothing casual about it. The Iona he'd first met would never have asked that. Did that mean there was a chance he could make her believe in love? That she might give them a chance?

"I want to, Iona, but I'm also realistic. I've duties here and at the pub. I could take you everywhere with me, but you're no' used to that. You're used to doing your own thing, and I want to take that into account."

"What are you thinking?" she asked, her tone just as serious.

"We watch the border between your land and ours. Always have, actually, and kept an eye on the Campbells that were there. But that isna enough now."

Her lips compressed. "How, exactly, do you keep watch?"

"Mostly at night, but there is usually a King nearby in case our enemies breach the doorway."

Comprehension dawned on her face then. "Ah, but that's near the border. That's not anywhere else on my land being watched."

"Precisely. I'm no' comfortable with that. Our resources are great, but we're stretched thin now. We let John down because we assumed that secret was safe. We know now that it isna."

She gave a tight nod. "Then what do you suggest? Me move in here?"

"I wouldna complain," he said with a grin, hope flaring in his chest.

She smiled and gazed at him with longing. "I don't think I would either."

Laith stilled, unsure if he heard her correctly. The longer he stared at her and her smile remained, the more he knew she meant her words. "You do know what you just said?"

"Yes."

Things were getting much too serious between them at the moment, and if Laith didn't do something soon, he was going to ask her right then to be his mate. That was moving too quick for her. "It was my making you scream. That's all it took to get you to change your mind," he said with a grin.

Her lips softened into the barest of smiles as she held his gaze with her deep brown ones. "I wish I knew what the cause was, because this scares me."

"I know." Laith leaned forward and reached across the table to hold her hand.

"You don't," she insisted. "I lied to Sammi. I was in a relationship once. I was a year into University when I began dating this guy. We were together for ten months. He was nice, but I felt suffocated, stifled. He wanted me with him all the time, and it was too much. That's how I knew I wasn't the type of person who wanted to be in a relationship. That is . . . until you."

Laith squeezed her hand. She was sharing a part of her past that he doubted she'd ever told another person. It proved once more that she was opening up to him. "I doona want to suffocate you, but I'll tell you that I want you with me all the time. I want to know you're safe, and the only way I can truly know that is to have you by my side. But it's more than that, Iona. I hunger for you."

"You've been alive for how long?"

He shrugged. "Too many."

"Thousands?"

Laith jerked his thumb upward.

"Millions?" she asked in a whisper.

"Does that make a difference?"

She gave a choked laugh. "I'm sure I'm not the first human you've wanted."

"A man has needs, even a dragon. I willna lie about that. Right before Ulrik's woman betrayed him, I considered asking my lover to remain with me."

Iona's dark eyes held his. "What happened?"

"I feared she might betray me. I knew then she couldn't be my mate."

"Mate? Don't you mean wife?"

He shrugged. "We have a ceremony, aye, but we're mated. A Dragon King has but one true mate. When I began to question her, I knew she wasna the one. My mate I will never question."

Iona swallowed, her gaze dropping to the table. "Is it this land that's changed me? Or is it my father's murder? I don't know if it's because I know the secret now or if I'm at a place in my life that I can let go of the things in my past."

"Does it matter?"

"No," she said with a chuckle as she looked at him. "It doesn't. I feel exposed, as if the walls I erected as a young girl were smashed. By you."

Laith tugged her arm until she rose and came around the table. He pulled her down onto his lap. "I willna push you on any of this. I want you. I want what is developing between us to continue."

"I can't believe I'm saying this, but I do as well."

"That makes me infinitely happy." He ran a finger down her cheek. He knew this could be all he ever got from Iona. He would never give up making her his, but for now, it was enough. "It's because I'm worried that I would like to bring someone to your place to help keep watch over you when I can't. He's a good man."

"Man?" she asked with a lift of her brow.

"He's a Warrior."

"The Warriors again? I think I'm ready to hear about them now."

Laith opened a bag of crisps and offered one to Iona. Once she had it, he took another out and ate it. "The Warriors began as men, humans. They were part of the Celtic tribes when Rome invaded Britain. The Druids did their best to keep Rome out of Scotland, but they were losing."

Iona took another chip. "This is where you tell me Caesar wrote history wrong?"

"Aye. One of many times."

She shrugged one shoulder. "Tell me more."

"The Druids have two sects. The *mies* are the Druids who use the magic from their birth. Then there are the *droughs*. They give their soul to Satan in exchange for black magic. The two sects didna interact, but with the fate of Scotland hanging in the balance, the *mies* realized they would need more than their magic to win against Rome. So they went to the *droughs*."

"Wait," Iona interjected. "Why didn't the Dragon Kings help?"

Laith handed her the bag of chips. "We watched over the fate of mankind, but we didna involve ourselves in their many wars."

"Makes sense. I'm guessing the *droughs* had an answer?"

He nodded. "They used their black magic and called up

long-forgotten gods from deep within Hell and asked the strongest warriors from each family to offer himself up. The gods took over their hosts and decimated Rome in a matter of weeks."

"So that's why Rome really left?" Iona said with a surprised look.

"The plan was flawless, until the Druids tried to put the gods back into Hell. The gods refused to give up their hosts. The Warriors began to slaughter anyone and everyone they came across. The *mies* and *droughs* then combined their magic to bind the gods inside the men. The men woke with no memory of what they had done as Warriors."

Iona raised a brow and eyed him. "That's not the end of the story. I know there's more."

Laith ran a hand through his still damp hair. "The spell to bind the gods was written upon a scroll, as was the spell to unbind them. Supposedly the Druids came to an agreement to burn both so that the gods could never be able to take over their host again. The Druids also assumed the gods would die with their host. In fact, the gods traveled through the bloodlines to the most powerful warriors, waiting."

"For?" Iona urged.

"There was a Druid, a *drough,* who craved more power than any *drough* before her. Her name was Deirdre, and she found the scroll to unbind the gods. This was centuries later, so she had no idea which families could have a god within their bloodline, but the scroll listed one clan— MacLeod."

Iona's eyes went wide. "MacLeod? There hasn't been a MacLeod clan in hundreds of years."

"Because Deirdre found the god. There were three brothers equal in every way. The god split itself into three so that each could have a piece of him. Eight hundred years ago Deirdre released the god within Fallon, Lucan, and

Quinn. There was something a little different with this spell, however. It allowed the men to take control of the god if he were strong enough. The MacLeods were such men, and they were able to overcome the evil of their god. They also broke away from Deirdre."

"There are just three Warriors?" Iona asked.

"No' hardly. Deirdre set out taking men she thought might house a god. Many were killed, and still many more had their gods unleashed. Some were able to fight and gain control, but most gave in and became her followers. The ones who got control eventually found the MacLeods and banded together, fighting Deirdre and any *drough* they came across who meant them harm."

"That's . . . some story," she said in awe. "Does it end there?"

"In some ways." Laith fingered a strand of her damp hair. "The Warriors found *mies* who they fell in love with and married. Those Druids are some of the most powerful ever, and they were able to hide MacLeod Castle from the world as well as put a protection around it. Because while the Warriors are immortal, the Druids are no'."

Iona grinned. "That protection allowed the Druids not to age, right?"

"Right. Some still live at MacLeod Castle, but after fighting three different *droughs,* we stepped in to aid them. In doing so, we used our magic to craft rings for the mortal Druids so they could go out into the world and live with their men instead of hiding in the castle."

"Like you hide," Iona said softly.

Laith hadn't ever thought of it that way. "I suppose."

"The Warriors hide who they are in a castle with Druid magic. You hide who you are in a manor using dragon magic. How have none of you seen the correlation?"

Laith looked into her dark eyes. "I doona know. Perhaps

we thought ourselves better, stronger, or any number of things. But I see the similarities."

"Are the Warriors free?"

"In some ways. They still hide who they are."

"And you want one of them to come here?"

Laith took her hand. "I do. You doona have to have him in the cottage with you, but he can keep an eye on you. His wife is one of the most powerful Druids I've ever known. She was forced to become *drough* to save her family, but since it was forced, her soul remained her own. The power of black magic combines with her pure magic to make her verra formidable."

"What's this Warrior's name?"

"Hayden." Laith left off his surname. He didn't want to do anything to keep Iona from agreeing to Hayden's presence. She had taken all he said stoically, but everyone had a breaking point.

The fact that Hayden was a long lost ancestor just might be that point.

Iona laced her fingers with his. "I admit, I'd feel better with someone there. It's just so strange being alone."

"I'll call Hayden then."

"What about his wife?"

"Isla?" Laith asked. "She'll come with him. If that's all right?"

"Of course. A wife shouldn't be separated from her husband."

"Iona," Sammi said in surprise as she walked into the kitchen. "I didn't know you were here."

Laith reluctantly rose, setting Iona on her feet as he spotted Tristan. "Sammi, could you stay with Iona while I make a call?"

"Sure," Sammi said and took his chair.

Laith winked at Iona before he walked out of the kitchen with Tristan on his heels. Once they were out of earshot, he turned to Tristan. "I think it's time Iona meets her ancestor."

"Hayden?" Tristan asked with a frown. "Why now?"

"A feeling. It may be for nothing, but—"

"No need to say more," Tristan interrupted while pulling out a mobile phone from his pocket. "I'll call him now."

Laith stopped Tristan before he could dial. "I'd like to talk to Hayden first. Iona doesna know who he is."

Tristan nodded and placed the call. They didn't have long to wait before Hayden agreed to come. "We'll meet in Con's office," Tristan said and ended the call.

Laith and Tristan took the stairs three at a time to the second level where Con's office was. By the time they walked inside, Hayden lounged in one of the chairs with Fallon MacLeod in the other.

"Damn, but you're fast," Tristan said with a smile.

The Dragon Kings might be able to shift and fly, but Fallon could teleport like the Fae, which made things easy for the Warrior and anyone around him.

The four greeted each other before Fallon looked around Con's office with his dark green eyes. "Where is Con?"

"Lately, who knows?" Tristan said tightly. "He's been gone more than he's been here, and he doesna tell us anything."

Laith closed the door. "I wanted to talk to Hayden before we went downstairs."

"About?" Hayden asked with his nearly black gaze locked on him. Hayden's blond hair was pulled back in a queue, the color an exact match to Iona's.

"There's a woman I'd like you to help protect."

Hayden chuckled. "A King asking me to help protect a woman? Why do you need my help?"

Laith exchanged a look with Tristan. "Her name is Iona Campbell."

That erased Hayden's cocky grin. He sat up straighter

in the chair. "You think because she's a Campbell that I'll say aye?"

"We think you'll say aye because she looks like you," Tristan said.

Hayden scrubbed a hand down his face, his gaze lowering to the floor.

Laith walked to the front of Con's desk and leaned back against it so he could look Hayden in the face. "Her father was murdered recently, and we think someone might be after her."

"Why?" Fallon demanded.

Laith sighed loudly. "Con wouldna want you to know this, and honestly, I doona either, but perhaps it'll allow you to see the urgency in this. The Campbells have been guarding an entrance into Dreagan that no' even our magic can stop. A doorway that your father guarded, Hayden."

"What doorway?" Hayden asked indignantly. "I never knew of such a place."

"The place where we killed the woman who betrayed Ulrik," Laith replied.

CHAPTER
TWENTY-NINE

Iona was wiping her eyes from laughing so hard at the joke Sammi told her when she spotted Laith out of the corner of her eye. She turned to him, still chuckling over the joke. "Hey," she called.

He entered the kitchen followed by Tristan, but there were two more men with him. She shot Laith a questioning look, but then her gaze was snagged by the last man, who entered and openly stared at her.

The man's dark gaze held a bit of shock. He was taller than the others, even Laith, and held himself like a man who wasn't afraid of anything. Much like any of the Dragon Kings she had met, but there was something different about him. She thought it might be because he looked a little like her father.

"Iona," Laith said from beside her. "I'd like to introduce you to Fallon MacLeod."

The other man stepped forward. He had a nice smile, long dark hair, the most unusual dark green eyes she'd ever seen, and a gold torc with boars' heads around his neck. That's when she grasped what name Laith had said.

"Fallon? The Fallon MacLeod?" she asked, looking from Laith to Fallon.

Fallon laughed and bowed his dark head as he clasped his hands behind his back. "I see Laith has told you about us Warriors. Aye, lass, I'm that Fallon. It's nice to meet you."

Iona was completely taken aback. She was surrounded by immortal Highlanders, something that wasn't supposed to be real. She then looked at the man with the blond hair and black eyes. "And you are?"

Laith cleared his throat and hurried to say, "Iona, this is Hayden. Hayden Campbell."

If she had been surprised before, the shock caused her heart to miss a beat. She looked at him again and saw the similarities between him and her father—as well as herself.

"It's truly a pleasure," Hayden said as he walked to her and gently took her hand in his. "We Warriors know our family lines continued after we . . . " He paused and waved his hand about.

"Were altered," Fallon supplied.

Hayden gave him a nod before turning his gaze back to Iona. "Quite right. Altered. But we've never searched our families out. I certainly never knew that mine had such a pact with Dreagan. If I had, I'd have gotten to know your father. I would be honored, lass, to stand as your guard."

Iona was speechless. One of her ancestors was standing in front of her. She wasn't without family anymore. Her eyes began to water. "I didn't think I had any more family."

Hayden's smile was bright. "You doona only have me, but you also have my wife, Isla, and every Warrior and Druid from MacLeod Castle."

"He's right," Fallon said. "Family is important to us."

"And to the Kings," Tristan added.

Iona sniffed and looked to Laith. "You knew he was related to me?"

"I did. I just wasna sure how you would react," he explained.

"I can no' wait to bring you to MacLeod Castle," Hayden said as he pulled her up to stand beside him. "I want you to meet everyone. You have a huge family, Iona, that also extends to the Dragon Kings since Tristan's twin is a Warrior."

Iona jerked back and swiveled her eyes to Tristan. "How is that possible?"

"He was once a Warrior," Sammi said as she rose from the table and walked to stand beside her mate. "He was killed, but came back as a Dragon King. Their newest King in millions of years," she said proudly.

Fallon smiled as he laughed. "Our family keeps growing. First we got Tristan back, which included Sammi. Then with Jane as Sammi's sister, we have Jane and Banan."

"The ties between Warriors and Dragon Kings are strengthening," Tristan said, but his comment was directed at Laith.

"I'm going to punch Con for no' telling me," Hayden growled.

Iona looked up into Hayden's black eyes and found her throat clogging with emotion. "I refused to speak to my father for two decades because of lies my mother told me. I never knew the man he was until recently, but I have a duty to fulfill. I owe him at least that." She shifted her gaze to Laith. "You gave me a family again. I can't ever thank you enough."

She pulled her hand out of Hayden's grasp and flung herself at Laith. He caught her and held her tightly against him. Something strong stirred in his chest. It warmed him, soothed him. And he knew it was all because of Iona.

"I swore I would protect you," he whispered low enough

only she could hear. "If I can no', then Hayden and the rest of the Warriors will. No one will dare try and harm you now."

Laith was loath to release Iona, but her bright smile soothed him. She was special, and not just because she was guardian for the Campbells, but because she was his.

She didn't know it yet, no one but Laith did. After their conversation earlier, he knew without a doubt he wouldn't be content until she was his. And by her own words, she was closer to that realization than she knew.

He reluctantly released her, but found his own smile growing when she remained by his side, her arm around him. Laith rested his arm on her shoulders and looked up to find Tristan staring at him.

"*When did you know?*" Tristan asked through their mental link.

Laith wanted to ignore him, but if he did, Tristan was likely to ask the question out loud. "*I think I've had a suspicion for a few days, but I knew today.*"

"*Does she?*"

"*Nay. With John dying, I was the one to tell her who we are and what she's guarding. That was last night, and then she discovers she has family who are immortal?*"

Tristan threw him a dark look. "*If she is your mate, Laith, then doona let too much time pass without telling her. Mortals can be taken in a blink.*"

Laith squeezed Iona as he thought of the life gone from her. As if sensing his dark thoughts, Hayden raised a blond brow at him. Laith gave a slight shake of his head, hoping Hayden would let it drop.

"I'd better go get Isla," Fallon said. "The others are going to want to come as well."

Hayden firmly shook his head. "No' now. Iona has too much on her plate. Once all this is settled, then she can meet them."

"You want to be the one to tell my wife that?" Fallon asked in dismay.

Hayden quickly threw up his hands. "You're on your own with Larena, my friend. Just bring me Isla as quick as you can."

Fallon threw him a black look and disappeared.

"Oh. My. God," Iona said with a gasp. "He's . . . he's . . . gone."

Hayden threw back his head and laughed. "If that shocked you, how did you react when you saw a dragon for the first time?"

Laith inwardly groaned when Iona looked away. He met Hayden's gaze and said, "She's no' seen us yet."

"Ah," Hayden said in understanding, drawing out the word. "I see. After all we Warriors had seen, it took us aback as well."

"What do you look like when you release your god?" Iona asked.

Hayden rubbed his chin as he considered her. "Lass, are you sure you're ready?"

"If I'm part of this world, I need to not just hear the details but see them as well."

She had a point, Laith conceded. He shrugged when Hayden looked at him. And then, in the next instant Hayden's skin was a deep red, small red horns protruded atop his head, red claws lengthened from his fingertips, and his black irises disappeared, to be replaced with red from corner to corner.

Laith felt the tremor go through Iona. He looked down at her to see the color drain from her face. For a moment, he thought she might bolt, but she swallowed loudly and held her ground.

"And each Warrior looks like this?" she asked hesitantly.

Hayden glanced down at the red skin of his arms. "The gods inside us favor colors as well as certain powers. My god, Ouraneon, is the god of massacre. His color is red, and my power is control over fire."

"Control?" Iona repeated in confusion.

Tristan motioned to Hayden to hold up his hand. "He can call it forth, use it as a weapon, extinguish it, or whatever he wants."

Iona's gaze shifted back to Hayden in time to see a ball of fire form in the palm of his hand. Her mouth fell open in dismay. "That's extraordinary."

Hayden extinguished the fire and tamped down his god so he returned to normal. "Lass, if you think that's something, wait until you see the Kings in their true forms."

"Hayden Campbell, you better not be scaring her," Isla said as she and Fallon appeared next to him.

Hayden bent and kissed his tiny wife. "Never, my love. Iona, I want you to meet Isla, the love of my life."

Iona and Isla said hello, and Laith watched as Iona took in Isla's hip-length black hair and ice blue eyes. Iona reacted better to Fallon and Isla's sudden appearance than she had when he teleported away.

"Let's go to your land," Hayden told Iona. "I want to check everything before night falls."

Laith saw Con standing on the stairs. Iona was too busy talking to Isla to notice him, which was fine by Laith. He pulled Iona aside. "I'll be by later. I've got something I need to do here."

"Is everything all right?" she asked, concerned.

Laith smiled and lied. "Of course. Do you still want to see what you're guarding?"

"Yes."

"Then I'll meet you at midnight at the waterfall."

She touched his face. "You've given me so much today, Laith. Thank you isn't nearly enough."

"Thank me later. Now get going before Hayden comes for you," he said and gave her a quick kiss.

She laughed and hurried to the others. As soon as she reached the group, they put their hands on each other and Fallon teleported them away.

After they left, Laith's smile dropped as he turned to Con who had removed his suit jacket and draped it over the banister. Tristan stood just outside the kitchen door alone, having sent Sammi away.

"What is it?" Laith asked Con.

Con's black eyes showed nothing. "When did you sleep with her?"

"When has that been any of your business?" Laith retorted.

"It became my business when she inherited the Campbell land and took the mantle of responsibility that goes along with it. The Kings have never dallied with the Campbells for that reason alone."

Laith walked to the stairs and slowly climbed them until he stood beside Con. "Mostly because it's been males that inherited the duties. Regardless, it's done."

"And if she refuses you later?" Con demanded. "Do you really think she'll feel so inclined to protect us?"

Laith made a sound at the back of his throat. "Are you angry because I slept with her because she's a Campbell, or because I want her as my mate?"

Con's silence was answer enough.

"Both then," Laith said and looked around him. "As I said, it's done. Hayden and Isla will be watching over her."

"You think she's in danger?"

Laith ground his teeth together to hold back his tide of anger. "John wasna killed for nothing. Iona could be next, because with her death the land is no longer in the hands of the Campbells."

"No' true," Con said softly. "Thomas MacBane let it slip that Iona had a will drawn up yesterday. There is a place for next of kin, and I'm fairly certain that will now be Hayden."

Laith knew where the conversation was going, but he wanted Con to say it. "Which means?"

"Which means the closer she is to a Dragon King, the more she's in peril. If you want to protect her, stay out of her life."

CHAPTER THIRTY

Iona looked up at Hayden as he smiled down at her, a twinkle of playfulness in his dark eyes. The group suddenly closed in around her. Fallon put his hand on her shoulder at the same time Hayden took her hand.

One moment they were standing in Dreagan Manor, and the next, Iona was outside her cottage. She staggered backward, her mouth open. It was one thing to hear that someone could teleport, and even see it. It was quite another to experience it herself.

She blinked as if waiting for her brain to catch up with her body. Isla nudged Hayden out of the way and wrapped an arm around her.

Iona looked down at Isla and took deep breaths to find her equilibrium once again. "I wasn't expecting that."

"It was probably for the best," Isla said as she watched Hayden and Fallon walk around the cottage. "Knowing what is about to happen is sometimes worse."

"You're probably right. What are they doing?" she asked about the men.

"Doing what a Warrior does best—protect." Isla dropped her hand when Iona regained her balance and looked around. "They're scouting to see where the best places are to hide and to determine where an enemy might try to attack."

"Oh." Iona crossed her arms over her chest and looked from the Warriors to Isla. Iona wondered if Isla knew she was acting like Hayden as well.

Isla threw her a smile over her shoulder, and explained, "Magic can be felt by a Warrior. A Druid can tell when magic has been used, but Hayden and Fallon can feel the difference in magic used by a Druid, a Fae, or a Dragon King."

"How is it the Warriors and Druids have remained as secret as the Dragon Kings?"

"The Druids haven't," she said and stopped near a tree where the Range Rover was parked. "There are those claiming to be Druids out there now, though they have no magic. That makes it easier for us to keep ourselves private because the world is focused on the others."

Iona shrugged, because that made sense. "Would it be rude to ask how old you are?"

Isla's ice blue eyes shifted to her. "I was already five centuries old when I met Hayden in 1603."

"That's . . . mind-boggling."

"And the fact Laith has been alive since the dawn of time isn't?" Isla asked with a grin.

Iona rolled her eyes. "Oh, yes, it is, but I try not to dwell on it. I can't seem to wrap my head around that fact or that he is a dragon."

"So you've not seen him?" Isla asked with a small frown.

"Everyone keeps asking me that. Should I be concerned?"

Isla contemplated her question for a moment. "I know I wasn't prepared for the sheer size of them. The Kings in dragon form are huge. They're also fierce looking. Just keep that in mind."

Iona would do that just. Laith was the first man she wanted to continue to be around. He had found the piece of her she locked away long ago. When no other men had even attempted to reach her, he set out to win her. And he had done just that.

It scared her, but she didn't push him away. Another first for her. If she weren't careful, she might find herself falling for Laith. Not falling in love, because she didn't believe in that, but falling for the idea of them as a couple.

That she could easily do. Already she counted down the minutes until she could see him again.

That was dangerous territory to tread upon. If she wanted to be with Laith, then it would be increasingly difficult for her to leave when she got a new assignment—if she wasn't already fired. She hadn't checked her e-mail in a few days.

Iona enjoyed what she did more than anything else in the world. She couldn't give that up, nor would she remain with anyone that asked her to. Laith was the first to make her even think along these lines. It was probably a moot point anyway. The odds of their relationship lasting long er than her time in Scotland was . . . well, frankly, slim to none.

Still . . . if she were to ever settle down, she could see herself with Laith.

Iona was befuddled with this new world she found herself a part of, but knowing she had family—an extended one by the sound of it—was something she had never counted on. Or realized she wanted.

Her mother was still around, and as much as she loved her, it wasn't the same as having someone like Hayden. It had nothing to do with his immortality and everything to do with how he welcomed her with open arms, no talk of money at all.

Iona had no illusions. She knew with the money she sent

her mother that she wouldn't see or hear from Sarah again until more was needed. Iona made sure to send over a huge chunk out of her own account that should tide her mother over for several years.

"Something wrong?" Isla asked.

Iona quickly shook her head. "Just doing a lot of thinking lately."

"Ah. About Laith, I gather."

"How did you know?" she asked in amazement.

Isla smiled and looked to Hayden. "Hayden and the others were battling Deirdre, who forced me to help her by holding my sister and niece, when the Warriors attacked her. I tried to get away, because I knew she wouldn't die as easily as they assumed. Hayden found me in the snow half-alive. Deirdre had bound me to her. Since I wasn't dead, I knew she was alive. I begged Hayden to kill me."

"He obviously didn't."

"No," Isla said in a soft voice. She swallowed hard and looked sadly around the area. "He didn't. He wanted to as soon as he learned I was *drough*. He hated *droughs,* you see, because they killed his family."

It was the sadness and regret in Isla's amazing blue eyes that clued Iona in. "It was you, wasn't it?"

She nodded and looked away, blinking quickly. "It's tough for me to return here, even after all this time. Deirdre had control of my mind and body, forcing me to commit atrocities, but the simple fact is, it was me."

"How did Hayden get past his hatred?"

She moved her long black hair off her shoulder. "With the same attraction I fought as well. We were like oil and water at first, each fighting not to give into the desire, but the passion was too great. Against all odds, we fell in love, and it was with Hayden's help that I broke the spell that linked me to Deirdre."

"And your sister and niece?" Iona asked.

Isla's gaze returned to her. "They died. The Druids at MacLeod Castle took me as one of their own. They gave me hope while Hayden gave me courage and love."

Iona looked away, unwilling to tell her new friend her thoughts on love. She saw Hayden wave Fallon over as they both squatted near a cluster of trees and moved the leaves of the ferns out of the way to look at the ground.

"Why did you turn up your nose at the mention of love?"

Iona glanced at Isla. "I didn't turn up my nose."

"Yes," Isla said with a chuckle. "You did. Do you not believe in it?"

Iona didn't like the way Hayden and Fallon continued to look at the spot. "I usually hide my disdain for the word better, but I've been besieged by it these past few days. I'm used to being on my own, and yet I've found myself surrounded by new friends, which has made dealing with my father's murder a bit easier."

For someone who liked being alone, Iona found herself surrounded by friends and family. It altered her way of thinking even more. She had fought against any constraints of having friends, but now she realized she had only been harming herself. She was stronger with friends around her, fortified by her new family.

"Being surrounded by friends is a good thing," Isla pointed out.

"I don't deny that." Iona dropped her arms and searched for the right words. "I think people want to believe in love. That want makes them think they feel something that doesn't exist, and then the couple is surprised when that 'supposed' loved ends and they divorce, separate, or break up."

"You've never seen love, then?"

"I do think the love between a parent and their children,

as well as a child for their parents, is real. Falling in love with another person, however, isn't. Lust? Desire? Yes, those things are real."

Isla raised a black brow. "So is it just lust and desire that had you standing beside Laith? Or was it the start of something more?"

"I honestly don't know." Iona sighed and squeezed her eyes closed for a second. "I used to think love was all made up in our minds. That there is no such thing as a soul mate or the other half of a person. That people want to believe in love because they need to think there is someone out there for them."

"But," Isla pressed.

Iona shook her head vigorously. "I've watched my mother go through men like tissues. I told myself there wasn't someone out there for me, that I was better alone. That put everything else into perspective and has allowed me to live happily. At least I thought I was happy."

"And now?"

Iona had said too much to Laith earlier. She hadn't been able to help it. The situation presented itself, and suddenly she was spilling her guts. The fact she wanted to be with him all the time scared her as nothing else could.

She swallowed and faced Isla. "I don't want to care for him. I don't want to need him."

"But you do. There's nothing wrong with that."

Iona smiled as she always did when she thought of Laith. "I don't deny there's a tidal wave of attraction between us. I also don't deny that he makes me smile or that I feel stronger when he's near. I'm not foolish enough to think it'll last longer than my time here."

Isla frowned. "You're leaving?"

"I don't normally stay in one place too long." Though she wouldn't be averse to remaining in Scotland. It was the first place that felt like home since she left twenty years earlier.

Isla studied her for a moment, and then shrugged. "Why not test what happens between you and Laith and see? Or are you afraid that you will fall in love?"

Isla's dare took Iona aback. She wasn't afraid of falling in love. How could she be when she didn't believe in it? Or . . . did she? "I—"

"Isla!" Hayden's shout interrupted her.

Iona followed as Isla ran to her husband. As soon as they reached Fallon and Hayden, Isla peered at the ground. Fallon's face was grim as he looked up at Iona and slowly got to his feet. Iona shifted her gaze to Hayden to see his brow furrowed in a deep frown. He shook his head of blond hair and let the fern leaves pop back into place.

"This isna good," Hayden said.

Iona watched the fern leaves sway gently until the momentum stopped them. She turned and looked over her shoulder to the cottage that was twenty feet away. The window to her living room was in line with them, giving her a view straight into the kitchen

"Dragon and Dark Fae magic mixed," Fallon said, his words clipped in anger. "I'll alert Dreagan."

"And I'll widen the search," Hayden said.

Iona turned back around, but Fallon was already gone. "What does the magic mean?"

"It means there was someone here," Hayden said with a scowl. "Dark magic is deadlier than black magic. Black magic has a sickening, cloying feel to it. Dark magic feels like death. It's sinister, nefarious in ways that I can no' describe."

Isla shuddered. "It's strong enough use of magic that even I can sense it. Dragon magic is the purest, most powerful magic in this realm. To be combined with a

Dark Fae's magic is . . . " She paused and looked help-lessly to Hayden.

"Disgusting. Repulsive. An atrocity. Take your pick," Hayden mumbled.

Iona's stomach revolted. "Someone was watching me? Someone was here?"

"Laith thought there might be trouble. It's why he called me," Hayden said. "Doona worry, Iona. Whoever this is willna get any closer to you."

She didn't like the fear that iced her veins. "Did this person go into the cottage?"

Hayden immediately walked to the front door. Iona tossed him the keys and waited outside with Isla while he checked the inside.

When he returned to the door, his face held a thunder-ous expression. "They've been all through the house."

Iona's knees threatened to crumple. "I thought I was misplacing things. I thought I was being forgetful with all that's been going on."

"Nay," Hayden said darkly. "Someone has been follow-ing you."

Hayden's head snapped to the left and his black gaze narrowed on something. A heartbeat later he moved so quickly Iona couldn't track him as he ran into the woods.

Isla gave her a soft shove toward the house. "Get inside while I set up a perimeter spell."

Iona stood shaking in the middle of the living room looking around the cottage. She still couldn't believe some-one had been in her house. But how? Wouldn't she have seen them?

She looked out the window at Isla standing outside with her eyes closed and her lips moving. Her arms were held at her sides at first, her palms facing out. A second later and her arms began to slowly lift upward until they were di-rectly above her head.

Her hands clasped together, and there was a bright light that burst from her hands. Iona ducked in reaction, and glanced around to see if she could spot the magic.

A few moments later Isla walked into the house, and Iona asked, "Will your spell work? Will it keep whoever this is out?"

"Probably not since it's Dark magic that's used," Isla stated grimly. "But it'll alert me if he tries to come inside."

CHAPTER
THIRTY-ONE

Laith wasn't about to let Con make the decision for him when it came to Iona. He glared at Constantine for long silent moments before Tristan walked up the stairs and shouldered his way between them until he was a few steps above them, then stopped and faced them.

"Con, you're being a wanker. You wanted one of us to get close to Iona so we could determine what she knew, and tell her of her legacy if John hadn't. You can no' just tell him to stop after he's gotten close," Tristan said. "And Laith, you're not thinking calmly. Con is trying to put things into perspective and doing it poorly."

"I'm doing a fine job," Con stated succinctly.

Laith walked past Con and Tristan on the stairs. He reached the top and then paused before he slowly turned to look at the King of Kings. "Is it that you can no' stand to see us happy?"

"I've done everything to make sure each of you have a place to call your own, a home where you can be yourselves," Con answered.

"But no' to be happy?"

Con's black gaze was penetrating. "When was the last

time you were truly, utterly happy, Laith? I can name mine. When my Golds were still here, when I could stand atop the mountains and see dragons in every direction. No female, no matter how beautiful, will ever fill that hole inside me."

"And you want each of us to feel the same," Laith said as he faced Con. "I feel the loss of my Blacks every second of every day. Nothing will ever change that. I was in agreement after what happened with Ulrik's woman no' to allow a human close. None of us balked against the magic we used to block ourselves from feeling anything. But that spell was broken. No one knows how or why, but you can no' stop the fact that the Kings are mating again."

Con's eyes widened in surprise. "Is that what you think? That I doona want you to have mates?"

"Shall I remind you what you did to Kellan and Denae? What about Kiril and Shara?"

"I'm King of Kings, Laith. Part of that job is to ensure each of you make the right decisions whether those decisions match what you want or not."

Laith took a step toward Con, fury building rapidly. "I'm no' a child to be ordered about by a controlling parent. I'm a Dragon King! I didna earn that position lightly."

"Enough! Both of you," Tristan said. He walked past Con and went to Laith and took him by the arm. "Come. You need to calm down."

Laith didn't want to let it go. He wanted to hit something, preferably Con, but it wouldn't do any good. Like Tristan said, he needed to calm himself. He was about to turn away when he spotted Fallon suddenly appear at the base of the stairs. He met Fallon's troubled gaze.

"We've got a problem," Fallon said tensely.

Con spun around to Fallon. "What is it?"

"Hayden and I scouted around Iona's cottage. We hadna

gotten far when we felt magic—dragon and Dark Fae mixed."

"No' again," Con murmured.

Laith hurried down the steps. "Where?"

"In a grove of trees near the cottage," Fallon explained. "Whoever was there had direct sight through the window to the living area and the kitchen."

Laith didn't need to hear more. "Take me to Iona."

"No' yet," Con said.

That was the last straw for Laith. He jerked his head to Con. "I'm going."

"Listen," Con said calmly as he removed first one gold dragon head cuff link and then the other before he rolled up the sleeves of his dress shirt to his elbows. He started down the stairs, a muscle jumping in his jaw. "Allow Hayden and Isla to watch over Iona. The person observing Iona willna ever see them if Isla can protect Iona and the cottage with spells."

Laith knew he was reacting with emotion instead of looking at it with cold, calculating strategy as Con did everything. He kept silent, waiting for Con to continue.

"Hayden and Isla willna be alone. Larena and I will be helping as well," Fallon interjected.

Con inclined his head. "As Hayden has brought Iona into the MacLeod fold, I'm no' surprised. We appreciate it. That will be three Warriors and one Druid protecting Iona on Campbell land. We're stronger on Dreagan. We'll patrol the border and the air."

"And corner the bastard," Laith said as he realized what Con planned.

Tristan's smile was slow as he rubbed his hands together. "The Kings and Warriors fighting together again. I like this."

Laith should feel better about the entire thing, but there

was something still bothering him. He looked at Fallon and asked, "Was the magic strong?"

"Verra," Fallon answered. "He had been there just hours before."

"Look by the waterfall," Laith said, a sinking feeling in his gut. "Tell me if the magic is there as well."

Fallon disappeared instantly. Laith closed his eyes, praying he was wrong.

"Laith?" Con questioned.

He held up his hand to Con and Tristan, letting them know to wait.

Not a minute later Fallon reappeared. "I found a spot. He was there. How did you know?"

"Aye?" Con asked in a hard tone. "How did you know?"

Laith opened his eyes and raked a hand through his hair as he began to pace the area. "Because Iona and I were there for several hours before I brought her here."

"Shite," Tristan mumbled.

"We were being watched, and I didna know it!" Laith was furious—with himself and the situation. "I should've known."

Fallon widened his stance as he crossed his arms over his chest. "Hard to know you're being watched when magic is used."

"Dragon magic," Laith said. "I should've known. I assumed because the border onto Dreagan was being guarded that Iona was safe."

Tristan pulled his long hair into his hand at the base of his neck and tied it off with a strip of leather. "They could've taken one or both of you."

"They were observing," Con said. "They were watching to see how close a King was with Iona. And they saw what they needed."

Laith didn't need to be reminded. It sickened him to

know someone watched them, saw Iona naked and screaming. That was for his eyes only. Then he remembered what had happened when they were leaving.

"Iona's camera case was in a different spot than where she thought she left it. She said that's been happening a lot lately with her misplacing things, but she thought she was just being forgetful."

"Which means whoever this asshole is, he's going through her things," Fallon said.

Con descended the stairs to stand beside Fallon. "Return to Hayden and fill him in. Set up a perimeter around the cottage as wide as you can. Isla's magic is powerful, but it willna hold up against what'll be coming."

"Then we'll need more Druids," Fallon said with a smirk.

Laith called Fallon's name before he could teleport away. "If we were being watched, then that means the jerk heard our conversations."

Con raised a brow. "I suppose you have a plan?"

"Aye," Laith stated. "I was to meet Iona at midnight at the waterfall. She wants to see what she's protecting, and I promised to show her. We carry through with that plan. If he's watching, he'll be there. We catch him then."

Con smiled coldly. "I like it."

"I do too," Tristan chimed in.

Laith's gaze snapped to Con, that sinking feeling returning tenfold. "I'll retrace my steps with Iona and see if I can detect anything."

"I hate these buggers," Tristan replied angrily as he walked in the opposite direction. "I'll start searching the boundary."

"I've alerted the others on patrol," Con called. He waited until Tristan and Laith were gone before he looked at Fallon. "How many of the Warriors do you think you can get here?"

"All of them," Fallon said. "What are you no' telling me?"

"The mix of dragon and Dark Fae magic has never been done, but this is the second occurrence in a few days. The main reason it's no' been done is that no Dragon King would ever associate with a Dark Fae."

Fallon's green eyes narrowed a fraction. "Phelan told us about Kiril and Shara. That was a Dragon King mixing with a Dark Fae."

"Shara chose her side. She was then able to throw off the mantle of a Dark Fae and become Light. Associate might no' have been the right word. The fact is, every King fought against the Fae."

"Every King?" Fallon asked.

Con held out his hand and opened his fingers to see the cuff links. "You lead the Warriors, Fallon. No one else who is in our position understands the decisions we have to make."

"Or the weight of those decisions," Fallon agreed.

"Do you have regrets?"

"All the time. I'm no' perfect. None of us are. My men understand that."

Con put the cuff links in his pocket. "I have just one regret that haunts me every day. For ages we went about our lives without a worry. As technology increased we took precautions, but we were spelled to ensure that none of us would ever again be swayed by a human. That spell was broken. I still doona know how, and nothing I've done has been able to put that spell back into place. Since then, humans and the Dark Fae have stepped forward to show us they are actively trying to expose us to the world."

"You've fought the Dark Fae before. Do it again."

"It's easier than that. I know who is pulling the strings. That's my regret, Fallon. I could've prevented this from happening if I had just killed him instead of banishing him."

Fallon briefly closed his eyes. "Ulrik. Are you sure it's him?"

"He told me he would get his revenge."

"So kill him if that's what it takes."

Con smiled tightly. "I doona have the backing of all the Kings. If I do it now, it'll divide us."

"And if it isna Ulrik pulling the strings then you've just given everything to your enemy," Fallon said with a nod.

"It has to be Ulrik. There isna another Dragon King out there, and that's what it would take to use our magic since there are no other dragons about."

"But you took Ulrik's magic," Fallon said in confusion.

"Exactly. If he somehow got it back, then the longer I wait to kill him, the more damage he can do."

Fallon let out a long breath. "So you're going to kill the man you considered a brother."

"What choice do I have?" Con asked.

"You doona. You're doing it for the sake of the Dragon Kings."

That's the reason Con would give the others, and for now, that's the only reason that would count.

He wasn't surprised when the mobile rang. He had been expecting the call for a few hours. "Yes?" he answered, careful to put his British accent in place.

"Sir, she went to Dreagan, just as you said they would bring her," came the man's voice on the other end of the line. "She also had sex with one of them."

"Who?" he demanded.

"Laith."

He smiled and sat up from the lounger in his office. Anticipation pushed him as he walked to his desk and hit a button on his laptop. The screensaver disappeared to show a bar of progression loading.

"Did you go with her to Dreagan?"

There was a slight pause. "I got fifty feet onto the property and one of them began looking for me. I remained on the border."

"I needed you inside to hear their conversations," he said tightly.

"Had I proceeded, they would've found me out. Whatever magic is being used to hide me wasn't working with them."

"But no one else has discovered you yet?" he asked.

The merc laughed. "No. I've been able to move about freely. Iona has some company, however."

That got his attention. "Who?"

"I don't know who they are, but they aren't Dragon Kings. They are able to use magic. There are two men and a woman, and they disappeared from Dreagan much like the Fae do."

"Warriors," he said with distaste. "I should've known Con would bring them in."

The Australian made a sound. "I'm almost back to Campbell land."

"Be careful. It willna . . . it won't take them long to discover magic was used. The Warriors can sense magic, so keep your distance."

"And Iona Campbell?"

"As long as she has her camera with her, I'll get what I need. Remain and watch, but don't be caught. I want a report of what the Warriors and Kings do in the morning."

He disconnected the call and waited until the first picture from Iona's camera came through. It was of inside Dreagan Manor. With the right technology and people, he could get everything he wanted without much effort.

"So close now," he mumbled to himself.

CHAPTER
THIRTY-TWO

As soon as word spread to all the Dragon Kings that an enemy wasn't just closing in, but had targeted Iona, everyone went into action.

When the last visitor collected their newly purchased whisky and headed out of the shop, Cassie closed and locked the door behind them. Employees were sent home early, and she spotted Rhys walking through the buildings to make sure everyone was gone. He was on his way back to the manor when Cassie joined him.

"I just got off a call with Lily. I still think she sounds frightened, but she assures me she's doing good."

Rhys nodded absently. "That's nice. You do realize my decision had nothing to do with Lily. It was simply a matter of a human who worked for us was in trouble."

"I didn't ask for an explanation." She wondered why he was lying, but she also knew the worst thing she could do was point that out.

"It doesna matter. I know what everyone is thinking, and they're wrong. Lily means nothing to me."

Cassie cut her eyes to him to see his jaw clenched. The fact Rhys had chosen to shift into a human—never to be able to return to his true form—because Lily had been in danger was telling. "I didn't ask if she did, and it's rather offensive that you would say such a thing. What if she heard?"

Rhys halted so quickly she had taken a couple of steps before she realized it. Cassie turned and found his aqua gaze narrowed dangerously on her.

But Cassie wasn't cowed, not after being mated to her own King. "Lily is a kind soul, Rhys. She's gentle and shy, and I fear there is something in her past that has turned her the way she is."

"I know." He said the words barely above a whisper, his gaze moving to the ground.

"I know Lily has to mean something for you to give up your true form," she said carefully.

His shoulders dropped and he ran a hand down his face, a haggard expression taking him. "As soon as I heard that it was Lily in trouble, I shifted before I even had time to realize what I was doing."

Cassie knew what that meant, but she also knew Rhys wouldn't want to acknowledge it or hear it, so she kept silent. She adored Rhys. He was fun and easygoing until someone threatened those he cared about. Then he was a beast, a feral animal who reacted instantly.

But he also wasn't right for Lily. Rhys was used to fast women. Lily was the exact opposite, and no matter what Rhys might feel, Cassie didn't think anything could come of it. Lily was just too timid.

Rhys looked to the sky. "I'll never fly again. It's only been a few hours, but I crave it like never before." He returned his gaze to her. "I wonder if that's how Ulrik feels."

"I don't know Ulrik, and I don't want to know him. It doesn't matter if you can shift. You can still use your magic, and you are still a Dragon King."

He looked away, disgust turning the corners of his lips down. "Of course it matters if I can no' shift."

She opened her mouth to call him back as Rhys walked off, but a large hand entwined with hers. She looked up at Hal and sighed. "Did you hear all of that?"

"I did," he said with a slight nod as he watched Rhys. "No other King readied to rush to Lily's side as Rhys did. He has no idea what that means. Or perhaps he does and just isna ready to admit it even to himself."

Cassie rested her head on Hal's chest. "I think he does, but I think he's doing the right thing in not admitting it."

"You doona believe Lily is the one for him?"

"Actually, I think she would do him a world of good. It's that I don't think Rhys is the right one for Lily. She's too shy, and she's not like the women he usually gravitates to."

Hal put a finger beneath her chin and lifted her face to him. "Have you ever considered that he chooses those other women on purpose?"

"Because he likes their blatant sexuality? Because he likes how their clothes barely cover them?" she said, distaste dripping from every word.

Hal smiled and kissed the tip of her nose. "There is much you doona understand about men, my love."

"Explain it to me then."

He turned her so that she stood before him, their bodies pressed tight. "I'd rather spend my time kissing you from head to feet, lingering in the middle."

Cassie brought his head down for a kiss. Hal always did know what to say to make her melt. Unfortunately, there wasn't time for a dalliance of any kind.

"Damn," Hal said with a groan as he ended the kiss. He smoothed her hair away from her face. "I have to go."

"I know. Be careful."

It wasn't the first time she had said those words, but it

was the first time she truly meant them. After Rhys was hit with dragon magic, every mate was on edge that the same could happen to her King.

Being a mate to a Dragon King meant that their mortal lives became immortal, to live as long as her King did. Since the only way a Dragon King died was by the hands of another Dragon King, it wasn't much of a worry.

Not so anymore. What Rhys had been going through brought it home to Cassie, Elena, Jane, Denae, and Sammi. Shara was the only nonhuman, but no one was sure how it would work since, as a Fae, Shara lived an extremely long life anyway.

Cassie held Hal a little tighter before she released him. He walked into the side entrance of the mountain, but paused to give her one last wave. She returned it, keeping her smile in place until he was out of sight. With dread weighing her down, Cassie walked to the manor where the other mates gathered to wait out the long, dark night.

Midnight didn't feel as free and magical as it had the night before. Now, it felt deadly and scary. Iona hated the fear that made her jump at every sound in the forest now. She adjusted the strap of her camera case and gripped it tighter. She had walked the woods dozens of times without a worry. How many times had she been watched? How many times had she walked past him?

Worse, how many times had he been in the cottage while she slept?

It was apparent that the items she thought she'd misplaced or forgotten that she'd moved had been touched by this unknown foe. It sickened her, but that emotion soon turned to anger. What gave anyone the right to trespass on her land, to come into her cottage?

And all because she bordered Dreagan.

As far as the people of the village knew, they were lucky

to be near such a famous distillery that brought in millions of dollars in tourist revenue each year.

None knew the truth about Dreagan. The few who did were either working to protect the legendary secret—or trying to expose it.

As Iona walked, she tried to think why anyone would want to expose Dreagan. It wouldn't give this hidden enemy any control over the Dragon Kings. If anything, it would turn the Kings' full fury on their nemesis. The entire world would want a piece of the Kings, whether it was to study them, use them for magic, or try to control their power.

No good could come out of revealing the Dragon Kings. Unless . . .

Iona stopped and put her hand on a tree as the world began to spin. She blinked into the dark, thankful that the moon was full and shed enough light that she didn't need a flashlight. She licked her lips and looked up at the sky through the thick limbs of the trees. Dragon magic had been used, and yet Fallon said none of the Kings at Dreagan were a part of it. Iona knew of only one other Dragon King—Ulrik.

If he'd had his magic returned somehow, and he was the one behind this, then it was perfectly clear what his motives were. Unmasking the Dragon Kings would return the world to the war that once raged between humans and the Kings.

The Dragon Kings wouldn't stand by and be taken. They would fight, which would only spur the war. Iona hadn't seen a dragon or witnessed the power of the Kings, but if the Warriors were any indication, the Kings could rid the Earth of every human.

There would then be nothing to stop the dragons from returning.

Iona took a deep breath and continued on to the waterfall. As soon as Hayden told her she would be meeting Laith as planned, she watched the clock, the hours drifting slowly by. Mostly because she would be with Laith again, but there was also the excitement of getting to see Laith as a dragon. That overshadowed everything, even the fact that she was going to get to see what the Campbells had been guarding.

Even though Iona knew she wasn't alone in the forest because the Warriors surrounded her, she was still shaken at the thought of someone spying on her. No one needed to tell her that meant her hours with Laith at the waterfall had been observed.

Iona glanced around, trying to find a glimpse of the Warriors and found nothing. They were good at remaining hidden, especially Larena. She was Fallon's wife and the only female Warrior. Her power was becoming invisible—literally.

The plan was for Larena to remain near Iona at all times until Iona was with Laith. A second Druid named Aisley arrived with the other Warriors teleported in by Fallon. Aisley was beautiful with her black hair and fawn-colored eyes. There hadn't been time for much talking as the Warriors took their places, and Isla and Aisley quickly hid themselves to do their magic.

Iona briefly spotted the Warrior Ian, who was the twin to Tristan, before he vanished in the forest. She had been so startled by him that, at first, she thought he was Tristan they looked so alike.

She couldn't wait to learn more about the Warriors, Druids, Fae, and Dragon Kings. For eight years as a little girl, she had been a part of a world without even knowing it. Her mother certainly hadn't. It explained why her father hadn't come after them himself.

It still hurt, but Iona understood. Now she could forgive him. Guarding such a secret wasn't an easy burden to take on. It was dangerous and full of secrets, and yet she embraced it.

Iona heard the waterfall and lengthened her strides to hurry and reach it. It wasn't full of childhood memories anymore. Now there were new memories, memories of sighs and screams of pleasure. She smiled just thinking about it.

That smile widened when she came to the pool and watched the moon reflected in the ever-moving water. Suddenly, the moon was blocked out in the reflection of the pool. Iona's head jerked up to the dark sky. She searched around her, turning this way and that. Then she spotted the dark shape. It was huge, even so high up in the sky.

The dragon tilted one wing and swung around to fly back low over her. There was a deep whoosh as the dragon's wing beat, sending her hair flying in her face.

She couldn't take her eyes off him. He gracefully landed at the top of the waterfall and tucked his large wings against him. With the moonlight shining upon him, Iona saw the jet black scales. A row of bony plates ran from the base of his skull to the dragon's shoulders. His tail flicked and settled behind him, splashing water up so high even she could see it.

So this was Laith. No wonder everyone was worried about her reaction. He was . . . terrifying. If she didn't know the man, she would certainly run away. But she did know the man. She knew his voice, his smile, and his touch.

Her hand shook as she lifted it and motioned for Laith to come to her. He leapt into the air, his wings spread, and glided down to land behind her. Iona followed his progression, and took a step back when she saw him up close. He was alarmingly large and frightening magnificent.

Laith extended a muscular limb—with four splayed digits that had very long black talons—before her. Deep purple dragon eyes blinked at her before he motioned to his back with his head.

"Get on," Larena's disembodied voice whispered in her ear. "Laith won't drop you."

With Laith watching closely, Iona knew whatever her decision was would affect her future with him. It was the perfect time for her to turn away as she normally would, to forget him and whatever feelings she was developing.

It was the safe thing to do.

Iona put her foot on Laith's limb and climbed up.

CHAPTER
THIRTY-THREE

A puff of breath left Iona when she settled on Laith's back at the base of his neck. She gripped the bony plate nearest her to have something to hold onto and was amazed it was as warm as his scales.

She buzzed with excitement and a thread of fear when Laith unfurled his wings. There was a brief pause before they were suddenly in the air.

Iona gasped, a cry of fright lodged in her throat. She began to shake and held Laith so tight her fingers began to go numb. She was hyperventilating, her gaze locked on Laith's black scales in front of her. Her legs gripped him until her muscles were trembling from the exertion, but she wanted to be prepared if she fell.

It took her a long time to realize that Laith was flying just atop the trees in a straight line. She blinked and glanced away from his scales to see the land below. Then she felt the wind upon her face.

Iona gradually relaxed her hold and simply enjoyed the fact she was atop a dragon flying over Scotland. She felt the subtle shift in Laith's muscles beneath her legs every time his wings moved. The steady beat from his wings' flapping was gentle and comforting. Ahead, she glimpsed Dreagan Manor, but Laith altered his course slightly, making a wide circle to take them back to the waterfall.

For the first time in her life, Iona wanted to experience something with her own eyes instead of through the lens of her camera. Then there was the fact that she didn't risk taking a picture for fear of Laith being in it. She would love to have a picture of him in dragon form, but she wouldn't dare attempt it for fear of it accidentally landing in the wrong hands.

From her vantage point atop Laith, the world looked greener, more peaceful, and infinitely more beautiful. It was no wonder the Kings preferred to be in their true forms. Iona was being given a rare gift, one that she would never forget.

The closer they got to the waterfall, the lower Laith flew. Iona glanced behind them to see the trees moving because he was hitting them as he flew past. When she turned back around, she caught sight of the waterfall. It was pretty from the ground, but from the air, it was spectacular.

The water tumbled down the sheer face of the cliff to crash upon boulders forming white foam. It then flowed into the calm pool of water. Iona spotted the semicircle of boulders where she and Laith had made love earlier. Then her eyes moved to the start of the stream and followed it until it disappeared into the trees.

Iona was mesmerized, captivated. How many times had her father lain near the waterfall, his gaze on the sky as he hoped to see one of the Dragon Kings? She knew she would be here most nights from now on. How could she not after such an experience?

She looked below her as Laith flew to the waterfall, close enough that water splashed on her jeans. Iona was smiling, but it froze in place when she saw it.

The spot the Campbells had protected for generations

was visible in the moonlight upon the granite. It was a seven-pointed star. It was beautiful and eerie all at the same time.

Iona swallowed hard, reminded of what the humans had done to the Dragon Kings—and the Kings' retaliation.

Laith landed atop the waterfall and carefully tucked his wings against him. He did his best not to look to his right where the unknown observer stood at the bottom of the waterfall.

The night had gone better than expected. In truth, he thought Iona might run from him when he first appeared, and she nearly had. Her fear had been evident. Yet she had motioned him to come to her and willingly climbed upon his back.

Her fear doubled once he was in the air. Laith thought for sure that she would never relax. It's why he decided to fly around for a bit to ease her discomfort, which seemed to work since she finally loosened up and enjoyed the ride.

If only he could have ended things there. He could practically feel her joy and happiness right up until he flew over the place where they had killed Ulrik's woman. He couldn't even remember her name, if he had ever known it. She had always been Ulrik's woman, and that's how she would always be remembered.

As soon as Iona slid off him, Laith shifted back into a man as he watched her stand next to the septagram that was a reminder of their broken vow.

Iona looked up at him somberly. "Why can't I see it during the day?"

"We see it always. In the sunlight it shines bright red, just as it did when her blood spilled out of her. At night, it shines white. A constant reminder," he answered.

"Can anyone else see this?"

"You see it because you're a Campbell. We see it because we're Dragon Kings, but others, nay, they'll never see it—day or night."

"That's a relief," she said with a soft sigh.

Laith wanted to go to her, to pull her against him and feel her warmth. He desperately wanted her arms around him, to have her lean on him. But he gave her the time he knew she needed.

"Does Ulrik know of this place?" she asked.

Laith frowned and spotted a bronze dragon in the distance. Kellan. Not far behind him was Hal, his green scales shining beneath the light of the full moon. Did Ulrik know? Laith assumed he did, but what if he didn't? "I doona know. Why? What are you thinking?"

"It's probably nothing." She tucked her hair behind her ear and faced him. "I mean, I just learned of you and your history."

If there was one thing Laith knew about Iona it was that she was intelligent. "Tell me," he urged.

"Why would anyone want to reveal your existence to the world? What would they gain? You all are too powerful to be controlled. They could try and kill you, I suppose."

Laith shook his head. "They can try, but the only way for a King to be killed is by another King."

"Then there really is only one thing to be gained."

He was wholly intrigued now. "What?"

"The return of the war between the humans and dragons."

Laith ran a hand through his hair. "Aye. We've come to the same conclusion, which leads us back to Ulrik. The Dark Fae gain nothing. They feed off the souls of humans, so if the humans are gone, what do they have?"

"That doesn't make sense," she said with a frown. "I thought I had it figured out."

"I wish you had. We've gone round and round with this

for months with no answer." He saw her camera case resting against her hip. "You know the pictures you took tonight will have to be erased."

Her forehead furrowed in confusion. "I don't know what you're talking about. I didn't take the camera out."

"I heard the shutter, Iona."

"I didn't take pictures," she said more forcefully.

Laith glanced at the camera bag again. "You're never without it."

She looked at him askance, her hand protectively on the bag. "No. Why would I? It's my livelihood."

"Did you buy the camera?"

"It was a gift."

He looked away, praying he was wrong. "Will you take it off and leave it here?"

"Are you nuts? This is a five-thousand-dollar camera."

"Iona," he said softly. "If you were no' taking pictures, then how was the shutter going off?"

She removed the strap from her shoulder and cradled the bag against her. "I didn't take any pictures."

"I believe you." Laith walked to her and put his hands atop hers. "You'll get the camera back. I give you my word. I just want someone to take a look at it and make sure it hasna been tampered with."

Several tense moments went by before Iona reluctantly handed him the bag. Laith set it carefully down beside him. When he straightened and saw Iona's broken expression, he pulled her against him.

The knot in his chest loosened when her arms wrapped around him and she buried her face in his neck. He closed his eyes and held her tighter as he moved his face so his mouth was near her ear.

"Listen carefully," Laith whispered. "The trap has worked. He's been watching. The others are closing in on him now."

"What if they don't catch him?"

Laith opened his eyes as he leaned back to look into her dark brown depths. "Then I will."

"Do your enemies know who they're messing with?" she asked with a small smile.

"They're finding out." He cupped her face. "Be ready. It's about to happen."

No sooner were the words out of his mouth than six Warriors surrounded the tree where the culprit hid. Aisley stood beside Isla, the two surrounded by Phelan and Hayden as they poured their magic atop the man, breaking through his spell until he was visible.

"I've got her," Larena said to Laith, her iridescent Warrior skin shimmering in the moonlight.

Laith gave a nod to Iona and took a running leap off the waterfall, shifting into a dragon as he did. He used his dragon magic of paralyzing gas to stop their foe before he could get away. A flash of jade scales could be seen as Warrick moved from the right out of the trees. From the left was Ryder, his smoke-colored scales muted in the darkness.

"Guess you'll be staying for a wee bit," Hayden said as he glared at the man lying unmoving on the ground.

Con stepped from the trees in only a pair of jeans after having shifted back into human form. He swiped a hand through his blond hair and sneered down at the intruder. "Let's make sure there're no poison pills hidden in your teeth."

Laith watched as Con and Fallon searched the man's mouth and found nothing. Con stood and dusted off his hands as he turned away. "That was offensive."

"Con!" Aisley shouted as the man suddenly rose up and went for Con.

Laith couldn't believe the human had already broken through his magic. It wasn't possible. Nor could he use his magic again without inflicting the gas on most of the War-riors in the process. Laith shifted into a human and lunged forward, but Con had already pivoted back around, his hand on the man's throat. Suddenly the human's eyes went wide and blood trickled from the corner of the man's mouth. Every eye turned to Rhi who stood behind the human, her sword buried so deep in the human that the tip touched Con's chest.

"Rhi," Con stated angrily.

She yanked her sword out and flicked off the blood as the man crumpled to the ground.

"We needed to question him," Phelan said as he stalked to Rhi. "And where the hell have you been?"

Rhi's silver gaze slid to Phelan. "I've been around, and trust me when I say you're better off not talking to him."

"We'll never know that now," Laith said, not hiding his anger. "We needed to know why he's been watching Iona."

Rhi bent and wiped her sword on the mortal's black shirt before she sheathed the blade at her back. "You don't need him for that. I can tell you."

"So tell us," Con said casually.

Too casually, Laith thought. The hatred between Rhi and Con had always been deep, but it was different now. There was something else added to the mix—resentment perhaps?

Rhi turned her head and looked over her shoulder up at the waterfall. "Iona is collecting data." Rhi's gaze returned to Con. "On Dreagan."

CHAPTER
THIRTY-FOUR

Iona wished she could hear and see what was going on. All she could make out from her vantage point atop the waterfall was a bit of movement. She knew where Laith was because he hadn't moved from his spot once he had shifted to human.

"We're wanted," Larena said as she came to stand beside Iona, nude.

Iona looked at the golden-haired Warrior, who was dramatic with her goddess released, and stunning as a woman. Larena's tight expression caused concern however. "What's going on?"

"The sooner I get you down, the sooner you find out."

"Me? How do you know?" she demanded.

Larena's smoky blue eyes shifted to her. "I'm a Warrior, Iona. My senses—sight, smell, and hearing—are five times what yours are."

"So you can hear them talking?"

"I can," Larena said softly.

Iona glanced at Laith to see him looking up at her. "Then tell me what is being said."

Larena shook her head as her skin began to turn iridescent with the release of her goddess. "Hold on tight."

"Hold on?" Iona repeated even as she locked an arm around Larena's shoulders.

She didn't have a chance to voice anything more as Larena jumped from the cliff. A scream never made it past Iona's lips as her heart lodged in her throat.

As soon as Larena landed them, Iona pushed away from her. "Don't do that to me again without more warning."

"Sorry," Larena said and walked to stand beside Fallon.

Iona saw Fallon hand a bundle of clothes to Larena, who disappeared behind some trees to change. With her hands on her knees, Iona bent over to calm her racing heart.

After flying atop Laith and jumping off the cliff, Iona had her fill of excitement for the next few months. What could be so important that Larena had to bring her down to the others so quickly?

That's when Iona realized how quiet everyone was. She lifted her head and looked at Laith, in all his naked glory with his dragon tat on his back, who was glaring at Con. Iona straightened when she caught sight of the black-haired woman from the pub. The Fae, Rhi.

Iona glanced at Hayden to see he was slowly making his way to her, as was Isla. The other two dragons suddenly shifted into human form, but remained where they were. If she hadn't known who the Kings were, she would at one glance of their naked bodies and the amazing dragon tats that graced them.

She couldn't stand the wait or the standoff that appeared to be happening. Iona cleared her throat, a frown forming when she saw the man lying unmoving at Con's feet. "What's going on?"

"Do you know this man?" Con asked, pointing to the male at his feet without taking his gaze from Laith.

Iona couldn't see his face. She started to go to the man when Hayden's hand on her arm stopped her. Her head swiveled to Hayden. "I can't answer without having a look." Hayden grudgingly released her. Iona's skin prickled with the intensity of the situation. Once she reached the man, she bent over him, but couldn't see in the darkness. "I need light."

Instantly Hayden was at her side, a large ball of fire held over her in his hand. She gave him a nod of thanks, and swallowed hard when she saw his concerned gaze on Con.

Iona returned her attention to the man. She rolled him onto his back and saw the dark stain on the front of his black shirt. After a careful look at his face, she stood. "I've never seen him before. Is he the one who's been watching me?"

"Aye," Hayden said and put out the flames in his palm.

"Someone tell me what is going on," Iona demanded.

Laith finally looked at her. "I need your camera."

"Why?"

"Because we want to see what pictures you've been taking," Con said.

Laith ignored Con and walked to her. "Will you allow me to look at your camera?"

She wanted to tell them no, because that camera was an extension of her. She couldn't stand the thought of someone else touching it that didn't know its intricacies. But she also realized it was important. Laith already claimed that he heard her shutter, yet she knew for a fact she hadn't taken any pictures.

Iona held his gaze. "I never took the camera out of the bag tonight."

"We'll be able to tell as soon as we look at the pictures," Laith said.

"You think I'm betraying you."

Laith gave a shake of his head. "I doona, but I have to prove that. Right now, it appears someone was collecting data on us."

"Through me?" she asked with a snort. "I don't like being used. I especially don't like being a pawn to be blamed for a betrayal. Take the camera. I left it atop the waterfall."

"It's here," Larena said as she stepped out of the trees, the camera bag hanging from her hand.

Con took the bag from Larena. "We need to analyze this."

"I agree," Laith said. "We do it here though."

Con bowed his head in agreement. He held out the bag and said, "Ryder."

Ryder walked naked through the group and grabbed the bag.

He had taken two steps when Hayden said, "I'd like to have Evie and Gwynn here to help."

"I'll retrieve them," Fallon said and vanished.

Iona watched Ryder head back toward the cottage with her camera. "I've never been without it."

"It'll be fine," Laith said and put his hand on her lower back, guiding her to follow Ryder.

If she hadn't been so distressed at what was happening, she would've been more shocked at the fact there were three naked men around.

Iona walked past Con as he turned to Rhi. She spotted his dragon tattoo on his back, the same as Laith's. But that's where the similarities stopped. Con's dragon was lying down, his wings spread, whereas Laith's dragon tat had it standing on its hind legs.

She halted beside Con and waited for him to acknowledge her. She lifted a brow when he let out a string of curses as Rhi vanished. Iona then asked him, "You think I'm the one behind this, right? What would I have to gain?"

"What does any human have to gain?" he asked sharply.

"Exactly. I knew nothing of your existence until recently, but even then I've seen the power you have. It would be ludicrous for me to even attempt to do anything against either the Dragon Kings or the Warriors. I understand you have something precious to protect, but if you can't see I'm not your enemy, then it won't be long until everyone is your enemy."

She left Laith standing with Con and started walking to the cottage. The day began gloriously and ended appallingly. The hours in Laith's arms were ruined by the fact that some considered her a potential enemy.

"I couldn't have said it better," Isla said as she matched Iona's steps. "The Kings are our allies, but Con can be narrow-minded at times."

"I would probably be as well." Iona smiled at Isla's shocked expression. "Put yourself in their shoes. It can't have been easy."

Isla sidestepped a fallen tree. "I imagine our ancestors felt the same way when it came to the Kings. Each side will have a story to pull the heartstrings. Neither is right, but neither is wrong. The Kings blame the humans for the betrayal, but what pushed Ulrik's woman to betray him?"

"It could've been anything. Or nothing."

"It was somebody, I grant you that."

They walked the rest of the way in silence. Halfway back to the cottage, Iona looked over her shoulder to see Laith beside Warrick with Con two steps behind them. There was no sign of Rhi or any Warriors.

"Hayden and the others are going to keep watch," Isla told her. "Everyone is here to ensure your safety."

"Unless I'm deemed an enemy."

Isla's lips flattened. "You say you didn't take any pictures. Laith believes. Hayden and I believe you."

"How do you know Hayden believes me?"

Isla's smile was full of happiness and desire. "Because

when two people are in love, they come to understand how the other thinks."

Love. That word seemed to come up a lot of late, and Iona wasn't sure how she felt about it anymore. Especially since every time someone said the word, she immediately thought of Laith.

When Iona reached the cottage, she stepped inside and immediately put on the coffeemaker. She was exhausted—both mentally and physically—and she suspected she was going to need to be on her toes when it came to Con. The coffee hadn't even begun to brew when Hayden opened the front door and walked in, followed by two women and Fallon.

"The stones are loud here," said the first woman. She had long, curly brown hair and blue eyes. Her lids closed over her eyes as she lifted her face as if listening.

Isla leaned close and said, "If a Druid has strong magic, then we can also have specialties. For Evie, she can hear the stones. They communicate and do her bidding."

"Do her bidding?" Iona repeated in surprise.

Evie's eyes opened and she smiled at Iona. "Yes. I can have them move or form in any shape that I desire. It's nice to meet you, Iona. You're all that's being talked about at the castle."

Iona liked Evie immediately. There was something kind about her that seemed to draw everyone. "So you're good with electronics?"

"I used to be a software programmer," Evie said in a soft Scottish brogue. "But I'm not the only one good at fiddling with computers. Gwynn has special skills as a hacker."

Iona's gaze moved to the next woman who had coal black hair and eyes the color of violets.

Gwynn's smile was radiant as she stepped forward. "Hello, Iona."

She was taken aback at the American accent. "Where are you from?"

"Texas," Gwynn said with a grin. She then looked around. "Where should we set up?"

Ryder walked out of her father's office wearing a pair of jeans and opened John's laptop on the oval dining table. "Right here."

Iona remained in the kitchen and watched as Gwynn and Evie sat down and pulled out laptops she hadn't even realized they had. A moment later and Ryder was inspecting her camera.

It was difficult for Iona to watch. She kept telling herself it was just a piece of equipment, that it could be replaced, but that camera hadn't just been a gift, it had become the one constant in her life she could trust.

The small cottage felt even tinier as Laith, Warrick, and Con stood in the living room watching the three at the table intently. Someone had supplied jeans for Laith and Warrick as well. Iona's gaze met Laith's. She tried to read his expression, but couldn't tell anything. He was closed off as he had never been before.

Ryder hooked up her camera to the laptop and began to scroll through the pictures. "There are pictures of Dreagan from the skies. You can even get a glimpse of Laith in dragon form."

Iona's stomach fell to her feet. How was she ever going to convince them she hadn't taken the pictures now? And how were the pictures taken if she wasn't the one snapping the button?

"They're fuzzy," Gwynn pointed out.

Evie tilted her head. "And not level."

Ryder leaned back and looked at Iona. "No' the types of pictures Iona takes."

She held her breath as Con leaned over Ryder to look

closer at the pictures. He finally straightened and sighed. "Nay. Those were no' taken by Iona."

Her knees grew so weak from relief that she almost crumpled to the floor. She wanted to celebrate, but the crisis was far from over. Though things surely couldn't get any worse.

Ryder continued to scroll through the pictures. He let out a curse that had every eye turning to him. "There's a shot of the doorway."

The doorway Iona was supposed to protect.

The doorway that was to remain secret.

The doorway that was an unrestricted way onto Dreagan.

Things had gotten infinitely worse.

CHAPTER
THIRTY-FIVE

Laith couldn't stop staring at the picture of the hidden doorway. It wasn't a particularly clear snap of the spot, but there was no denying it was atop the waterfall. Suddenly the picture disappeared, as did the others Ryder had downloaded. Laith could only watch as Ryder, Gwynn, and Evie frantically punched the keyboard to halt whatever was happening.

Laith glanced at Iona to see her face go pale. At least they knew she wasn't the one taking the photos. He hadn't doubted her, but Con certainly had.

"Fuck!" Ryder shouted and slammed his hands on the table, rattling the computers. He shoved his chair back and raked a hand through his short blond hair as he stood and paced.

Con's voice was calm, belying the fury shining through his black gaze, as he asked, "What happened?"

"Someone erased the pictures," Gwynn said, her head shaking as she stared at the blank screen.

Evie was still rapidly entering code. Her fingers moved so quickly that it was difficult to tell what she was typing. On the screen it looked like gibberish to Laith. Apparently it was something brilliant because Ryder stopped pacing and stood behind her chair. Both Gwynn and Ryder were staring at Evie's computer screen raptly.

Evie punched the enter key hard and sat back with a smile. "I couldn't stop them from taking the pictures, but I was able to put in a virus on the tail end of the last picture that will track where the photos are being uploaded next."

"Quick thinking," Ryder told Evie with a grin.

They all watched as the screen on Evie's computer flashed and pulled up a map of the world in black. A bright green line appeared in Scotland and then zigzagged at a rapid rate all over the world countless times.

"Well, that didna get us much," Warrick said.

Gwynn made a sound at the back of her throat. "Whoever this guy is, he's damn good. He's making it very difficult to track him. Nigh impossible for some people."

"But not us," Evie said as she flexed her fingers. "Ready?"

Ryder returned to his chair and pulled up another screen. "Count me in."

Laith didn't break their concentration to ask what they were doing as the three began typing. To his surprise, Iona came to stand beside him. She held out a mug of coffee to him. He'd rather have a bottle of whisky, but the coffee would do for the time being. Laith wrapped his arm around Iona's shoulders after he took the coffee. As she laid her head on his shoulder, he saw Con look at them out of the corner of his eye.

"I almost had them," Gwynn said with a loud sigh. She banged her hands on the keyboard in frustration.

Evie stopped typing as well. "My virus won't be detected, but it could continue to bounce off servers for days."

"Until then, we have something else to look at," Ryder said as he reached for the camera.

Laith felt Iona stiffen and decided to take her outside so she couldn't see them tampering with the camera. She didn't fight him when he walked her out the back door and sat her in one of the chairs.

"The past few days have been . . . indescribable." She wrapped her hands around her mug of coffee and looked into the distance. "I feel as if everything is out of my control."

"It is," Con said as he walked out onto the deck and closed the door behind him. "That's how most feel at any given time. I hope you doona think too badly of me for what I said earlier."

It wasn't an apology. Laith couldn't remember Con ever apologizing for anything, but it was the closest he had ever come.

Iona nudged the chair next to her with her foot and motioned to it with her hand. "Of course not. The weight of all of this must rest heavily upon you."

"It does," Con said as he sat. "It does on all the Kings' shoulders."

Laith remained by Iona's chair, his hand on her shoulder with her hair tickling the back of his hand. "I can no' help but feel that all of this was orchestrated."

"Obviously," Con said as he laced his fingers over his bare stomach.

Laith shook his head. "Nay. I mean from the time Iona got the job with the Commune to now."

"That means my bosses are part of this," Iona said, disbelief deepening her words. She set her mug on the table and looked up at Laith. "You asked about my bosses because you were suspicious. I should've been as well."

Con turned his head to Iona. "You had no reason to. They took advantage of you, but now we need to know everything you know. We need every contact you have, every e-mail."

"You'll have it. I don't like being used."

Laith fisted his other hand. "I doona take kindly to it either. They killed John. Who's to say they willna do the same to Iona now that they have the pictures and know where the doorway is located?"

Iona hated the anxiety that statement caused her. She wasn't alone anymore, though. There was Hayden and Isla and the rest of the Warriors and Druids.

Then there was Laith.

She couldn't begin to describe how it felt to have him near, to know that he would look out for her. Iona prided herself on being self-sufficient and capable of handling any situation, but nothing could have prepared her for magic, dragons, and immortality.

There was a war waging around Iona that was just getting started, but there was nothing in her years of experience that she could pull from to handle what she was experiencing and feeling. All she could do was cling to the ones who offered her safety. Namely, Laith.

"What would happen if there wasn't an heir to take over this land?" Iona asked.

A vein in Con's temple throbbed. "It would go to someone else, probably one of our enemies."

Iona reached up and covered Laith's hand that rested on her shoulder. "Then I guess it's a good thing I texted my attorney earlier to have Hayden named as my heir in case something happened to me. It should've been his anyway, right?"

"Aye, it was meant to be his," Con said with a half-smile.

Laith squeezed her shoulder. "That was clever of you."

"I'm a clever woman," she said with a smile as she looked up into Laith's gunmetal eyes.

How she loved the way his dark blond hair fell across his forehead. His locks were windblown, wild. Much like she felt. Perhaps it had something to do with her ride upon the back of a Dragon King. Whatever it was, Iona could feel that something was different about her.

Her heart accelerated when Laith's gaze lowered to her mouth and his fingers tightened slightly at her neck. Her lips parted as she hungered for his kiss. Just before Laith bent to kiss her, Con rose to his feet. Iona ducked her head, embarrassed that she had forgotten Con was even there. That's what Laith did to her. He made her disregard everyone and everything.

"Y'all are going to want to see this," Gwynn said after she threw open the back door.

Iona jumped up, her hand entwined with Laith's, and followed Con inside. She moaned in despair when she saw her beloved camera in pieces on the table.

"I can put it back together," Ryder assured her.

Laith winked at her. "I promised her a new one anyway."

"What did you find?" Con asked.

Ryder smoothed a hand over his mouth. "A new camera might be the best thing. What I found isna good. It seems someone attached a device that allows them to no' only upload any and all of Iona's pictures of their choosing, but to operate the camera themselves."

"That can't be right," Iona said in bewilderment. "I'd have known. I mean, that technology isn't even feasible."

Ryder held up the microchip as proof. "It's no' just feasible, lass, but workable."

"That's not all," Evie said, her expression as grim as her voice. "I dug through the software on the camera, and the chip was implanted when the camera was manufactured. It received an update once a year until three weeks ago when the software was upgraded twice in a fortnight."

Iona was thankful she had ahold of Laith. Otherwise she wasn't sure she could have remained standing. Was there any part of her life that hadn't been tampered with? "Right before my father was killed. The Commune gave me the camera, and that means . . . the Commune murdered him."

"We'll get revenge," Laith promised.

The room began to spin. She held his hand tighter, but still it didn't calm her racing heart. But Iona knew what would. She looked up into his eyes.

Laith was a rock, solid and sturdy. He gave her security and shelter in the tempest that continued to erupt around her. She couldn't believe that fate had delivered him in the worst sort of circumstances, but she was never more grateful than in that moment.

Gwynn lifted her hand to get everyone's attention. "Iona, I'm sorry, but I searched your laptop. I had a notion there might be something on it, and I was right."

"What now?" Iona asked no one in particular and took a deep breath as she looked to Gwynn.

Gwynn shot her a remorseful look. "There is spyware on your computer. I've dismantled it, but I don't know how long it'll take them to realize that."

"What did they see?" Warrick asked worriedly.

Gwynn shrugged helplessly. "Everything. They read every e-mail, saw every site she visited on the Internet."

"That's my private computer," Iona said weakly. "How did they get to it?"

With a stroke of a key, Gwynn pulled up the virus. "It was attached to every e-mail coming from the Commune's assistant. So if you read e-mails on your phone or another computer, they would have access."

"My mobile," Iona said and rushed to her purse. She pulled it from her purse, but it was yanked out of her hands by Laith who tossed it to the floor and stomped on it.

He shot her a crooked smile. "I owe you a new mobile as well."

Iona looked around the room. "Was nothing of my life private? Did they have their fingers in everything?"

Warrick crossed his arms over his chest and frowned. "It appears so."

Con walked to the back of the couch and braced his hands on it. "What was on your mobile, Iona?"

"Contacts, text and phone messages."

"Anything important?" Laith asked.

She started to shake her head, then stopped. "I texted Thomas MacBane the addendum to my will."

"I'm on it," Warrick said as he hurried out of the house.

Iona pulled out a chair at the table and sank into it. "This is a nightmare. I thought I had all this freedom to do whatever I wanted while having amazing assignments and getting paid an obscene amount of money to do what I love. I'd have taken the pictures whether I was paid or not."

"You know the truth now." Laith jerked his chin to the camera and computer. "Are you sure they can no' hear or see us?"

Ryder waved his hands over the parts. "I've taken care of the camera, and you smashed the mobile."

"The spyware and camera have been properly disabled on the laptop," Gwynn said.

Evie nodded. "Twice over."

"Then for the time being Iona is free of their watch," Laith said.

Con raised a blond brow. "Your point?"

"Now's the perfect time to gather all the intel on the Commune that she has."

Iona shook off her woe-is-me attitude and scooted a chair closer to Gwynn as she sat down. "Go into my e-mail. Everything will be in a file labeled Commune. Inside that file are separate files for each assignment."

A minute later and Gwynn let out a soft whistle. "There are hundreds of e-mails."

"I keep everything," Iona replied with a scrunch of her face.

Evie leaned over Gwynn's other side to look. "I'll connect the two computers and start looking through the e-mails with you."

Iona's heart pounded in her ears like a drum. Her life was being dismantled one piece at a time. What was she going to be when it was all said and done?

Laith squatted beside her and cupped her face in his hands. "Look at me. Look into my eyes. What do you see?"

"You," she said. "I see you."

"Remember that, Iona Campbell," he whispered before he kissed her.

CHAPTER
THIRTY-SIX

Fury raged through him. The Dragon Kings had meddled again, but it didn't matter. He had what he needed. The infamous doorway onto Dreagan land.

It had been a myth whispered about in dark corners, though none of those doing the whispering had any notion of what they spoke about.

But he did.

The moment mutterings reached him about a place where no magic could touch, he knew.

He looked at his chessboard and moved his rook sideways four spaces. His pieces were continuing to move, even as the Dragon Kings thought they were gaining an advantage.

There were always casualties of war. Luckily the never-ending parade of mercenaries to his door kept him in supply of men who liked to kill. As for others, he paid handsomely to get whatever he wanted for the select few who weren't already indebted to him.

Another piece on the board had fallen right into his trap as well, though Con wouldn't realize just how deep Rhys was in until it was too late.

He eyed the bishop. The next piece was coming. He could hardly contain his excitement, because when that slid into place, it would put Dreagan in check.

With a little stirring up of the Dark Fae, the Dragon Kings would have enemies attacking from both sides. He wanted to celebrate, but it was too early yet. The time would come soon enough, and the first thing he was going to do was kill Constantine. He would be King of Kings, and the other Kings would bow down to him.

Or be slain where they stood.

He could hardly wait. He rose from the couch and walked to his desk. Choosing the sixth mobile, he texted a single letter—N—and hit send.

Laith stared out the window as he held Iona. She was asleep on her feet by the time he returned to the cottage and brought her to bed. She hadn't uttered a sound, simply turned on her side and drifted off. He wished it was that easy for him, but his mind was full of all that was happening. Every time they thought they had beaten a foe, another arose. Just as Con said from the very beginning, everything pointed to Ulrik.

Ulrik must have found a Druid who was able to return enough of his dragon magic so that he could cause damage, but even that little bit was plenty to disrupt things. Rhys was case in point. Because of his injury, he was now human, unable to shift without ripping himself in two. Who would be next? Because Laith knew Ulrik wouldn't stop there. His hatred was centered on Con, but it spread to anyone who wasn't with him—which meant every Dragon King.

Then there was the Dark Fae. Of all the beings Ulrik had to have an accord with, why did it have to be them? For a King to mix his magic with the Dark Fae was . . . criminal. Then again, Ulrik hadn't been a part of the war with the Fae. He had no idea what they were capable of.

Laith knew they hadn't seen the last of the Dark Fae. Kiril had delivered a huge blow to them in Ireland, but that only meant they would strike harder the next time. Which could be at any time.

As powerful as Taraeth, King of the Darks was, he was nothing compared to his right-hand man, Balladyn. Already the Dark had taken three Kings, but had been unable to hold them. When Balladyn kidnapped Rhi, she had managed to free herself—even if she wasn't the same. When the Dark came at the Kings again, it was going to be twice as hard as before.

"You're brooding."

He looked down and found Iona's dark gaze on him. He caressed a finger down the side of her face. "Just thinking."

"Brooding. There're little lines on your brow to prove it."

That brought a smile to his lips. "Lines, huh? Should I be concerned about wrinkles?"

"Definitely." She rolled over to face him. "Did you rest at all?"

"I was with you."

She ducked her head as she yawned. "I should've stayed with the others."

"Gwynn and Evie are human, despite being magical. They needed rest as well. As soon as I brought you in here, Logan came for Gwynn and Malcolm for Evie. Ryder, on the other hand, is still working."

Iona's eyes darkened with desire. "You're in my bed."

"I am."

"With me."

"Aye." He cupped her butt and brought her against him.

Iona's hands roamed over his bare back. "Is it wrong that I don't want to think about what's going on outside my door?"

"No' at all," he murmured before he kissed her.

Desire consumed them, devoured them. Iona fumbled

with the button of his jeans while he shoved her shirt up and over her head. Laith tossed it aside and rolled her onto her back as his jeans were being tugged down his hips.

All Laith wanted was to be back inside her, to feel her tight, wet sheath surround him. The need, the yearning was more than he thought to ever experience, and yet the longer he was with Iona, the deeper the emotions and feelings became.

He unclasped her bra at the same time someone pounded on the door. Iona's body went limp as she moaned in frustration. Laith fell back on the bed and stared at the ceiling.

"We found something," Ryder said through the door.

Iona turned her head to Laith. "You should've woken me earlier. I'm not going to be able to concentrate now," she said with a wicked smile.

"You?" Laith asked. He lifted his head to look down at his swollen cock. "I need a cold shower."

Iona threw off the blanket and rolled out of bed. So much for keeping her occupied for a while. He yanked his jeans back into place and stood before he buttoned them.

Laith waited at the door for Iona to put her shirt back on and comb her fingers through her hair. They walked into the living together to find Ryder all but tackling Logan in his effort to grab the box of donuts.

"Geesh. You're as bad as Galen. Warn me next time," Logan grumbled. He then turned to Iona and smiled. "You've already met my better half, Gwynn. I'm Logan Hamilton."

Iona returned his smile. "Hi, Logan. Where is Gwynn?"

Logan's hazel gaze momentarily met Laith's before he replied, "She's still resting. I had a hell of a time getting her to stop last night. It wasna until she fell asleep typing that I was able to get her home for a wee bit."

"No' the castle?" Laith asked.

Logan shrugged and watched Ryder stuff an entire jelly

donut into his mouth. "We're close enough to the castle it doesna matter. The Druids are strengthening the protection spells. The children have already been moved there."

"Speaking of children, how is your son?"

Logan beamed like a proud father. "He's amazing. From the first moment Bran entered the world I've been astonished by him. Gwynn and I were talking about another child when all of this happened."

Laith glanced at Iona. "You know we willna let anything happen to any of the Druids or any of the children."

"I know," Logan said with a nod. "Gwynn wanted to feed Bran before she returned."

The front door opened and Malcolm walked in, raking a hand through his windblown blond hair. His blue eyes scanned the cottage before he stepped aside and Evie entered.

"There's a storm coming," Malcolm said. His gaze hardened for a moment before he touched the scars running from the left side of his face horizontally to his right side when he noticed Iona staring. He told her, "I was attacked by Warriors when I was still mortal. I'd have died if it hadna been for the Druids."

"I didn't mean to stare," Iona hurried to say.

Evie waved away her words. "He's fine, aren't you, honey?"

Laith watched as Evie rose up on her toes and pulled Malcolm's face down so she could kiss his scars. The smile on Malcolm's face transformed the Warrior, his love for Evie evident in his every action.

"I didn't mean to stare," Iona whispered again as she moved closer to Laith.

Malcolm lifted his eyes to meet Laith's. He gave a small nod, and Laith knew Malcolm wasn't upset. Laith took Iona's hand and pulled her to Ryder as he said, "Doona think twice about it."

Ryder finished off his third jelly donut then dusted off his hands and glanced at them. "It took more finesse than I've had to use in a verra long time, but I was able to trace all of the e-mails to one place—Madrid."

"That's not right," Iona said. "My bosses are all over the world, but Abby, their assistant, is based in London."

Ryder pointed to the screen of his laptop. "The proof is right there. If they lied to you about everything else, why would they no' do the same for where the assistant is?"

"Is there even an assistant?" Laith asked.

Ryder punched a few keys and a new screen popped up on the computer showing a picture of a thirtysomething attractive woman with big blue eyes and light brown hair. "There's Abigail Durham."

"Abby has a British accent," Iona said, her face mottled in confusion.

Laith asked, "So that is her? That's the assistant?"

"Yes, I've met her several times. She's delivered assignments and travel documents to my flat on occasion. We even had lunch together. She's a Londoner."

Evie pulled out the chair next to Ryder and sat as she looked at the computer. "Her address is Madrid, and has been for ten years. Did she tell you she lived in London?"

Iona was so tired of the lies, of trying to find her way through them. "Yes. We talked about neighborhoods, restaurants, and shopping. Why wouldn't she tell me she really lived in Spain?"

"Good question," Laith said. "As curious as that is, we really need to find the people behind the Commune. She'll know how to reach them."

Iona was walking to the phone in the kitchen before Laith finished. She lifted the receiver and dialed Abby's number. Iona listened to the first ring before there was a loud beep with a computerized voice that said, "We're sorry, but this number has been disconnected."

"They know we're on to them," Ryder said with a scowl. "I had a feeling."

"Which means they'll start wiping their existence," Malcolm added.

Iona touched Evie's shoulder. "Look up Paul Woods."

"Who is that?" Laith asked.

"A molecular chemist I know who works for the Commune."

Evie shook her head after three unsuccessful tries. "I can't find a record that he's dead or alive. The last place there is evidence of him is four weeks ago in Uganda."

"That could mean anything," Logan said.

Ryder crossed his arms over his chest and leaned his chair back on two legs. "Or it could mean he's dead."

"Look up Rebecca Turner," Iona asked Evie.

They went through half a dozen names before Iona realized it wouldn't matter who she tried to find—everyone was gone. Whether they were hiding or dead, however, was the question.

"What now?" she asked Laith.

He looked around the room before returning his gunmetal gaze to her. "You have what they want."

"The doorway," she said with a nod.

"They'll come intending to go through it."

Malcolm's smile was cold and calculating. "Then they'll be in for a surprise when we Warriors are there to stop them."

"You've no' fought the Dark Fae, Malcolm," Ryder pointed out. "They're much worse than any *drough*."

Evie looked at Malcolm and took his hand. "The Dark Fae won't be expecting Warriors and Druids to aid Iona."

"Doona count on that," Laith cautioned. "If anything, we need to go on the assumption they know exactly what we're planning."

Iona sighed. "So what do we do?"

"We give them what they want," Laith said.

Iona widened her eyes in surprise. "You can't mean to let them through the doorway?"

"Why no'?" Ryder asked with a sly smile. "That's the easiest way for us to kill them."

CHAPTER
THIRTY-SEVEN

He walked along the windswept hills to an isolated valley. The tall mountains stopped any sound from reaching him. It made him recall the days when there hadn't been the deafening noises of modern day like cars, airplanes, trains, or even mobile phones ringing.

In truth, he detested the sound of all the humans who were overpopulating the world. All the movies, books, and television shows depicting various apocalypses made him laugh. He was going to show them just what a true apocalypse was.

At one time the humans had run from him, screaming in terror as he dove from the sky, breathing fire to burn them where they stood. Very soon, he would do that once more.

All the so-called dictators and leaders of nations would realize how feeble they truly were compared to him. This time Con wouldn't be there to stand in his way. This time, he would make sure there wasn't a human left. Man, woman, child. They were all going to die.

He reached the valley, and within seconds was surrounded by Dark Fae. Standing before him was Taraeth with his long hair with only a little black visible in the silver. Taraeth's red eyes bore into him as if trying to bend him without words.

His first instinct was to squash Taraeth where he stood, but he had need of the king of the Dark Fae. For now.

He glanced down at Taraeth's missing left arm and raised a brow. A human had done that, a human who was now mated to Kellan. Beside Taraeth stood Balladyn. He moved his gaze to Taraeth's right-hand man and grinned at the fury sparking in the Dark's red eyes. Balladyn's hair was long, the mix of silver in his black hair plentiful.

"I hear you had Rhi. And then lost her."

Balladyn's lips pulled back over his teeth, glaring. "I caught her once. I'll catch her again."

"How did you find the Chains of Mordare?"

"That is none of your concern," Taraeth said, his voice raspy and his Irish brogue deep. "You called this meeting. What is it you want this time?"

He clasped his hands behind his back and didn't bother to give the rest of the Dark even a glance. His eyes held Taraeth's. "It's not what I want. It's what I can give you."

"And what might that be?" Taraeth asked.

"I hear you're looking for the weapon the Dragon Kings have hidden." He smiled when he saw the surprise flicker over Taraeth's face and Balladyn's skeptical look.

Balladyn's nostrils flared as he drew in a large breath. "How do you have it?"

"I don't. I do, however, know where it's hidden."

"What?" Taraeth thundered and took a step toward him, his face mottled with fury. "You know I've been looking for that for years. Why haven't you told me before now?"

"Because I didn't have a way for you to get there undetected until now," he answered calmly.

The Dark loved to show their anger any time they could.

It was all bluster as far as he was concerned. The humans, stupid fools, had no idea what they meddled with when they flirted with a Dark.

Taraeth's red eyes narrowed into slits. "You're willing to give me this information in exchange for what?"

"Nothing. For now. There will come a time when I'll call on you. I want your promise that you'll deliver every Dark Fae you have to me."

Balladyn chuckled as he cut his eyes to him. "Do you plan on going to war with the Dragon Kings, because once we have the weapon, there won't be anything left of them. Or you."

"If you think your petty threats scare me, let me ease your mind. They don't, so you might as well stop trying." He turned his eyes to Taracth. "Are you in charge? Or is Balladyn?"

Taraeth shot Balladyn a quelling look that only angered the Dark. "I am," Taraeth answered. "Before I agree, I want you to spell out exactly what you'll be giving us."

Leave it to a Dark to try and corner him. He swallowed a snort. "I will tell you the place where the weapon lies, and I will tell you how to get there undetected."

"Or we could torture you until you give us that information anyway," Balladyn said and quickly closed the distance between them.

He looked into Balladyn's red eyes and gave him a little shove. The shock on Balladyn's face when he was able to move him was priceless. He returned his hand to the other behind his back, the feeling of magic rushing along the tips of his fingers.

"If you try something that idiotic, you'll never get what you seek."

Taraeth growled. "Step back, Balladyn." Once Balladyn returned to Taraeth's side, he turned his head back. "You're offering quite a bit."

"And when the time comes, you'll be delivering your entire Dark army. Do we have a deal?"

Taraeth gave a jerky nod. "We do."

"Your word, Dark. In magic."

Taraeth rolled his neck as he stared. "You ask for my vow in magic. How did you even know that was possible?"

"I know many things. Now, your promise in magic or I walk away."

Several seconds ticked by before Taraeth lifted his right hand palm up. A ball of magic began to swirl in his hand, a mix of silver and black within the orb. "I give my vow that when the time comes, I will deliver my army to you without question or hesitation."

He nodded in acceptance. The ball of magic disappeared in a flash. He then said, "The weapon you seek is on Dreagan."

"The Dragon Kings wouldn't be that stupid to hide a weapon to be used against them so close," Balladyn said.

"How else could they keep a close eye on it?" he asked, quirking a black brow. "Stupid? That's called intelligence, actually."

"You said there was a way to get on Dreagan undetected," Taraeth said. "How is that possible?"

"The how isn't your concern," he said tightly. "The fact remains that you can. It's a doorway that is invisible to you or anyone other than a Dragon King. It's atop a waterfall that borders the east side of Dreagan. Stand on the north side of the waterfall and take five steps forward and then three to the right. You'll be at the doorway."

Taraeth cocked his head to the side. "Have you used it yourself?"

"I have other ways onto Dreagan."

Balladyn crossed his arms over his chest. "Of course you do."

"Careful, Dark," he cautioned. "The Kings will be on patrol, and there could be . . . others . . . waiting for you."

Taraeth gave a snort. "As if we worry about any others. Where on Dreagan is the weapon?"

He shrugged. "I don't have a clue."

"You said you would tell me where the weapon was," Taraeth said in a low tone filled with righteous anger.

He smiled and let his arms fall to his sides. "I did. I told you it was on Dreagan."

"We could search there for years," Balladyn stated. "We need a location."

"If you had listened to the Dragon Kings you've recently captured—and lost—they told you they didn't know. They weren't lying. They don't know. Only one does."

"Con," Taraeth said as understanding dawned.

His smile grew. "Exactly. Now, since our business is concluded, I'm sure you'll want to test out the doorway to ensure I'm not lying."

Balladyn gave him a scathing look. "You think you have everything covered, from your expensive clothes and British accent, but we know who you truly are."

Which was why he would happily kill every Fae—Dark or Light—once he stamped out the humans.

"Good hunting," he said and turned on his heel.

He didn't slow as he reached the Dark soldiers, and as expected, they hastily moved aside for him. How he detested the Dark, but they were enemies of his enemy, which made them an ally.

For the time being.

They also had their uses. If it hadn't been for him combining his magic with the Dark, he wouldn't have been able to spy on Iona Campbell as he had or kill her father so effortlessly.

It might have taken several millennia, but what was rightfully his was about to be returned.

Balladyn barely held in his rage as he watched the Dragon King walk away. "Do you trust him?"

"Not at all," Taraeth said. "He has his own agenda. I've known that from the beginning." He turned to face his lieutenant. "Never forget that, Balladyn. An enemy is always an enemy, even when they're an ally."

Balladyn glanced back at the King to watch him disappear over the top of the hill. "I didn't tell him about Rhi, and I know none of the other Kings told him."

"We have a leak apparently," Taraeth said. "Find it and squash it."

"My pleasure." He nodded to four of his men, and they teleported away immediately. "When do we go to Dreagan?"

Taraeth scratched his chin. "I'm not going to take his word. Send men who can remain veiled the longest to scout the area and report back."

Balladyn pointed to two of his men nearest him. "Go now."

"Sixty thousand acres is a lot to search, especially when we don't know exactly what it is we're searching for," Taraeth said, gazing off into the distance.

Balladyn covertly looked at Taraeth's missing arm. The king hadn't been himself ever since the human female had taken his arm. Other Dark had noticed it as well. It was only a matter of time before Balladyn took command. He hadn't yet determined how he was going to do it, precisely.

"You want revenge for your arm. If we find Denae, it could bring Con," Balladyn said.

Taraeth's red eyes swung to him as he frowned. "You have no idea what you're even considering. Constantine is stronger than the other Dragon Kings. His magic is greater.

It's what makes him King of Kings. We're only going to have one try in taking him. It needs to be planned perfectly."

"What do we do then?" Balladyn asked crossly.

"We go through the doorway and have a look around."

CHAPTER
THIRTY-EIGHT

Rhi waited until night fell before she appeared in The Silver Dragon, not bothering to veil herself. The lights were dimmed, a signal that the store was closed. She gave the front a cursory glance before she walked to the back. Rhi stood there for a moment. Ulrik lived upstairs. There had to be a way to get there from inside the shop.

With a roll of her eyes she went to the first wall covered in thick wood panels with intricate molding. She ran her hand along the wall as she walked around the small hallway. It wasn't until Rhi reached the opposite wall that she heard the telltale click of a hidden door. She immediately stopped and pressed harder on the panel.

The entire wall swung open to reveal a wide spiral staircase that led up to the second floor. Her black combat boots made nary a sound as she ascended. When she reached the top, she paused for a moment and took in the grandeur.

The rich, dark silver-colored walls were accented with black baseboards and crown molding. The floor was a deep espresso wood that had one rug, massive in size with various grays and blacks in a modern design set before the fireplace with a black couch and two dove gray chairs.

Rhi spotted a tall table behind the sofa that was lined with crystal decanters filled with various liquors. An ancient tapestry hung on one wall while two smaller pictures of ancient Roman architecture hung on either side of the stone fireplace.

A small, modern kitchen with lots of stainless steel and minimal cabinets was to one side of her while she spotted a doorway to the other that she was sure was Ulrik's bedroom.

Rhi hastily took a step back and retreated to the first floor. She closed the hidden door and found an overstuffed chair at the front of the store. Once seated, she crossed one leg over the other and considered Ulrik. The fact he wasn't there didn't bode well for him, mainly because she knew who was coming.

Rhi wasn't sure why she even concerned herself. Did it really matter if it was Ulrik who had taken her out of Balladyn's compound? She's the one who broke the Chains of Mordare. She's the one who had the entire stronghold collapsing around her. Or at least that's the rumor she heard whispered. She didn't know for sure, and she didn't want to know. It was better if that part was locked away for all eternity.

Then why did she care that Ulrik found his way onto the Fae realm? Why did she feel she owed him a debt for carrying her out? She still hadn't discovered how he knew of her secret house. Being around him made her . . . uncomfortable. Yet, if he found his way onto the Fae realm and learned of her house, what else could he do?

Rhi was still mulling that over when she heard the lock on the door of the shop turn. She propped her elbow on the arm of the chair and leaned her head onto her hand. The door swung open, but stopped before the little bell above it could ring. A moment later a large shadow of a man stepped inside and quietly shut the door behind him.

"No reason to be quiet," she said. "He's not here."

There was a long moment of silence before Con said, "What the hell are you doing here, Rhi?"

"A good question. One I don't have to ask you. You've come to kill Ulrik. Do you know what will happen to the Kings if you do?"

He stepped out of the shadows into the fall of light from the lamppost outside the nearby window, wearing nothing more than a pair of jeans that hung precariously on his trim hips. Con didn't bother to hide his anger. "It's a chance I'll take to save us."

"Hmm," she said and swung her leg. She couldn't believe he had flown to Perth and dared to walk the city in a pair of jeans, barefoot. Unless he flew straight to the store. Surely not. "I don't think that explanation will work for all the Kings."

"You think you know us so well," he said softly, all his anger contained once more.

He always did know how to piss her off. Rhi lifted her head from her hand, and said in an equally soft voice, "I know the Kings better than you in some ways."

"So you say. You can no' really know us. You were no' there when we fought the humans or had to send the dragons away. You were no' there when we banished Ulrik."

"No, I wasn't there, but we've been around long enough, watching the Dragon Kings," she stated. She waved her hand around the room. "This moment was destined to come sooner or later. Everyone knows it, including Ulrik."

Con's black eyes narrowed. "Where is Ulrik? Hiding?"

"He's not here, but I'm sure he's going to be upset that he missed you. You know he wants your death as much as you want his. I don't blame him, you know. What you did to him was beyond cruel."

"I couldna kill a friend."

Rhi rolled her eyes. "Pul-eeze. You put a friend out of

their misery. You condemn an enemy to eternity as the thing he hated most. And you wonder why Ulrik loathes you and the others as he docs."

"You know what he's done to Rhys!" Con thundered.

That brought her up short. Rhys. He was one of the few Kings that she missed terribly. Rhys was a good King, even if he did let his emotions rule him at times. "I gave Rhys the choice. He made it."

"He shouldna have had to."

"If you think killing Ulrik will reverse what has happened to Rhys, you're wrong."

"You doona know that," Con said, almost daring her.

Rhi drew in a deep breath. "What happens if you're wrong about Ulrik?"

"Why? Do you know something? Now's the time to tell me if you do."

"I'm not saying that. I asked a simple question."

Con gave a loud derisive snort. "As if anything with you is simple."

"It used to be." The words were out of her mouth before she realized it. Once released, she couldn't take them back. Rhi uncrossed her legs and stood. "Good luck with your killing."

Con shouted her name as she vanished before him for the second time in one night. He clenched his hands into fists and fought the urge to hit something. Rhi infuriated him. She interfered when she shouldn't, and she constantly harassed him. She was a plague that beset the Kings.

He put the Light Fae out of his mind and took stock of the interior of the shop. All he had seen before was the outside since no one had gotten cameras set up inside—until now.

Con had come to kill Ulrik, but on the off chance he wasn't there, he'd brought several wireless cameras. He dug into his pocket and put the first one near the door so they could see right to Ulrik's desk. Three more were put on the lower floor, and three more upstairs.

As Con walked to the back, he put more surveillance cameras along the way. He opened his hand and saw there were only four cameras left. It took Con less than a minute to find the panel that hid the stairs. He hurried upstairs and set the cameras about, and then took a few moments to look for any information Ulrik might have on them, or his connection to the Dark.

Con found nothing, which didn't help his sour mood. He went back downstairs and took more time riffling through Ulrik's desk, but still he found nothing.

He put everything back in place and opened his telepathic link to Ryder. *"We have new cameras in place."*

"Are you kidding?"

"They're on. Check them and you can see me." Con waited a moment and then waved toward the camera above the door.

"He's going to find them," Ryder stated flatly.

"Until then, we'll get what we can."

"This could send him over the edge, Con. I doona think this was a wise move."

Con slowly rose, his gaze directed at the camera. *"Every King is in danger. Do you want to endure what is happening to Rhys? I will do whatever is necessary for the survival of the Kings."*

"Careful. There are those of us who doona want Ulrik dead. You kill him, and you destroy what we have."

Con knew all too well that if he killed Ulrik that it would fracture the Kings, possibly for good. But if it meant the threat to them was gone, then he would do it.

"Being King of Kings means making the hard decisions. Is everything set for our visitors?"

"Aye."

Con severed the link and moved aside to roll the chair

back in place. He strode to the front door and walked outside. With a wave of magic, he locked the front door before he hurried to the shadows.

Ulrik pushed off from his spot against the building across the street from his store and watched Con fade into the night. The magic surrounding The Silver Dragon alerted him the moment someone entered.

He was on his way back to the store when an image of Rhi flashed in his head. As soon as the alert hit him, he hurried. He was curious about what would bring Rhi to him. Whatever she had to say would be good. It always was.

Ulrik was at the corner about to cross the street to the store when he spotted Con entering. A moment later, he got another alert, this time it was an image of Con that flashed in his head.

It took Ulrik a full minute to get past the haze of fury. His nemesis was in his place of business, his home. Ulrik had been counting down the days until he could confront Con and get his revenge. He wanted to kill Con right then, but it wasn't time.

As soon as Con was gone, Ulrik smiled. It was obvious that Con had set up cameras throughout the building. With only a thought, he deactivated every one.

"I'll be damned," Ryder said in shock.

Elena tucked her dark blond hair behind her ear and cut her sage green eyes to him. She sat beside him in the computer room at Dreagan helping to monitor everything. "What is it?"

"All the cameras Con just installed are gone."

"Gone? How's that possible? And what do you mean, 'Con just installed'?"

Ryder ran a hand down his face. "He was at Ulrik's. He set up cameras."

Elena let out a long whistle. "Was that wise?"

"It's a moot point since they're no' active."

"Did something go wrong with them?"

Ryder shook his head as he leaned back in his chair. "My equipment never fails."

"Then what?"

He turned his head to her. "No one was in the store. There were no wires to cut the cameras, and there were over a dozen set up. They all went out at once."

"Magic," Elena said with a frown. "At Ulrik's? That's not good news."

"Nay." He stared at the screen with all the squares blacked out. The cameras hadn't been operational for more than five minutes.

Which meant Ulrik had seen Con.

Ryder slowly sat up as his mind went through all the scenarios.

"Go," Elena urged. "They're waiting on you anyway, and you need to tell the others what you've found."

"It might be too late," he said, even as he stood and turned to throw open the doors to the balcony. He jumped from the balcony and shifted, his wings catching the current.

CHAPTER
THIRTY-NINE

Iona drummed her fingers on the table and stared at her camera that Ryder had reassembled hours ago. A camera she hadn't let out of her sight for years. She grabbed it and threw it as hard as she could at the refrigerator. Several pieces fell off, but it was still intact.

"If you want to do that again, I can add some magic behind it and make sure it shatters," Isla said as she leaned on the counter.

Iona shook her head. "I don't usually let my anger get to me like that."

"It's understandable."

"This waiting is unbearable," Iona said testily as she rose from the table and began to pace the kitchen.

Isla made a face. "It certainly is. The men never understand that because they're in the midst of battle."

"And I'm keeping you here," Iona said with a sigh.

"I volunteered," Isla reminded her. "Just as Hayden volunteered to remain near you in case something happens."

"It's the doorway they want."

"Yes, but if you're dead, they can get the land and have access to the doorway as often as they want."

"Killing me won't solve that problem," Iona said with a sly smile. "I had the will changed to name Hayden as my heir."

Isla's face went slack before a slow smile formed. "Does he know?"

"I haven't had a chance to tell him."

"That's very kind of you, Iona."

She shrugged and came to a stop at the counter across from Isla. "I had to have an heir."

"And if you have any children?"

She shrugged, unable to answer. At one time she hadn't ever even considered that as a possibility, but now . . . she was reevaluating everything.

"Does Laith know you love him?"

Iona jerked. "I don't love him."

"Don't you?" Isla said gently. "You don't have to believe in love for it to find you. You just have to recognize it when it's there and grab hold."

"I admit that I want to be with him. I think of him constantly, even when I'm not with him. I . . . care about him, but that's not love."

Isla tilted her head to the side and a curtain of black hair fell over her shoulder. "You have feelings. That's the first step. Open your heart and your mind, and you just might find that it is love you feel."

Iona looked into her ice blue eyes. "If there was a man who could make me want a family, it's Laith." It was Isla's quick look away that made her ask, "What? What is it?"

"I probably shouldn't be the one to tell you."

"Just tell me."

Isla pursed her lips for a moment. "The Kings do take wives, or mates as they're called. It isn't done lightly, because once a female binds herself to a King, it is for eternity."

"I'm human. Eternity isn't possible," Iona said with a chuckle.

"You've seen the Kings, you know they have magic. Do you think they would take wives who would die? Being bound to a King means that a female lives as long as the King does. You've seen Sammi. She was bound to Tristan not that long ago. She'll never age, nor will she die unless Tristan is killed by another King."

Iona could only stare in mute astonishment at Isla. The Kings expected their mates to love them for eternity? That was asking the impossible in an age where very few remained married.

"As for a family," Isla continued. "Back before the war with the humans, a few became pregnant with a King's child, but not one of the babies lived. Most died in the womb, and if they were carried to term, they were still-born."

"Laith never told me," Iona mumbled.

Isla lifted one shoulder in a shrug. "The Kings usually don't unless they're considering a woman for their mate."

"Oh." It stung that Laith didn't consider her. How ironic when she'd never considered a single man before him.

"Did you tell Laith you don't believe in love?" Isla asked.

Iona wrapped her arms around her middle. "I might have. Laith said he wanted whatever we had to continue. So do I, and I can't tell you how much that scares me."

"Take it one day at a time," Isla advised. "If you're happy with him, then be happy."

Iona opened her mouth to respond when a ball of fire was hurtled at the living room window. Isla turned and held up her hands as the fire smashed the window. Whatever magic she used stopped the ball from reaching them, and a moment later, it was gone.

"Move!" Isla said as she grabbed Iona's arm and brought her around the counter only to shove her down the hall.

Iona ran into her room and turned to the door. Isla stopped just outside her door in the hallway. "What's going on?"

"The battle," Isla said without looking at her. "That was Hayden's ball of fire." Suddenly Isla's face turned pale and a shudder went through her. "They've just crossed my barrier as if my magic didn't even exist."

Laith saw the fireball from his flight in the clouds. A growl rumbled through him as he fought to remain where he was and not go to Iona.

"As soon as they get through the doorway you can go to her," Con said through their link.

Laith wasn't sure he could wait that long. He wanted Iona at the manor, but she and Con both thought it a bad idea. Con because he was an ass, and Iona because she reminded him that everything needed to appear normal.

Normal. When had anything been normal? Laith couldn't remember what that even felt like. The closest he came to that was when Iona was in his arms.

"Con!" Ryder shouted. *"Ulrik simultaneously killed every camera you installed minutes after you left."*

Laith turned his head to look toward Con as he remained in the clouds. What had Con been doing at Ulrik's? Was that where he'd been going lately?

"That means he is using magic," Con stated furiously.

Two more balls of fire flared through the inky darkness in quick succession. There was a loud bellow, distinctively Hayden.

"It wasna a smart decision to leave Hayden there on his own," Laith told Con, pushing thoughts of Ulrik away for the moment.

Con chuckled. *"As powerful as Hayden is, Fallon wasna about to allow that to happen. Arran and Malcolm are with him."*

"Good. I still wish one of us was there."

"They'll have no trouble fighting humans, but the Warriors are no' alone. Rhys is with them."

No sooner had Con spoken than Rhys sent out a shout through the link, *"It's the Dark!"*

They barely had time to digest that before Laith turned and flew back through the clouds toward the waterfall. He glanced down and saw a dozen Dark standing atop the waterfall.

"It's Taraeth and Balladyn," Kellan said.

Kiril flew past Laith shouting, *"Balladyn is mine!"*

Laith saw Taraeth immediately with his one arm missing. He stepped through the doorway, and was quickly followed by Balladyn and the rest of the Dark.

"Now!" Con bellowed.

Dragon Kings dove from the clouds straight to where the Dark were crossing onto their land. Laith inhaled and felt fire stir within him. He opened his mouth and let it free while he sailed over them.

He immediately turned around and delivered his paralyzing gas on his next pass. Laith let out a whoop when three Dark fell.

Iona screamed as someone burst through the window. She raised her arm to shield her face from the glass as she turned away.

"Isla!" shouted a deep voice Iona didn't recognize.

She lowered her arm and spotted a man with long, wavy, dark brown hair. He held a sword, the blade curving slightly and becoming wider toward the point.

"We need to get out of here," he said as he approached Iona. "I'm Rhys. The Dark are closing in quickly."

Isla was suddenly beside him. "Let's go."

Iona was unceremoniously grabbed by Isla and pulled forward. She was amazed that such a small woman like

Isla had such strength. As soon as Iona was out of the window, Isla started running and pulled her once more. Iona glanced behind her to see Rhys plunge his sword into the abdomen of a man with black and silver hair.

Iona's heart was pounding. Fear swallowed her whole, weighing her down so that she felt as if she could hardly move. The next thing she knew Hayden stood ahead of them, a massive ball of fire held between his hands. Iona felt someone take her arm and looked over to see Rhys.

Iona's lungs burned, but she didn't slow. True evil was right on her heels. She was dragged after Rhys who moved just as fast as the Warriors. When they reached Hayden, they split, going around him as he lobbed the fireball at the group of Dark Fae coming for them. Iona happened to look up and spotted a dark shape moving quickly toward them in the sky.

"Laith," she said.

Rhys looked up when she spoke. "Shit," he said and grabbed her around the waist as he dove to the side.

Iona couldn't take her eyes from Laith who crashed through the trees, fire bursting from his mouth toward the Dark in an amazing display. The more fire he breathed, the more Hayden used it with his power, turning it toward the Dark who hadn't gotten blasted with it.

"It's hot," Iona said. They were at least fifty yards from the Dark, and the fire felt as if it were next to her skin.

"That's dragon fire, lass," Rhys said as he came up on one elbow. "It burns hotter than anything else on Earth."

By the screams of the Dark, it also killed them, something that Hayden's fire hadn't been able to do. The fear that consumed her began to lessen as Laith gained the upper hand on the Dark. Rhys got to his feet and pulled her with him. He then shoved her toward Isla and the Warriors while he went to cut down the Dark in his path.

Back and forth Laith flew, breathing fire each time. Hayden prevented the fire from moving to the trees and destroying the forest.

"We're winning," she said and turned to Isla.

Iona grunted when Malcolm with his maroon skin shoved her to the ground, and was then promptly thrown backward thirty feet. She looked up to see more Dark coming at them. Iona realized Malcolm had saved her life by taking the blast of magic meant for her.

"Iona," Isla called.

She looked to the side and saw Isla waving her to them. All around them Warriors with their different colored skin were coming out of the woods and fighting. Iona wasn't sure if she could make it to Isla in time, but if she remained where she was, she would certainly die. Iona jumped up and started running. Out of the corner of her eye, she saw Laith diving toward her. A blast of fire fell past her as he arched his back and flew upward.

She reached Isla and gasped for air. Another Warrior, Arran, flexed his hand, his skin and claws white as snow. He shifted slightly and struck out his hand while a Dark was rushing past, behind him.

Iona jerked at the violence before her, but she held back her gasp. She looked up into Arran's white eyes and said, "Nice going."

Arran smiled and jerked his chin to where Hayden was once more being surrounded. Iona could only watch in amazement as lightning began to zing everywhere. It didn't take her long to find the source—Malcolm.

While Hayden used fire and Malcolm used lightning, a spear of solid ice formed in Arran's hand before he threw it at a Dark.

As remarkable as the Warriors were, Iona had something else she was interested in—a Dragon King. She lifted her eyes, searching the skies for Laith.

He circled back around and was joined by an amber-colored dragon. Just as Laith opened his mouth to breathe fire, Iona saw a Dark with black and silver hair hanging midway down his back throw a ball of swirling black and silver magic right at Laith.

Iona's breath locked in her lungs when Laith wasn't able to dodge it. His dragon form disappeared in a blink as he fell naked to Earth.

"Nooooo!" Iona screamed.

CHAPTER
FORTY

Iona couldn't get to Laith fast enough. He wasn't moving, which spurred her to run faster. Above her, she heard the roar of a dragon, but her attention was on him. She turned her head and spotted the Dark responsible for bringing down Laith. For the first time in her life she wanted to really hurt something.

That's when she saw Rhys come up behind the Dark and swing his sword. Just before the blade connected with the Dark, the Fae vanished.

Iona reached Laith and knelt beside him. She looked him over but couldn't find any wounds. She touched his face, smoothing his hair back. "Laith? Laith, can you hear me?"

He couldn't be dead. Iona refused to even contemplate the possibility. Isla said a King couldn't be killed by anyone other than another King, but no one said anything about him being wounded.

She swallowed hard and gave him a shake. "Wake up, Laith. Please. I need you."

Did she ever need him, and not because there were Dark after her. She needed him because she knew life would be dull and tedious without him. It took seeing him plummet from the sky to bring it to full, rich awareness.

She shook him harder. "Laith!"

He suddenly took in a deep breath and then slowly released it. His eyes opened before focusing on her. "Iona?"

"Thank God," she mumbled as she bent and kissed him.

He held her for a moment. Then he looked around and jumped to his feet as he shoved her behind him. That's when Iona saw the two Dark Fae approaching them.

Iona wished she had some magical power to use for herself, but she was the most useless being there. Fury skated through her. Rage over her father's murder, anger over being spied upon, and resentment for being used.

"I don't want you on my land!" she screamed to the Dark. "Get off."

They paused, a confused look flashing in their red eyes.

As silly as it was, her words made her feel better. "Get off my land," she said louder.

The Darks' steps faltered, but still they came.

"Say it louder and with more force," Laith said over his shoulder.

Iona inhaled deeply. "Get off my land! No Dark is welcome here!"

There was a shout of pain from one of the Dark, and then they were both gone. Iona looked around to find the Dark disappearing one by one with looks of bewilderment and wrath directed at her.

"What just happened?" she asked Laith when he turned to look at her.

He smiled and pulled her into his arms. "That was your power. This is your land. You have the authority to decide who is welcome and who are no'. You told the Dark to leave, and they had no other choice."

"That's no' to say they willna return," Rhys said as he walked up.

Iona rested her head on Laith's chest as his arms held her tight. "I'll be ready for them."

It wasn't long before Isla, Hayden, Arran, and Malcolm walked up. Isla was frowning at the three Warriors who were all smiles as they talked of the battle.

"Men," Isla said with a roll of her eyes.

Hayden yanked her against him. "Now, my love, it does a Warrior good to battle."

"I know," she said softly and rose up on tiptoe to touch her lips to his.

Iona watched them with interest, mainly because she was so content in Laith's arms. She didn't want to think about the fear that had taken her when she thought he might not wake up. It had been real. Too real.

Isla had told her to open her heart and her mind. With dragons, Fae, Druids, and Warriors, was it out of the realm of possibility that love did exist?

"The Dark have been driven out for now," Laith told everyone.

Iona lifted her head to look at him. "Even from the doorway?"

"They didna get far once they went through the doorway," Laith said. "We were waiting for them."

Rhys wiped his sword off on his jeans. "The ones that escaped the doorway came here."

"Why did they no' just teleport away?" Isla asked.

Laith smiled widely. "Because once on Dreagan, they couldn't use that ability. A neat idea when we discovered they'd be coming. The only way to save themselves was to run back through the doorway."

"That's brilliant," Iona said with a chuckle.

"I can no' take credit. It was Rhys's idea."

Iona turned to Rhys. "Thank you for everything. That blade is wicked, as are you using it."

His smile was sad, as if her words were painful

somehow. Iona inwardly cringed when she spied the dragon on the hilt of the sword. With a nod, Rhys walked away without a word.

Iona turned back to Laith. "I don't understand."

"Rhys is a Dragon King. He was wounded by dragon magic that was mixed with dark magic, He'll never be able to shift into a dragon again," Laith explained.

Malcolm stared after Rhys as he tamped down his god. "What kind of bastard would do that to him?"

"The kind that willna live long," Arran said.

Laith took Iona's hand. "Let's get you to the cottage."

"Ah," Hayden hedged. "There might be a wee bit of a problem."

Iona shrugged and said, "I know some of the windows are gone."

"That's no' all that's gone," Arran mumbled as he walked past them. "Sometimes we Warriors doona pay attention to what we're destroying in a fight."

Iona lifted a brow. "How much damage?"

"Most of the house," Malcolm said as he finally pulled his gaze from Rhys. "No' all of it entirely our fault."

Iona waved away his words. "It's a house. It can be replaced. My life couldn't. Thank you all for helping to keep me safe."

"Ditto," Laith said.

Hayden slapped Laith on the shoulder. "It's what we do for family."

The four walked away to join with the other Warriors. Iona followed Laith's gaze to the sky to see dragons flying around. "Won't they be seen?"

"Isla and Phelan have taken care of that tonight. We can no' always be so close to your land."

"What did that blast of magic do to you?"

Laith looked down at her and smoothed her hair away from her face. "It's one of the only things a Dark can do to us. That magic prevents me from shifting for a short time. If in dragon form, it reverts us to human instantly."

"Which is why you fell?"

"Precisely."

Iona fidgeted, unsure of what to say or do now. It was her first battle. She didn't know if there were protocols that needed to be followed or what. "I need to gather what's left of my things."

"Aye, you do. You're coming with me to Dreagan."

Happiness erupted inside her, but she quelled it from showing too much. "Am I?"

"You doona have a house," Laith pointed out. "Then there is the fact that I want you in my bed so I can make love to you all through the night."

Iona couldn't find any fault with his thinking.

"Plus, we need to finish our conversation from the other day."

She grew nervous then, mostly because he was right. They did need to talk. She just wasn't sure what to say, or even how to go about it. She hadn't been in this position before. "I know."

"Are you ready for such a talk?" he asked, looking deep into her eyes.

"I honestly don't know. I'm scared, but I'm more frightened of losing you."

Laith knew exactly how she felt. Iona didn't know just how close she had been to dying, and he wouldn't tell her. She came out of it alive, and for that he would be forever grateful to the Warriors and Isla.

He was loath to move to bring her to the cottage where he was sure Hayden and Isla awaited them. Nor was he ready to bring her to Dreagan and be bombarded with everyone wanting to meet her.

"What is it?" she asked.

"There is much you doona know about a Dragon King."

She wrinkled her nose. "Isla explained the mating and the children."

"And?" he pressed.

Iona smoothed her hands over his bare chest and looked down. "And what?"

"Does that scare you off?"

Her dark eyes jerked to his as her hands stilled. "No."

"I doona want to frighten you, Iona, but I want you to know that I'll do whatever it takes to have you as mine. If that means I wait years, then I'll wait. I'll woo you and seduce you."

"Will you?" she asked with a teasing smile. "I'd like that."

"Whatever it takes."

She nodded, her smile widening.

"I mean it. I love you." Laith groaned when he saw her smile drop. He hadn't meant to blurt it out so soon, but there was no denying what he felt. "I love you."

"I don't know what that kind of love is."

Laith should've known it was too soon. He hated that he hadn't waited, but he wanted her to know his feelings.

"Will you show me?"

He blinked, surprise and delight filling him. He felt as if he could burst out of his skin he was so happy. "I would love nothing more."

Laith plunged his hands into her hair as he kissed her with all the passion, the need, and the love within him.

"They knew we were coming," Balladyn repeated yet again as he paced in front of Taraeth's throne.

Taraeth watched his lieutenant. "It appears they did."

"We lost many tonight."

"That can be replaced," Taraeth said. "We've more

pressing concerns. Namely discovering how the Kings were waiting for us."

Balladyn halted, his red eyes blazing with interest. "That's easy. It's our so-called friend. Let me bring him to you so you can take his head."

"That might be difficult. We had a pact." Taraeth fisted his right hand so he didn't reach for his left arm. He could still feel the appendage, even though it was gone. "He gave us the location of the doorway as well as the location of the weapon."

"That doesn't mean he didn't set us up," Balladyn insisted.

Taraeth drummed his fingers on the arm of his black throne. "He wouldn't be that stupid. He knows I would strike back immediately."

"So we just wait to see how the Kings knew?" Balladyn asked in disgust.

Taraeth smiled. "I didn't say that."

"What do you have in mind?"

"Our friend always asked us for help. I think it's time we ask him for some."

Balladyn nodded in approval. "I like it, but you promised him your army. What if he calls upon that promise?"

Taraeth hadn't thought of that. Still, it was a gamble he was willing to take. "I suspect he wants the army for when he attacks Dreagan."

"Which won't matter if we find the weapon."

"True, but we need to get on Dreagan first."

"Not such an easy feat," Balladyn said.

Taraeth laughed as he found the answer. "I think we need to send one of our females to him. Have her use glamour so he doesn't know."

"You want her to kill him?"

"I want her to learn who is in his life that we can hurt.

I want to know who his associates are, his enemies, and everyone he has contact with."

Balladyn grinned with delight. "I'll have someone sent right away."

"Wait a few weeks," Taraeth cautioned. "Let him think we're cowed. Let him think he's invincible."

CHAPTER
FORTY-ONE

Laith managed to get Iona to his room without anyone stopping them. He went to get her food, and when he returned, found her asleep. He stood in the doorway with the tray of food, smiling like a fool.

"She's been through a lot," Con said from behind him.

Laith turned his head to look at Con, surprised to find him there. "Aye, she has. She has power as well. It was Iona who forced the Dark off her property."

"I hate to admit that I forgot the Campbells could enforce that."

"We all did," Laith admitted and set the tray down on the table. He then walked out of the room and softly pulled the door shut before turning to Con. "Is this where you convince me I'm making a mistake?"

For long minutes, Con starred at him with his black, emotionless eyes. "Would it do any good?"

"Nay."

"Then that's no' why I'm here."

Laith frowned. Since when did Con give up so easily? "Why are you here?"

"Your woman's life was put in danger by our enemy. Her employers were part of it."

"They could be one and the same."

Con nodded in agreement. "I've come to the same conclusion. He got those pictures and the location of the doorway and gave it to the Dark."

"He?" Laith crossed his arms over his chest and regarded Con. "You mean Ulrik."

Con lifted one blond brow. "Does that bother you?"

Laith considered everything that had happened since the Silvers first moved three years ago and Hal was the first Dragon King to fall in love with a human. "I wanted it to be someone else, but I think it's Ulrik."

"He must be stopped," Con stated in a low, dangerous voice.

Laith glanced at the door behind him, thinking of Iona. "She's mine in all ways but the ceremony. I willna have her in danger like that again. What do you need from me?"

"I need to know that when I do confront Ulrik that you'll stand with me."

"You have it."

Con clapped him on the arm and strode away.

Laith remained where he was long after Con was gone. He knew it was the right decision to make, and yet he couldn't stop the disappointment and distress that engulfed him. Ulrik had been one of them. It should never have come to the point that they would have to kill one of their own.

He walked down the stairs to the hidden door in the manor that led straight into the mountain. Laith didn't stop until he reached the cavern that held the Silvers. His steps slowed and halted altogether when he reached the cage. The Dragon Kings' magic had made and enforced the cage, just as their magic kept the Silvers sleeping.

Laith reached through the cage and rested his hand on

the dragon nearest him, the silver metallic scales smooth and warm beneath his palm.

He searched his memories for the Ulrik that had laughed easily and often, the Ulrik who loved to play jokes on everyone. That Ulrik had been loyal to a fault, and the most giving of any Dragon King.

Ulrik had been the first of them to take a human as a lover. He didn't hesitate to trust the humans. Ulrik went so far as to also be the first to build a human house to bring them onto his land and protect them. Shortly after that, he became enamored with a human female, and she for him. Ulrik loved her completely. They would have been mated earlier had his duties not taken him away from her.

Ulrik was with Con, putting the final touches on their ceremony when they discovered she was betraying him. It was because Ulrik trusted with such certainty that the rest of the Kings were devastated at the news. It was because of Ulrik's friendship, his loyalty that each of the Kings wanted revenge before she could hurt him.

Looking back now, Laith knew it was a mistake for them to take matters into their own hands. It should've been Ulrik's decision to make regarding his woman. Laith hadn't understood before, but now that he loved, he realized just how grave their mistake was.

When he backed away from the cage and turned, he found Iona standing at the entrance. He frowned, wondering how she had found him.

"Warrick brought me," she answered his unasked question. Iona's dark eyes were troubled as she watched him. "Are you all right? You look . . . sad."

"I always am when I come here." Laith walked to her and took her hand. "Let me show you the Silvers."

"I don't think I should be here," she whispered and hastily looked around.

Laith smiled and kissed the back of her hand. "Of course you're supposed to be here."

They stopped before the cage, and Laith watched her move this way and that to take in the dragons. She walked slowly around the giant cage until she returned to him and gave a shake of her head.

"I've seen you shift. I know what you've told me is real, and yet it's all brought home by seeing these Silvers," she said and looked at him.

Laith tucked a stray strand of blond hair from her pony-tail behind her ear. "I understand."

"I could talk about these magnificent dragons all day and how sad it is to see them locked away, but I'd rather know what's really bothering you."

Laith sighed and squeezed the bridge of his nose. "I can no' deny who our enemy is any longer."

Iona glanced at the Silvers. "It's Ulrik, isn't it?"

"It is." Just admitting it out loud was like a dagger piercing his heart.

Iona threw her arms around him. "I'm so sorry."

He held her tight, taking the comfort she offered. It was new for him to share anything, and yet it eased him. "Con asked me to stand with him when he goes to kill Ulrik."

"Is there no other way?" she asked.

Laith pulled back to look into her eyes. "Nay."

"You won't do this alone. I'll be with you," she vowed.

He smiled, because whether she knew it or not, Iona had just pledged herself to him. Laith found himself smiling once more, the sadness from earlier falling away in Iona's presence.

"What?" she asked skeptically. "You're smiling now."

"Next month is the annual celebration Dreagan hosts for the village. Want to be my date?"

She looked upward and bit her bottom lip. "Hmm. That means I'll need to do more shopping."

"Is that an aye?" he asked as he jerked her hips against him.

Iona laughed and slid her hands into his hair. "Definitely."

"You do realize that means you'll stay here for a month?" he asked with a knowing look.

She shrugged and said offhandedly, "I know. I don't have a job anymore, remember?"

"Oh, I'm fairly certain we can take advantage of your expertise. Besides, the village needs a photographer for weddings and such."

"I used to thumb my nose at such jobs, but oddly enough, the thought of doing that appeals to me more and more. You've changed my world, Laith."

He caressed her cheek, amazed that she was really in his arms. "It wasna me. You were destined for this role, and you were brought home when you were ready to accept it."

"I'm ready for whatever is next."

"Including being mine?"

She pulled his head down until her lips were almost touching his. "Especially being yours."

Laith moaned and claimed her lips in a scorching kiss. She hadn't yet agreed to be his mate, but he was willing to wait. For Iona, he would do anything.

EPILOGUE

A month later . . .

Laith held Iona close as they danced to a slow song, their bodies swaying to the music. Normally, he hated the annual party, but he had been looking forward to it for weeks. He smiled at the envious looks from other men as they gazed at his Iona. She wore a spectacular black one-shoulder dress with elaborate silver beading around her waist that also followed the single strap across her back.

Iona kept her blond locks wavy as she pulled them back in a loose, side bun. She wore no jewelry, which made everything even more elegant. Laith couldn't wait to take her hair down and get her out of the dress.

"What are you grinning about?" she asked as the song ended.

Laith spun her twice, her laughter making him smile. As soon as the next song began, he pulled her tight and kept dancing. He then reached into the pocket of his tux jacket and pulled out the white velvet box.

She gasped, looking from the box to him. "Only jewelry comes in those little boxes."

He bit back a grin, because he knew that little worry frown of hers meant she thought he was asking her to marry him. It was coming, but not yet. Besides, he had something special planned for that.

"So it does."

"No one has ever given me jewelry," she whispered. She stopped dancing and took the box in both hands.

Laith covered her hands with his. "I like being the first."

She flashed him a smile. "You've been my first for many things."

"And I'll continue to be. Now, open the box."

Iona hesitated for another second before she popped open the lid, her eyes going wide. Laith glanced down at the pear-shaped black diamond earrings. "They're absolutely beautiful, Laith. Thank you."

He held the box while she put on the new earrings. She was glowing when he took her back in his arms to complete the dance.

"I'm going to have to thank you properly tonight."

Laith glanced at his watch. "We've been here for two hours. I think we could leave now."

At her nod, Laith took her hand and led her out of the building. As soon as they were in the night air, she lifted her dress with one hand and they began to run, laughing, to the manor.

Lily watched Laith and Iona disappear into the night. There was no doubt what they were going to do. Over the past few weeks Lily had seen more and more of Iona, and then she learned Iona had moved into the manor.

At first Lily had thought she was Rhys's. He did like them tall and blond, after all. But it turns out, Laith claimed the pretty photographer.

She wasn't sure what she thought of Iona. She was nice, but she had put Lily on edge by taking photos of her without

Lily being aware of it until after the fact. The last thing Lily wanted was for those pictures to get out. Iona assured her they wouldn't, and Lily prayed she could trust her.

Lily glanced down at her cream dress. It was the fanciest thing she had owned since she left her family. The silk was soft against her skin, though she was self-conscious of how form-fitting the dress was after wearing such loose clothing for so long.

She walked to a window and looked inside the warehouse to the guests within. The music was loud, and the guests smiling. A week before the warehouse had been filled with casks of whisky, but they had been distributed to other warehouses on the property just for this party.

A party she wasn't part of. Not because she wasn't invited, but because she felt out of place. If it had been up to her, she wouldn't have come, but Sammi, Jane, and Shara had produced the gown and shoes.

And though Lily wouldn't admit it to anyone else, she felt like a princess in the dress. It had been so very long since she had let her girly side come out that she was reveling in it. However, instead of doing it in a room full of people who didn't know her and wondered why she was standing by herself, she had chosen to watch everything from outside.

"Should you no' be inside with the others?"

Lily shuddered at the sound of Rhys's voice. He was forever walking up behind her, not that she minded. She turned to him and gasped at the sight of him. He was breathtaking in his tux jacket paired with a kilt. The man could wear anything, but she loved him in his kilt. "Perhaps. Shouldn't you?"

"Perhaps."

She smiled and glanced away. Lily could never look in his aqua eyes for too long for fear that he would see just how much she lusted after him.

"What are you really doing out here?" he asked softly.

"I don't do well with crowds."

He held out his hand as a new chord of music began. "How about with me?"

Lily's heart missed a beat. Was the most handsome man she knew actually asking her to dance? As if she would refuse.

She put her hand in his, noting how large it was compared to hers. His touch was tender and warm. She stared at the white shirt beneath his tuxedo jacket as he moved them around the small patio.

The music was slow and had a sensual beat, which made it even more difficult for Lily not to fantasize about Rhys. He was just being nice, that's all this was. She needed to remind herself of that every few seconds lest she begin to think something more might come out of a simple dance.

There were no words between, just the music and the night. It was the most romantic, most amazing moment of her life.

All too soon the music ended. Rhys drew them to a stop, but he didn't release her. Lily looked up into his face, her lips parting as her lungs seized. The raw desire she saw there made her stomach clench with excitement and need.

She refused to move when his head lowered to hers for fear that he would change his mind. Then his lips touched hers. It was just a soft brush at first, before he returned a second time and pressed his lips to hers.

Lily sighed as his hand delved into her hair to cup the back of her head. The next instant his tongue slipped through her lips and touched hers. Rhys kissed with sexual abandon that startled Lily as much as it thrilled her. He deepened the kiss, a moan rumbling his chest. She held him, basking in the euphoria of his taste, his touch.

And just as suddenly as he had begun it, Rhys ended the kiss.

Lily blinked up at him while trying to get her bearings. He gazed at her with fathomless eyes for long moments. Then he slid his fingers through the length of her hair.

"I love your hair," he whispered. As if that confession surprised him, Rhys promptly released her and strode away.

Lily touched her lips that still tingled from his kiss. She didn't know why Rhys kissed her, nor did it matter. She had been in his arms, had tasted him.

And it only made her wish for more.

Read on for an excerpt from
the next book by Donna Grant

NIGHT'S BLAZE

Now available from St. Martin's Paperbacks!

On the lift up to Lily's room, she and Rhys stood in the back while a group piled on with them. Rhys looked down at her while she watched everyone else.

Lily's eyes were so full of . . . eagerness that Rhys found himself watching her to see the play of emotions on her face. There were times she hid her feelings well, but others where she wore them on her sleeve for the world to see.

Tonight, they were visible, and he was glad. One by one the other occupants reached their floors. When the lift arrived at her floor, Lily glanced at him and walked out when the doors opened. Rhys followed, appreciating the sway of her hips—and thankful for the dress that no longer hid all of her beautiful curves.

It wasn't until the door shut behind him in her suite that she laughed. "Shall we resume our conversation now?"

Rhys wanted to continue his perusal of her—with her clothes off. Desire ran thick and hot in his veins. It was a mistake to think he could be alone with her in her room. He'd nearly taken her last night on the trail. There was no one to interrupt them in her suite, no one to stop him from marking her as his.

"Rhys?" she called his name, a small frown marring her face.

He looked beyond her to the living room and the numerous bags that filled the space. She followed his gaze and groaned aloud.

"I can't imagine what this looks like. I haven't done anything like this in years," she said while shoving aside bags so they could sit on the sofa.

Rhys stopped her and gave her a little push so she sat. He walked to the bar area and claimed a stool. The broader the distance the better if he was going to have to think and carry a conversation. "Forget the clothes. Let's continue where we were below."

"All right." She sat back on the sofa and crossed on leg over the other after she kicked off her heels. "Tell me something about yourself."

"I have enemies."

Her gaze lowered to the half-empty glass of champagne in her hand. "So do I."

Now that wasn't something he expected her to say. "What do you fear?"

"Not finding my courage when I need it."

Once more he was taken aback by her words. "Why would you need courage?"

"My enemy, remember," she said with a wink. But the truth was there in her words. "Your turn."

Rhys wanted to ask her so many more questions, but he'd begun this game. "I fear that I willna gain back part of myself that I've lost."

"Hmm," she said with a nod as she drank. "I can relate. What do you hope for?"

"To vanquish my enemies."

"I want to be free." Her voice was full of wistfulness.

He thought over his next question for a moment, then asked, "If you could be anywhere, where would you be?"

"Here. With you. You?"

He stared into her eyes, his balls tightening with need. "Right here."

"Tell me something you've never told anyone else, a secret we would share between us."

Rhys set aside his warm champagne. He couldn't tell her his biggest secret—that he was really a dragon. But he wished he could. "That I'll fail those who need me most."

"My given name is Lilliana Eleanor Ross, the Earl and Countess of Carlisle's third daughter."

"You're nobility?" he asked in shock. That certainly wasn't something he saw coming. It explained why she wore the clothes as she did, as well as her elegance.

Lily bowed her head of black hair and pushed the length off her shoulder. "I am. The friend I saw today called me Lady Lily. I just knew Denae was going to ask about it, but she didn't."

"That's no' her style."

"No, it's not."

"That is some secret," Rhys said. "I feel my response was quite inadequate."

Lily laughed and finished off her champagne before she set it on the coffee table. "You could tell me more."

"My friends count on me. I . . . I'm no' as I once was. I'm more focused on vengeance."

"You're still there for your friends. That's what matters."

Rhys glanced away, because he knew that unless he could shift, he was useless in the coming battle. But he shoved those thoughts aside as he remembered who he was with. He thought of her new tattoo and the scar Cassie mentioned seeing. Suddenly, he wanted to see the scar himself. "Show me something no one else has seen."

Lily held his gaze for several seconds as she swallowed nervously. Then rose gracefully and walked to him. She turned her back to him and moved her hair. "Unzip me, please."

Rhys hesitated, his hands shaking at the thought of touching her bare skin. He revisited their kisses every night in his dreams. He couldn't have her this close and not take her, but if Cassie was right and Lily was once abused, he had to let her make the first move.

He grasped the zipper and slowly pulled it down. The neck of her dress gapped and creamy bare skin became visible. Then he saw her red bra. He swallowed, desire riding him hard.

Lily shifted so that the dress fell from her left shoulder. Rhys saw the vertical mark that ran over four inches from her shoulder down her back and about an inch wide. The scar was leathery, indicating it was a burn.

Fury, deep and dark, surged. The longer Rhys stared at the wound, the more he wanted to find the bastard and envelope him in dragon fire. Nothing burned as hot as a dragon's fire.

Rhys ran his hand along the scar. He knew the answer, but he asked, "Who did this to you?"

"Someone I trusted. Someone I gave my love to. A boyfriend I lived with."

Rhys was about to zip up her dress when he spotted something else on her back. He gently moved aside the dress from her right shoulder and saw more scars. They were thin, white, indicating they were older.

His hands shook from the ferocity of his wrath. "He did all of this?"

"Yes."

"With what?"

Lily took a deep breath. "The largest scar was from a

fire poker. The others were from whatever was in reach. Sometimes his pocket knife, sometimes his cigarettes."

Rhys finished unzipping her dress and got the full view of her back. It was riddled with scars. Some burns, as she said from the ends of a cigarette, and others cuts.

"Only your back?" he asked around the emotion thickening his throat. He couldn't understand why someone would want to hurt a person as sweet and beautiful as Lily.

Lily stepped away before she faced him. She let the dress drop. "He made sure never to hurt me where others could see."

In all his eons of years, the only time Rhys had ever felt such outrage was when he sent his dragons away. Now, as he looked at Lily's stomach, as scarred as her back, he couldn't comprehend anyone doing something so heinous.

The amount of courage it took her to show him was staggering. When Rhys asked his question, he wasn't sure what he would show her. Now he knew. Now there was no doubt what he would let her see.

Rhys took off his jacket and carefully folded it to lay it across the stool next to him. Then he unbuttoned his shirt and removed it. He didn't take his eyes from Lily's face, so he was able to see her lips part and a look of awe fall over her face.

Lily couldn't stop herself from closing the distance and putting her hands on such an amazing piece of artwork. The dragon, a curious mix of black and red ink, was intricate, the shading masterful.

She was mesmerized by the tattoo, running the pads of her fingers along it. The head of the dragon was on Rhys's right pec. The body of the dragon stretched across Rhys's impressive chest almost as if it were lying down with its wings tucked. The tail however, went over Rhys's left shoulder and then wrapped around his left arm, stopping at his elbow. The planning and drawing of such art must have taken months, not to mention the time it took to get the tattoo.

Lily lifted her gaze to Rhys's blue eyes. "This is . . . I don't have adequate words. I've never seen such beautifully elegant, and yet fiercely intense work. Still, I can't be the only one to see this."

Though she hated to admit it, Lily knew Rhys bedded other women. They had to have seen the tattoo.

"I doona willingly show this."

"Why?" she asked in disbelief. "It's gorgeous."

Rhys shrugged. "I have my reasons. When I take a woman to my bed, it's either too dark for her to see, or I take her from behind."

Lily returned her gaze to the dragon, but that's not what she saw. She indulged herself on the perfection that was Rhys. Hard sinew, flawless and impeccably shaped, warmed beneath her palms from his thick shoulders to the washboard stomach to his narrow waist.

She slid her hand along the bulging muscles of his arm where the dragon tail was and imagined those arms around her, holding her close. Not so long ago that dream had been reality. It was a fleeting moment in time, but it was branded upon her mind for all eternity.

"If others have seen this, it wasna because I wanted to show it," Rhys said in a low voice.

"This art was meant to be seen. Why would you get this and then hide it?" she asked and tilted her head back to look at him.

Rhys's chest expanded as he drew in a breath. "It's . . . complicated."

"I show you scars. You show me beauty."

"Those scars are part of you. They tell a story of your courage and strength."

Lily felt her eyes sting with unshed tears. "It took me years to get up the nerve to leave him."

"But leave him you did."

"Yes." If only she'd found someone like Rhys—no, if only she'd found Rhys—instead of Dennis, how different her life would be. "I walked away from my family for him."

"Focus on the part where you left him."

It was good advice, because the last person Lily wanted to think about being so close to Rhys was Dennis. The bastard had no place in her life in any way, shape, or form.

Rhys's gaze intensified as he stared down at her. "It takes a special kind of bravery to do what you've done."

"If I was as strong as you think, I'd take what I really want."

"Which is?"

As soon as the words left his mouth, she rose up and placed her lips on his. Lily wasn't sure where such daring came from. Perhaps it was standing in her bra and panties after allowing him to see the ugliness of her body. Perhaps it was how gently he ran his fingers over her scars, causing her eyes to fill with tears. Because how could anyone look or touch her and feel passion?

Perhaps it was because he showed her his tat.

Regardless, she wanted another kiss, and she wasn't going to let the night end without it.

Lily began to pull away when Rhys wrapped an arm around her, bringing her close. He rested his forehead against her while he let his fingers trail lightly down her arm.

"I've been craving that all night," he whispered.

Chills raced over Lily's skin. She slid her arms around his neck, shivering when his caress traced down her side to her hip around to her buttocks. Her breath was coming rapidly, her body heating from the need coiling within her. She sucked in a breath when he cupped her ass and pulled her against the hardness of his arousal.

Rhys's other hand shifted upward, delving into her hair. "Doona tease, sweet Lily."

Lily realized then that he was letting her take the lead. A man who was always in charge was giving her the reins. She knew it was because of her past, but that didn't matter. The simple fact that he was thinking of her when no one else had made her breath catch.

Rhys was able to reach into her very soul in one instance and repair years of damage Dennis wrought. If there was any doubt in her mind that Rhys wasn't unique and exceptional, it was gone now.

She looked into his eyes. Her heart thumped, her blood hammered in her ears. The desire was no longer hidden in his gaze. It shone bright for all to see. This was her moment, her shining instant where her wish to have Rhys was granted.

Lily lifted her mouth to his, but it wasn't for the chaste kiss from a moment ago. All of her desire, all of her longing . . . all of her yearning was poured into the kiss.

And Rhys's answering moan was all it took to spur her onward.